I0660452

An Aesthetic Education

ALSO BY CATHARINE SAVAGE BROSMAN

POETRY

Watering (1972)
Journeying from Canyon de Chelly (1990)
Passages (1996)
Places in Mind (2000)
The Muscled Truce (2003)
Range of Light (2007)
Breakwater (2009)
Under the Pergola (2011)
On the North Slope (2012)
On the Old Plaza (2014)
A Memory of Manaus (2017)
Clara's Bees (2021)
Arm in Arm (2022)

CREATIVE NON-FICTION

The Shimmering Maya and Other Essays (1994)
Finding Higher Ground (2003)
Music from the Lake and Other Essays (2017)

CRITICISM

André Gide: l'évolution de sa pensée religieuse (1962)
Malraux, Sartre, and Aragon as Political Novelists (1964)
Roger Martin du Gard (1968)
Jean-Paul Sartre (1983)
Jules Roy (1988)
Art as Testimony: The Work of Jules Roy (1989)
An Annotated Bibliography of Criticism on André Gide, 1973-1988 (1990)
Dictionary of Literary Biography, volumes 65, 72, 83, 119, 123, edited (1988-1992)
Simone de Beauvoir Revisited (1991)
Twentieth-Century French Culture, 1900-1975, edited with an introduction (1995)
Retour aux Nourritures terrestres, edited, with David H. Walker (1997)
Visions of War in France: Fiction, Art, Ideology (1999)
Existential Fiction (2000)
Albert Camus (2000)
Louisiana Creole Literature: A Historical Study (2013)
Southwestern Women Writers and the Vision of Goodness (2016)
Louisiana Poets: A Literary Guide, with Olivia McNeely Pass (2019)
Mississippi Poets: A Literary Guide (2021)

An Aesthetic Education and Other Stories

Foreword by Jonathan Chaves and a New Story

CATHARINE SAVAGE BROSMAN

GREEN ALTAR BOOKS
SHOTWELL PUBLISHING

AN AESTHETIC EDUCATION AND OTHER STORIES
Copyright © 2019, 2022 Catharine Savage Brosman

ALL RIGHTS RESERVED. No part of this book may be used or reproduced in any manner whatsoever without written permission except in the case of brief quotations embodied in critical articles or reviews.

This book is a work of fiction. Names, characters, businesses, organizations, events and incidents either are the product of the author's imagination or are used fictitiously. Any resemblance to actual persons, living or dead, or events is entirely coincidental.

Produced in the Republic of South Carolina

by GREEN ALTAR BOOKS,

an imprint of SHOTWELL PUBLISHING, LLC

POST OFFICE BOX 2592

COLUMBIA, SOUTH CAROLINA 29202

www.ShotwellPublishing.com

Cover: Image by Llambrano from Pixabay. CC0

ISBN: 978-1-947660-71-7

SECOND EDITION

10 9 8 7 6 5 4 3 2 1

To those I love, both the quick and the dead.

Contents

ACKNOWLEDGEMENTS

THE AUTHOR IS GRATEFUL to the publishers of the following print and internet journals, where the stories indicated first appeared.

Chronicles: A Magazine of American Culture, "A Day with Cyprien"; *Concho River Review*, "Chiaroscuro"; *The Evansville Review*, "Along the Danube"; *LISA* (an internet magazine), "Cubist Angles," "Icons," "Knights of the Nile," "A Summer Sketch"; *Louisiana English Journal*, "Dora's Dying," "Virtual Art"; *Louisiana Literature*, "Family Values," "A Mirage on the Road," "Petroglyphs," "Two Gray Hills"; *Southern Gothic* (an internet magazine), "An Aesthetic Education"; *The Xavier Review*, "The Thomas Grant." A portion of "Petroglyphs" first appeared in Brosman, *Petroglyphs: Poems and Prose* (Thibodaux, LA: Jubilee: A Festival of the Arts / Nicholls State University, 2003).

The author wishes to thank likewise the editors of *Modern Age: A Conservative Review* and Professor Jonathan Chaves of the George Washington University for granting permission to reprint as a foreword his review of the first edition of this collection (62, 3, Summer 2020).

She appreciates the kind support of the book by Randall Ivey, Martha Mackenzie, Donald Maginnis, Olivia Pass, Donald Mace Williams, and R. V. Young.

Foreword

The Art of Character

by Jonathan Chaves[1]

CATHARINE SAVAGE BROSMAN is highly respected for her elegant poetry, as well as for her scholarship in French literature and Louisiana literature. She is Professor Emerita of French at Tulane University, having held the Kathryn B. Gore Chair in French at that institution. With such a career, she might well sit back, relax, and enjoy the views she describes so well, a good cocktail in hand. Instead, she publishes this, a collection of eighteen short stories, everyone of which contains an unforgettable epiphany of human truth. I have not read so fine a work of American fiction in decades. The characters and situations in this book will remain with me for the rest of my life.

There is a cast of characters who reappear in the stories, including the same narrator throughout, almost producing the effect of a novel, except for the fact that the stories are not organized chronologically in the life of the narrator. The result on one level is a kaleidoscopic revelation of the narrator herself as a character. She is a painter, and a professional art historian, working as a curator at a fictional New Orleans art museum, frequently traveling to France as well as Austria, both for work and for pleasure. And then there is the American Southwest, a magical place to which she loves to withdraw for camping and hiking expeditions. The atmospheres of all these venues are conjured up with a combination of piercing insight, aesthetic sensibility of the highest order, and sheer sensual experience, all conveyed in an English prose that is revelatory in a

---

1   Originally published in *Modern Age*, 62, 3 (Summer 2020).

nearly Proustian fashion. This is not merely a poet's prose, although there are poetically charged passages; it is the fully developed artistic medium of a true master of fiction.

In dealing with the art and museum worlds, Brosman presents a panoply of pretentious, even completely phony *poseurs*, at least one of whom is outrightly psychotic (in "A Little Nightcap," a terrifying yet amusing story that is a unique variation on the mystery genre). Such persons are rife in these areas, especially at a time in history when on the one hand, there are no accepted standards for what is "beautiful" or "good," and yet certain "postmodern theories," usually just cited as "theory" as if they were the only ones in existence, command lip-service by young scholars hoping to gain tenure in academia, or prestigious curatorial positions in the museums. Norma Wurmser, in "Virtual Art," is a perfect portrait of the type of woman who succeeds in such an atmosphere. Despite a lack of solid knowledge about artistic photography, she manages to worm herself (pun possibly intended) into the directorship of the museum's photography department, and goes on to dominate her colleagues by organizing a conference on a bogus topic, "Indo-European Technological Evidence on Women and Art." The mere use of the word "women" ensures that even the suspicious director of the museum cannot say her nay.

Then there is the wonderful Julius Wallace, in "The Thomas Grant," clumsy, awkward, hyper-anxious (with a flying phobia, for example), and yet a true scholar of Mesopotamian and other ancient art. His close colleagues, seeing past the surface to the man's underlying sincerity, and admiring his undoubted scholarship, band together to help him obtain travel money in response to an invitation to pursue research in Europe. This character was painful for me, and yet compelled self-deprecatory enjoyment of the humorous side, because—I am afraid I recognized certain of his characteristics in myself...

Another character whose portrait moves gently but rigorously inward, from surface to innermost soul, is that of Cyprien, in "A Day with Cyprien." The narrator meets again with a French friend from thirty years ago, now a museum curator in Bordeaux, who comes up to Paris to see her. Together they visit a museum dedicated to the eighteenth century, displaying such painters as Hubert Robert and Guardi (the author's knowledge of European painting and art in general is prodigious). But as the day unfolds, it is not memories or great art that galvanize Cyprien's feelings and therefore the narrator's enriched grasp of his nature, but a seemingly trivial incident, his loss of his glasses (one of several pairs he always carries with him). The day is transformed into an urgent hunt through the labyrinthine Parisian Métro system for these, to no avail until they appear, almost miraculously, perched on a car parked in the street. Cyprien must have dropped them, and some good Samaritan picked them up and placed them on the car. Cyprien's relief is so great that his anxiety is transformed into a joy that even the ebullient capriccios of Guardi could not inspire in him. And so Cyprien is "happy again," liberated somehow to enjoy truly the presence of his old friend. Have we not all been held captive by the demon anxiety, over some trivial thing which unawares had become a key symbol for us of our own being?

One way that Brosman conjures up her characters is through their clothing, as Gogol does in "The Overcoat," but in the eponymous "An Aesthetic Education," she tops the mark in her description of the "pink poodle lady." This airhead appears at a bar frequented by the narrator and her friends, in a dress of "Pepto-Bismol pink," adorned with a huge poodle whose movements as she walks, sits, stoops become indelible images of her surface character (apparently the only one she has). Eventually, to everyone's amazement, she is hired and transformed by a gallery owner into an avant-garde artiste of impeccably awful taste. The development of this one is hilarious, but returns joyfully to true beauty in the end as the narrator, back home, gratefully contemplates her own landscapes on the wall.

It is in the Southwestern stories that Brosman reaches the peak of her art. The three of these that move me to the depths of my heart are "A Mirage on the Road," "Petroglyphs," and "Two Gray Hills". The first gives us Carole Magnin, lone proprietress of a small guest ranch in the remote Colorado mountains. When the narrator comes upon her, she has hired a couple, a middle-age man and a young woman, who have recently moved in and helped her enormously by renovating several of the aging, seedy cabins. Carole has invested her hopes for future revival of this business in the help of the two. But she has misinterpreted them as people. They are wanderers, called by the road, and they abruptly desert her, although that is not how they see it. Carole is left faced with the realization that her hopes were a mere "mirage on the road," and the evocation of her feeling is one of the very finest things in this book. At the very end, Brosman does something that immediately brought me back to the classical Chinese poetry I study and translate, with a brilliant oblique closure, from the human heart off into nature: "I looked past the trees, whose branches shook excitedly in the wind as if they were about to fly off. Beyond, rocky patches in the timber shone, brilliant, almost silvered, in the late morning sun." So ends the story. In the eighth century, Chinese poet (and painter) Wang Wei (701-761), gives us this:

In Response to a Poem from Chamberlain Chang

In my late years, I'm only fond of peace;

The world's affairs no longer touch my heart.

I look within: no further long-range plan,

I only know, return to the old woods.

Pine-breezes blow loose my waist-band;

The mountain moon shines as I play my lute.

You ask me, "What's the secret of success and failure?"

—The fishermen's songs sound far across the bay.

Chamberlain Chang in his original poem sent to the poet (now lost) must indeed have asked, how does one know whether one has succeeded or failed? Carole Magnin feels like a failure. Wang Wei has accepted the age-old Chinese option of purposeful withdrawal from the world of turmoil in quest of serenity. And yet, when he directly addresses Chang's question in the final couplet, he points us off to the bay, over which can be heard in the distance the singing of fishermen making their living at this humble trade. The question cannot be answered; meanwhile the world of nature and those who work within her continues, unaffected and beautiful.

"Petroglyphs" follows our narrator and an English couple who have lost their son to leukemia "in early adolescence" as they drive off the map in remote regions of the Four Corners. On the simplest level, the story is an exciting adventure, yet shot through with the poignancy of the couple's terrible loss. It becomes unclear whether the three companions are lost or not, whether they will run out of gas. Eventually, they come upon a set of numinously radiant petroglyphs, perhaps one thousand years old. Hunters are shown, and a woman; between them is a child, a radiant sun above his head. Brought to tears, "Anne reached over and touched the stone just below the child's figure, then put her fingers to her lips." It is as if this ancient image of a child has blessed her and her husband, and somehow conveyed that their own beloved son has joined something beyond time and space.

The book ends with the third of these three masterpieces, "Two Gray Hills." Here too there is an element of mystery. The narrator and her English friends have driven to a Navajo campground near Chinle, a Navajo town in Arizona. They are approached there by an old Navajo man who tells them he had noticed the Louisiana license plate way back at a gas station and had been able to trace their movements to the campground. But why in the world would he have done this? He explains that his daughter had left years before, for New Orleans. He has not heard from her. (There may have been some sort of falling out between them.) Full of sincere emotion, he wishes to present the narrator with a particularly valuable Navajo rug, of the type known as Two Gray Hills. But she declines the gift, insisting that she cannot accept it; she has done nothing. But, learning that the daughter is a painter and potter, the narrator tells the father she may at least be able to make an effort to track her down, because she is herself an artist and museum curator. Upon returning to New Orleans, she begins her search, writing to the old man to tell him so; whereupon he has the rug shipped to her. Through a series of events, she succeeds in finding the young woman and in persuading her to write to her father. At the narrator's suggestion, she effects a reconciliation with him and later goes with her husband to visit him. To the narrator they bring back gifts from themselves and the old man, who sends another Two Gray Hills rug of great value. She hangs it in her study next to the other. She loves "its stylized black shapes, suggesting the monumental basalt rock formations of the Four Corners, where I can imagine the crimson sun glowing at sunset, coloring the sky, like the thick blood of love." The seemingly huge gaps between cosmopolitan New Orleans and the remote hills of the Arizona terrain, as well as between a seemingly constant past and an ever-changing present, have been transcended by a father's love for his daughter, of which the Two Gray Hills rug is the perfect icon. Art becomes a bridge to the transcendent.

Jonathan Chaves

The George Washington University

Washington D.C.

Author's Note

THE INITIAL LAUNCH of this collection of short fiction took place in 2019, to much acclaim in Louisiana and elsewhere. Bookshops, public libraries, and universities around the state provided opportunities for publicizing it through readings and signing events. The momentum of that reception could not be maintained, however, beyond February 2020, the last month in which such events could be held, before the lockdowns dictated by the corona virus were imposed. The renewal of cultural activity and the enthusiasm of readers have prompted the publishers to issue this second edition, with a foreword by Professor Jonathan Chaves of The George Washington University. Readers will find a new story, "The Charm of Love." The edition incorporates corrections of inaccuracies and typographic and technical errors in the first edition.

Rooted in the real—places, times, mores, human nature and human possibility—these stories spring also from what Edmund Burke called the moral imagination, the faculty that allows for recognition and appreciation of truth, goodness, and beauty. As Russell Kirk wrote, such imagination "aspires to right order in the soul." That certain lives are marked by obvious disorder in behavior and views, and various characters display moral anomalies, while others, alas, are physically misshapen does not invalidate the presiding ethos and its goals; rather, it underlines them. Farce is a revealing mode, and a healthy one; satire brings out points, edges, and contours of the real.

The action is seen and related by a narrator who appears throughout, Harriet (Harry) D'Aquin, née Hamilton, an art historian and painter. She is both an observer and, usually, a participant. Her vision and the comments and reflections it inspires dominate the account of things; but of course that vision is frequently qualified, even contested, by others'. It must be stressed that, despite overlaps, not all facts of her background, life, and character are to be taken as those of the author.

The stories are not arranged in the chronological order of the events they depict. The time of the action varies, from Harriet's youth as an art student well into her maturity. Those stories in which she appears as an adult, practicing her profession, are set in the 1990s and around 2000, at the turn of the century. Various features of that period, now a quarter-century past, contrast with today's uses. The names and offerings of bars and restaurants, for instance, may have changed. With the advent of near-universal cell phone towers, usages concerning telephoning and the instruments themselves are radically different. Certain details here concerning a funeral establishment in New Orleans and a transatlantic crossing would no longer fit the picture.

The settings for the stories include the American Southwest, the Florida Gulf Coast, Paris and Austria, and, chiefly, New Orleans. Well-known locales there such as bars, restaurants, and neighborhoods appear under their true names. The museums and galleries mentioned are, however, wholly invented. Similarly, all characters save the narrator are entirely fictional, and any apparent resemblances between them and actual persons living or dead are completely coincidental.

An Aesthetic Education

IT ALL STARTED AT THE BAR at the Columns Hotel on St. Charles Avenue. The question ultimately was, *whose* education?

On Friday nights, from Happy Hour time on, the bar is crowded with locals and visitors, and full of *Gemütlichkeit*. Tourists who pop in from the avenue and hotel guests are delighted to discover what the locals know already: that they'll find fried catfish snacks as well as inexpensive drinks, and that if you're interested in extending your social circle, that is, in picking up someone, it's not a bad place to start. Young and not-so-young attorneys drop by after they leave their offices downtown; doctors, technicians, and nurses from the hospitals in the neighborhood use it as a watering and mixing place; some of the cream of city government can be seen there; and dozens of others from Uptown treat it as a sort of club. Maybe some of the tourists have found out that this old mansion served as the setting for a French movie about a New Orleans bordello.

That November evening, we were seated close to the bar, in the sort of comfort you'd expect at home—a low table, a sort of divan or padded bench, and four chairs. Usually we sit on the open veranda, but this time the weather drove us inside, to the coziness of low lights, mirrors, dark wainscoting, old furniture, and alcoves, where the autumn wind shook the sash of a floor-to-ceiling window and made the old lace curtains shiver at the edges.

Three of us from the museum and a couple of acquaintances had met there before going to an opening at *Vision*, a large gallery downtown—not quite a command performance for us, but a gesture of professional courtesy and support for the arts in New Orleans. It was the fall juried show of the Guild of Graphic Artists—amateurs, more or less. In fact, I had already seen the exhibit prior to the *vernissage*, because I'd agreed to serve on the jury; but I was willing to go again to help swell the crowd, along with my colleague Elinor Perrin and her husband Roger, Greg d'Hannis—also on the curatorial staff—and a new acquaintance of Elinor's, a young neighbor named Jennifer Stevenson, accompanied by somebody she called Richard, of whom she seemed quite enamored. Jack, my husband, had stayed home; no art openings for *him*. We supposed that the buffet at the show would be very scanty, so starting out at the Columns seemed like a good idea. Anyhow, it had been a wearisome week and a drink at 5:30 sounded appealing. After the opening, if we were still hungry, we'd go eat somewhere in the Faubourg Marigny.

Standing at the bar, almost under the television set, where someone was relating the scandals of the day, was a cluster of men who sounded like trial attorneys—not because they were talking about the law, but because the manner and tone of each revealed the public self-assurance required for one who, unless he is to fail, generally must make *his* interpretation of things prevail over that of others— by rhetoric and deviousness, if necessary. (Roger, a lawyer, would not have been insulted by my reflections on certain members of his profession; he doesn't like some of them much himself.) Completely engaged in their conversation, which was like a tennis match without rules, balls being lobbed every which way, not often returned, they were paying attention neither to the news nor anything else, and did not notice a woman, no longer entirely young but wishing to appear so, who approached the bar at their left, apparently alone and trying to order a drink. She had blond hair, bleached and teased, big rhinestone earrings, and a small, heart-shaped face, heavily made-up. I like painting but think that canvases are more suitable than faces for the thickly-layered stuff put on with a palette knife.

The woman was dressed in a suit of Pepto-Bismol pink, over the front of which paraded something that looked like a dog, embroidered in black yarn. Her shoes were thin-strapped sandals of patent leather on stiletto heels—the sort of creation that, when put on a human foot, seems intended to make walking almost impossible, like the binding of Chinese women's feet. She looked inquiringly, one might say hopefully, toward the cluster of lawyers at her right, but they seemed unaware of anything but themselves and she couldn't manage to distract them. That just illustrated what I'd been thinking about their preoccupation. She then turned, got the barman's attention, and ordered a martini, which she proceeded to sip, one elbow leaning on the six inches of bar she had managed to homestead, her gaze turned outward toward the room and what it had to offer. I saw that the hind legs of the woolly poodle—that's what it was—began more or less at the right hem of the fashionably-short skirt. Its body crossed onto her jacket at an angle, its forepaws on the bodice, so that its head reached over where a pocket might have been, all the way to her left shoulder. At its neck was a collar of white yarn, with rhinestone studs, to which was attached a small leather leash—a real leash, dangling down the jacket, its other end hooked onto her left sleeve. She was walking her dog across her suit, in other words. Maybe, I reflected, instead of going to the art show we should just look at her and any acquaintances who might join her later, who might afford some similar sort of visual entertainment.

Her glance, on a longer leash than the poodle, wandered around the room, pausing here and there to sniff, as it were, then moving on. Listening idly to the general chatter around me and sipping my wine, without attempting to follow what Jennifer and Richard were saying to each other or engage my other companions in conversation, I could watch the poodle woman as she watched everything else. Thus I saw her eye alight on Greg. It stayed there.

Greg is a big, beefy man, with a large head crowned with wavy chestnut hair and a deep, virile voice. He was wearing Italian tassel loafers and a good-looking brown tweed suit, somewhat classier than his usual dress at the museum; the tweed seemed to bring out his masculine strength. Since his divorce, he hasn't worn a wedding ring. The woman in pink, who herself didn't have one, may have observed that his finger was bare, though maybe a ring wouldn't have been much of an impediment anyway. To my mind, he looked like the intellectual he is. Of course, even if bits of our shop talk had floated over to her, she couldn't know that he is curator of our Italian and Northern European collections and has an impressive portfolio of publications. Still, though her choice showed good taste, I couldn't help supposing that she undervalued him. Oh well, in brains as in lots of other things, it takes one to know one. In the meanwhile, no friend had come to join her; perhaps she had been stood up, or simply had come alone in the hope of meeting someone.

Greg's gaze, I could be confident, was not wandering. Badly burned once by the flames of love, he was anxious not to fall into the bonfire again. I think he wasn't even aware of her, or of much else, needing instead to empty his mind for a few moments; good friends are those who let you absent yourself a while from felicity or other emotion, even in their presence. So the Pink Lady, as I thought of her, would not find his glance seeking hers; she would have to act somehow on her own. Without planning it, Elinor's friend Jennifer Stevenson, who turned out to be a shade too spontaneous, furnished an opportunity when she got up to order another beer from the bartender, since the waitress was busy elsewhere. Richard could have done it for her, but he had just seen someone he knew across the room and had stepped over to talk to him. So many people were sitting or standing at the bar that Jennifer needed to squeeze among two or three bodies; she picked the spot by the woman, who at least wasn't big enough to block her completely.

As she elbowed her way through, I heard above the din a high-pitched, rather coy voice, with a local accent we call Yat, attached to the pink-and-poodle wool suit. The remark was directed toward Jennifer. "It's awfully crowded here; I can't find a free table and it's hard to keep a place at this bar."

"Yes, it's packed," Jennifer answered. She got the bartender's attention and ordered another Abita Amber, then, while he drew it, said a few more words to the poodle woman.

The same yapping voice, emanating as if from the dog itself, spoke again. "I saw you at the table, with the others... and that handsome man. I mean the one in the brown tweed suit."

Jennifer must have been relieved to hear that the particular "handsome man" was not Richard, to whom she gave an adoring sidelong glance; "Richard is mine," it said.

They exchanged a few more words before the barman handed Jennifer her beer.

Did I hear correctly then? As Jennifer was getting out her wallet, it sounded as if the poodle woman said, "I'd like to meet him."

Jennifer replied, rather loudly, "You're not with anyone? Why don't you come over to our table—we've got room enough for someone else on the bench."

She is young; that's her excuse. Graciously giving up empty chairs is one thing; inviting a stranger to sit and drink with you so that she can make eyes at someone in your party is another. Jennifer couldn't know, of course, what complications would ensue; maybe she wouldn't have seen them as complications, anyhow. Glass in hand, she came back with the Pink Lady in tow. Just then Richard returned, with the friend he'd seen, Al somebody. There was pushing of chairs, followed by squeezing of bodies to let the two new ones into the company. Brief introductions followed. The woman's name seemed to be Carrie or Corrie, short for Corinne, I supposed. Presently I discovered that it was Kori—one of those names with a sound and a spelling suggesting a commercial product, maybe a hair dye or tonic or laxative for the older set. Al, the fellow Richard had brought over, cast his line for Kori right away.

"Do you come here to the Columns often?" he began.

"Oh, sometimes" (non-committal); "do you?" (polite in a bored fashion).

"No, I usually go to the Pontchartrain, or sometimes GB's, because I live nearby, but just happened to come by this evening and ran into Richard, here."

She was interested neither in Al and Richard nor those watering places—unless Greg, whose name she now knew, went there sometimes. Ignoring Al, she turned toward her left. "I like this place, don't you?" she said to Greg. "But I don't know GB's; is it nicer?"

Greg showed little sign of wanting to converse with Kori. I guessed that he had been put off by the voice, the Pepto-Bismol pink, the makeup, and above all the poodle, now having to bend at the middle and sit, so to speak, as its wearer did. Greg wasn't exactly gruff—courtesy was too much ingrained in him for that—but he gave her very short shrift. "Friends of mine go there sometimes on Saturdays for mimosas and Bloody Marys—but I've rarely been there myself."

"Are you in business?" Kori inquired.

He hesitated a moment, and again Jennifer helped her out. "He's with the museum—the Orleanian Institute, you know." (I wondered whether Kori *did* know of it.) "These people—Greg, Harriet, and Elinor, I mean—all work there. I'm just a friend of Elinor's, and Richard, here, he's a broker."

"Oh, I simply adore modern art!" exclaimed Kori, the same way she might have said at dinner with a date, "Oh, I just love French fries." Her feathery, mascaraed eyelashes seemed about to take wing, and her eyes swept over Greg with a *suivez-moi jeune homme* look. If beauty is in the eye of the beholder, maybe she thought that what was on her suit was art. She got her art one way, we at the museum another.

Small shoots of conversation sprang up around the table, though Greg contributed little to cultivating them. What Kori did in the way of work was not quite clear; she seemed to be a free-lancer of some sort. Her talk was vapid. If we didn't want her company the rest of the evening, we needed to keep our mouths shut about going to the exhibit opening. Greg wouldn't say a word, nor I, nor Elinor, I was confident; having, out of friendliness, invited Jennifer to come, she doubtless felt a bit responsible for the way Jennifer had let Kori attach herself to us, and wouldn't want to encourage it further. Roger would follow Elinor's lead: he has his own life in his law firm, but with the museum crowd he graciously leaves things in her hands. But Jennifer, obviously, could not be relied upon. Before long she had told Kori that we all planned to attend the opening of an art show, a little after 7:00. "Wouldn't you like to go with us? It may not be very good," she added apologetically, wheezing a little as if she were allergic to the thought of it.

Her prediction about the exhibit was not unfair, though I wondered what she knew about it—perhaps she'd heard Elinor make a remark to that effect earlier—and especially whether Kori would care.

"But, you know," Jennifer continued, "the worst you can do is lose."

"Oh yes, that's what Dear Abby says, isn't it? Or is it someone else? Anyway, I'd just *love* to come."

Kori then got out a small white telephone, dialed a number, and murmured a few words into what I took to be an answering machine at the other end. We started to empty our glasses and eat the remaining scraps of fish on the paper plates, and then had to talk about who was going to ride with whom to the gallery and where we'd park. Al helped us out. "Well, if you're all going to that show, I'll come along too and I'll bring Kori here. I know that gallery. I've got my parking place in a garage near there, twenty-four hours a day."

Maybe that will impress her, I thought; whatever he did, he had a fourteen-carat advantage in that parking space. I managed to suppress the impulse to ask him whether he minded having dogs in his car. He threw down a couple of dollars as a tip and gestured to Kori, who was obliged to follow him in the absence of any other invitation. Then Roger, Elinor, Jennifer, and Richard paid and went off together; Richard was driving the four of them. Greg was relieved to be paired up with just me. Though lacking vanity, he had seen that Kori had picked him out. "What on earth for?" he asked, as we walked out. "I never even looked at her. She's not my type at all, and I can't believe she could think I was hers. After all, I'm an art historian, not a lawyer or banker or successful car dealer. I'm not a swinger or 'cool,' as she'd say."

"Maybe she likes the idea of knowing an art expert—it has cachet. Or maybe it's that tweed; it makes you look serious." I was only half-teasing; perhaps the creature, having known too many free spirits in sports cars, really did yearn for a man who looked solid and stable. Moreover, she might have a fantastic idea of the salary range of museum curators.

"Well, it *is* a good suit, I'll admit. Where could she find that creation she had on? Clothes *do* make the man—or the woman."

"I don't know where one would buy something like that," I answered, as we got in his car and started down the avenue. "Maybe in the French Quarter? From a catalogue? Maybe she made the thing herself! I suppose it could be considered as sartorial aesthetics—but it's worse than those strange Surrealist creations by Arp and Dali."

By the time Greg and I parked on Camp Street and arrived at the gallery, the others were already there and had gotten glasses of an ordinary California wine and a few peanuts. As Jennifer had predicted, the exhibit was very uneven; Greg and Elinor were rolling their eyes. If the worst you can do is lose, most of these aspiring artists had the worst of it, in my view, having lost time, money for supplies, and standing in others' eyes. But maybe they really had gained, or thought so, which would be enough for them and their friends: I couldn't assess the *experience* of their painting, only its results. In any case, it would have been unbecoming of me to say anything, since I had already participated in the judging; so I just wandered around, looking again at the few canvases I had admired and seeing how people were reacting to them, and exchanging greetings and pleasantries with the gallery owners and a few of the artists. Kori was accompanied by Al, but showed little appreciation for his attentions. She kept glancing toward Greg, I noticed, but he managed to evade her, moving from section to section, hiding behind panels, or mixing with others.

The winner of first prize was standing by his painting, a still life with vegetables—one of the few pieces of high quality. He and I engaged in conversation. Some time must have passed; he went to refill our plastic wine glasses. Behind me, I heard a man's voice saying indignantly, "He worked and worked all his life, and supported his wife and children, and then he was killed by a truck, right in front of his *aunt.*" Whether the aunt's presence added to the injustice, I wasn't sure, but being reminded of what is, at best, our precarious human condition is always fitting. As the painter returned with our drinks, a very different voice, across the gallery, gave a sort of squeal and pronounced the name *Viagra*.

It was Kori, all right. She had managed to shake Al; the man to whom she was speaking turned out, thank heaven, to be not Greg, but instead a tall, dark-haired fellow with a small mustache. To my delight I recognized Mario d'Angelo, who works at another gallery in town, owned by someone from California who probably uses it as a tax write-off. Leaving aside the possible pertinence of Viagra to his case—about which I knew and wished to know nothing—I realized that he was perfect for her: superficially sophisticated, artificially blasé, silly. He might even like the poodle. Mario caught my eye just then; I smiled in encouragement. I said goodbye to the prize-winner and looked around for Greg. I had to maneuver around an old hag with blue hair and three shades of rouge, and then a woman so ample in proportions that she must have gotten Omar the Tentmaker to do her dress. She was attempting to converse with a huge, lusty-looking man, a living Brueghel figure; their stomachs stuck out so far that they almost needed megaphones to reach each others' ears.

Greg was engaged in talk with someone I didn't recognize.

"Well, that's not really pertinent, since I'm divorced now," I heard him say.

The man at his side nevertheless thrust into his hand a business card. "But you might get married again, or know some young couple who's having problems, or an older couple for that matter ..." He then walked off.

"Who was that, Greg?" I inquired.

"Some fellow who does marriage counseling—he's got an office on Maple Street. He's going around trying to drum up business. He wanted to enroll me among his clients, though I told him I wasn't interested—it's too late for my first marriage, and I don't plan on a second. Of course maybe I should follow the principle of—who said it, supposedly, Dear Abby?—'The worst you can do is lose!'" He laughed.

"What nerve! I wonder how many times *he's* been married. Most of those people are cranks anyhow." I certainly didn't think he could do anything for Jack and me. "Oh, well. Listen, I want you to look back there, over to the right; see who Kori is talking to?"

"It's Mario d'Angelo, isn't it? Good—maybe he'll keep her off of me for a while. What happened to Al?"

"I don't know," I answered. "Oh, there he is, with Richard and Jennifer."

"Well, I think he's lost out; she's batting her eyelashes at Mario."

"They were speaking ... very personally, you might say. I heard her squeal 'Viagra.'"

"Good Lord! How could they get on that topic so fast? Surely she hasn't recommended it? It may have been a speculative crack about Al."

"I don't want even to think about it. If Mario likes her, fine; I hope he'll take her away."

I was writing the script. Soon, she came over to Greg, with Mario at her side. Syrup dripped from her mouth, rounded and dark like a bing cherry. "Oh, Greg, *so* good to have met you. But I'm afraid I'm not free the rest of the evening—*sorry*. Mario here and I are going down to Galatoire's."

"You lost out, Greg, and you didn't even want to be in the running," I said when they'd walked off.

"Thank God. Let's go find Elinor and Roger and head downtown. Imagine what the waiters at Galatoire's are going to think when they see the poodle suit! Though," he added as an afterthought, "maybe it's no worse than what some tourists wear."

Leaving the exhibit and the few artists still standing around, hoping for compliments or a sale, the four of us walked to Greg's Explorer. Jennifer and Richard had told us goodbye and gone off. As

10

we were driving down to Canal Street, Greg put on a tape—one of the Brandenburg Concertos. He rolled down his window and turned the music on high volume, sending into the streets a baroque blast that competed quite well with a car alarm not far away and the cacophonous racket of a couple of boom-boxes carried by youths on the sidewalk. "Sorry," he said to us, raising his voice, "if it's a bit loud. After Kori and now this awful show, my nerves are a little raw. I just need to ... well, make a statement, as people would say!"

"If you keep blasting like that," shouted Elinor, "it will reach as far as Galatoire's sidewalk, and Kori and her swain will have to listen to Bach while they're waiting in line."

"Oh, I just love Bach!" I said, imitating her voice.

We got to Canal Street and Greg turned down the volume.

Roger remarked, "You all are a pack of snobs. But of course I agree with you. That's why Elinor and I get along so well." He gave her a tender pat on the shoulder.

"Maybe, though," Greg replied, "we get what we deserve when we run into someone like Kori. Don't we need to be brought down from our ivory towers and into reality? Her kind challenges our claim and our ability to bring art to the people—since that's what a museum is for, isn't it? 'Sweet are the uses of adversity ...'"

"'Which, like the toad ... wears yet a precious jewel in its head,'" I continued. "But notice that tonight the rhinestones were on the poodle's collar, not its head!"

"Do you think Mario will invite her to his gallery sometime?" asked Elinor.

"Perhaps," Greg answered, "and there are some tacky things there she might like. Maybe he'll take on her aesthetic education." That would be something: he was known for outlandish taste. "Then she'll tire of him, or he of her. She might try to ... seek me out again. For heaven's sake, warn me if you ever see her again while we're at the Columns, or wandering around any of our museum rooms!"

"Pearls before swine...or dogs. But New Orleans wouldn't be the same without Kori and her ilk. The 'city that taste forgot,' you know."

"True," added Elinor; "better bad taste than no taste at all. In fact, we need it; it sets off finer things."

Later that evening, after we'd had gumbo and poor-boys at a place on Frenchman Street, we were again driving uptown. Greg put on a tape of Erik Satie's "Gymnopédies." Their pure, spare lines and cool augmented chords flowed over us. I thought of the man who been killed by a truck in front of his aunt. A feeling of *caritas* made me feel a bit ashamed of our snobbery. Greg was right to say that we needed to be brought down occasionally from our ivory tower. After all, light does not belong under a bushel ...

Three weeks later, we learned by chance that Mario, promoted manager at the gallery, had hired Kori as an assistant. Far from abandoning her aesthetic education, he was, apparently, continuing it.

"Or maybe," suggested Elinor, "she's taken on his! Can you imagine what they might cook up at the gallery? Poodles on the walls, Pepto-Bismol pink on the stationery, in the restrooms, maybe an Andy Warhol soup-can on her dress, or her face made up like a Jackson Pollock canvas."

"If so," I added, "the gallery scene in New Orleans will be shaken up a bit. Greg, are you sure you don't want to sacrifice yourself and try to attract her to something more tasteful?"

"God forbid," he answered, "that I should interfere with Mario's lessons."

The irony is that, some months afterward, a leaflet arrived at the museum announcing a coming exhibit at Mario's gallery of work by a new artist named Korith. No last name was given—as if the person were Michelangelo or Raffaello—but a picture revealed that it was our

Kori, her hair restyled and her name altered to suggest seriousness. Her career, if that's what it would be, was getting off to a meteoric start, certainly. The exhibit was titled "Living Images: The Body as Art." What? Body as art—or at least body *in* art, and you can't necessarily distinguish—is as ancient as art itself—Assyrian and Egyptian bas-reliefs, Greek and Roman statues, pre-Columbian statuettes, not to mention European painting and sculpture. So what did she have in mind and what was new?

Greg, understandably, refused to go see the show, but Elinor and I, motivated by both courtesy and curiosity, went to the opening, albeit with some misgivings. Mario and Kori were presiding jointly. Mario was in evening dress. There was a crowd of extravagant people—for instance, a man wearing a velvet beret, suit, and cape, rhinestone earrings, and pointed dancing shoes. Strains of Wagner's "Siegfried's Rhine Journey" were playing in the background—Mario must have made the selection, which struck me as incongruous—and strobe lights cast blue, green, and red dyes on everything.

I am accustomed to object lessons in the outlandish—bastard assemblies of elements from high and low culture, the low always more abundant, being the dominant gene. But this was the most gruesome I'd ever encountered. What "body art" turned out to be was mostly anatomy, exteriorized. Except for cheap pictures of the Sacred Heart of Jesus and medieval renditions of the torture of Christian martyrs, including Saint Erasmus, whose intestines were pulled out and rolled up on a wheel like a garden hose, I couldn't recall any previous art that was so dependent upon interior organs of the body and some normally thought of as "private parts." Kori, the prime exhibit, was clad in a toga-like garment, with appliqués of organs: true-to-life pictures, in full color, of heart, lungs, stomach, and liver. Her shoes, made of plastic, had an x-ray picture of foot bones on the top. On her forehead was affixed a drawing of the inside of the cranium.

On the walls were silk-screen renditions of kidneys and other body parts, some of which I didn't recognize, all dark and bloody-looking. One exhibit niche was devoted to "Headgear Art"—including an arrangement of small bones affixed to a cloche hat, and something called "Chapeau-Coeur," made of red plastic and showing the valves and arteries. Displayed on stands were three-dimensional organ models, distorted and surrealistic, including the "Lover's Liver," as well as feet and hands—I mean, plaster casts of the bones—and molded imitations of other body parts. Suddenly I remembered the name *Viagra*, as pronounced by Kori that night at the show. Good heavens—had she been inspired by a prescription? Sex shops in the French Quarter not more than two blocks from where we stood sold the same sort of things, made in China, I supposed. No art collector would possibly purchase any of the stuff I'd seen—it was too outrageous. As if in response to the objection, I noticed some other items—painted silk, canvas, cotton, plastic—where the organs were so stylized that they could pass for abstract designs; they were the only ones that had prices listed.

Kori was a sensation, to judge by the exclamations and the crowd of admirers surrounding her like Secret Service men. Elinor and I, rather unnoticed, continued examining the displays. Suddenly she saw us. "Harriet! Elinor!" she exclaimed, breaking from her circle of admirers and rushing to our side. Art historians have an advantage: we are the certifiers, even if most of those we certify are dead. No matter that we were dressed conservatively, unlike most of the others present: our opinion implicitly counts for something. "How *wonderful* to see you!"

"Thank you, Kori," I managed to get out. "This is quite a show you have here!"

"Oh, do you like it?"

"It is extraordinary," I replied. "You have a good crowd."

"Yes, Mario does so well at getting out publicity—and he knows so many people. By the way, where is Greg this evening?"

Elinor spoke for us both. "Oh, he's home, writing his articles, as usual."

"Well, I'm *so sorry* he isn't here. But I hope you will tell him ..."

"Oh, yes," I assured her; "and thank you for inviting us." We'd seen enough; we made our way toward the door. Impulsively, as we walked down Chartres Street to Canal, I clutched my stomach, as though to protect that vital organ from predatory artists.

The next day, a review appeared in the *Times-Picayune.* It turned out that Kori Falgout, aka the suddenly-famous Korith, was, or had been, a free-lance medical illustrator by profession. All through that season and the next, she continued to be a sparkling success, having acquired the marketing manager she'd always needed to put her training to new uses—more flamboyant uses than illustrating medical textbooks and charts. She and Mario had educated each other aplenty. As for me, I'd seen more than I wanted of body art, that was certain. What did Cocteau say? "Art is knowing how far you can go too far." That evening I went home and looked again at my still lifes and landscapes—God, they were beautiful.

The Thomas Grant

JULIUS WALLACE WAS ALREADY on the staff at our museum when I arrived. He had been there for some years, and remained until the end, not just of his career, but of his life, since, his heart literally worn out, he collapsed and died right on the front steps. Yet, as a native New Yorker, he could never reconcile himself to living in the South, with its steamy climate, drawl, and provincial ways. New Orleans, for all its historic importance and charm, struck him as benighted, and the local accents appalled him. Since he did not like to fly, he had to take the *Crescent* or the *Southerner,* until it was abolished, in order to get back home, see his mother, and reestablish contact with Manhattan streets, concert halls, museums, and baseball. He didn't drive either. Imagining a dog behind the wheel would be scarcely more preposterous than picturing Julius cruising down the road. He always lived where he could take the streetcar and busses—for a while in the French Quarter, then in a high-rise apartment building on St. Charles Avenue.

He was the only son of a Jewish couple. Nature had favored him with a splendid intelligence and spectacular memory but an unprepossessing physique. He had thick lips, weak, bug-like eyes, not much in the way of chest or shoulders, and splayed feet. He had never married—probably never had a girlfriend—and was a mama's boy in some ways. Yet his attitude toward women was, to judge by his manner with me, basically normal. What would have been his sexual energies had been channeled elsewhere—into his studies, then his career. He was married to his work; for him, art was life, or most of it, music and baseball being the only other things that counted. No woman could have lived with him anyway. His field was ancient art, particularly of the Eastern Mediterranean and Mesopotamia. He had gone to Columbia for undergraduate work and then the University of Chicago, where he had taken full advantage of the Oriental Institute. He'd also spent time at various institutes and museums in Europe. Those were the days when one could still cross the ocean by regular liner.

Our little museum was not really suitable for his talents and interests; our holdings in his areas are thin. He spent most of his time writing on other collections and doing historical investigation, publishing his articles in our *Bulletin*, the *Journal of the American Oriental Society*, and foreign journals. When he could not avoid it, he would deal with matters at hand, obliging himself, to the degree it was possible, to focus on them. Why he hadn't found a permanent position at a big museum in a larger city was never entirely clear to me, though I could guess. He spoke sometimes of disputes and unfair treatment in two earlier positions; but maybe that was just Julius, always unhappy with the management and half of his colleagues. His intellectual snobbery could not have helped him (even baseball was, to him, a game of the mind), nor his resistance and indecisiveness, even inertia, when it came to dealing with practical questions. Perhaps chance accounted principally for his staying in New Orleans; there are few curatorial positions in ancient art, and one has to wait for a vacancy through death or retirement. As for teaching—well, Julius was entirely unfitted for that; he would not have lasted a year at a university, still less the seven required for tenure. At the Orleanian, he was protected by a contract that would have made it difficult for him to be dismissed.

He did not get on well with Reginald Mullins, the director, whom he referred to as *Mullet*. Why would he? Though both were from New York and had in common the fact that they always wore dark suits, winter and summer, they were otherwise opposites: the tall, gray-haired Gentile from an old family, who (whatever his shortcomings) was recognized in the community as an important figure in the arts, and the pudgy, unprepossessing Jew, who had no social life to speak of, no contacts, nothing but his intelligence. Anyhow, Julius would not have liked *any* director; for the director, with the board, sets the budget, and Julius always considered himself underpaid. Perhaps he was; his salary seemed more a function of his lack of importance on the local scene and unpopularity with certain colleagues than of his real achievements. Moreover, *any* director, in the course of things, would have made requests of Julius, set down policy, required that certain tasks be carried out in a certain way, and Julius would have found that unreasonable. Not that he was lazy or unwilling to give his time; that's almost *all* he did, work at the museum, then continue working at home. He simply could not collaborate well with others and had no sense of organizational requirements. His mind was like a rubber band that has been stretched and then must release, quickly, its accumulated energy; he did so partly through a stream of talk, brilliant but digressive, and ill-suited for exchanges on practical matters.

With Greg, Elinor, and me, however, Julius got on well. He had a nose for the party out of power. We were on the same footing, as colleagues, and, fortunately, there were few occasions on which one of us had to work closely on some venture with him. We formed a sort of substitute family for him. Greg was certainly his closest friend, and they spent a great deal of time together, especially after Greg separated from his wife and subsequently was divorced. They were two lonely men, one having to reacquaint himself with the single condition, the other never having left it.

It was Greg who told me one day that Julius had been invited to join a team, based in London, that was going to launch a major research project on Assyrian art, underwritten by the British Academy and some big donors—probably Iranian or Iraqi money. Julius himself was, as usual, holed up in his office, the messiest of them all, by far, with art journals, art books, catalogues, fliers, leaflets, newsletters, clippings in disarray, overflowing shelves, desk, and filing cabinet, and piled on the floor. He was far too much in a dither to bring the news himself. So Greg came down the hall with the announcement.

"Harry! Good news! Julius has just gotten a splendid offer."

"Grand! What is it?"

Greg explained, adding that much of the work could be done by correspondence. "At the outset, though, Julius will have to spend one month in England, this coming June, with the other team members."

"Will he do it? I mean, is he willing to go, and will Reginald let him?"

Greg said that, since the invitation constituted a significant honor and would bring prestige to the museum as well as Julius himself, Mullins was willing to let him take a short leave of absence. "Perhaps he even relishes the prospect of a few weeks without Julius here."

"He won't consent to fly, will he?"

"That's so, though he didn't tell Mullins so; he wanted at least to shove the letter of invitation under his nose to impress him, and make him think he'd accept. But in fact I have just explained to Julius that, although most of the liners that used to provided transatlantic service have been retired, the *Queen Elizabeth 2* still has regular crossings from mid-May until September. Five days for each crossing, thirty hours or so on the *Crescent* to New York and then back—he can do the entire thing in six weeks. He is overjoyed at the idea of going; the chance seems to him like a vindication of his abilities and his research, which so many people in Europe know about but doesn't get him very far here."

"There's another problem: Julius cannot work with a team—as part of a team. He will drive his collaborators to the madhouse."

"Well, yes. But in fact, as I understand it, the month in London is more for orientation and initial ground-laying, led by the team director. Of course you know how Julius talks, with his machine-gun delivery, always ahead of itself; I may not have a clear picture of how things are to be organized, and maybe he doesn't himself. Anyway, he wants to go."

"He deserves the chance, certainly. And if you're right in thinking that the essential work is to be done later, each researcher taking on one aspect of the project, which the team head will then bring together, perhaps it can work. Who is the head researcher, anyway?"

"A certain Professor Destuttes. I've heard of him but know nothing more."

"Well, give Julius my congratulations if you run into him this morning before I do. I've got to settle down here and get this report done, so I'll probably close my door. I want to hear more about it; let's get together soon."

Two days later, not having seen Julius, I went to his office, where, I reflected, the disorder revealed his temperament, always stirred up about something. As soon as I mentioned the trip to London, he put on a sour face and began to whine. "I can't go, Harry."

"Why not? You know about the *QE2* crossings in the summer; you won't have to fly."

"But I cannot afford it. Where would I get the money for my passage by ship? The cost is enormous; one of the office assistants inquired for me. In London we'll be taken care of—put up in some hotel near Russell Square and fed—and there's a small travel allowance, enough for airfare; but it's not much more than the cost of a train ticket with sleeping accommodations and thus can't pay for the Atlantic crossing."

I had never known what resources Julius had other than his salary. He was always complaining about being hard up, saying that he couldn't afford a better apartment, didn't have money for some expensive catalogue or other book he wanted, or couldn't go to Chicago to see the newest show at the Art Institute and watch the Cubs play (they were his favorite National League team; he had felt betrayed when the Dodgers left Brooklyn and had never accepted the Mets). Since his mother was still alive, she must have had, at least in usufruct, any small assets his father had left. Still, Julius should have been able to live on his salary: he was unmarried, had no car, did not have expensive habits (except for art books and subscriptions to journals that Mullins refused to order for the museum because they were too specialized). I supposed he never saved anything, never invested, just spent it all on books, yearly trips to New York, occasional visits to Chicago, concert and opera tickets in New Orleans (he subscribed to every series), and eating out—since he never cooked a thing, or even opened a can, as far as I knew. He may have had medical bills also;

while we all had group insurance, he sometimes consulted doctors in New York about his heart, and insurance probably didn't cover costs of out-of-state physicians.

My speculations were pointless; Julius kept repeating that he couldn't afford to go by ship and wouldn't fly.

"You've got to manage somehow! This is too important. After all, Mullins has agreed to a leave, and he will be piqued if you do not accept his generosity. Think, also, how much pleasure it will give some around here, especially Emily, if you must turn down this chance."

Emily Blankenship, like so many others, gives great value to her "perception" of things. The real standing Julius had in his field did not impress her; the "perception" was that he was a loser, a fussbudget, a pedant concerned with details—as if art and art history weren't just that—and she would feel vindicated by any setback he had.

"Not to mention the importance of this opportunity in your own career," I added. "It fits so well into your interests, and should give additional exposure to your work—maybe lead even to other projects. Perhaps you could get a loan?"

The notion wasn't very sound: I imagine he had no collateral other than an art library. He dismissed it impatiently.

"What about a grant then, Julius, a travel grant? There might be something that would fit these circumstances, although, with June just a few months away, the application dates for this summer may have passed. I know, I know" (he had gestured as if to brush aside the suggestion as absurd), "it is horribly tedious to look up these things. But it would be worth it." I made him promise not to tell Mullins nor, certainly, the British professor that he could not go, and assured him that I would look into the directories of foundations for a suitable grant.

On the following weekend, Greg, jogging in Audubon Park, ran into Will Thomas, the son of a deceased museum benefactor, whose family still made donations from time to time. Will and Greg know each other from their exercise club. As Greg reported it to me, they stopped to chat, stepping off the track for a few minutes, under an oak. Greg is not the sort to hit on someone for money; he's in art history, not development. But the topic did turn to museum finances. By chance Will, admitting that, under the pressures of his business, he hadn't kept up well with things at the museum, happened to ask whether Greg knew who had gotten recently the travel fellowship that old man Thomas had endowed.

Greg had never heard of this fellowship, and said so.

"Well, I realize that you don't handle this stuff, though still I'm surprised you aren't aware of it. It is supposed to go to a staff member, for research at a museum or library or architectural sites, or similar projects, either here or abroad."

Greg immediately thought of Julius. It seemed providential, this discovery. Perhaps someone else had won the award for the current year, but he couldn't imagine who. Emily and her friends would have bragged to everyone; and Greg knew that neither he, Elinor, nor I had gotten anything, then or earlier. Greg promised Will that he would look into the matter and telephone him.

On Monday, when Greg inquired of Sharon Lively, Mullins's secretary, about the fellowship, she expressed ignorance of it and said Thomas must have been mistaken. Sharon is in good faith; she really thought that such a fund didn't exist.

"Well," I asked Greg, "did you suggest that she look into the files on endowments?"

"No, though maybe I should have. But that seems insulting to Sharon."

"You're right. Maybe Will is wrong about this endowment, but if not, it bears investigation. You're not going to drop this, are you?"

Greg is tenacious, like a dog with his teeth in a trousers cuff. "Certainly not."

So he made an appointment to see Mullins. He couldn't get in before Friday afternoon.

Around 11:00 on Saturday morning he called me at home. "Harry, can you come meet me for coffee at the Rink? I want to tell you what I found out yesterday."

"Sure; just give me a half-hour or so. Is Elinor coming?" But then I remembered that she and Roger were going across the lake for the weekend. "Oh, no, she'll have left by now."

So the two of us had coffee, with no one else around except a few tattooed and earringed students and bohemians and some Garden District tourists. What Greg had to say was almost incredible.

"I saw Mullins all right. He denies that there is, or ever was, such a fellowship endowed by old man Thomas. I made him look in the files— at least he pretended to—and he claimed he found the documents for other gifts from the Thomas family—you know, lots of gifts to support purchase of paintings as well as the small sculpture gallery—but no travel stipend."

"Well, I suppose Will is just mistaken."

"Oh, no. I called him as soon as Mullins and I finished, and we met this morning in the park, by the fountain. He brought the original, notarized copies of the documents making the donation, with the precise description of the award, all the conditions set out, and the total sum indicated. They are signed by his father, of course, by his father's attorney, Robert Andry, by the chairman of the museum board, and by the museum director."

"It wasn't Mullins himself, was it? When did all this take place?"

"No, at least it wasn't Mullins himself. It was in the late 1950s. The board chairman was Charles Everett—ever hear of him?—and the director was Aloysius Becnel."

"I know that name, of course. But he's been long gone."

"Yes. But that Mullins! Always preaching to us 'institutional memory, institutional responsibility.' And then he himself doesn't know who has donated what."

We were indignant, seeing Mullins's ignorance, or deception—I didn't know what to believe—as one more directorial sin. I had to admit, however, that it could be simple error on his part, not conspiracy.

"Of course it may be!" Greg retorted. "But since when have you, Harriet D'Aquin, been so tolerant of others' errors—errors that have repercussions? You *know* you expect perfection from everyone, including yourself."

"Sorry, Greg," I answered. "Mea culpa. You're right: such mistakes are unacceptable. What did Will say when you reported that Mullins denied there was such a fellowship?"

"You can imagine; he exploded. He would have had apoplexy if he weren't in such good physical condition. After all, that is *his family's* money, and it was to be in his mother's honor; that's the way his father set it up."

Will had resolved to go see Mullins, taking all the papers; the terms of the donation would allow the Thomas family to retrieve the endowment if it wasn't used according to the conditions. Greg also wanted to speak to Mullins, who would have to be informed that Julius needed extra travel support because he wouldn't fly. Though it was risky to broach the subject with someone so temperamental, Greg decided to say something to Julius about the existence of the fellowship, to keep him from despairing; he easily fell into depression and might write back to refuse the offer, especially if I couldn't locate soon a plausible source of grant money.

By mid-morning on Monday the museum offices were in turmoil. Fortunately, on Mondays doors do not open to the public until 11:00; otherwise, visitors might have heard the commotion. On the strength of his family's connections to the museum and the major donations it had made, Thomas had been able to put an early call through to

Mullins, who, according to Sharon, canceled other appointments in order to free time for him. Shortly after I arrived, I saw Will enter the building, explaining to the guard that the director was expecting him. It could not have been comfortable for Mullins to see written proof that a grave mistake had been made—and hear that he was considered at fault. I had difficulty believing that Mullins was directly responsible for the oversight. He is foolish sometimes, easily swayed by visions of prestige or pseudo-prestige, and overly concerned with appearances; but I did not believe him capable of misuse of funds, or even the mismanagement that would lead to it. Something else must have happened in the years between the gift by old Mr. Thomas and Mullins's arrival. It was quite possible that Becnel never activated the fellowship, through indolence and neglect, or worse; I had heard that he did not keep very good records. This is, after all, the most easygoing city in the country, and one of the most corrupt. As for Everett, the board chairman then, his task wasn't that of overseeing operations in detail.

No sooner had Mullins gotten rid of a very irate Will Thomas—by blandishments, I guess, though the heart of the matter still had to be elucidated—than he ran into Julius. I had seen Mullins accompany Thomas to the central foyer and escort him out, taking pains to show as much courtesy as possible. As Mullins returned, Julius emerged from his office and confronted him by the bulletin board, where I had been posting things. Julius was beside himself; paranoia came easily to him. I stood listening to the accusations, which, with drops of saliva, flew out of his mouth like grapeshot.

"What is this about a stipend you've been hiding—funds to support travel and research? What do you mean by not telling anyone? You *knew* I had an offer to go to England."

Mullins just stood there for a moment, trying to find words to confront this new rage. I noticed that he tugged on his shirt cuffs, pulling them down below his coat sleeves.

Julius stamped his foot. "You despise me because I'm just a Jew boy, and I don't have any connections here ... In your eyes, I'm just a harmless drudge" (even in his rage, he remembered Dr. Johnson's phrase) "whereas you are the *director*, in thick with old New Orleans society—clubs and dinners and Mardi Gras balls and all that."

Mullins tried to protest. "Now, Julius, none of this was deliberate. I suppose Greg told you everything. If so, he must have said ..."

"That makes no difference, none at all! *You* are responsible for things in this third-rate place. You really don't care very much about any of us—about what *we* care about and you are supposed to—our research, the reputation of this museum, what we've given our lives to."

Allowing for exaggeration, there was some truth in those words; Mullins frequently made protestations about the importance of our work and the value of the museum to the community, but most of what he said constituted a superficial window-dressing directed to the public.

"And I do believe you're jealous of my success—because my work is very well known in Europe and the Near East, whereas you're just an *Americanist*." He said it with a sneer and stamped his foot again. He was very red in the face.

I knew it was a strain on his heart for him to get so excited. Worried, and feeling for him—although the scene would have appeared comical to some—I interrupted. "Julius, be reasonable for a moment; let Reginald talk to you and tell you what he knows, and what he's going to do." That last phrase was a broad hint.

"*He's* the one who's unreasonable!"

Greg had probably heard most of this from his office. He stepped out, took Julius by the arm, and led him back into his own office, trying to calm him down. It didn't work immediately—I could hear him screaming about "Mullet"—but at least it gave Mullins a chance to collect himself, and me to speak again. "Look, Reginald: Greg, and Elinor, and I, and you too, I'm sure, despite what he claims, are concerned about Julius. Whatever happened to that endowment in the convoluted financial records here—you have to admit they are terrible, or else we wouldn't be in this fix—you need to look into the matter, find the funds, and see to it that Julius is the first recipient—the first within anyone's memory, at least. As for all the opportunities we've lost in the past—think of those trips to Paris I paid for myself—it's probably too late. The important thing is to see to Julius, and soon. I've been searching for foundations that might give him some support, but the deadlines are mostly past, and some of them have strange requirements that Julius can't meet. Where *is* that money, anyhow? In some Swiss bank account?"

He made his characteristic gesture of wiping his brow, although, to his credit, it was not damp. "I don't know, Harriet. Will Thomas's documents make it clear that the fellowship was set up, but don't help me locate our records, still less the money itself. God, what a way to begin a week! *I* didn't do this; *I* didn't steal the money, for God's sake. You don't think so, do you?" And he walked away without waiting for my answer.

He didn't need to be pressed any more; the point had been made. I knocked lightly at Greg's door, half-open. Julius was still there. "Julius," I said, "we're with you. Reginald will find that money somehow; we'll get you over to London."

This episode had left us all agitated. And people think that a museum is a separate world, an oasis of calm and beauty, where you gaze quietly at pictures, examine prints, or walk around the sculptures, admiring the stone or bronze, and then go to the café for a sandwich and coffee, under the unmoved eyes of the past! All these representations of life on the walls, whether born of light or darkness, whether sublime, grotesque, classical or romantic, cluttered, cautious, brazen, healthy, or insane, were purchased with the cold cash of life. It is a struggle, too, to keep them visible and clean and try to decipher their meaning, so that others' visions may become ours.

Back in my office, I reflected that, whatever happened, Will Thomas's family would probably never make another donation. Will had not been the supporter his father was, but still, from time to time, some Thomas money continued to trickle in, underwriting the purchase of a good painting that turned up on the market or a few architectural or botanical drawings for the Louisiana collection. We wouldn't see that again. I just hoped that Mullins could locate the missing funds, which, since the interest had not been paid out under his directorship, should have increased substantially, and persuade Will to leave them in trust rather than taking them back on grounds of breach of contract.

Greg, bless him, offered to mediate, if necessary. Mullins told Sharon to put aside everything else she was doing for the whole week; a low-level assistant would take calls. The idea was that she would look through every file in the entire office; Mullins himself was to help her. They even planned to work on Saturday. For Mullins to go to the office on Saturday was a novelty. Elinor and I tried to keep Julius in the nearest thing he had to equilibrium. We made him promise to send his written acceptance to London before the week was out. It was by no means certain that the funds would be found—someone might really have purloined them in the past—and grant prospects weren't good; but I was convinced now that Reginald would arrange somehow for transportation on the *QE2*. Let him get down on his navy-blue-clad knees and ask an angel for the money! Just not someone who was a close friend of the Thomas family...

Greg, meanwhile, did not cease pressing Mullins. "I told him," he reported, "that Julius needed to know—and needed to know *now*. Think of it, Harry: Mullins *could* be accused of careless handling of museum funds, at the least... He's perfectly aware that he's in a tight spot; so I think he is giving it his full attention. Blackmail would be ungentlemanly of me, of course." He chuckled.

We kept after Julius, the way you check up on a child, and on Friday, he and Greg walked to the postbox together with the letter of acceptance. It was decided that we would all have dinner the next evening at the Upperline; Jack, my husband, would come, and Roger would accompany Elinor. Julius didn't drink, but the rest of us would meet at the Bayou Bar at the Pontchartrain Hotel; he would join us at the restaurant, just off the streetcar line.

The Bayou Bar, that Saturday, was not crowded; the conventioneers were all downtown. We were just chatting about the week when the bartender came over. "There's a telephone call for someone named Greg. Sorry; I couldn't catch the last name. Perhaps that's one of you?"

We were astonished; who knew where he was except us? Greg calmly stood up and went to the phone. As he spoke, I could see he was getting excited—anger, indignation, pleasure all show quickly on his big, ruddy face. He was back at the table in no time.

"That was Sharon."

"Sharon!" said Elinor. "How did she know you were here?"

"Oh, I just happened to mention to her yesterday that we were coming here—and then would go to the Upperline to meet Julius—and that we'd like good news to talk about."

"And what did she say?" two or three of us asked at once. Even Jack was interested; Julius irritated him, but he had always considered Mullins something of a fraud.

"The money has been found, and there's a lot of it! Sharon and Mullins, down on their hands and knees today, pulling out old files on the bottom shelf in the back storage room, found the records and the pass book to the account."

So Mullins really had been on his knees, after a fashion. The image was not unpleasing.

"What's curious is that the money is in a trust fund in a little bank in Terrebonne Parish. It doesn't seem to bother with sending out yearly reports! Or maybe Mullins just pays no attention; maybe he gives them to a part-time worker to file, and they get thrown out instead."

"A lot of Becnels live down there," I pointed out; "Aloysius Becnel probably stuck it in the bank of an uncle or cousin. Maybe it doesn't exist anymore—taken over by some other; it may have changed its name two or three times, and its own records may be lost."

Greg knew no further details; Sharon had told him just the bare bones. We finished our drinks, got into our two cars, and headed up the avenue for the Upperline. As we turned on Bordeaux Street, I saw Julius getting off the streetcar. After we'd parked, we waited on the sidewalk till Julius got there.

Greg had the pleasure of telling him that the money had been found. "Surely you will get enough to take care of your ticket on the *QE2*. Sharon says the account is very large, so the interest should be sizeable. And Mullins won't dare cook up some pretext not to give it to you. Did I tell you that, according to Will, the director and the board decide who gets the grant? He does his best to keep that board happy; they better vote with him on this."

Julius was ecstatic; we had trouble reining him in and getting him inside the restaurant. We were shown to a table halfway back. Jack, Roger, and Greg immediately asked for the wine list, and started looking it over. Julius could hardly sit still; Elinor and I listened as he talked on. For once, he was not pessimistic; he said that "Mullet" couldn't weasel out on this.

The waiter took the wine order, brought two bottles, opened them, and filled our glasses. Julius asked for a Coca-Cola. Then the menus came. "Do you think there's mullet on the menu tonight?" Julius asked, with an innocent air. We burst into laughter. As it was subsiding, I heard a familiar voice by the bar, where a small line of those waiting for tables was forming.

"Good heavens!" I exclaimed. "That sounds like Mullins."

Sure enough: there he was, with his wife, Gladys. It was coincidence, of course: Sharon would not have told him our plans, nor would he have sought us out—far from it. Soon Reginald and

Gladys were seated almost beside us. We could not help but greet them. Pleasantries were exchanged. With Gladys, conversation is easy; she says and thinks nothing but commonplaces anyhow. With Mullins, further talk might have been a bit delicate: we knew what he'd been doing all day, and all week.

Greg, a bit bull-like himself in a nice way, simply took the bull by the horns. "Reginald, we hear that the money has been found; Sharon telephoned, since she knew how anxious we were and how much Julius deserves this grant. I'm sure you don't mind her calling instead of waiting for you to tell us." (He didn't say she'd phoned us at a bar.)

"That's right, I'm pleased to say. One of my predecessors obviously hadn't filed this material very well, and the money is not with our other accounts at the Whitney; it's in an anonymous numbered account, in a small bank in Terrebonne Parish. I will not conceal from you the fact that I am very much relieved."

"So," Greg pursued, "now that you have copies of Will Thomas's documents and the money itself, I assume you'll see to it that the award is reinstated—and that Julius will be the new laureate."

"Of course; I believe that can be taken care of very soon. Just some … formalities with the board, and then looking into the account itself; I don't know whether that bank still exists under that name."

"You have gotten in touch with Will, of course?" Greg continued. "Excuse me; this is not my business, directly, but I've become involved in spite of myself."

"Of course; I telephoned him immediately."

"Did you find any record of whether the fellowship was *ever* awarded?" I asked.

"Yes, two or three times in the early days."

Sic transit gloria mundi, I thought; who had won the awards, and what had ever come of it all?

"By the way," Mullins continued, "the Thomas family has agreed not to pursue any legal action against the museum for letting these funds sit idle—but on conditions."

"What are those?" asked Julius, suddenly frantic: he could already imagine that new strings attached to the award would keep him from getting it, just as he thought it was his.

"They insist—and Will was adamant about this—that our auditors calculate the interest not paid out in the years when those on the current staff" (and he looked at Greg and me) "made research trips not funded by the museum or any foundation, and see to it that appropriate reimbursement is made for travel expenses then. Retroactive support, in other words."

"You know that I'm something of a friend of Will," observed Greg. He is scrupulous.

"That makes no difference. The grant is specifically for those on the curatorial staff; it would be expected that they would be known and have friends in the community."

It was plain that the waiter was anxious for us to order. We thanked Mullins in conciliatory words, and turned to the menus. The entire meal was celebratory; Julius was all sunbeams. We talked about London and his marvelous opportunity, and then about the Saints' season, which had ended without glory, as usual, and prospects for Cubs baseball, and lots of other small topics.

Things happened as Mullins had said: Julius got a large grant, more than enough for his ship passage to England, enough, in fact, to underwrite also a week's trip to the continent, Mullins having given him extra time off. Greg and I eventually were handed checks partially covering expenses for past trips to Europe, and each of us, along with some other staff researchers, got an award for the coming fall. We saw Julius off at the train station in mid-May. His big suitcase had been checked; he would have to get a porter to help him with it in New York. He carried a briefcase and a little overnight bag, but also an armful of back issues of journals and newspapers that he intended to read in his compartment and on shipboard. He would be a spectacle there, walking into the salons in his dark suit with a passel of reading matter for intellectuals, poring over the pages for hours, while casually dressed, pleasure-seeking passengers were playing bridge or conversing or going out for shuffleboard. Greg gave him such a thumping on the back, by way of affectionate farewell, that he almost dropped his load. After his death, I could still remember him clearly, standing on the steps of the sleeping coach, waving to us. "Goodbye, goodbye," he called. He seemed fragile—all that intensity of mind, attached to an unreliable heart, in an unreliable world. His vulnerability made me think again of those distant sculptures, reliefs, and mosaics to which he had devoted his life, all witnesses to a consciousness trying to understand, and leave something of itself, as it looked out over the shifting dunes and the blue indifference of the sea.

A Mirage on the Road

WE HAD PITCHED CAMP the previous evening under tall pines in the San Juan National Forest, west of Pagosa Springs, and I had rested well, with my sleeping bag spread on pine needles and the triangle of the open tent flap crammed with stars. We had washed with water heated over a small fire and had made a simple breakfast of coffee, orange juice from the cooler, and rolls. Leaving the tents set up, since we planned two more nights there, we had put a few things in our backpacks and started hiking on a trail that should lead us to a back road and from there to a property Cal wanted to look over. The three of us—my cousin Cal McDonald, his wife, Jane, and I—had organized this camping trip not only for pleasure but so that he could investigate various old lodges and dude ranches in southern Colorado with an eye toward buying one and getting back into the business of renting out cabins or rooms to hikers, fishermen, and hunters. He had owned a successful accounting business in town for most of his career, but missed the rougher and more varied life, which he had known second-hand as a young man, of those who run rustic tourist operations; and now, thinking ahead to retirement, he was seduced by the idea of returning to life partly outdoors, with an income but also the rewards of looking out in the evening over his own pasture, creek, and forest. He did not want the sort of property near a town that developers buy to make "ranchettes" or "rancheritos"—small acreages for building mostly second homes; he wanted an isolated site, but already built and established, which could be advertised, genuinely, as a hostelry run by a Coloradan, in the traditional manner, with a stream, horses, cabins, and other rustic features. Through a connection, he had learned about an old resort well off the highway, not far from our campsite, owned by a woman now getting on in years and without any family; he was determined to visit it.

For some while we hiked along the trail, dappled in alternating sunlight and the shade of Douglas firs and aspen. It connected with a county gravel road, well-rutted and washboarded by recent rains. Following it uphill for a mile or so, we came to a gate. "Lazy River Ranch," proclaimed the rather worn sign; "Cabins, Fishing, Riding, Home Cooking." That was it. The gate swung open easily, and we proceeded up a rough track running along a grass pasture on one side and sagebrush range on the other. Past a small rise, we could see the place, or guess at it, in a grove of conifers and some Lombardy poplars. Back of the buildings and trees, hills rose sharply, their stands of pine and firs scalloped darkly onto the dusty-green sage.

A few cars with out-of-state license plates were parked over to one side of the open space in front of the main lodge, a neat log structure, not very large; farther left, under the trees, I noticed an old, battered pickup truck and a newer one. The cabins were set in a row to the right; three or four cars were visible farther down the row. A dog barked briefly somewhere. The three of us went up the steps of the lodge and crossed the wide porch. Cal knocked at the screen door; it wasn't clear whether one should enter or not. In a bit a sturdy woman clad in a denim shirt and women's work trousers appeared. I wondered whether she was the owner, a housecleaner, or the cook. She was about the right age, as I understood it, to be the proprietor. She looked at the three of us, then at the front yard, taking in very clearly the fact that no new vehicle seemed to be parked there, and looked back, rather quizzically. Cal introduced himself and said that he wasn't interested in taking rooms but instead had walked over from the nearby forest campground in order to look around the place, because he had heard that she might be interested in selling it. He added that he supposed he was speaking to the owner.

"Not at all," she retorted somewhat sharply. "Well, yes, I *am* the owner, but what makes you think I want to sell my business? This land has been in my family since my great-grandfather's days. Who did you say you were, anyway?"

Cal repeated his name, said he was from Colorado Springs, and added that he had worked at a guest lodge years before.

"Well, I don't care. My place is not for sale."

We were still standing on the porch, in front of the screen door, three-quarters ajar and filled with the woman's frame. Flies buzzed around, making their steady summer music, and I noticed two or three darting for the opened door; one settled in a curl of the woman's gray hair. I was half-turned around, anticipating things as always, ready to go, when I realized that Cal was saying, "You see, someone you know spoke to me about you—my wife's friend in Colorado Springs, Alice Hopkins." I had heard of this woman, some connection of Jane's who had worked in the alumni office at Colorado College, but I had not realized, nor had Cal and Jane, that merely mentioning the name would make such a difference.

"Oh!" the woman answered, as sharply as before but with a distinctly different tone. "Oh—so you know Alice? In that case, come in, do come in." Standing aside and gesturing for us to enter, she showed us past the reception desk, designed, like the rest of the lodge, in mountain cabin style, and then into a sitting room to the left. It was decorated in the Western tradition, with simple pine furniture, a pine-board floor, bearskins in front of the chairs, a few hunting trophies, and what I recognized as very fine Navajo rugs, some hung on the walls, others suspended from a half-balcony at one end of the room. The fireplace was empty, but one could see that a full-bodied blaze could be lit there in the colder seasons.

After the bustle of our entry and our sitting down—I chose an armchair that would put me just on the edge of the conversation—a few more diplomatic preliminaries had to take place. We voiced a "thank you" or so, commented on the pleasing features of the room, and settled back politely. The owner then picked up the topic that had brought us there. "Well, you know then, since you know Alice, that I am Carole Magnin; she and I were at the university together." She gave a wry chuckle. "That was some years ago, yes indeed." Turning to Jane, who was seated on a broad couch next to Cal, she added, "And you are—this man's wife, the one who really knows Alice?"

"Yes, I'm Jane McDonald, Cal's wife, and yes, I've known Alice for a long while, since I too worked at Colorado College, in the art department. I knew her even before that. She and my parents grew up near each other in Manitou Springs, and my family still lives there, just up the road from her."

Carole Magnin turned to me. "And you are ...."?

"Oh, sorry, I'm Harriet D'Aquin—Cal's cousin. Please call me Harry. I've come along on this trip just for the company." Thinking then that she might notice my accent, I added, "I'm originally from El Paso but have lived in New Orleans for many years. I'm with a museum there, but I find time to visit Colorado, in order to see my cousins and paint, since I'm an artist also and do landscapes, among other things."

She turned back to Cal and Jane. "I didn't want to let you in, you know." (We knew.) "I am too proud." There was a silence. "It is true, what Alice must have told you; not that I really *want* to sell the Lazy River, but that I *must* think of what is going to become of it—what is going to become of me. This place—and a lot more land, which I've had to sell off, over there" (she gestured) "was originally ranched by my great-grandfather, then my grandfather. They had cattle, which made money for them some of the time but not always. My grandfather had the idea of building the cabins that you see and creating a sort of fishing ranch—not really a dude ranch, because not many Easterners came around and he didn't furnish entertainment or attempt to teach anyone outdoor skills; just a place where people who didn't require much could stay for a few weeks in the summer and fish or ride if they wished and already knew how, or look at the mountains if that was all they wanted. Then my parents ran the place, and ran it well. The war hurt the business, of course, not just then but in the fifties, because ideas about vacations changed and different, fancier places sprang up and continue springing up ... Pagosa Springs resort, Breckenridge, Aspen, all that sort for the moneyed set ... But my parents held on anyhow and I was able even to go to the university in Boulder. I was their only child—the Depression, you know. Now here I am, over seventy years old, and I have trouble running the place—it has often

38

been hard to get domestic help, and the income just barely meets my expenses. And, since I never married, there's no one to leave it to ... no one. Alice was right."

Her melancholy note did not call for an immediate comment; a person her age has a right to her regrets. Suddenly, her tone changed entirely. "But why do I say that? Now things are different! Did you see that pickup truck at the front—the newer one, the red Ford? That belongs to my new helper, Johnny McIntosh. I call him my foreman. He'll be around later; I'll introduce you to him. Oh, he's not strictly *new*; in fact, now he seems to belong around the place as much as I do." Johnny had been working there for almost a year, she explained. He too had come through the national forest—but not the way we had come, and not for the same reason. He and his "little wife," as Carole put it, had driven up the road in an old van one day at the end of the previous summer season, asking for work. They had been at the forest campground all that past summer, supervising the place as camp hosts for a nominal payment, living out of their van and a tent, along with their dog. Then the campground closed for the season and they were hard up. He had explained to Carole that they did not want to leave the area and would do any sort of work. Why they had picked the Lazy River Ranch—certainly not very imposing and reached only by two gravel roads—wasn't clear; but Carole looked upon them as a godsend. The place needed all sorts of attention, both the routine maintenance that must be done in the autumn to clean up after summer use and protect against the winter, and other work long overdue; and her summer help, not very good anyway, had left. Carole had hired them on the spot, given them a cabin to live in, and put Johnny to work. "Why I agreed, I'm not quite sure," she added. "Of course I *did* need help—there is always so much to do, just to keep things as they are so that guests come back, at least—but I usually don't hire people just off the road."

The "little wife," Ellie, had taken a job at a store outside of Pagosa Springs, to which she drove the van, wheezing even in low gear, in good weather and bad; and Johnny, who apparently could do anything, had worked much of the winter, painting, plastering, plumbing (there were no longer outhouses, Carole explained, as in her grandfather's day, but the minuscule sanitary facilities in the cabins were old and required frequent repairs), chopping wood, cleaning up the grounds, even doing some roofing. His wife had helped too on occasion, sorting linens, assisting with painting. Now the new season was drawing to a close, and he was still at it. "Business has been even a little better this year, with people staying longer, and I think that he is part of the reason; the cabins look nicer. I have even been able to get back some of my horses. I used to have to board them at a ranch farther down the river, and my guests, if they wanted to ride, went down there. But Johnny has fixed up the corral and stables behind the trees, there, and I've brought back six of the horses for riding and a couple of pack horses."

"Then, that pickup you mentioned..." began Cal; "but you said he came in an old van?"

"The truck's his now, or almost; in the winter, he and Ellie got a loan from the bank and bought it. She usually takes it to work, but this morning he drove her in—some business he had. You see, he's doing well. I hope he'll stay; he can stay here as long as he wants."

"Then you really are not interested in a buyer for your property, if one came along—if I were that one?" asked Cal. "Not that I'm sure this set-up would do; I might like to consider it, though, after a look around."

"Not right now, certainly. Johnny's arrival has changed so much. He and his little Ellie—they have made such a difference. I feel like going on now, not just for my father's and grandfather's sake, but for them; they need the ranch as much as the ranch needs them."

"Still," Jane intervened, "we might like to look at your cabins and the rest of your set-up here. We might find some business for you when we run into out-of-state visitors, or among Cal's friends, or Harry's down in the Louisiana swamps."

"Of course. Look, why don't we have a cup of coffee and wait till Johnny comes back from working on a cabin; I'm expecting him. Then we'll all go see the rest of the place here, and the horses, if you like them."

Carole Magnin—I don't know why, but thought of her more comfortably by both names than by one, perhaps because of her age—did not invite us into the dining room, where, she explained, only breakfast and dinner were served, lunches being always box lunches prepared ahead of time; instead, she brought in cups from the kitchen and a large old-fashioned coffee pot, as big as an urn, made of flecked blue enamel. We drank the potent brew, all of us adding sugar and milk. I tried to make small talk; Cal and Jane, with their Colorado background and acquaintance with Alice, did better than I. Pretty soon, from the back of the lodge, we heard a door slam and then what turned out to be Johnny's voice. "Miss Carole, oh Miss Carole!"

"In here, Johnny—in the lounge."

He came in shortly, an older man than I had supposed—close to fifty, one would guess—with a black tee shirt, ordinary dungarees, and heavy scuffed boots. He had smudges of dirt on his arms, and I could see, even from my seat, that his nails were stubby and dark with dirt. But he was not ill at ease; and after all, we too were very informally dressed, in our hiking clothes.

"We have company, Johnny, you see," said Carole.

"Oh, hello," he said; "how did you get here? I didn't see another car parked outside."

"They walked, Johnny, from the campsite—you know, the forest campground where you and Ellie worked."

"Oh, really? Do you want to stay at the Lazy River for a while and fish or ride?"

"No," Cal explained, "we just came over to pay a call here; I'd heard about this lovely spot from someone my wife knows in Colorado Springs."

"Let's be frank; they wanted to look the place over to see whether they might buy it."

Johnny did not blink. "It's not for sale, is it, Miss Carole?"

"No, Johnny, not now. Anyway, let me introduce you: Cal and Jane McDonald, and his cousin Harriet—no, Harry, she said."

We shook hands. Cal added, "I understand you are Johnny McIntosh; we are fellow Scotsmen, or rather, our ancestors were, a good while ago."

Johnny's smile was telling. "Scotland! I've always wanted to go there. Maybe Ellie and I will get there someday. But I know nothing about my ancestors, nothing at all, not even much about my relatives ..."

"Johnny's originally from Delaware," added Carole.

"Yes, but I've never even been back there since I came out west. Anyhow, I don't belong there. My mother died when I was born, my father picked up and abandoned me, and all I know is that there's a half-brother McIntosh somewhere in Philadelphia ... or at least there used to be."

I found the admission odd—coming from a stranger, at least, one we'd had conversation with for only about two minutes. But what to me might be a bit shameful, or at least the sort of thing you don't spill out easily, was to him fact, perhaps even fact of pride; one makes one's destiny and sense of self from the materials at hand.

"And how did you come to Colorado?" asked Cal.

The answer would have to be very long, or very short. "I was on the road, on the road all the time. The road led here." To say what his rather wry tone signified, whether a vein of satisfaction, or a touch of bitterness, would be to know him much better than we possibly could then. Brightly, he added, "I found Ellie along the way, too."

Carole explained that she was going to give us a tour of the lodge and cabins, the corral, and the pasture leading to the river. "I want them to see how good things look here, after you've fixed them up." He discussed with her briefly a couple of practical matters and excused himself, not offering to come along. We saw the upstairs of the lodge and one of the bedrooms; then Carole ushered us outside and took us into the nearest cabin, unoccupied, in very good condition, it seemed to me, with pine furniture, blankets folded at the foot of the bed, rag rugs, a tiny bathroom, and a small corner kitchenette. Cal asked a question or so about the construction, not as a prospective purchaser, I think, but out of courtesy.

Again outside, we walked around the back under the trees toward the corral. The horses were keeping each other company at the far side; at the sound of our voices, they came over, eyes bright and tails swishing in the air. Carole gestured around and said something about still owning the near hills and all the pasture visible upstream. I could see the river—really, just a middling stream—cutting across the near pasture. Farther on, the slope was steep, and I admired again the outlines of dense stands of trees. The sky was enormously vast and high, the sort I love, holding with ease massive fortifications of white clouds that would have pleased Constable.

A sudden desire, which turned immediately into a plan, seized me. "May I ask how long you will remain open in September? I have a few extra days, after our camping trip ends, before I must return to New Orleans, and I could come down here and sketch and paint for a bit. I brought my acrylics with me. I also want to get back to watercolors— mountains, trees. I have not done enough this summer."

"The lodge will be closed after Labor Day; but I keep some of the cabins open until the first of October, for those who can prepare their own meals."

"Well, I've got my Jeep, and I could easily get into town for supplies and fix myself simple fare."

It was decided that we would speak about it more upon returning to the lodge. Cal and Jane began to talk to Carole about water and mineral rights, always important around there.

"Mineral rights are entirely mine but useless, since there is nothing here." She then went into the arrangements about water, more crucial. We walked meanwhile to the river and its crude wooden bridge, "still strong enough for a pickup truck as well as horses," and then headed back to the lodge. Carole wrote down my name in the reservations book for one week, starting after Labor Day. Cal, deciding he could not find out anything more about the place and having concluded that she intended to hold onto it anyway, thanked her for the tour and expressed his pleasure at meeting her. Jane and I added our word of appreciation, of course, and Jane assured her that she would call Alice to report the visit. We then bade Carole goodbye, explaining that we had lunch things and drinks in our backpacks and would have a picnic under the trees somewhere on the trail. As we headed toward the road, I could see Johnny beside one of the cabins, with a bucket that could have held paint or caulking material.

A week or so later, after our camping trip was over and Cal had looked at another property or two, I said goodbye to my companions and again headed southwest for the Lazy River Ranch. Being alone for a few days and concentrating on problems of rendering the imposing scenes of skyscape, range, and forest, in different lights, and brushing up my watercolor technique, would be good for me; much of what I had seen during our trip had held my eye and was preserved in my memory as painterly material, but I had not had enough solitude for concentration on technical questions, still less for going deeper into my vision.

The first days at the ranch were uneventful, except for meeting Ellie the evening of my arrival. To my surprise, she looked like a girl; she could not have been more than half Johnny's age. She was wearing a loose Hawaiian dress of bright blue and yellow, but her figure did not foretell maternity, and in fact the waistless smock looked quite incongruous on someone so young. I thought about other Ellies Johnny might have known in the past and wondered whether she represented for him in her freshness a renewal of young love or a denunciation of earlier experience. Each day I spent a few moments with Carole, simply chatting on the porch or at the corral, where I would go to visit the horses, and I greeted Johnny and Ellie when our paths crossed; but generally I kept to myself, walking to various vantage points, working with my portfolio on my knees, hiking farther on, reading in the evenings after supper in the last daylight or by the low lamp in the cabin. No one bothered me; only two other cabins were occupied, by some fishermen from New Mexico, and they left me alone, thank heaven.

On the fourth day I drove into Pagosa Springs early in the morning, needing to pick up some fresh things for my meals the rest of the week. It had occurred to me also to look around for an art supply store, to get some more paper, even if it was not very good quality. A town that size might have one, or at least a hobby shop or a printer who sold drawing paper. I stopped at the City Market, where Cal, Jane, and I had gone together and where I'd gotten my first groceries before settling in the cabin. As I started to pull into an angle space half-way down the parking lot, I saw in the opposite row a red Ford pickup that looked like Johnny's. I stopped and got out, and then I saw Johnny himself, coming around to the back of the truck, with Ellie at his side, wearing shorts this time. My first thought was surprise that she was there with him and not at work. They started arranging some boxes and bulky canvas sacks in the cargo space. I think they didn't see me at first. Ellie turned aside and pulled up a grocery cart, from which she unloaded several plastic sacks and a couple more boxes. I stepped across the lane and spoke to them.

"Hi, Ellie, hi, Johnny. I'm surprised to see you but glad—I've come in for groceries, but I could use some more drawing paper. Do you know by chance whether there's a little art or hobby shop here, or somewhere else I might look?"

Ellie looked startled at seeing me. Johnny had composure, all right. "There's a print and copy shop not far; it might have good paper. That's your best chance, at least. Go west on the highway a bit and then turn right, where you see the liquor store. It's back from the road a block or so; I think you'll find it easily."

"Thanks, Johnny. I'll go after I get my meat and fruit and so on. It looks as if you two are loading up for the month; you won't have to shop again for a while." I glanced again, rather tactlessly, at the load in the back of the pickup. There was a large tool box, I noticed, its lid open, and Johnny was stuffing some of the sacks into it. I noticed also a big keg or drum—gasoline? water? "Oh, of course, you must be getting supplies for Carole also."

Ellie's face twisted, for a moment losing its freshness. Johnny's barely changed. "Not this time. Miss Carole doesn't even know I came into town with Ellie this morning—unless she's looking for me now and figured out. We're not going back, Ellie and I. I've paid off most of my debts, and we're leaving."

"Why, Johnny! Of course, it's none of my business, really ... but ... I'm so surprised! Didn't you like working there? Carole seemed to like having you around; she said all sorts of good things about your work."

"Work is work; it is the same everywhere. Ellie and I are pulling up stakes; we're hitting the road."

Did I imagine that I saw a light film of tears over Ellie's eyes? She said nothing, just stood there for a moment, and then turned back toward the grocery cart. It was not my place to remonstrate, but I could not let them go like that, without intervening, as it were, for someone's expectations, someone's hopes.

"And she doesn't know—you didn't say anything to Carole? She will be crushed; she's genuinely interested in you and Ellie, you know. And she has counted on you so much to work during another winter, maybe rebuilding some of the cabins entirely if you could. She relied on you. Where would you find a better place?"

The implication was clear—disloyalty, impracticality. It was really not my place to pass judgment on these people I barely knew, whose life was their own—had to be their own. But Johnny did not judge me in turn for meddling or trying to impose my way of seeing. He had probably heard before many comments not too different from mine;

I suppose he was beyond them. He acknowledged at least how hard goodbyes would have been.

"It's true that Miss Carole was good to me, to us; that's why I cannot really tell her. She wouldn't understand, I know; she thought we would be there ... well, more or less forever ... unless she sold the place, of course. I never said so; she just wanted to imagine it that way."

Maybe Ellie wanted to, also. Young as she was, she could have pictured buying some of the property when Carole became incapacitated or died—they had a loan for a pickup, why not land?—and building a stable life there. But the road had won out—not Scotland (how could they ever get there?—that journey was only in Johnny's mind), but simply somewhere else.

"Johnny, may I tell Carole at least that I've seen you, and what you said? Not that it will be easy; the very thought ..."

"Of course; that will help, that will help a lot. You'll be doing me a favor."

It was a charge I could have well done without. I wondered whether disappointments were duller at Carole's age, after the precedents that experience must inevitably have afforded, or keener, in the knowledge that little time might be afforded for fate somehow to make up for them. I said a hasty goodbye, wishing Johnny and Ellie well, and headed for the supermarket. Later, my groceries in the Jeep, I found the print and copy shop Johnny had described; its stock in paper was no better than what you'd expect, but at least I could get some large sheets. I headed then for the Lazy River Ranch, my tranquility of early morning quite shattered.

Carole was on the lodge porch when I drove up and parked in front of my cabin. I hurried over. She was obviously distraught. "Harry, have you seen Johnny this morning? I can't find him anywhere, and he didn't come to get his work orders for the day."

"Yes, Carole, I've seen him ... and Ellie. I met them just now—I mean, a little while ago—in the City Market parking lot in Pagosa Springs."

"Did he say why he'd gone in with her? I wanted him to start some more repairs around the corral this morning. What are they doing in town—why wasn't she at work?"

I had to pour out the story, somewhat hurriedly but with interruptions, first my own, then hers. She took the news bravely, in her way, but the shock was written on her features.

"Oh, why? Why did they leave? It doesn't make any sense. I was going to pay him throughout the winter and have him make some major improvements; then we could have had even a better season next year. It was ... it was... in my heart ... a little bit like the old days ... the expectation of good things. I suppose I am too old for that; life has punished me for hoping. Oh, but ... you know, it was almost like having a family."

My further attempts at explanation were useless; I had already told her most of what Johnny had said, putting it in as favorable a light as possible, granting him for Carole's sake some of that justification born of sympathy—a sympathy I did not wholly feel, however—but not wishing to justify him too much, since that would have devalued the hurt she felt. To it, at least, she had an entire right.

"Carole, I'm very sorry. This leaves you in a difficult position, doesn't it? Practically, I mean—for work this fall and winter—and somewhat ... undercut in your plans. It is most unfortunate. Of course you may get some other good help; but I know that Johnny could do so many different things ..."

"It will not be the same, even if I hire someone else. Everything I told you, or your cousin Cal, rather, about the ranch and the future I truly meant; I felt I could go on here, with Johnny and Ellie helping—running the lodge, keeping my land. Those dreams of mine, those foolish old woman's dreams! They were a dry well, a mirage of green on the road to death."

48

Johnny and Ellie had doubtless gotten well down the highway by then; they had not said which direction they were going, but I could picture them driving west toward Durango, then into the canyon area—camping perhaps for a while in an isolated spot on the great sage range belonging to the Bureau of Land Management, gazing through the shimmery distances at the unearthly reds and purples of the mesas. The fishermen from New Mexico would leave the Lazy River by the end of the month. I had four more nights in the cabin, then I too would be gone; and I wasn't sure that meanwhile I would feel quite so much like crossing the old bridge and choosing a spot for sketching. Cal, having given up on the Lazy River, was talking about fixing up an old lodge northwest of Woodland Park; even if I told him what had happened, he couldn't very well bring up again with Carole for a long while the possibility of buying her place. Carole would be alone for the off-season, as she had been before Johnny and Ellie came along. She wasn't the only one, I reflected, taken in by a mirage, fixing her eyes on something shining up the road, something that moves as we move, always out of reach. Painting itself ...

I turned back toward my cabin and got my groceries from the Jeep. The pad of drawing paper lay on the seat. I picked it up, then looked past the trees, whose branches shook excitedly in the wind as if they were about to fly off. Beyond, rocky patches in the timber shone, brilliant, almost silvered, in the late morning sun.

Mr. Mullins's Funeral

WE WERE SEATED on hard chairs in one of the larger parlors at Bultman's. The rest of the furnishings and decoration were meant to reassure, even soothe us: highly polished sideboards, heavy curtains that draped flowingly and puddled on the floor, subdued colors and soft lighting—everything in good taste, as in an elegant reception room in one of the mansions not far away on St. Charles Avenue. But the chairs were unyielding: this was, after all, a funeral, and we would have to suffer a bit in acknowledgment of the unbending fact of death.

It was Reginald Mullins's father who had died. Almost everyone on the curatorial staff of the museum was in attendance, as well as Reginald's secretary, Sharon, and one or two other long-time office employees. We scarcely knew the deceased, of course, but when a parent of the director dies, it is looked upon as a death in the family. Old man Mullins was in his late eighties, and his death was not unexpected, since for extreme old age there is not much of a cure. He had moved down to New Orleans from New York, the Mullins home state, ten or so years before, following his retirement and his wife's death, and had lived alone in an apartment house near Napoleon and St. Charles. Reginald had kept a watchful eye on him.

Despite my lack of esteem and affection for Reginald, I did have genuine sympathy for him. The loss of a father or mother—even an aged one, when the survivor is an adult in middle age—shakes the foundation of one's life; to lose the author of one's being is a metaphysical scandal. Then there are often feelings of failure and guilt. Reflections on his own mortality were bound to gnaw at Reginald; he was henceforth on the front lines. For that matter, everyone there was doubtless thinking of mortality, and if, on the one hand, at a funeral one can always rejoice not to be the corpse, on the other, there is no escaping the thought, buzzing around the room like a hornet, that at some similar gathering in the future one will be the unwilling, mute, immobile centerpiece, the position occupied in this case by Mr. Mullins, enclosed in a huge dark oak casket with mounds of flowers on top and large standing sprays at the side.

I was seated with Greg d'Hannis and Elinor Perrin. Elinor's husband, Roger, had taken an hour or so off from the law offices of McKinley, Melançon, and Perrin to accompany her, even though Elinor could have said, truthfully enough, that he was under great pressure from current cases. We had spoken briefly with Reginald in the foyer when we arrived, had signed the book of condolences, and had found chairs at the left side. Waiting for the service to begin, we shifted positions on the hard chairs, whispered a word or so to each other, surreptitiously looked at others present, and stared at the walls and ceiling. I was able to identify the wreath that we had ordered in the name of the museum staff—red carnations. I watched as various others came in, signed the book, then found seats. Few of these people had known Mr. Mullins, I supposed; maybe some were in a bridge club with him, and presumably a few lived in his apartment building, but most were probably members of Reginald's circle, including a large number of Friends of the Museum, some of whom, in fact, have little to occupy them and could look upon the funeral as a distraction. They were, it turned out, to be well entertained.

After some minutes, as one old couple was shuffling toward chairs near us, Reginald and his little mouse of a wife, Gladys, accompanied by a collared clergyman, entered from a side door and took seats on the front row, cordoned off by white ribbons. Another man, who followed an instant later, was, I supposed, Reginald's brother from New York, Walter, of whom I had only heard. Like Reginald, he was tall and graying, though his features were very different. He was dressed impeccably in a dark blue pin-striped suit with an appropriate tie; but he looked out of sorts, even angry. Was it the stress occasioned by his father's death, and the attendant travel and ceremony? Stress can be expressed in various ways. Was it genuine grief, denial of an unbearable fact, or anger at heaven for creating us mortal? All those sentiments take their toll on the body. I knew little about the man, assuming merely that his experiences and outlook would be much like Reginald's.

As I was musing thus, a staff member closed the main parlor doors, through which we had entered. There was a rustling among the audience, as dresses and suits were slightly displaced, then smoothed out, to accommodate the erect posture that people felt obliged to adopt. An almost imperceptible sigh rippled through the rows, whether of feigned or real distress on the occasion, or relief that the service would finally start.

The clergyman, whom I recognized, from having seen him officiate at a wedding, as the rector from the church of St. James the Less, on Napoleon Avenue, began very simply by announcing that he would read the burial service from the Book of Common Prayer, "the 1928 version," he specified, "because the deceased preferred it to all other rites." Good for him, I thought; he hadn't been taken in by novelty, unlike Reginald, who, despite a conservative bearing, was often swayed by fads, not to say frauds, in art. The service proceeded, without music, following the written text of the Prayer Book, except for a short homily on death and a eulogy of the old man, in very general terms. The usual formulas appeared: "his fidelity to God and his country, his upright life in his profession and the community, and his role as a devoted husband and father." Whether Reginald and Walter, or the late wife, or the man's former colleagues would have agreed with these encomia I could not know. It would make little difference, I supposed; since the faults of the dead lose some of their power (not always *all*) to irritate us, overlooking them is the rule.

No mention was made of the deceased's having attended St. James's assiduously; perhaps, like so many others, he was just a nominal Episcopalian, or maybe he was put off by innovations in the church. Apparently, however, the clergyman knew or had been told by Reginald that the old fellow liked the traditional service, was fond of music, and had enjoyed sailing in his younger days. Speaking of Mr. Mullins's prowess as a sailor and enjoyment of the open waters, the rector of St. James foresaw the "Day of Resurrection, when with all the saints, including his late beloved wife—and with those seated here, his sons and all his friends" (and he gestured, first to the front row, then, vaguely, to the rest of us) "he will be raised from the waters of the deep and will embark on his eternal voyage, sails afurl, over the vast heavenly seas." The incongruity of raising from the depths one who had not drowned or died at sea and the image of all the blessed, including some who do not like the water, sailing as if on Lake Pontchartrain struck me as ridiculous; despite the seriousness of the occasion, I barely suppressed a smile. Walter, I thought, gave a start.

After the final prayer had ended, there was a pause, and Reginald rose to his feet to announce that in a few moments there was to be an hour-long "memorial concert" given by a string quartet in the solarium of Bultman's. Sharon had earlier warned us about this event, which Reginald called, following the current fashion, "a celebration of life," so it was no surprise. Roger Perrin would certainly skip it and return to his office, but the rest of our group were obliged to attend. Behind us, the large parlor doors opened, as if mechanically. Greg, Elinor and Roger, and I rose and, with the others, started moving out into the foyer, where Reginald and Gladys stood to receive condolences. The brother was standing somewhat toward the side. We were among the first to approach Reginald. We said the sort of appropriate words you would expect; I tried to make mine sound as sincere as possible, while pressing Reginald's hand. For Gladys, a grave look and a few repetitious phrases were sufficient.

I turned and saw Walter, still standing apart from the others. He looked more displeased than before. It seemed proper to speak to him, however, since no one else had approached him. "You are Reginald's brother, Walter, if I am not mistaken. I'm Harriet D'Aquin, one of the curators at the museum. Please accept my condolences on the death of your father. There is no good way to lose a father."

"Thank you," he said, rather coldly. He then stunned me by adding, in a matter-of-fact voice, "I do not agree with these funeral arrangements." Elinor had come up beside me and must have heard his remark. It was an awkward moment. I hazarded an uncontroversial, if slightly inaccurate, observation, inspired by my supposition that he was shocked by the coming concert. "I am very sorry. Things are done somewhat differently here sometimes—differently from what one would expect in New York, I mean. Music is very important in New Orleans." (That depends, of course, on what one means by music. There's much more string quartet playing in New York than here.)

"That is not what I meant. It would have been better simply for Reginald to have our father cremated and dispense with everything else. Nothing good is going to come of this."

What could he mean by that? One doesn't expect much from a funeral; it's mostly a formality, the public recognition of death and its implications, fulfilling an ancient need of the human race and perhaps assisting with grieving. The law takes care of the estate and God presumably handles the rest. And why was Walter making the remark to *me*? Perhaps he looked upon me as a crony, a confederate of Reginald in these plans. But what had been done was, in fact, very ordinary—a simple service, a few trite and rather silly words on the dead, and a musical tribute—much better than one of these events where all the survivors and friends read a poem of their composition or saccharine passages they have copied from literary works or religious tracts.

His objections emboldened me. Not out of any loyalty to the dead or living, just from a desire to understand, I asked, "Then may I inquire why you came from New York for this event?"

"It was a mistake. Please excuse me." He turned abruptly.

Others were still speaking to Reginald and Gladys, or milling around, talking in low voices, or moving gradually toward the solarium, a large hall at the rear with potted palms and a great deal of glass. Greg and I made our way there, Elinor following shortly after Roger left. Folding chairs, harder than those in the parlor, had been set up, along with music stands. A cello lay on the carpeted dais. I noticed that a door to the back parking lot was ajar, affording a bit of the October breeze. We found seats at that side, to take advantage of the fresh air; with all that glass, heated by the early afternoon sun, the room would be warm.

"Did you hear what Reginald's brother said to me?" I asked Elinor.

"Yes, I was astonished—that is, if I heard right. He didn't like the funeral arrangements? But wasn't he consulted? Perhaps he and Reginald do not get along. What did he want instead—a service in New York?"

"He just said that Reginald should have had the body cremated and been done with it. But why on earth did he come down for the ceremony? He looked angry throughout. You're right; they can't be on very good terms now."

"What are you saying?" whispered Greg, at my right.

"We can't tell you now; wait until later."

Others had filed in—not quite so many, I thought, as at the preceding rite. Reginald and Gladys were on the first row. Walter sat behind them, on the far side, away from the windows. Shortly the musicians, in black tie, entered and took their seats. A low hum of conversation diminished, then ceased. There was no introduction, nor any printed program; they simply picked up their bows and began playing what I recognized as Haydn's "Emperor" quartet.

Walter's attitude was on my mind, even as I tried to listen well to the Haydn. Death and what follows often do create or reveal deep differences of views and prompt some very shabby behavior, especially quarrels about money; but this case did not appear to involve a dispute over the inheritance. Still, maybe that was the undercurrent—or something else.

Suddenly, at the left, where the outside door had remained open, I saw a strange figure emerge from the sunshine. It was a man of indeterminate age—perhaps sixty—wearing thick glasses, very ill-kempt, and dressed in a crumpled shirt and a stained pair of painters' pants. He must have entered from the parking lot. Surely others saw him also, but few could have known, I thought, what I knew: that he was a common drunk from the neighborhood, whom I often saw ambling on the neutral ground in front of the Rite Aid drugstore at the corner of St. Charles and Louisiana—diagonally across from

Bultman's—or making his way slowly down the sidewalk carrying a plastic sack that contained, doubtless, a pint of whiskey. If I was close enough on those occasions, I could hear him humming tunelessly to himself. Once on a Saturday morning, returning from Harry's Ace Hardware on Magazine, I had spied him weaving across Louisiana Avenue—wearing something that looked like a pair of pyjamas, and already very intoxicated. On another occasion, a friend and I, walking back in the evening from the bar at the Columns Hotel, had come upon him leaning against an oak tree, engaged, I fear, in an activity that is supposed to be confined to the washroom. He always looked wild-eyed. This time his eyes shifted back and forth, as he stood near me—not moving, but seeming interested in the proceedings. He had no plastic sack, but he looked intoxicated enough, and swayed slightly. After a moment, he took a few steps toward the nearest potted palm. He seemed to be mouthing sounds—a primitive, drunken sort of karioke.

No member of Bultman's staff seemed to be present to escort him out, and no one else approached him. The musicians probably didn't notice, nor those seated at the far side. Reginald must have seen him, I thought. What would Walter think at the sight of a drunk, sneaking in the side door while the memorial concert was going on? It was certainly going to confirm his objections to his brother's choices about the ceremony. The scene was not without humor, the sort that an Irishman might appreciate; but this was a staid, Uptown funeral at Bultman's, not an Irish wake.

I did not have time to wonder long about what would ensue, for, against the background of Haydn's second movement, there was a sudden outburst. First the fellow made a sort of whinnying sound and launched into a bar or so of song, quite loud. "Nearer, My God, to Thee" would have been appropriate, but in fact it was a phrase from "Glorious Things of Thee Are Spoken," inspired obviously by the Haydn quartet, from which the tune was borrowed; he must have remembered it from Sunday School long ago. He then shifted his weight a bit, did a gig step, and shouted, in somewhat slurred speech, "Glorious things ... All foolishness. Let the dead bury their dead, the Bible says! Stop all this ceremony. Stop it, I say." The musicians did indeed stop, their bows in mid-stroke, as if frozen. "The old man's dead, and I'm glad. He was a mean old man, a cruel, mean old man and a hypocrite ... He..." His words trailed off, in drunken syllables, although he finally proved to be sober enough to get out his grievances.

By this time Reginald had run over to him and grabbed him. "Get out! Get out and don't come back, Carlson! How dare you interrupt us! I have told you before ..." A few other men from the audience similarly rose and went toward the door. Walter did not move. Greg, who is heavily built and strong, could have helped, but he is singularly sensitive and did not want to embarrass Reginald any further by intervening. A man in a brown suit assisted Reginald in holding the fellow, in an attempt to turn him around and push him out. But unwilling, angry drunks are not easy to remove. He shook loose of the two.

"Take your hands off me, Reginald, you sneaking ..." I could not quite hear the next words; they could not have been polite. His voice rose. "This is just like you to do something like this. That old man was mean and you know it. Oh, you, you always got everything—Lawrenceville, Princeton, Yacht Club, all that, because you were his favorite—and a wimp—and because ... because... But as for Walter and me ... Look at me! And Walter, with his breakdowns ... You ... hypocrite, you ... prig ... just like him ..."

Walter, hearing his name mentioned, rose abruptly and, passing in front of the musicians, joined the *mêlée*. Upon seeing him, the drunk shouted, "You here too! Why aren't you back in New York? You shouldn't be here after what he did to you. You're probably not even his legitimate son! You must suspect that ... I *know* I'm not. Why don't you face facts? He took us in ... to save face. Bastards, that's what we are. And Reginald here ..."

There may have been audible gasps from some; or perhaps I just imagine it. Walter blanched. Reginald, losing his self-control, shouted, "Damn you, Carlson, damn you! How *dare* you insinuate anything of the sort! You are a liar as well as a drunk. Get out!" By that time, the brown-suited man and two others were able to get hold of the drunk again and started pushing him out. Walter glared at them, not helping either side. No one else moved. The fellow grabbed hold of the large potted palm, pulling it along with him. Then a staff member—his face, though trained to gravity and false sympathy, showing real apprehension—ran in from the foyer and joined them. There was an enormous commotion as shouts, curses, questions, and a few answers were exchanged, and the potted palm was dragged along farther, serving as both a shield and a cumbersome weapon.

Finally, the men got Carlson out the door and down the steps to the parking lot, with the potted palm tumbling after. There was a crash as the ceramic cache-pot broke. Walter disappeared outside for a moment, then returned and, with admirable self-control, went back to his seat. We could still hear the shouts, though I could no longer catch the words. All of the audience felt, doubtless, an extreme embarrassment, for which there was no suitable expression, since it seemed inappropriate to walk out of a memorial service, even at a moment of unplanned, scandalous drama, and leave the bereaved, now embarrassed by unsavory revelations and verbal abuse. But staying seemed equally awkward. I wondered whether the musicians would resume playing; they made no gesture toward doing so. Whispers, then snatches of talk began eddying through the audience; soon there was no more pretense of quiet and everyone was talking.

"I know that man," I told Elinor and Greg.

"What! You *know* him? You knew that Reginald had another brother—if he really is his brother?"

"He must be in some sense; Reginald called him by name and didn't deny his ... relationship. But I didn't realize he was his brother. What I meant was that I see him often, shuffling along St. Charles, sometimes coming out of the Rite Aid or trying to cross against the traffic; and he's always drunk. Of course I had *no* idea there was any relationship between him and Reginald. I can't believe it."

"What is he doing in New Orleans anyway?" asked Greg. "Reginald came to be director at the museum, and his father moved down from New York because he was getting old. But Walter still lives up there."

"New Orleans is a good place for drunks," Elinor answered. "Seriously! Lots of bars are open twenty-four hours a day, life is less expensive here, the weather is milder, and the city is full of his kind. They usually seem to survive."

"Perhaps," I added, "he came here originally with the hope that Reginald would get him a job—not at the museum, I suppose, though maybe so; he must have been educated. Or else he didn't want a job, just support ... enough to get by ... from either his father—or his supposed father—or Reginald. Maybe he even indulged in blackmail. Or he may have a little income from somewhere. I just wonder how he found out about the funeral. When I see him in the mornings he already seems too drunk to read the obituaries in the newspaper. Maybe, though, he sometimes picks up a paper from someone's trash and looks at it."

A few people had risen to leave. There was still commotion in the parking lot, and, through the glass, I saw an NOPD squad car pull in. It may have come upon the fracas by chance: police cars often cruise in that neighborhood. Or someone from Bultman's staff may have telephoned for help. I gathered the man would be taken down to Central Lockup and booked with disorderly behavior and public drunkenness. We remained in our seats, somewhat uncertain, though the prospect of having more music seemed dim. Gladys too, looking blanched, sat still; she would never take the initiative. Presently, Walter appeared at the dais and went up to the musicians. After saying a word or so to them, he turned to face what was left of the audience and announced, "The concert will not resume."

That was certainly a signal to leave, and we all got up. Ahead, I could see Walter at the row where Gladys was seated, bending over her; he took her arm, pulled her up, and escorted her out. Others followed, still talking among themselves, though not too loudly. The musicians folded their sheet music, picked up their instruments by the neck, and filed out through a door at the far right. As we made our way toward the large central foyer, I saw the squad car pull away. Reginald came back in, his hair still in place after the scuffle but his tie awry and his cuffs, usually so primly arranged, sticking out unevenly. He had lost his composure; he looked crazed. One had to wonder what he had known, or suspected, of Carlson's revelations, if they were that and not merely lucubrations. Probably a great deal; but he had rationalized them away. He cast a glance, possibly unseeing, toward the clusters of people still trailing out and the empty dais where the quartet had been set up. Greg, who was near him, told me later that he heard him mumbling, "Where is Gladys?"

In the foyer, I said a few words of greeting to one or two people— museum supporters, surely humiliated for Reginald, who was standing to one side, looking distraught. He still hadn't found Gladys, it seemed. But, abruptly, he turned and moved across the floor in front of me—without noticing me, of course—and reached her on the other side of the room, where she stood with Walter. As we approached the door, I could hear him say, "Gladys! Come, we must go home. Clearly, it was a mistake to hold this ceremony, and I shouldn't have sent word to Carlson about Father's death. What has happened can't be helped. But do not believe a word about ..."

So it was he who had informed his brother! An old feeling of family ties, despite everything, and a sense that so radical an event as a father's death must be shared, even with the unworthy, the resentful, the envious—these had been his motives, doubtless. But he must have warned him to stay away from the service. Either he had told Walter that he'd spoken to Carlson, or Walter had guessed it and had predicted, correctly, that there would be trouble. As I looked back on it, it seemed fortunate that the fellow, who had probably been lurking around the place for a while, hadn't burst in during the religious service itself, interrupting the prayers and the clergyman's pious words. Maybe he had tried to get in the front door and been turned away; then, with a drunk's persistence, he had found the open door by the parking lot.

To Reginald's words, Gladys said nothing, but gave a little whimper. Walter, in an angry voice, interjected a few words; I caught "told you this ..." and "you should have known he might..." When Reginald said something in reply, Walter lost his temper and shouted back. "What difference does it make, now that Father's dead? But it makes a difference to *me* to have skeletons come out of the closet. Carlson was right: you always liked to flatter and appease and put on airs, and this is what you get for it—public scandal." I could not hear any more, since Elinor, Greg, and I were moving out onto the tiled porch, where a few people, who obviously knew each other, were parting, their voices still low, subdued somewhat by the strange events. I said goodbye to Greg and Elinor and started walking down St. Charles toward home. This time, at least, I would not see the drunk, whom I now knew to be Carlson Mullins, but I would think all the way of the expression I would have to assume when I next saw Reginald at the museum—we were to have a meeting later in the week, but I'd probably run into him in the hall before then. Elinor would be thinking the same thing, even as she looked forward to telling Roger what he had missed. The other people present were certainly talking over the episode as they drove away, thinking of its various interpretations and relishing in advance the moment they could recount it to their friends.

As for Walter, he would surely exchange some very sharp words with Reginald. Any differences they had before would be magnified by the events. Moreover, they would have to face together the question of the estate. Since Mr. Mullins was a resident of Louisiana, the state code, basically still Napoleonic, would apply; it does not allow one to disinherit a son or daughter entirely, no matter what the circumstances. Assuming, as seemed plausible, that the old man had acknowledged both Carlson and Walter as his sons, whether they were or not, Carlson would inherit a substantial fraction of his assets, which must not have been negligible, and the brothers would have to deal with him in that connection. Maybe someone at McKinley, Melançon, and Perrin would handle the matter for them. Carlson would have ample funds for his whiskey. Bultman's would recover: a new potted palm would be set in the solarium, and the startled employee, who was doubtless retelling the event right now to others in the back office, would assume again his grave public mien. Reginald would pay the musicians from the estate, and he and Walter could have it out face to face, or by letter and telephone, rattling the skeletons even as old Mullins, the cause of it all, was barely cold in his grave.

PETROGLYPHS

"THIS MUST BE IT," Nigel said as he climbed back into the Jeep on the passenger side. I had pulled over where a dirt road, barely more than a wagon-track, went off from the highway to the right, and Nigel, who usually served as map-reader and navigator, had gotten out to look. We had been searching for an unnumbered, unpaved state road (yes, in Utah there are such) angling almost due west from state highway 279, which runs along a section of the Colorado River between Moab and Potash. Climbing through Long Canyon and over Pucker Pass, it would give us a shortcut to a highway leading to Dead Horse Point State Park and the Island in the Sky section of Canyonlands National Park. There was no sign, but it still seemed to be the road we wanted.

Nigel and Anne Robertson, friends from England, had joined me that summer to explore the Southwest. I had driven to meet them at the El Paso airport. From there we had worked our way north through New Mexico, looping into southern Colorado, then zigzagging back and forth through the Four Corners area before we got to the Canyonlands. At the end of the trip, they would fly out of Denver. We had chosen to rough it; they had been warned about the heat. The summer had been one of the most brutal in recent memory. Texas was burned up with drought, its crops dead and its wild animals and stock hungry and thirsty or else fed on imported hay. The Four Corners area was regularly recording temperatures of 110. We had been fortunate enough to be in high, forested territory part of the time, but on other days we felt the full force of the desert sun.

We had already camped out for ten nights straight, the previous one at a Bureau of Land Management campground to the south. I did the driving; Nigel and Anne were supposed to look at the scenery. And of course we all contributed to pitching and then breaking camp and doing the shopping for groceries and ice every day or so. We had gotten on well as a trio, though at times I sensed between the two of them some tension, which usually remained vague and under control but occasionally surfaced in their cold, edgy manner. Its source was unclear.

Nigel is a fellow art historian; Anne is an archivist. They had chosen to accept my invitation of several years' standing and come to America that summer, despite some reluctance on their part to allow themselves the enjoyment such a journey signified. Two years earlier, their only child, a son, had died of leukemia in early adolescence, and for a while they had refused to leave home or to do anything else that seemed, to their distressed hearts, like an infidelity to the dead child. I was both gratified and relieved that they had agreed finally to join me. At least it was wholly alien territory, which the boy had never known; that may have helped.

Taking care to stay off the interstates, or motorways, as they called them, we had already driven hundreds of miles, hiked up mountains and down caverns and canyons, and visited numerous sites of ethnological and geological interest. Nigel and Anne took photographs of landscapes, geological curiosities, and ruins, and bought books and maps to study in the late afternoons, after we'd set up camp. I did some sketching. We had been especially thorough in visiting Anasazi archeological sites that contained petroglyphs. My interest in them had developed in previous years as I experimented with incorporating stylized designs into my painting. Nigel had begun to share this interest, and now both he and Anne wanted to see them. We had visited Chimney Rock, Canyon de Chelly, Newspaper Rock, and numerous other sites. That very morning, shortly before reaching the intersection with the dirt road, we had stopped at a small site along the river and studied the pictographic inscriptions.

The road we were considering didn't appear much worse than others we had already taken, including a precipitous climb on Utah 261 north of Mexican Hat and the laborious Navajo route that starts south of Shiprock, New Mexico, crosses to Red Rock, Arizona, then ascends a rugged pass through the Chuska Mountains to Lukachukai.

"Are you sure this is right, Nigel?" asked Anne. "There's no indication at all." It's the sort of thing anyone might have said; still, it sounded a bit accusatory.

"That proves nothing, just because there isn't any sign. According to my calculations, we've come about the right distance from Moab. If we go on much further, we'll get to Potash, which is too far."

I agreed, adding, "It doesn't look like a ranch road; there's no indication that it's posted." So, after a bit more discussion, we agreed to give it a try. It was mid-morning. We had a nearly full tank of gasoline, along with food, water, and other supplies, so that backtracking or other delays would mean nothing more than wasted time.

The road climbed sharply away from the level of the river, into a wilderness of white rock, streaked with strange minerals—uranium, potash, and others. There was little vegetation; I doubted anyone could have ranched there. It was plain that we would have to gain a great deal of altitude in order to reach the paved road on the mesa. Steep inclines, passages cut into the rock, and narrow gullies alternated with hairpin turns and shelves, precipitous and exceedingly rough. We would make it around one bend, turn sharply up into another, then find ourselves on another shelf road or in a canyon. I had the Jeep in the lowest gear most of the time, and was taking things very easy. Still, since we ran the air conditioner and the inclines were steep, I was concerned about the engine. We got our water bottles out of the ice chest from time to time to drink, and after a while ate some fruit and cheese, but didn't stop anywhere for a real lunch because there was, literally, nowhere to pull over. And what would we have used for shade?

After another hour or more, during which our conversation was mostly about the condition of the road and the heat and the brutal sun, Anne asked, "Do you think this road really does climb to the mesa-top?"

Nigel has a man's ability to visualize space and orient himself easily. "It can't go anywhere else," he answered, sharply. He turned to me. "Don't you agree?"

"I suppose so. Even with all these horseshoe bends, I think we're still headed in the right direction. It seems endless; but we might as well continue on, since we'd lose so much time by going back now, and anyhow, there's no good place to turn. I don't mind driving on as long as the track doesn't peter out completely; that's a possibility, you know."

It wasn't long after that when I saw steam rising from under the hood. Even the toughest of vehicles can break down, I reflected. "Look at that, you all—something like steam or smoke coming out."

"I see it," said Nigel. "Overheating, that's sure. Has your warning light come on?"

As I looked, there was a red flash. "Yes, there it is—the temperature light."

We were at that moment, thank heaven, not on a ledge but in a pinched-in gully, part of Long Canyon, I supposed, comparatively straight and enclosed by sandy banks. There was extra space at one side, so that I could pull over a bit. I cut the engine and we all got out. Nigel lifted what he called the bonnet, and we could feel the intense heat of the engine as we looked at the rising steam, laden with strange fumes. There was nothing to do but wait; you can't open a hot radiator to look inside. We got some more drinks from the cooler and picked on the rest of the cheese, fruit, and rolls. Since the track itself was rutted and extremely rocky, there wasn't a comfortable place to sit down, so we just leaned against the gully bank. Then Anne and I put back the water bottles and other things. I used the time to straighten out the cargo area a bit, and Anne collected the back seat trash in a plastic sack. After a while, I asked, "Do you think that radiator is cool enough for you to take the cap off now?"

"No, let's wait a while longer. Meanwhile, let me count the jugs to see how much water is available."

"Anne," I said, "why don't we look around to see whether we can climb one of the banks and find a few trees, especially if there's something seriously wrong with the Jeep and we have to wait a long while." A dozen yards away, some straggly sagebrush could give a handhold. I stepped across the road to try to get a better view. "There seem to be some bushes or trees up there; I can't tell how high, but it might be worth climbing up to see." The soil was friable, but the bank was not particularly high. So, digging our boots into the sand and pulling ourselves up by the brush, we half-climbed, half-crawled up the bank, reached a small ledge, and then continued up.

"Yes," Anne said in a moment, "you're right, Harriet; there are some of those trees that we've seen frequently, juniper and—what kind of pine is it?"

"Piñon." We found ourselves on a sizeable plateau, which, I thought, might be a lower spur of the main mesa. We walked over to the clump of low trees, not very far, and saw that they were filled out enough to create quite a pleasant patch of shade. Moreover, the ground underneath and near them was mostly firm sand, with small tufts of grass, rather than rock. Instead of exploring further, we went back towards the road, carefully got ourselves down the bank, without slipping too much, and walked back to the Jeep, where Nigel was about to open the radiator. Removing the cap gingerly, he waited a few more moments, looked in, then started pouring in water from a gallon jug. "We don't have as much water as I thought," he said—"that is, by the standards of this radiator, which is huge compared to what I'm used to. I think you've lost a great deal, Harry," he added.

"I can't understand why. Do you think the mechanic at the Quick-E-Lube could have forgotten to check the level?" (We had stopped for service back in Moab.)

"Maybe so. We'll see how far this goes." He emptied one jug and poured in two others.

But it did not go very far, apparently. Almost as soon as I turned on the ignition and we started again, the temperature light flashed once or twice, then remained lit. I stopped and turned to Nigel and Anne. "Look," I said, "this isn't going to work, I'm afraid. The engine is still over-heated, and you say we can't spare any more water, since we'll need it for ourselves if we have to stay here for a while more. There may be other problems also; those fumes worry me. Don't you think we'd better just wait until someone comes by and we can send for help?" I wasn't sure, of course, than anyone would come along; we had seen no other vehicle. It occurred to me that we might have to walk out.

It was agreed that we'd better not try to drive farther; we might damage the engine. Nigel volunteered to put the Jeep in reverse—I supposed a few more moments wouldn't be crucial—and back down a few yards to a better spot. Anne and I got out. It made me nervous watching him take my $20,000 investment down that steep incline, but since he was confident enough to risk his life also, I could trust him, and pretty soon he had positioned the Jeep so that another car could pass.

By that time it was mid-afternoon, but sundown wouldn't come for a long while and it was still blazing hot. After Nigel had cut off the engine again, there was no sound other than the occasional crackling of an insect and the dry brushing of wind along the sand and through bits of brown grass and wizened sagebrush. I was concerned that my British guests would feel some resentment against me or the anonymous mechanic who might have omitted to check the coolant and water. In fact, they did not appear to. But the heat and desolation—rather Inferno-like, I felt—and our inaction probably fed the hostility I could sense between them. Occasional glances were like burning brands, and the few words they exchanged were clipped and sharp.

After a few minutes, Anne asked, "Doesn't that sound like a car to you?"

Nigel said nothing. I answered, "Yes, it does, climbing up. It's a good thing Nigel managed to get us out of the track." Shortly a Suburban came into view. It would be, it turned out, the only vehicle we'd see. Two men were in the front seat. When they had pulled up nearly abreast of us, they stopped. There was a Colorado license plate, I noticed. The driver left the engine running but the passenger got out and came over to us.

He was a burly man, thick-thighed and barrel-chested. He wore a denim shirt, blue jeans, and heavy-duty outdoor boots. He had a hat, of course—we all did—but his was dingy and worn-looking. Neither young nor old, as I recall. The skin on his face and arms was burnt a dull brick red, and his features were large. I don't remember quite how he spoke; maybe he said "Howdy." Then he asked Nigel, "Something the matter here?"

The question was predictable, if not entirely reasonable. You can't imagine anyone choosing that spot for a picnic, especially when it was 110 degrees, so one could assume right away that we'd had some sort of car trouble.

"Well, the engine overheated. At first I just thought it needed to cool down and the radiator needed water, but we didn't have enough really to replace what had blown out. There may be some other problem too; we all smelled fumes. I'm beginning to suspect a broken hose."

From the first, the man must have noted my Louisiana license and been surprised that someone from the Gulf Coast would have ventured onto a dirt track across such barrenness. He probably chalked it up to foolhardiness. He must have been even more astonished to hear Nigel's British accent. About that time the driver got out, cutting off his engine first, and came close to where we were standing. He resembled his companion, though he was less burly in the chest and slightly taller. Each had a vaguely sinister appearance. "What's going on here?" he asked, more to his friend than to us.

Nigel answered nonetheless. "Well, we were trying to get to the mesa-top, to the road that goes to Dead Horse Point. But we've had radiator trouble, maybe something else also. We're spending some time here looking around the Canyonlands before we return to the Abajo Mountains."

The men looked at us very strangely, I thought. But what was odd about the situation? It was clear that we were sightseers, two women and a man—"tourists," in a word. The others seemed concerned about our presence; perhaps we should be concerned about theirs. Suddenly I recalled that, the previous month, four armed men had killed a Colorado state patrolman after an aborted attack on an Indian casino, then murdered two other officers of the law before taking refuge somewhere in the innumerable caves and canyons of the Four Corners area. One of the attackers had been shot subsequently during an attempt at capture, but, despite an intense search by the police of four states, plus the Navajo authorities, no one else had been found. I had warned Nigel and Anne before they arrived from England, knowing we would camp in the very territory where they were hiding out. We had agreed we would run the risk. It was understandable that, having lost their son, they did not seem disturbed by threats to themselves.

Now, in a moment of panic, I thought these fellows might be two of the outlaws. But why would they use a road, if they were trying to hide out? Of course, if they *did* get onto the roads once in a while, to replenish supplies or, conceivably, get away from an area the police were searching, the one we had taken would be the right kind for them—empty, almost impassable. I couldn't see into the back of the Suburban to tell whether it looked loaded. I wondered whether it had been stolen. Anne looked alarmed, I noticed. We had a gun, but it was under the seat and might prove useless.

"Look," I said, "could you help us out? If you have a lot of extra water, that would be a start; we think the radiator is still very low. Or, if you know anything about engines..." I added, as much for our own benefit as the stranger's, "I can't understand how this happened."

Anne intervened then. "Because otherwise we just have to wait here until someone else comes along, and you're the first ones who have passed—or else we'll have to walk up to the mesa this evening ..."

"That wouldn't work," Nigel interrupted; "if I understand correctly, there's no town on the mesa top, just the park offices, and they'll be closed after dark, won't they, Harriet?"

"Yes, I'm afraid so. If we don't get help soon, we'll have to spent the night, then walk out in the morning and call for someone to come round from Moab."

The men both kept staring at us strangely. I think now that they may have been involved in something illegal but were probably not the desperadoes who had murdered the Colorado patrolman. They were suspicious of any vehicle and wanted to be sure we were just tourists. "We don't have any extra water—nothing that we can spare," answered the driver finally.

"Well, can you telephone for us when you get up to ... is it Dead Horse Point where you're going?" I continued. "You could call a service station in Moab and ask that a truck be sent tomorrow morning— maybe the roundabout way, coming down from the mesa. I think it cannot be much higher. Or you could ask the ranger to call for us. This isn't park land; still ..."

"I'm afraid not," the first man answered. "We'll be on our way now." Clearly, they didn't want to get involved.

There wasn't any good-bye, any "good luck"; they just got back into the Suburban and started off, crunching their tires over the gravel and rocks as they ground their way upwards.

"That was odd, very odd," I said, summing it up. Nigel and Anne didn't know as well as I the unwritten laws of Western neighborliness, but they understood what I meant. "I think they're not going to do anything to help us out, even make a phone call. They just want to get away."

"We don't have much choice now, do we?" said Anne, in a rather nervous voice.

"Looks that way," I answered. "Unless someone else comes along, we're stuck here for the rest of the afternoon and the night. It's a good thing we've got our camping gear and food, and that water we saved. Why don't we climb up again where you and I went, Anne? We can set up camp under the trees. If a car starts up the road, we'll hear it in time." I wanted to reassure her. "Nigel, don't you think we can manage to get our supplies and tents and sleeping bags up the bank?"

They agreed that it was a good idea. We found a somewhat better path than the one I had chosen earlier. Working efficiently, we carried up everything that we needed for one night of camping. There was plenty of dead juniper around for fuel, and we would have a very simple meal out of cans—chili and corn—along with carrot and celery sticks, fig bars, and half a magnum of leftover wine. We locked up in the Jeep everything we didn't need; I supposed it would be safe, since, once night fell, no one would think of taking that road. Nigel took my pistol. Even though there's not much of a gun culture in England, he had a bit of familiarity with firearms.

Once set up, our camp, though hasty and makeshift, looked attractive under the trees: two little tents with their sleeping bags, a picnic cloth held down on the sand with rocks, jackets hung on branches (we might need them later in the evening, despite the heat of the day), a box of pots and other supplies, water jugs, and the ice chest, all arranged near a small ring of stones we'd made for the fire. We would not be able to wash much—perhaps, at most, our hands and faces. The dishes would have to wait. Maybe a rapid brushing of teeth after dinner ...

The afternoon was not quite at an end. Stretching off to the left was a patch of slickrock, almost flat, with scattered potholes, completely dry. A half-mile or so away, I could see what appeared to be a draw, with larger trees, which looked inviting. There might even be a small spring and grass. "Why don't you and I go for a walk over there?" I asked Anne, gesturing to the slickrock. "Nigel can watch our things, if that's all right—not that anyone is around here to bother them!"

With sunglasses and hat brims pulled well down, we started over the slickrock in a westerly direction. Anne was quiet and seemed morose. "I'm sorry about all this delay," I said finally. "We've lost a half-day at least, and I'm not sure when we'll get going again. It will be quite a hike tomorrow. We'll probably have to cut out some stops we wanted to make later. I hope you are not too bored. And I certainly hope also that you are not ... nervous, because of those strange men we met."

"No, Harry," she answered. "We're both patient, Nigel and I, and we know it's not your doing; these things can happen, even when you think everything is in order. I don't mind, really. And I'm not afraid. It's just that... Nigel and I have had some very serious difficulties. You probably realize that we are not on the best of terms. It has nothing to do with you, I assure you, and we're glad—at least I am—that we've taken this trip. But the undercurrents ... doubtless you can feel them. It all comes from our son ... our disagreements about our son—Adrian, you know."

I waited to hear more. After some while, she continued.

"We have not had a good two years. What should have been a bond between us for life—since we made him and remember him from before birth and love him deeply—has not been enough; instead, his death has driven us apart."

"But you both miss him dreadfully," I interjected.

"Yes, but not in the same way, and not together. Marriages break up over accidents and losses and disasters that should ... should act to cement them. The stress is too great. I have accused Nigel of ... not caring—I know that is unfair—and ... well, being aloof and harsh with Adrian—before he was sick, I mean. He seemed to think he should act like those authoritarian fathers from Victorian times, as *his* father did. Maybe ... I don't know... it's some strange sense of rivalry, an old competitive instinct of the race, this way in which fathers and sons compete with each other, occasionally hate each other. Nigel in turn has accused me of Adrian's death—as though I had anything to do with it! The doctors couldn't save him; could I? It's his way of punishing himself, really, through me—since he feels guilty; we both feel guilty. It is ironic: separated from our son, we are almost alienated from each other also."

What can be said to the disclosure of such intimate dramas? At least my silence fit the landscape, where the stone and sand were dry and inhumane and the sun was like a refiner's fire. We continued making our way over the slickrock. Soon I could distinguish fir and ponderosa pine in the draw I had guessed at earlier, with a steep cliff beyond, which might rise to the principal section of the mesa. "Look, Anne, at those fine trees. They seem to be growing out of the far cliff, and perhaps some of them are, but the tallest ones must be down in a wash. Do you want to walk on and see?"

It wasn't far; Anne agreed. There was indeed a broad, rather deep wash, with cleared patches where crops could have been cultivated and, at the edge, huge ponderosas and their compelling shade, with fir and piñon pine growing on the sloping cliff side. No stream was visible, but there would be frequent runoff down the cliff and probably some springs not far below the surface. Suddenly, as I looked past a few trees clinging to the cliff side, I noticed a hollow, and in its shadow a small ruin. "Oh, look up, near those piñons, over to the right—there's a shallow cave, with what look like cliff-dwellings!"

We were much pleased by the discovery. I was confident that the site was not marked on any of our maps nor written up in our books; sometimes these finds are deliberately unpublicized, since, while there are thousands of such ruins in the Southwest, those unprotected by the government have often been vandalized, even destroyed. I suppose that, although these were well off the road, other hikers had discovered them before, perhaps taking some of the artifacts; but at least the site had not been wholly dismantled. Yet access to it did not look difficult. "Let's go back and tell Nigel what we've found," I suggested. "If we eat supper early, and simply leave things as they are, we could come here afterwards and show him."

We turned back, walking quickly along the slickrock. When we told Nigel of the find, he was even more enthusiastic than we. "Let's not wait until after supper," he suggested. "I'd like to take pictures, and it may get dim in the canyon. Let's just arrange things for later—the fire all ready to light, cans ready to open, and so on, and go now. Here, Anne, take your flashlight, just in case we get delayed; you too, Harry. Plus your water bottle. I'll get my camera."

We threw the things into our backpacks and started out. Now that Anne and I knew the way, we weren't long in reaching the wash, which had begun to take on more shadow. "There, Nigel," she said, pointing, as soon as we were in sight of the cliff.

He almost broke into a run. We moved quickly into the wash, past some large Douglas firs, then up the other side to a small ledge that ran toward the ruins, higher. Surely the original inhabitants had used ladders, which they would withdraw at night. Numerous small trees had taken root between the ledge and the cave, holding down soil and affording a way of access. "Let's climb up through here," Nigel suggested, pointing to a strip with good footing.

The ruin was very small—only three separate dwellings, or rooms, barely protected by the shallow overhang. But its condition was excellent, the mortarless walls nearly intact and the broad *vigas* or beams, made probably from ponderosa pine, still in place. Dark smudges on the upper walls and shallow roof indicated fires of centuries ago, and small apertures in the walls for ventilation or human egress gazed at us like the eyes of the dead. It would have been, I reflected, a convenient hiding place for those fleeing the law, but we saw no evidence of recent human presence.

It was Anne who saw first the petroglyphs, slightly farther along on the rock face. "Look," she exclaimed, "petroglyphs—over there! Oh, Nigel!" Her tone was almost tender. It was a good thing we hadn't waited until later to come; they would then have been devoured by shadow. Even as it was, we could not see them well until we were almost upon them; something in the coloration of one—a slightly greenish wheel—must have caught the light differently and thus attracted Anne's attention. I started working my way along a narrow shelf. Behind me, Nigel had grabbed Anne by the hand—I noticed that with pleasure—and was pulling her along.

When I reached the petroglyphs and started examining them, reading, as it were, left to right, I was amazed by their number, richness, and quality. Together, they created a stunning presence out of the past. Anne and Nigel began to exclaim over the inscriptions and their excellent condition, more or less at shoulder level, which would have been slightly above the heads of the Anasazi. There were many individual figures—though fewer than at Newspaper Rock, which has been carved and recarved in historical times. Deer, turkey, birds on the wing represented the animal kingdom; the plants included trees and unidentified smaller vegetation, with various leaves, some of which might be corn. The radiant sun was accompanied by another circular shape, which I took to be the moon. Vertical lines of dots, resembling Apollinaire's ideogram "Pluie," seemed intended to represent, and perhaps invoke, rain. There were hand prints and numerous stylized designs I could not identify. Human figures, well proportioned, took their place among the other elements of earth and sky: although the bodies were drawn very crudely, one could easily identify hunters, and others who were perhaps priests, wearing what looked like ceremonial headdresses.

Finally, there were women and—most astonishing of all—what must have been a child. He was positioned between, but at some distance from, the hunters on one side and the women on the other, so that he seemed to occupy the center. I noticed a sun emblem just above him. He was standing, his arms outstretched, the palms upward. Whatever it meant to the Anasazi, the iconographic value of the figure to me was enormous, suggesting Christian images—which the Anasazi had never known—of invitation, blessing, invocation, or possibly sacrifice. The sun radiating above his head make me think immediately of the Light of the World. The fact that it was a child who occupied such a central position—in a culture which, like the European Middle Ages, apparently gave little direct place to children—struck me as especially significant. Son of man, son of woman, the figure seemed to offer reconciliation between the sexes and their two spirits, as well as communication with the celestial elements above.

All this flashed through my mind, but I said nothing, for Anne and Nigel, slightly behind me, had not yet reached the figure. Suddenly she gave a gasp. I turned and watched them. Certainly they must see the figure as I did, its striking Christian suggestions of reconciliation and unity blending with its even broader significance as a quintessential figure of vulnerable, yet enduring and universal humanity. After nearly a thousand years, the figure spoke to us still, almost as if it were alive. Art is never merely individualistic, not even in our own time, and there are few people, no matter how skeptical, who discount all suggestions of transcendence.

Finally it was Nigel who felt the silence was full enough. He spoke gently. "The figures seem so alive—despite the destructiveness of time. Think of that child, preserved here for centuries. Oh, Anne! He is like our son—dead, dead, but the center of our lives, once, the evidence and image of our union."

Anne said nothing. I saw Nigel turn directly toward her. "We let him come between us, in the wrong way. Look how the boy stands here, with outstretched hands, not separating, but bringing together those on either side."

Anne gave a small sob, and I saw that the tears had started to come. She made no effort to hide them or wipe them away, but Nigel took out his bandana handkerchief and dabbed at her cheeks.

She got out a few words. "Perhaps he too died as a boy and never grew up. It is as if he were somehow ... close to us—the way Adrian is." She stopped, choked, and more tears flowed. Her face was flushed. We'd been in terrific heat all day, sometimes in direct sun; but it was surely feeling that made her color that way. Her eyes were extraordinarily bright.

I stepped closer to my friends. "These figures have such presence! This is how stylization works: the plainest lines, the most fundamental meanings. It is truly transcultural. We do not need to know everything about prehistorical peoples; we recognize and respond to this."

We stood for many more minutes in front of the petroglyphs. All this time, the sun was declining, and the entire canyon was taking on shadow. Using a lengthy exposure, Nigel took several photographs, before suggesting finally that we should start back. Anne reached over and touched the stone just below the child's figure, then put her fingers to her lips. We picked our way back along the shelf, through the trees down to the wash, by then almost wholly obscured, and up the other side, finally along the slickrock in the direction of our camp. Though there was no trail, we traced our way by the potholes that we'd passed. Above us, the sky was clear and of a rather pale blue, with a few gauzy clouds and vague yellowish lights coming from the west. There was no need for the flashlights, but when we got back to the camp I hung mine on a juniper branch, and Nigel propped his on tree roots, to illuminate us later. The things for supper were as we had left them, and any apprehensions we had felt about intruders had been dismissed in the wake of our discovery and the sense of calm it had created. We hastily started the fire, opened cans, put out our plates and utensils, and filled our wine cups.

As the fire took hold and, later, the kettles were heating, Anne went to sit by Nigel, who was leaning against a large rock. In the low western sun, the wind-twisted trees cast long, fantastic shapes of dancing figures against the pale sand, and the shadows of our tents spread like those of some Arabian sheik. The trees were aromatic in the growing coolness. Cicadas and cedar wrens made little noises in the brush. I saw Anne take her husband's hand, as he had reached for hers when they ran toward the petroglyphs, and press it to her lips, where earlier she had laid her fingers after touching the rock. We would sleep well, I trusted, perhaps imagining we were in the cliff dwellings, among our brothers of a thousand years before. In the morning, having repacked our things in the Jeep, we could start on foot for Dead Horse Point. With luck, a vehicle would pass us and someone would offer help. It had not been such a lost day, I reflected. In their dreams, Anne and Nigel might feel reconciled to each other as well as closer to their lost son. Over beyond the draw, a child preserved in stone was looking out through the trees, as if in blessing on these three visitors who came by chance, out of time, into his land, his peace.

Virtual Art

WE NEVER SHOULD HAVE hired Norma Wurmser at the museum. The day the personnel committee met on the matter was the closest we've ever come there to seeing blood flow. When the committee was deadlocked on her candidacy, despite vigorous campaigning by her supporters and hyperbolic praises of her obviously inflated resumé, I supposed that her name would be stricken from the list. How wrong I was, again.

Emily Blankenship, of our staff, a crony of hers, it turned out, nominated her for the directorship of the photography department; supposedly, that was her strength. In fact, she doesn't know much about either the techniques or the aesthetics of still photography; what's more important, she is ill-trained in curating collections of historical photographs, which is mostly what we have. Her weaknesses had been concealed, but not so skillfully that several of us weren't suspicious. Moreover, she shortly proved to be a meddler and a busybody, stepping onto others' terrain while neglecting what was supposed to be her own. She apparently wanted, for unknown reasons, to come to New Orleans, and played the connections game well enough to get here; carrying out what she was hired to do certainly wasn't part of her plan, however.

Greg d'Hannis was the one who first found out she'd been offered a contract, despite the split vote. He came down the hall that day in a rage and burst into my office, closing the door behind him. His ruddy anger filled the place. "Do you know what's happened? That imbecile director of ours has just offered the photography curatorial position to Norma Wurmser!"

"Greg, I can't believe it. Are you sure? Who told you?"

"Sharon herself." (She is secretary to the director, Reginald Mullins.) "She says the announcement will be made tomorrow; but it's not a secret, even now."

"But why? How? How can he just overlook the committee's decision—a hung vote? She didn't have majority support, after all. And he had said that he would not choose anyone without it. What a mistake, what a terrible mistake. He'll see."

I was so beside myself that I didn't quite know what I meant by that prediction, "He'll see"—the belief that Norma herself would prove him wrong, or the delusion that life would provide other retribution.

Greg agreed. We were usually of the same mind, anyhow, and had sustained each other for years, proving that men and women *can* have honorable professional friendships. "Of course he'll see. She'll turn the place upside down and bring disgrace on us all. What a prima donna, and at the same time a sycophant! You remember how she put on airs, yet cozied up to Mullins at that reception—and tried to insinuate herself with us all during the interview. That jackass Bill was taken in, and the sisters of Lesbos. I wonder if she really knows anything about historical photography; her resumé is mostly sugar-icing. Mullins's decision is outrageous." He had begun to breathe a little less noisily but was still rather red in the face. I had probably turned white; indignation always makes the blood leave me for a minute.

We spent a few more minutes turning the matter over in our minds and conversation, until my telephone rang and Greg returned to his office. The next day the announcement of the appointment was circulated among the museum staff, and it appeared shortly in the monthly museum newsletter and even the *Times-Picayune.* And a few weeks later Norma moved in on us, like a squall or, better, a disease.

We called her the Taupe, because of her mole-like profile, her underground ways, and her coloring. She was originally from Philadelphia. As Greg had predicted, she proved to be a *poseur* of the first order, or *poseuse*, to use the gendered word she would prefer.

Her speech is clipped and her accent affected, and, although my other colleagues all call me Harry, she always addressed me as "Harriet," pronouncing the first syllable wrong by rhyming it with *car*. She fancies herself to be sensitive—an artists' artist—and her bohemian appearance seems intended to give that impression, as though that would make her superior to us who dress ordinarily in street clothes of unremarkable styles. Her skin borders on the jaundiced; how does she do it? Her hair, treated with henna, I think, hangs limp and apparently unwashed; dramatic gestures throw it back when she believes she has made a point. She adds no color to her lips or cheeks, but outlines her eyes with heavy mascara and kohl. Her garments, dragging around her ankles, are usually loose and shapeless, of a dung-brown hue or faded black; I can imagine her playing the part in a medieval play of someone with scrofula, attempting to get close to the king.

She did not take long to make her presence oppressive. With those who had supported her, especially Emily, who, unfortunately, is here to stay, she formed an axis of which she was, if not the chief, at least the newest star. (We later learned from Sharon, in a top-secret admission, that those supporters had gone to Mullins on the sly, violating procedures agreed upon by all, to persuade him to ignore the committee's vote, which they claimed was invalid by reason of improper politicking and "prejudice against the candidate.") By the logic of his own position, in having selected her despite assurances that no one would be named without majority support on the personnel committee, Mullins had to give her and her allies quite a free rein, assenting to initial demands that went beyond the ordinary and seeming to share viewpoints she put forth about her department and the museum as a whole. Eventually, I suppose, this axis would have broken apart from the play of contradictory forces; there were too many different reasons—among them sheer laziness and job-shirking as well as an ideological agenda—for which its members had agreed to her appointment and acted together for a while. But she herself helped do it in. What were her supporters to her? Merely a means, a train she would ride for a while. And she rode it to her advantage.

Not long after she came, just after we had finished organizing a big show, Greg and I were having tea with Elinor Perrin in my office. Since Elinor is in charge of historical maps, etchings, and drawings, and prepares general historical exhibits, she has to work with the photography department. "So how is the Taupe?" I asked. "I haven't seen her, but of course I've been closeted here."

"You've missed her for good reason; she's in London," Elinor replied.

"In London? What on earth for?" The Orleanian Institute, which is both a museum and a research center, has few connections there; we have representative holdings of American and European art, especially French painting, Northern European, and Italian, but our greatest strengths are Louisiana graphic art, especially architectural drawings, photography, maps, and other documents.

"Her mother needed a companion for a while."

"What do you mean, needed a companion?" interjected Greg. "Is she having surgery? Even then ... Norma's supposed to be here working, isn't she? Is the old woman dying?"

"Anyhow, does she live there?" I added.

"She went there from Philadelphia to spend some time... a sort of whim, it appears to me. Then she decided she wasn't feeling well and asked Norma to come over. I got all this from Norma herself; she didn't see how strange it sounds."

"Strange indeed!" I commented. "Is she getting paid meanwhile?"

"No, she's on unpaid leave. But of course work in the photography department is more or less on hold."

"Absurd. The woman just arrived."

Some weeks later, Norma returned, breezing in as if she'd been gone for a day to have her teeth worked on, stirring up things, pulling rank on the secretaries (amazing how those who complain all the time about patriarchal oppression are so keen on asserting authority, once they get the chance). Elinor, who was in charge of an exhibit planned for the following season on "The River and Its Representations," needed to consult her about the holdings; but Norma, fractious as ever, was more hindrance than help, vetoing choices, maneuvering on the sidelines, attempting to impose her views—a regular butinsky. An assistant in the photography department tried to be useful, but, as a college student in art history, he was a novice and just part-time. After a while it became clear that Norma was opposed to the entire exhibit—though it wasn't hers to decide, having been agreed upon before she arrived. Sharon reported later that she'd heard Norma in Mullins's office, screaming, "Where are the women in this exhibit? Women make up more than half the population! Does she" (she meant Elinor) "realize that? All I see is paintings and engravings of ships, and the port, and captains and seamen, and photographs taken on the wharves showing the stevedores loading and unloading things—just an occasional Creole woman selling watermelon or some such. This is absolutely sexist" (*absolutely*, with an affected pronunciation given to the *u*, was one of her favorite words) "and you should cancel the whole project."

Even with some subsequent ruckus by Emily, Bill, and the sisters of Lesbos, alerted by the Taupe and always ready to raise the feminist banner in even the least suitable context, Mullins didn't give in on that one—he really couldn't at that stage; but Norma ceased completely to cooperate, and finally the photographs were selected and mounted by Elinor alone with some help from the college student. We noted with irony that, while Elinor is a woman, she and her opinions didn't really count in her adversaries' eyes; despite the feminist truisms they mouth, to be worthy of consideration you have to be *their* kind of woman.

The exhibit was launched; Norma didn't show up for the *vernissage*. I don't know what she occupied herself with, generally, but we detected interfering and plotting from time to time. Mullins kept his own counsel on her. Some months later, I learned that she had asked for another leave, to go to California for a while. This time it was I who broke the news to Greg. He was indignant. "Why in heaven's name …?"

"Mullins admitted to me that she has a boyfriend out there."

Greg burst into a great guffaw, a Falstaff half-amused, half-incredulous. "What benighted son of woman would be attracted to *her*? Good God, I pity him; he must be an untouchable."

"Yes, it's hard to believe. And why did she try so hard to come to New Orleans, if her love interest is on the West Coast?"

"Maybe she met him just recently; maybe she picked him up in London among the gaping American tourists in Leicester Square."

Elinor came in then, and we had to bring her up to date. She felt some relief but even more outrage. "Who is supposed to run her department? I can't understand it."

Even though we had no authority—the personnel committee and others help make certain decisions, but Mullins runs the place generally—Greg, Elinor, another friend, and I decided to go see him, in our role as curators of departments, to protest against his granting the second leave, for such a purpose. I was astounded at his explanation.

"Oh, but she's going for professional reasons."

"You mean this is a *paid* leave?" My voice rose. "What on earth for?"

"She is going to try to set up contacts in the Silicone Valley."

It was getting more and more preposterous. "That's ridiculous," bellowed Greg. "You mean she's going to try to get money out of Bill Gates and his ilk to support a museum in New Orleans? I thought she was in charge of the photography department, not fund drives. She'll alienate anyone she talks to and we'll be ridiculed."

"No, no," explained Mullins, soothingly (he thought); "she is going to investigate new ways of imaging photographs—turning them into computer-generated holographs, a kind of virtual reality. Then she'll come back here and start on our collections."

I could not believe it. Like all mid-sized museums, we are constantly trying to make ends meet as we carry out our ordinary tasks of preserving, displaying, and enlarging our collections, getting visiting exhibits, doing research, and serving the public through various programs. We have no funds for extraordinary projects like that; only the Metropolitan in New York and a few other huge institutions can afford to digitalize a whole collection. Norma had done very little to take care of and enhance the collections already here; her airs and appearance had not won her friends among the patrons and collectors in town, who could have donated additional historical or artistic materials. Now she wanted to spend money (it would cost tens of thousands, I supposed) to turn perfectly good photographs into virtual reality—as though the real objects, on paper, some signed by major artists, were somehow wanting. She would get in with that crowd of nerds in California and come back crazier than before.

I protested. "Look, Reginald, we are in the business of caring for and exhibiting *art* and historical material, right here. That's what the public and the patrons who give money to us expect. We don't have grand holdings, but they still represent an important part of New Orleans culture. We shouldn't spend money turning them into electronic wonders and putting them on the internet, like a holograph museum. We're not the Met or the Louvre, which serve the world. Where is the enjoyment, anyhow, in looking at a computer screen? For myself, I like to turn over the leaves in a portfolio, examine the works one by one, touch the paper, just as I like *painting*—something textured on the wall, in a frame, the spectator in front of it, studying it, *flat*. What she proposes," I added, with biblical indignation, "are vain simulacra!"

My argument had flaws, of course. I wasn't unmindful of Malraux's idea of the Museum Without Walls. Art books, with their reproductions, have brought paintings to many and played an important role in modern art history; historical photographs, copied, are a major source of information for researchers and pleasure for readers. Computer reproduction would do the same, I supposed, if the nerds didn't turn it into a toy. But no committee had met on this project, as Mullins admitted when Elinor challenged him, and I knew that the staff had not been informed. There really was no money for such, unless other undertakings were reduced and the very rationale of the museum changed. Mullins had just been seduced by the Taupe, that's all, *totus porcus.* Seduced by an idea and her airs, I mean.

We lost again; Norma left for California. I wasn't sure whether, in fact, it was the imaging project or the putative boyfriend that counted more for her; she might easily be involved with both, of course, especially if the man was himself a software guru. I'm not certain even that she was there during the entire period of leave; Elinor tried to get in touch with her once at the telephone number she had given and was told that Norma was not available and had not left other numbers at which she could be reached.

Some weeks later an announcement was circulated, the sort of thing that would be sent out widely: the museum would sponsor late the following year a "global conference" on "Ethnological Approaches to Technologizing Art." What in heaven's name could that mean? All art depends on technology, in the broad sense, except oral poetry, unaccompanied song, and performances in dance and drama, based on memory and where the body is the instrument. Even in the caves at Lascaux there had to be suitable materials for creating the mural figures, and anything literary or musical that's written down requires papyrus or some other material plus writing instruments, or their modern equivalents. "Technologizing art" was, I supposed, jargon for imaging, but how would that be approached ethnologically? Some sort of McLuhanesque analysis of the internet and its effects? I couldn't imagine *race* being interjected into the subject, and didn't believe there would be emphasis on primitive materials, transmission, and so on; only a small number of trained archeologists could deal with such questions. The conference organizer was, of course, Norma Wurmser. The keynote speaker would be a certain Scott Bernstein, said to be a specialist in computer design and virtual reality. He might be the boyfriend. Who and what would make the conference "global" was not clear. Papers were solicited from all those interested. Greg, Elinor, and I were not; we were, instead, aghast. I wondered what the museum's patrons would say about such a conference; but my business is taking care of the French holdings, not public relations.

The conference did prove to be the Taupe's undoing. At least we looked at it that way. But you know how these things work in institutions, frequently in politics: someone comes in, a self-styled *expert* (the newspapers always use that term), talks of the cutting edge, redesigns things to fit some fashionable trend, spends a lot of money, alienates many and creates divisiveness, gives birth (sometimes) to a project that as often as not is deformed or stillborn—then, leaving the others with the afterbirth, moves elsewhere, boasting of new accomplishments and thus getting a higher salary.

We had to put up with the Taupe for over a year before the crisis came. Whether Mullins began to lose patience with her during that period, I can't say. Somehow, he had manipulated the board members into underwriting the conference, probably deceiving them a bit. Greg, Elinor, and I stayed out of the way. When the final program was printed, we saw that Norma had succeeded in creating a veneer of globalism: in addition to numerous Californians and some from other parts of the U.S., there were speakers from Korea, Japan (some new application of technology, I wondered?), and Holland, of all places— well, they take up with anything radical, and of course they do have marvelous paintings, if that has anything to do with it.

Bernstein's name didn't appear on the list, however. If he had been the fond lover, that must have ended. Instead, as keynote speaker, there was a woman with a very foreign-sounding name, whose address was given as New York. "Greg, have you heard of this Biljana Tadeusz-Gapa?" I asked, as we were standing at our pigeon holes, looking at the program. Greg, especially now that he's divorced, is a reader, with very vast knowledge.

"Certainly not! I suppose she's some sort of anthropologist, or maybe a linguist, though she isn't attached to a university. Look at that title: 'Indo-European Technological Evidence on Women and Art.' If that isn't the most pretentious trash I ever heard of! What does it mean, anyhow? Indo-European evidence—that could be anything or everything, from the Hittites on, linguistic, archeological, historical, but where on God's green earth would the technological part be? She can't distinguish between men's and women's technology! If she really knew anything about Indo-European archeology, she wouldn't want to get involved in something like this; she'd be doing legitimate research."

Norma fluttered about throughout the final weeks of preparation, speaking to me airily, as though, a non-participant, I didn't count—someone from the rear when the real battle was going on at the front lines. I didn't care. My thought was to stay out of the way completely. But Mullins invited all the curators, along with the board and museum angels, to a black-tie cocktail buffet the evening the conference opened, after which we would adjourn to the lecture hall. The thing would be catered and held in the museum itself. I didn't care about pleasing Mullins, for my position is secure, but my absence would have been remarked by board members and patrons, whose goodwill is genuine and to whom my own department owes a great deal. In the event, we all showed up.

Greg, Elinor, one or two others, and I formed a little cluster, as often, around the bar and then the buffet table. Mullins was there, looking distinguished, with the noisiest of the patrons and the two stars of the evening—Norma, as conference organizer, and the keynote speaker. The sisters of Lesbos were much in evidence, their mannishness exaggerated in, and perhaps for, the social setting. The speaker was not hard to identify. Abnormally thin, she was clad in a long black gown—the sort of aggressive, soulless garment that Lady Macbeth might have worn; in their tight sleeves, her elbows seemed to turn into weapons and her hands stuck out like claws. Unlike Norma, she had on violent make-up—deep magenta on her lips and blue all over her eyes. It was a strange get-up in which to give the opening speech at a conference.

Moreover, it soon became obvious that she was quite intoxicated. Above the general line of conversations and cocktail sounds, her voice rose in spikes, and she stabbed someone with an elbow. Her accent, unidentifiable to me, was thick, and few could have followed her words, but she was in the limelight and people gathered around as at a seance. Norma, in a burlap-textured gown that fell shapeless to her ankles, its brown plainness relieved only by a necklace of heavy dark stones, was shepherding her star at the same time that she was displaying her.

Elinor and I agreed that the woman had been drinking. "Do you think Norma realizes *how* drunk?" Elinor added.

"I doubt it."

Just then Greg, who had gone for another whiskey—he can absorb a lot without its showing—returned beside us. "You see her, don't you? I caught a few words—not hers, but Norma's. The Taupe is nervous but she doesn't dare show it and can't do anything."

"Does Mullins realize something's amiss?

"Can't say—he practices urbanity to the point of cover-up."

We returned to the buffet, trying to get enough of Mullins's offerings onto saucer-sized plates to see us through the evening, and I got another glass of red wine; *I* didn't have to speak and wanted to anesthesize myself against the coming performance. Greg and I drank up, and we emptied our plates. As the platform party moved laboriously toward the lecture hall, we darted in and got seats on the front left, close to the exit. Patrons, some in tuxes and cocktail dresses, were taking their places, but the crowd seemed small to me. As for the other conference participants, of course I couldn't identify them; they may have been among the nondescript people trailing in. When Norma, Tadeusz-Gapa, Mullins, and the board chairman moved down the aisle, a little ripple of attention followed them; it grew as they approached the steps leading to the platform. Norma assisted her guest, who seemed to be weaving and stumbled at the top, then bumped into a potted palm before falling onto a chair.

There were long introductions; Mullins made a fool of himself, first by speaking too long and in rapturous phrases, then by introducing the introducer, that is, Norma, who herself gave a lengthy and florid presentation. Innumerable phrases concerning the importance of the conference and its topic (still very far from clear) flew from their lips, in addition to encomia about Tadeusz-Gapa, but with a striking absence of hard facts about her credentials and publications. Finally it was her turn. Her stilt-like limbs seemed reluctant to carry her to the podium. She scarcely acknowledged the effusive praise of which she had been the object, and said nothing about the conference as a whole, which she was supposed to launch, but instead mumbled a few phrases where I could discern the words *goddess, ethnology,* and *authentic.* She then paused, dramatically. Suddenly she burst out: "O Woman, the artist of the world!" If any members of the audience were dozing after their drinks, they must have been startled, like Haydn's listeners during the Surprise Symphony.

What on earth, I wondered. She then explained that it was the opening line of an old Indo-European poem. An Indo-European poem? She didn't seem cognizant of the fact that there is no language by that name. The line sounded phoney to me, anyhow. No reference was made to the source or time of the work; it merely was a launching pad for some nonsense in the feminist vein, pseudo-historical, pseudo-anthropological, concerning women's great place in art in the distant past and the betrayal of that tradition by the later patriarchal tradition—as though there had been a race of women artists parallel to the Amazons and, like them, done in by history. It was difficult to follow her, given her accent and a somewhat thickened tongue, as if she had Turkish paste in her mouth—though what difference does it make if the material is bogus? But she managed to stay on her feet, leaning on the lectern, and after a while I thought she might be sobering up a bit.

Elinor, Greg, and I exchanged glances and raised an eyebrow or so. Mullins kept on a mask of placid attention. Norma looked a bit uncomfortable, though her jaundiced complexion always gives the impression of unease. Finally, I stopped listening. After some more rambling, the speaker sat down, without any concluding words, as far as I could tell. Norma, surprised, nevertheless popped up and thanked her for her "seminal speech" (with unintended irony, doubtless). Mullins himself rose to conclude the proceedings and remind listeners of the sessions the next day. He had to announce, however, that the Korean was unable to come. Before he had even finished, we three darted for the exit and from there to the parking lot. We could scarcely contain ourselves for disbelief at what we had witnessed.

"Can you imagine?" exclaimed Elinor. "The woman is a charlatan—or she's out of her mind."

"A fraud, all right, one way or the other," Greg agreed. "A thing like this makes a terrible impression on our patrons. No matter how little they know about most of what we do"—he chuckled—"they know a drunk when they see one and most of them will suspect that the feminist stuff she was mouthing was baloney."

"Mullins knows that. Even Norma does. She was edgy, you saw," I added. "She let that old buzz-word *seminal* pop out. She wasn't prepared for how this turned out—a half-drunken lecturer, who declaims some bogus quotation, expounds preposterous pseudo-historical stuff, and doesn't even conclude, but just sits down. Where did she find that creature, anyway?"

We talked about it a bit more, then continued the next day, when the morning conference sessions had begun and we were in our offices. It was Greg, we decided, who would go to Mullins, once the conference was over and the feathers had settled in the henhouse. Meanwhile, he would do some investigating of the lecturer—although tracing her might be difficult, since no publications had been mentioned and she had no professional appointment. He found that her name did not appear as an author in on-line catalogues. Searches of journals where an Indo-Europeanist might have published turned up nothing. I helped Greg go through bound library catalogues from various European countries; no trace of her. One membership list—a feminist art association—bore her name and a New York street address; that was useless. Armed with this knowledge, which made her suspect, though it did not really prove fraud or even incompetence, and keeping well in mind that evening performance, Greg made an appointment and confronted Mullins.

It turned out that Greg did not have to argue our case lengthily. "I challenge you," he said (as he reported to us later) "to defend your approval of this conference and the keynote speaker. You realize how badly she performed, don't you—not just her condition, but those ridiculous claims about women in pre-patriarchal art and that poem? I suppose she was Norma's choice, but you are the one who gave carte blanche for Norma to organize this thing. The woman brought disgrace on the museum; besides, I think she's a phoney. The rest of the conference didn't look very legitimate to me either." He brandished some papers he had brought—the program and some on-line index printouts.

Mullins sighed deeply and, according to Greg's memory, ran his hand over his brow. "I know, I know." He glanced toward the papers. "The whole thing was deplorable—the conference theme, that keynote speech, some of the other papers ... Norma admitted as much. It's even worse than you know, Greg. That lecturer doesn't even have an advanced degree!"

"How did you ascertain that?"

"She admitted it to Norma the night after the speech. They went back to the hotel and the woman insisted on having a drink in the bar. She'd already had too many, as you surely saw—doubtless started before we picked her up for the cocktail buffet. I don't know what Norma said to her—whether she humored her or finally lost patience—but anyhow, the woman, while protesting that she *was* deeply involved in the research and everything she'd said was true, admitted that she had no credentials and had never published a single article."

Greg didn't mind repeating that we'd thought all along that the conference was hare-brained and that anyone involved in it was suspect. "And that includes Norma—she cooked up the whole thing when she was in California on that foolish project; she chose the papers and the speakers; she threw away some of our money on this idiocy."

"I know. Why did I let her do it? I was taken in." He sighed again. "She has been disastrous from the beginning." He could admit his error, at least.

"What are you going to do about it? Is Norma going to stay? She's been a plague all along. But this is serious; I'm sure the fund-raisers will tell you that."

"Yes, of course. It's ... it's a difficult case."

The conversation ended on that admission, Greg having decided that he shouldn't say more; Mullins was cognizant of the mistake he'd made in hiring Norma, but wouldn't be pushed.

Some days later, I met her in the front lobby. "So, *Harriet*," she said, with a snooty little lisp, "you and your friends, the big ox and Elinor, I hope you're pleased with your little conspiracy. You have made life impossible for me here; I'm leaving."

"Norma, I have never interfered with what you did, or what you were *supposed* to do, and no conspiracy was necessary; your troubles here are your own doing. You would not cooperate with Elinor on the exhibit, you were rude, you meddled in others' affairs, you were gone a lot—and then you organized that ridiculous conference with that awful woman who turns out to be a scholarly fraud, as well you know. If she deceived you, it is not our fault. Where did you find her—in the side streets of Soho?"

She turned away without a word. The prospect of her departure, which I announced to the others, was immensely heartening, although it meant another search; the three of us agreed that, when the day came, we would celebrate it, maybe at Commander's Palace. As it turns out, though, she has even more to cheer about: she has gotten a position as a division curator at a big collection in California. Well, she's gone now, and her allies, if not chastened, are a bit discomfited and are lying low. We'll drink to that, at least.

The Knights of the Nile

IT WAS ANOTHER OF THE FAMOUS Carnival balls of New Orleans, one of those events, including innumerable parades, Jazz Fest, and countless other festivals, along with a generally hedonistic attitude year-round, that justify characterizing the place as The City That Care Forgot. We were in the ballroom of the Hilton, at the foot of Poydras at the Mississippi. Most Mardi Gras balls still take place in the Auditorium, on Basin Street, but the Knights of the Nile, a Carnival club or "krewe," decided last winter to hold theirs elsewhere. My host for the evening was an unmasked krewe member, Hughes Legendre, called Hugh, a former Marine officer and an old friend of my deceased husband, Jack. He is ten years older than I, a fine figure of a man, looking at bit like Charlton Heston, but with one bad leg. He jokes about it facetiously as "an old war wound"; indeed, it really *is*, but he makes light of it, out of modesty, one may suppose, or possibly fearing hostile anti-military reactions from members of his children's generation. First, we had attended the Queen's Reception in a side room, met the queen and her court, had champagne, and then had taken seats to watch the pageant. I had volunteered to get drinks at the bar across the room to save Hugh's stiff leg.

The pageant began with a grand march, to the suitable music of "Aida," played by a small orchestra, and other pseudo-Oriental strains. Lilies of the Nile decorated fake pedestals and a small gauze-draped platform. The colors of costumes, plumes, masks, and other appurtenances were as brilliant as trumpet calls. Motifs varied, from garments in the Far Eastern style to more nearly Egyptian ones. After the march, most masked krewe members sat on the floor, creating a parting of the waters, so to speak, for the entry of ladies-in-waiting, princesses, and finally the queen, escorted to the throne platform to join the king, clad in gold and white, and his dukes, the "Duke of Green," the "Duke of Orange," and so on. A certain amount of bowing went on, but the show was not excessively formal, and we could chat amiably instead of having to keep still, as at a religious rite. Hugh used the moment to pass to me a favor in a black velvet bag: a "member's favor," one usually given during the first dance. It was a small pyramid in gold, hung on a golden chain. I put mine around my neck immediately.

During the pause after the revelers had seated themselves on the floor and were awaiting their queen's entry, I happen to glance across the open space to the left, and to my amazement recognized Sylvia Croft, dressed in black, with pearls at her throat. That she should be at a Carnival ball was noteworthy.

Sylvia is afflicted with a congenital deformity that sets her apart and makes many activities difficult. True, she went to college, studying art and art history; that's how I knew her, one semester when St. John's College sent students to enroll for credit in lectures given under our auspices at the Orleanian Institute. That year it was a course on Southern art, by James Gordon. Sylvia had driven to class in her specially-equipped sedan, with high floor pedals, low seat and a small wheel. For she is a hunchback, very short, with thin little legs and a shapeless middle, a bit rounded like a keg, draped always in some loose garment, often a sweatshirt, hanging down to her knees and worn with tights. Nothing is wrong with her brain, of course, and her arms and hands, while a bit small, are not deformed; our staff discovered that she was an excellent draughtsman. Her temperament is as sweet as they come, and I remembered her winsome smile.

A discreet gesture let her know, if she was looking my way, that I'd seen her; I was unsure. Later, after the coronation, I would go speak to her. Hugh and I chatted, sipped our drinks, and watched the spectacle. When it was over and there was a general moving-about and mingling, just before the dancing began, I returned to the bar to fill Hugh's glass, looking around as I did so for Sylvia. There she was, at some distance, surrounded by a large group, visible at waist height between two men. Well, that was grand; she obviously didn't lack for company. She wouldn't dance, I imagined, but neither would Hugh, with his game leg; one could enjoy the evening anyhow.

Some while later I excused myself to go find the women's restroom. Entering, I immediately caught sight of Sylvia, bent over a wash basin. Her black dress was of silk jacquard, and she was wearing little Mary Jane shoes, doubtless bought at a children's shop, since her feet were so small. Another woman, stunningly dressed in emerald green, stood beside her, looking very much concerned. I noticed that each had a golden pyramid, identical to mine; Sylvia's dangled over the basin. She was coughing, or choking. When she straightened up, her dark eyes, which seemed to have been chosen to match her dress and contrast with the pearls, had a wild look. It was not clear whether she recognized me. Nevertheless, not wanting to pass by as though we were unacquainted, I greeted her, or attempted to, normally.

"Hello, Sylvia. It's been years since we saw each other at the museum. How are you?"

She appeared startled. "What ... what ... ?"

"Sorry—I should have given my name. Harriet D'Aquin, you'll remember, from the Orleanian Institute."

The woman in green spoke to me. "Sylvia's not herself; she's ..."

There was a retching sound, and Sylvia bent again over the basin, her friend holding her a bit through the middle.

"Oh, pardon me," I said hastily. "I'm very sorry that I spoke now, if she's not well. Please forgive me. I'll try to talk with her another time."

"Yes, please do that."

Toward the end of the evening, I glimpsed them again across the room. Someone seemed to be chiding Sylvia. The woman in green then went to the dance floor with a masked partner; other maskers continued talking in an animated manner to Sylvia, one of them leaning over her. Then, at the close of the ball, she left amid a small group.

It was at James and Irene Gordon's house that I saw her next. Strange: it had been years since we'd run into each other, and here it had happened twice in four months. The Gordons are kind enough to invite me to dinner on occasion in their nineteenth-century house on Prytania Street, with a huge modern kitchen suitable for entertaining informally during the period of meal preparation. They had invited me to bring a date. Date? I don't date. But some masculine company would be nice, and I had thought of Hugh.

So the two of us were there, along with a half-dozen or so other guests, including Sylvia. In a peasant-style top and dark tights, she looked like something from a toy shop. For a moment I fancied her painted by Velásquez in one of his portraits of dwarfs, those dark eyes of hers set off perhaps by a *mantilla* or a lace collar; but then I realized that the image, though graphically pleasing, was offensive socially, since she needed to be treated and thought of not as a curiosity nor court buffoon, as surely the Habsburgs viewed those miniature people, but in her full personhood. The woman in emerald green from the K of N ball was there also. This time, she wore a white eyelet blouse and an ankle-length skirt of blue lawn, embroidered in white, with stylish espadrilles.

Introductions were made all around. "Harry, you remember Sylvia Croft from the museum, don't you?" said James, "the time I taught that course there."

"Indeed I do; and in fact, James, we saw each other not long ago." I turned toward her. "How are you, Sylvia?—well, I hope?" The tone of my voice was intended to convey that I truly meant it but didn't want to say "Better than last time?"

"Oh, yes, Dr. D'Aquin, thank you." The statement wasn't made with great conviction, but she added a resolute smile.

"And Sylvia, please meet my friend Hugh Legendre." The tall figure bent to shake her hand, murmuring something about knowing her father.

James, who was still at the edge of the group, added, just before turning to answer the doorbell, "Sylvia, you'll have to introduce Roz to everyone for me."

Roz, the woman from the ball, turned out to be Rosalind, "my wonderful sister." Some of the guests moved into the front room, an old-fashioned parlor furnished with fine Victorian furniture. Others turned toward the kitchen. I followed, to chat with Irene over her cooking islands. While we were sipping a dry wine and nibbling on Spanish olives, as a shrimp dish simmered on the shiny steel range, Sylvia came up to me. "Dr. D'Aquin, may I ... may I talk to you a bit ... later, after dinner, I mean—just the two of us?"

"Why certainly, Sylvia." It was not a conversation to be dreaded, but I wondered what was on her mind.

Dinner was lovely, the shrimp, flavored with bay, chili powder, and marjoram in a tomato sauce, light enough for summer, the rice dry and grainy as we like it in Louisiana, the salad crisp, and a dessert so fluffy that it barely weighed on the tongue. Coffee was served then in the parlor. Afterwards, some of the guests stepped through an enclosed rear porch to the garden, steamy and tropical with its moonflowers, hibiscus, and palms. Sylvia and I followed as far as the door.

"Let's stay here and chat," I said; "you can bring me up to date."

The porch was cooled by a slow, dreamy overhead fan as well as air conditioning vents and its own greenery; in the garden, small colored lights made the great elephant-ear leaves and palm fronds glow, creating a private feeling. We sat on casual white-wicker furniture upholstered in white with green stripes. Sylvia took a chair with an extra cushion, which helped raise her eyes to the level of mine.

"I don't know quite why I feel the need to explain, Dr. D'Aquin, but I do. That incident in the women's restroom at the Knights of the Nile ball ... I *did* recognize you, you know, and later told Roz who you were, but I was just unable to say anything."

"That's all right, Sylvia. Don't think anything of it."

"But I don't want you to believe ... that I was *drunk* or that I take tranquillizers or drugs! I do take many medicines, because of ... all my troubles inside that come from being so ... misshapen; but I am very careful about the prescriptions. But I *was* sick."

"It can happen to anyone—a virus, or food poisoning from the Ptomaine Palace Café!"

She managed to laugh briefly. "But that wasn't it. I was sick because of my family. They have made me ill." This was said in a darkly serious tone.

I waited for her to go on. Just then James popped his head in with the coffee pot. "You girls doing all right in here?"

"Yes," I replied quickly, "we're having one of those catch-up conversations that women love. But you may pour a little more coffee for us. I hope Hugh is managing without me; please tell him I've not forgotten we came together!" In fact Hugh, I knew, wouldn't mind. He could talk to anyone, meet new people, fit into any group.

Resuming her narrative, Sylvia said, "My grandparents and my father—I must explain that my mother died some years ago—are furious with me. Some months ago I met a man named Peter Kouri, and we became engaged. But everyone is against it—everyone except Roz, that is. I have money of my own, left to me by my mother from *her* family's fortune—because she wanted me to have it all, seeing that ... well, there is the expense of therapy and medication, and there might be other high medical bills. I'm working now—at Präger's Antiques on Royal Street—but the salary is low. Anyhow, my father and paternal grandparents have declared that I must not marry this man. He's of Lebanese descent. My grandparents are very old-fashioned."

Putting down my coffee cup, I dared ask, "Is it a matter of religion?"

"No, not really. He's a Maronite Christian. But to my grandparents he's a *foreigner*. It's not blood, in the strict sense: I can never have children" (she gave a wry glance at her deformed self) "and I wouldn't wish to if I could, because of the ... risk. As for Daddy—well, he says he agrees with them; he also claims that Peter is not worthy of me."

"What does he mean by that?"

"He won't explain clearly," Sylvia answered. "It's not money; Peter has large holdings around Crowley. Daddy just keeps repeating that Peter is not trustworthy, that he isn't the sort of man one wants as a son-in-law."

After a pause, Sylvia continued. "There had been quite a scene at home the evening of that ball. My father is a krewe member, as are two of my cousins. Apparently he had been drinking in the krewe room before the pageant, and had spoken his mind to them, saying that I would *never* marry Peter—or that if I did he would disown me. The worst part is that Peter was there also in the krewe room; he's an out-of-town member, through his own connections. He heard everything, apparently. I don't mind about Daddy's money; I have Mother's, and Roz will just get more from Daddy if I'm disinherited as far as the civil code will allow. But to be banished—cursed, the way people did in the old days when a daughter went against her father ... Peter then told all this to Roz in the ballroom. He was very angry. She would have kept quiet, but Daddy himself came up and started carrying on about it right to my face. It made me sick; I have always gotten ill easily. I was frightened to death that Peter would ... leave me, you know."

"You're speaking," I said, "to someone who knows that same feeling under stress: the constriction in the throat, the knot in the stomach, the trembling of all the nervous system. It's not that I don't have courage and self-control! But my body makes me pay for it. I feel for you."

For a moment, we were silent. The group from the garden opened the door, letting in steamy breath, and returned to the parlor.

"Roz," Sylvia went on, "has been wonderful. She has defended me, risking Daddy's displeasure. She also tried to explain things to Peter. She believes he honestly loves me."

Presumably he did, though I was a bit suspicious, knowing in particular that "large holdings" around Crowley or anywhere else might not mean quite the fortune that a young man might want—perhaps might mean no fortune at all, but debts—and that her money could appear very attractive. Her father might have similar misgivings.

"Peter would have been here tonight—the Gordons asked me to bring him along—but he's in Crowley this week."

Anyone who is not overcome by passion and the hope it inspires can't help seeing the other side of such a relationship. "You don't think ..." I offered tentatively, "that your father ... might know something specific—about Peter's finances, or ... well, I hate to say it, but his *character*?"

"Well, no! He has never cited anything in particular. It's all suspicions—unfounded suspicions, and prejudice, just as with my grandparents."

Ordinarily, I do not encourage the young people who talk to me (God knows they do! I thought I was an art historian but turn out to be a counselor to all the museum interns) to go against their parents' views; we are not there to seduce young people away from their families, their religion, their upbringing. But Sylvia was thirty, if anything, and surely had a human as well as a legal right to make her own decisions. "Well, how good at least that Roz has been so supportive. Surely, you must decide for yourself; it is just unfortunate that you find yourself displeasing your father so greatly."

James popped in again at that moment. "Brandy, anyone?"

We had been away from the group long enough. "Let's go join the others," Sylvia said. "Mr. Legendre must be looking for you."

"Oh, Sylvia, call him Hugh! He doesn't want this *Mister* business. And I'm to be Harry from now on, or Harriet if you prefer. But you're right; let's go get a little brandy and see how the conversation is proceeding in the other room. Have you seen Irene's Wifredo Lam painting, by the way?" And we went back into the parlor. Before long, Sylvia was seated on a rose-colored love seat, with Hugh, in a nearby chair. She was listening intently as he talked, very simply, about his own art collection, particularly a series of André Masson drawings.

It was the Knights of the Nile that brought us together again and furnished a scene of semi-tragic opera. The function was an autumn cocktail party given by Hugh for a large number of his K of N colleagues and their wives, daughters, and others. The Crofts—father and daughters—were invited, plus Peter. Hugh lives in the French Quarter, on Ursulines Street, very close to the old Ursuline Convent and the Beauregard-Keyes house, in an ancient building that has served variously as private residence, convent, school, and house of ill-repute. In recent years it was turned into a condominium, "The Hof," with five residences opening onto the central courtyard, all somewhat gerrymandered. Hugh's consists of a small entrance foyer on the ground floor, with stairs and an elevator leading to a spacious entertaining room upstairs with a balcony, along with a library, dining room, butler's pantry, and kitchen, and, on the third story, his bedroom area, with mansard windows and another balcony cut into the hip roof. He could easily entertain sixty people at a stand-up party. It was catered, of course.

I'd gotten there a bit late, having waited a long while for the streetcar (two passed me by, filled with tourists from Audubon Park) and then having walked along Chartres to Ursulines Street. Most of the other guests, I'd assumed, had taken taxis, since there is little parking available. Approaching Hugh's corner, I caught sounds of some sort of commotion. Turning, I saw a small group of people in the street and others on Hugh's balcony just above. Indistinct shouting rose above a bass of other voices and there was much movement. Drawing closer, I realized that a figure on the balcony was clinging to the wrought-iron railing; it was Sylvia, not much higher than the railing but visible amid the others because she was so close to it, with her arms hanging over. A low center of gravity favored her; still, it looked as if she might be sent tumbling into the street. Perhaps they all would: the small balcony, cantilevered, wasn't meant for more than three or four people, standing calmly, not jostling each other. I thought I heard her voice: "No, no!"

Past some rather shopworn statuary in the courtyard, I entered Hugh's open door and walked up the stairs. The catering company butler admitted me into the main room. Almost everyone was standing near the windows and French doors. I looked around.

The butler thought to explain. "Mr. Legendre is out on the balcony. He's trying to get that … that young lady to come in."

I hadn't noticed him out there, but no wonder, in the confusion.

A waiter carrying a drink tray turned up at my elbow just then; I picked up a glass of champagne. A server emerged from the pantry with napkins in one hand and a tray of hors-d'oeuvres in the other, and offered oyster patties; I took one, almost mechanically, and started nibbling on it. In the adjacent dining area, a few people were drinking and talking together. Suddenly there was movement, and James Gordon appeared in the French doors. "Make room!" he shouted. More movement, and then Sylvia, disheveled and thrashing a bit, was dragged by Roz and Hugh into the room. Well, the balcony had held, at least.

"Roz, let me go. Get *off* of me! Let me go."

Verbal and physical confusion followed—Rosalind's protests, Hugh's words as he clutched Sylvia, her struggles. But she could not shake off her sister and a tall man, even one much older than she and lame. Butler, waiter, guests—we were all witnesses to this drama, unwilling voyeurs, fascinated as snakes by a fakir: there is something inhuman, almost sacred, in great anger, perhaps all the more striking in so small a person. But we were anxious too, of course. I supposed she had tried to throw herself from the balcony to the sidewalk below, or threatened to and frightened the others. Had she had a bad reaction to some new medication?

Having apparently expended all her energy and passion, Sylvia allowed herself to be pushed into a chair, where Rosalind held her by the shoulders, half-restraining, half-protective; Hugh stood before her, looking stern. "Sylvia! Don't try that again, for God's sake!"

Her rage was suddenly transformed into a spasm of sobbing. "You don't know what it's like! You can't *possibly* know! That was my only chance. Look at me!"

"Oh, Sylvia," Roz pleaded with her, "don't think about *him* anymore. Look, all the rest of us love you; *I* love you, just as you are; it makes no difference."

So there was a man involved. Peter Kouri? Her father? Neither one appeared to be present.

James and Irene were beside me then, and we said hello, properly, for the first time, since it hadn't been possible before. We turned; it seemed discreet to step aside from Sylvia and Roz.

"James, do you know what happened?"

"Yes," he replied; "I got there quickly, thank heaven; I realized, as I was standing by the open French doors, that something was amiss. First I thought perhaps Sylvia had become dizzy."

"She takes lots of medication," I interjected. "And her system ... well, it isn't strong. Once, I remember, she fell ill ... when things weren't going right." I didn't want to reveal the circumstances or speak of her father's threats.

"Yes, we know about the medication, don't we, Irene?"

Irene nodded in agreement. We were in the library by that time, so that James could pour himself a whiskey. "Heaven knows I need it," he observed. "But—to get back to Sylvia—it wasn't just a case of nerves or medication, I think; it's clear she heard something this evening that caused her to rush out there."

Just as at the K of N ball, when she'd gotten sick. Words can be knives, tearing at the soul; worse, one remembers them, hears their echo, and suffers from their wounds long after they are spoken, unlike physical pain, which, when ended, leaves only unsure mental images.

At that moment, two or three people appeared from the staircase—guests who had gone down after Sylvia had threatened, or tried, to hurl herself into the street. Following them was a swarthy man with an aquiline nose; exclamations made me realize that it must be Peter Kouri, arriving late.

"What are you doing here?" shouted Rosalind. "Look at what you've done. She's tried to *kill herself* over you!"

Hugh moved toward him. He spoke in a strong voice but not dramatically. "Peter, you don't belong here. I know you were invited, and the law of hospitality would ordinarily demand that you be treated as a guest. But, under the circumstances ... What Roz says is true; that is, we think so. Sylvia tried to throw herself down into the street, just a few minutes ago, saying that she realized she had been duped, and that ..."

Rosalind, who had come to stand by Hugh, interrupted. She was in a rage. "You are to blame for all this, Peter; you courted her, asked her to marry you, made her quarrel with Daddy, who was suspicious about you all along; he wouldn't even come this evening. And now at this very party we have found out—*she* found out—just *by chance,* from a friend of Hugh's, that you have filed for bankruptcy in Crowley and have boasted over there of your engagement to a New Orleans woman, though her father objects to you—a woman who won't cause you much trouble and has lots of money!" She broke off, then continued before Peter could protest. "You called her a *cripple*! You are despicable; you could have been responsible for her death!"

By this time, Peter had managed to overcome his first surprise. "But ... but ... how could *I* know? I just arrived." Then, as though social niceties were important at such a moment, he added lamely, "Sorry I'm so late."

"Whether you knew or not what she just did, or tried to do, isn't the point!" Rosalind countered. "You knew your own motives, didn't you? And that you would break her heart? Look at her! Do you deny what we heard?"

Rosalind turned and pointed to the chair where her sister was still seated. Sylvia had already gone through a range of emotions, from despair to anger; a moment before, she had been crying quietly—a good release. The expression on her face now was one almost of terror.

Peter may have been on the point of saying something, but then Hugh spoke. "You may choose to deny it, Peter, but we know it is true, unfortunately; my guest, who did not realize the import of his information when he spoke, is an old friend and an unimpeachable source; he assures me he heard your very words. It is just most unfortunate that Sylvia had to find out this way. She is distraught, and your presence is making it worse. You will have to leave. As host, I apologize."

Peter's countenance expressed dismay—that of someone whose machinations have been found out and who is about to lose advantages long coveted.

"I ... I don't know what to say, Hugh. There must have been some misunderstanding ... I'm not quite sure why... It is true about the bankruptcy, but ..."

"No matter. Please leave. The butler will see you out."

The butler was right there, at the doorway leading to the landing and the staircase. Like everyone else except Rosalind and Hugh, he'd been mesmerized, unable to move until then.

Peter turned, was ushered out, and disappeared; the butler came back with a dignified demeanor. The spell of silence held for a moment, then gave way, as Rosalind moved back to Sylvia's chair and attempted to comfort her and Hugh looked around at his guests, who became human again as their wax-statue poses were released.

"I'm very sorry about that," he said. "Please—go into the dining room, where the buffet is set up, and Charles here will bring more champagne. And you know that mixed drinks and wine are available too—the bar is set up in the library."

He then moved toward Sylvia, whose paralyzed face and frightened eyes had softened a bit under Rosalind's ministrations. I could hear Roz saying to her, "Do you just want to sit here a bit? Have something to eat? Or shall I take you home right now?" I didn't hear the answer, but shortly could see that Rosalind was offering her a sip of wine and an oyster patty from a nearby tray. Sylvia probably wouldn't eat anything, but the wine might help.

To leave soon would be discreet, I thought, but not in such great haste as to suggest that Hugh's party was a failure. We milled about a bit, got sandwiches from the buffet table, and returned to the main room, where a number of guests were saying their goodbyes. The French doors were still open: it was a blessedly pleasant evening.

Suddenly a man's voice rose from the street. He sounded drunk, I thought, but maybe it was my imagination. Or was it the intoxication of anger? A few shouts flew up; then we heard Hugh's name. "Hugh Legendre, you have ruined my reputation and my chances! If you repeat any of this, if you tell what happened, I shall make sure that *your* reputation too is ruined forever."

It was an idle threat; Hugh's standing is so high and his character so good that attacks from someone such as Peter would do nothing. Hugh stepped again onto the balcony. "Go away, Peter, or I shall call the police immediately. They're on Royal Street; they'll be here in two minutes. Go away and do not come back!"

The tone from below was mocking, now, as well as aggressive. "I shall, I shall. And tell her that I never want to see her again!"

Whether Sylvia, about to rise now with Rosalind at her side, heard clearly I don't know. Nor have I ever found out who it was who told about the Kouri bankruptcy and quoted Peter's words about his engagement. Hugh had confidence in his source; that was all that mattered. And of course the marriage did not take place. The scene at Hugh's now belongs to private annals, joining countless other New Orleans dramas, public and private, in which the glitter cracks and gives way to falsehood and unhappiness.

Hugh closed the French doors suddenly and said, "I'll put on the fans." But everyone prepared to leave, putting down glasses and pulpy wads of paper napkins, thanking Hugh, waving feeble little goodbyes to Sylvia as a pathetic substitute for doing anything else.

I couldn't go without speaking to her: her unhappiness resonated in me, another among life's unlimited supply of sour notes. "Sylvia, Rosalind," I said, looking at both of them, "I am so sorry this has happened. Please, Sylvia, take care of yourself ... Do not despair. You have many concerned friends."

"Yes," added Irene, just behind me.

Hugh approached at that moment. "I apologize deeply, Sylvia, for this awful scene and what you were exposed to earlier. It is most unfortunate."

"May we drive you home, Sylvia and Roz?" James asked. "The car's in a hotel garage near here."

Rosalind accepted, and soon they all four went down the stairs, Sylvia hobbling a bit, leaning on James. I lingered a moment to say something more to Hugh, then left. Outside, the cicadas and evening birds were busy fretting the moist night air. A ship called, very close, and, farther away, one could hear the river calliope. Traffic in the Quarter was light; people were at dinner or in bars. I walked down

Chartres and then along Canal Street to catch the streetcar home. Lovely, it was, the city in its peaceable twilight mode, lights on, a few strolling tourists looking carefree, the streetcar turning the corner at Carondolet; all seemed in order, "a beauteous, evening / calm and free." But, like the cardboard backdrop and flimsy colored gauze draped at the Knights of the Nile pageant, the impression was ersatz; behind it, someone whose body was already deformed was going home now with a badly broken heart as well. It, at least, would not show so plainly, but it would ache for a long while. Aren't many of us, I reflected, similarly creatures of disgrace, cripples in one way or another? And hadn't we, on occasion, broken others' spirits, adding to the burden of the world?

A Summer Sketch

"I'M QUITTING FOR NOW; see you later."

The June sunlight of Texas—a monster with fiery claws, reaching down from a molten sky and reflecting off the surface of the water—seared through me and tore at my eyes, even through sunglasses. I didn't want to go back to New York with a sunburn and skin peeling off my nose. Nor did I wish to go blind, as Monet had and Degas feared he would in New Orleans when the dazzling light of 30° latitude struck him. Musicians go deaf; painters lose their sight. I didn't want to follow that pattern.

A group of us had been fishing all morning in the Rio Grande, near a little riverside community downstream from El Paso. In good seasons, when the water wasn't too low, one could find bass and catfish there. But for me, fishing was usually futile; I didn't have the touch. This time, I'd caught nothing at all, and the sun had caught *me*. So I'd decided to reel in my line and go cool off under a cottonwood tree, my eyelids doubling the shade. There's nothing wrong with a woman trying the sport, and I had lots of patience, but something was missing—coordination, quick reactions, maybe instinct and desire. But that made little difference, since this was an outing with friends and family, and I wasn't the only one without much skill in the water. My mother didn't even make a show of trying, though my aunt Dora always put on her hip boots and stood in the river for a while, at least. She was high-spirited, sociable, and youthful for her age—around fifty—and, with my uncle Joe dead and no children, she valued the family into which she had married and enjoyed outings tremendously. I supposed, however, that the heat would finally seem too much for her also and that in a while she would go inside and rest.

My father had organized this little trip. We were staying at a riverside motel on the U.S. side that had cabins with one or two bedrooms and a little kitchen and sitting room. In addition to my parents, Aunt Dora, and me, there was my father's friend Tom Martin, a colleague from the newspaper office, with his wife, Susan. Tom had towed his boat down from Elephant Butte Dam, above Las Cruces, though you don't need a boat to fish the Rio Grande where we were. We had driven down in two cars the previous afternoon, settled into our respective cabins, and all crowded onto the boat to cross to the Mexican side for drinks and dinner at a cantina there. Fishing had begun in the morning, and would continue for a week. Tom and Susan were on the boat, the rest of us on the riverbanks. Now that I'd gotten my tackle together and gone out once, to be sociable, I wouldn't bother again, since mainly I wanted to work. I'd taken my drawing materials and planned to do some river sketches and cloud studies—the sort of outdoor scene that I didn't practice much in New York. I also had two or three important books and articles that I needed to digest. Anyone who didn't want to fish was free to do other things—rest, draw, read, as my mother did, or walk along the sandy banks of the river. We would all go to dinner together in the evening, taking the boat, or driving twenty miles or so to another Texas town or crossing the bridge at Tornillo or Ft. Hancock to eat at some spot on highway 2 in Chihuahua.

I gathered my gear and settled among the python-like roots of the large cottonwood. In a while, after letting the shade cool me down and soothe my eyes, I would walk the half-mile or so to the cabin, get a quick sandwich from the makings my mother had brought, and then think about work. Drawing in the midday sun was out of the question; it would have to be reading on the shaded porch to the east or in the sitting room, which had a swamp cooler as air conditioning. Later in the afternoon, I could return to the riverbank and look for a suitable spot for sketching. The others would trickle back, I supposed, as their drinks and sandwiches ran out or they got too hot or burnt by the sun and wind.

About three I was on the shaded porch, taking notes from some articles. (Maybe I shouldn't mention the time of day at all, for we had discarded the routines of working life for this *dolce far niente* of the summer. Furthermore, we were almost on the line where Central Time turns into the Mountain Zone; we could drive a short distance and the hour would change. So we went mostly by the sun anyhow.) Dora, who had returned to the cabin not long after me, was reading in a chair close to the steps. As always, she looked lovely. Her dark hair, cut short, was glossy, even in the shade, and she had changed into sandals, white slacks, and a fuchsia-and-white striped blouse, with a cream-colored woven belt that accented her narrow waist.

As I looked up to empty my mind and rest my eyes for a moment, I saw an older man coming along toward our cabin, carrying a small ice chest. Stopping on the bottom step, he said to Dora, in a twangy West Texas drawl, "Excuse me, Ma'am, I saw you sitting here and just thought you might like to have one of these cold Cokes in this cooler. I'm staying in another cabin, over there" (and he gestured) "but I brought more than I can use, really. It's awfully warm." And, as if to prove it, he put down the cooler, removed his Stetson with his left hand, and, pulling out a red bandana from his pocket with his other hand, wiped his brow.

He'd seen me too all along, I imagine; in fact, as I reflected later, he was probably encouraged by my presence, which made it less awkward and less bold for him to address Dora: I could act as a kind of chaperone, a youthful *dueña*. After putting his hat on again, he added hastily, looking at me, "Oh, excuse me, you too, Ma'am. I saw y'all fishing in the river this morning; pretty sunny out there, wasn't it? Did you catch anything?"

Neither of us had yet spoken to him; he couldn't have continued his monologue much longer. Dora finally said in her delightful accent (she had been born in Ireland), "Oh, no, I rarely do; and my niece here wasn't out very long—you came back before noon, didn't you, dearie?"

I nodded. It was up to them to decide what to do next, I thought. Picking up his cooler, the man opened it, pulled out two cans, and repeated his offer. "So why don't you have these?"

"Why, that's mighty friendly of you." (That is one of the Texas colloquialisms Dora had learned.) "Thank you. Won't you come up here in the shade of the porch?"

Wes Lamb, as he turned out to be, was an impressive man: tall, tanned, dressed in the Western style, with his Stetson, a blue checked cowboy-style shirt with mother-of-pearl buttons, a wide tooled-leather belt with a large silver buckle, dark denims, and cowboy boots in very good condition. Surely he hadn't worn those down to the riverbank; he must have changed. His hair, which I'd noticed as he took off his hat again to sit beside us, had a lot of silver in it, but it had not thinned much, and he was lean through the middle, unlike most men his age. That Dora was willing talk to him didn't surprise me: in her position at the bank, she dealt every week with dozens of people, men more than women, and would not have thought it compromising to strike up a conversation with a stranger. Still, we weren't at a bank, and it was clear to me that he had come up to talk to Dora because ... well, because she was *Dora*, an obviously attractive and apparently unaccompanied woman more or less of his age. But how had he known she wasn't married to one of the men around—my father, or Tom, or somebody else? Maybe it was a hunch, the sort of instinct developed by men who have lived in the world a good while, gambled a bit with circumstances, as you have to, and learned to take in a situation at a glance.

Wes had introduced himself, and Dora gave her name. I added, "I'm Harriet Hamilton. I was named for my grandmother, but I don't like the name very much; everyone calls me Harry. I'm here with my family. My mother is inside, reading or resting, and my father is still down at the river, I think, or maybe with some friends, who have brought their boat." Wes had opened our cans and taken out a third for himself. We sat there in the shade, with summer sounds, colors, and light all around us: insects buzzing, car tires crunching on the gravel road now and then, hibiscus by the walkway and climbing talisman roses on a trellis, a sky that resembled a blue Byzantine mosaic, and the light streaming on the sand like golden lava. It was the sort of moment that goes slowly and fully. We exchanged a few more comments on the fishing and the scenery, and I took some sips, savoring the icy flow and letting the bubbles tickle my throat.

After names, it's always where you live, if that isn't obvious, or where you come from, and what you do. Wes explained, "I've come down here for some fishing for a couple of weeks, while I have some time off between jobs. My boat is down there at the launch. All this territory is familiar to me; my family was in sheep ranching downriver in Terrell and Brewster counties."

How appropriate, I thought, given his name.

"And do you still ranch some?" asked Dora.

"No, I'm in the oil and gas business. I work mostly out of Jal and Hobbs, New Mexico, but at one time or another I've had jobs in almost every oil patch in West Texas, and lots in Oklahoma, Colorado, and Wyoming. I also get down to Venezuela pretty often."

A moving man, then, if not a restless one. He could have had one wife or four.

"We're from El Paso," Dora explained. "That is, I live there now. You can tell from my accent that I'm a foreigner—Ireland."

"There are Lambs—I don't mean just sheep!—in Ireland; I had ancestors from there."

"I know the name. My maiden name was Lynch. I came here years ago and married Harry's uncle; but he's dead now. I work at the West Texas National Bank. My brother-in-law is with a newspaper. Harry" (and she gestured to me) "is an art student in New York."

That gave me a pretext for leaving. Picking up my clipboard, pen, and glasses, I excused myself, explaining: "You'll have to pardon me. I do art history as well as studio art, but I've had enough note-taking for the afternoon. I've brought some sketching materials along on this trip and I want to work at least some every day. It was too hot and bright at midday, but now I think I'll go down among the cottonwoods and athel trees along the river and try my luck. I'll do better than at fishing, certainly. 'Bye, Aunt Dora; see you later, for cocktails. Did Dad say we were going across the river to eat again this evening?"

"I don't know what the plans are, dearie. *Hasta luego.*" (She had learned Spanish too.)

By six or so, when I got back, hot and dusty, from the riverbank groves, Wes was gone, but Dora was still on the porch. "Your parents are inside, getting cleaned up, I think. We'll leave for dinner across the river around 7; you have time for a shower. Tom and Susan will take your parents with them in the boat; would you like to come with Wes Lamb and me in his boat?"

That was Dora's way of telling me that he had been invited to join the group for dinner.

We gathered at 7, all cleaned up, the sun still brilliant in the northwestern sky and glowing on our complexions. We drove to the boat launch in two cars, then got into the two boats, crossed the river, and tied up. We started walking toward a little cantina, the hole-in-the-wall type, within sight, but Wes said he knew another, just down the road, with an open deck over the water. It turned out to be everything you would want in a border place—neon beer signs, wooden tables and benches, Mexican beers, and excellent enchiladas, tacos, and chiles rellenos. There was even a mariachi band. We started off with margaritas at the bar, then moved to a big corner booth, with the river practically under us. Was it the margaritas and Tecate beers, or the steady river with its cool blue shadows, or the summer evening, or simply the charm of Wes Lamb that seemed to work so well? We were in the best of moods. Dora seemed quite taken with Wes, who paid her every attention possible while maintaining the discretion necessary to one who had attached himself, without quite having been invited. Perhaps, past middle age, love must work faster, there being less time ...

"When did your family settle in Terrell County?" I asked.

120

"My grandfather came over from Ireland in the 1870s. He knew nothing about ranching or Texas and hadn't intended at all to emigrate to the U.S.; even during the worst of the famines, his family had managed to hang on. But he won some land in a poker game."

"In a poker game!" my father exclaimed.

"Yes, he won it off an Englishman, one of those fools who gamble away their fortune. Of course *he*, the Englishman, that is, had never set foot on that land, but owned it somehow. You know there are places over there in Terrell County and a bit north, just wide spots in the road, if that, that have English names—Pope, Dryden, Sheffield, and Fort Lancaster. There was some sort of connection between his family and that territory. God knows nothing on this earth could look less like England! But anyhow, this fellow owned some land—hundreds and hundreds of sections. He was foolish enough to bet at poker without much money, and when he lost more than he had, he paid off with this land. My grandfather came over. He had thought that Ireland was poor: seeing Terrell County was a revelation! The chief difference was that West Texas was *truly* a wilderness, where you couldn't grow *anything*—no chance of blight! But, since it wasn't worth much, until oil was discovered—and Terrell County has very little—you could own a lot of land and not pay much in the way of taxes. He got some goats and sheep, which can live off sagebrush and greasewood and cactus, and hired Mexican ranch hands who crossed the river back and forth, and managed to make a living. Of course the cougars did a lot of damage in those days, and the bottom went out of the wool and mohair market more than once, but my family hung on; a brother of mine and his wife still ranch down there. So I'm really at home on the river; but I suppose Ireland is in my blood too." He looked at Dora as if to invite her to join him in paying homage to that green island.

The rest of the week passed rapidly. My father went down to the river in the mornings; my mother sat on the porch and read; Susan and Tom went out in their boat; I took early walks, then read and jotted down notes in the morning, and drew or read some more in the afternoon. The fish were put on ice, then taken to a little freezing plant to be frozen and packaged; dipped in cornmeal and fried, they would be delicious. Dora went down to the river once with my father but spent the other days with Wes, either on his boat or at the water's edge, walking or picnicking among the trees. She wore a gauzy long-sleeved shirt and a woman's Stetson, in a gaucho style, and wrapped her neck in a light kerchief to keep from burning her Celtic skin; she looked wonderful. I don't know how far downriver they went; one day they left at 9 didn't get back until well after 6. Every evening we ate together, all of us, at a café or cantina on one or the other side of the river. Tom, Wes, and my father exchanged accounts of their experiences and told anecdotes and jokes, of which they had an endless supply. Dora, Susan, my mother, and I constituted an appreciative audience, sometimes a chorus; occasionally we furnished repartee or made a few observations of our own. When Saturday came, the men stopped fishing at noon and sat on the porch all afternoon with beers and a baseball broadcast going on the radio. All appeared harmonious, particularly between Dora and Wes. You could see the progress that love, if I should call it that, was making. What woman of Dora's age, alone, would not have considered Wes's company a pleasure, a prospect, conceivably a promise? One must be *very* old, I believe, to exclude the possibility of beginning again.

Surely in everyone's mind the question arose of what would happen with Wes and Dora at the end of our week. We were scheduled to leave the camp on Sunday and return to El Paso, where Tom, Father, and Dora had to return to work, and I would fly back to New York a few days later. Wes had said he would stay on a while more, then return to Hobbs and, later, fly to Venezuela. When Sunday came and we packed up, Wes came out of his cabin to say goodbye. He had already helped Tom get the boat hooked up to his car. Tom, Susan, my parents, and I all shook hands with him; Dora stood on her toes, kissed him on the cheek as he bent down, and said, "Hasta la vista."

In the car, driving back, with the four of us, there was talk about all the fish my father and Tom had caught, and what I good time we'd had, and my sketches (I had worked especially on cactus—ocotillo, cholla, and prickly pear—and trees in scattered clumps, the sort you find close to water sources), and what good company Wes was over a beer on the porch or at dinner. No one said anything further on that topic, even after we dropped off Dora at her house.

A day or so later, I mentioned Wes to my parents. I was young then, and assumed that the equation of love would hold: interested man + interested woman + suitable circumstances = a match.

"But we really don't know much about it," my father said. "Certainly, it's too early to tell. Dora would like to marry again, probably; she is lonely, and her vitality is being wasted. But we don't know whether she would choose *him*. Though I don't have any evidence of it, spending the day on his boat may have shown her sides of his character or experience that she wouldn't find quite... congenial. Or, she may discover at some later date that he's not suitable for her. We know *nothing* of his interest beyond his attentiveness to Dora this past week."

"Doesn't that mean something?"

"Not necessarily," my mother answered, with a knowing smile. "Just remember some of your experiences with boys in high school ... and a few men you've run into. Of course *they* are young; one wouldn't expect serious commitment from most of them. Still, older men are just boys grown up ... a little."

"And in fact," Father continued, after a smile of acknowledgment at my mother's observation, "even if Wes has told Dora a good deal about himself, she can't have yet much corroboration. I will say this: it is true that there is a huge spread owned by a Lamb family in the Big Bend, straddling the Brewster-Terrell county line."

Newspaper men have stores of information, and what they don't know they can find out.

"And I believe," he added, "that in other respects also the man is genuine—that is, what he says he is. But he's basically an itinerant, though an employed and apparently prosperous one. Often the manner of living makes the man."

My father was the finest judge of character I had yet met, or ever will, I believe; his assessment was sterling for me. Yet I did not understand fully its import.

All this about Dora and Wes was speculation anyhow, concerned but pointless. All I learned before returning to New York was that Wes called her from Hobbs and had made plans to come see her the following weekend. He had two more weeks before leaving for Venezuela. She told me herself about the plan, feeling perhaps more like confiding in me than in my parents—despite the understanding they always showed—since I too was single. "I like him, Harry," she said to me with her winsome Irish smile, "and I'm glad I'll see him again."

What information I got concerning them during the rest of that summer and in the fall was scanty. As planned, Wes had visited Dora in El Paso; they had gone out to dinner more than once, and one afternoon they even dropped by my parents' house. Then he had left for South America. Some weeks afterward, she had received from a jeweler's in Caracas a silver pin in the shape of an orchid, with a pearl in the middle. But by Christmastime, when I flew back for ten days or so, she had heard nothing further. She was, of course, much too self-possessed and proud to attempt to reach him through his business address in Hobbs, or even to make inquiries.

What, I wondered, had gone wrong? That was how I put the question to my father.

"Perhaps *nothing* went wrong. It depends on one's understanding and expectations. What if one or another of them thought all along that it was merely a summer interlude, which they enjoyed and appreciated at its value—*they* would decide what that was—but which could not or should not have a sequel? What if *both* thought that way?"

"I'm not confident that Dora didn't have ... something else in mind. You said yourself that you believed she'd like to marry again. I keep wondering why he just fell silent like that."

"Well, if you're looking for a reason, better look for *several* reasons. Often there is no single one. The causes, if you can call them that, of our actions may be deep within ourselves, multiple and sometimes invisible, like cottonwood roots, or rivulets in the rock and earth in the high peaks, which turn into streams and finally into the Rio Grande. What one sees is the river, or the thick, hardened roots at the tree base, but that's only the most obvious aspect. There must be a personal truth in this hidden motivation—maybe it's the most authentic part of us—but often we don't recognize it in either ourselves or others, and our explanations are ... incomplete. That's why I tell my staff at the paper: 'Don't assume any *because*. There may be two, or five, or ten different reasons.'"

"And I suppose there may be ten different desires," I said. "Is it true that men are essentially different from women, in their multiplicity of desires, their need for action on the world?" The lines from Byron's *Don Juan* came to mind: "Man's love is of man's life a thing apart; / 'Tis woman's whole existence ..."

One might think I was putting my father on the spot; but he could talk of anything dispassionately.

"Whether you look at it biologically, or anthropologically, or historically, or socially—that is, in terms of today's society—there seems to be ... a difference. In order for the species to survive, men needed to hunt and fish and fight and reproduce themselves, and that meant conquest. You say yourself that you don't quite have the instinct for fishing. Perhaps, though, it's better to see this difference without judging. Perhaps reason has two genders."

That was a startling way to look at things. I had a sudden vision of the wisdom of men, the wisdom of women interweaving and contrasting, like light and shade in the groves of cottonwoods and athels that I had sketched along the river, almost clashing in their strong effects of *chiaroscuro*. So, I thought, this is what I'm in for, the rest of my life. I'd had intimations before, and a few disappointments, but hadn't reflected enough on the way there could be two kinds of rationality.

"Of course," Father added, "folly is of both sexes also!"

The following year, I was home for the entire summer. Dora was at the house often, and sometimes the two of us went out to lunch. She herself brought up the subject of Wes. "I think you know, Harry, that I was disappointed when Wes didn't write to me from Venezuela. Before he left, he didn't even say anything very precise about seeing me when he returned. Why am I embarrassed to tell you that I've never heard from him since? And I even found out by chance at the bank that he had been back in Hobbs for a few months. You see ... It seems as if ... I've failed somehow."

"You shouldn't take it that way, Aunt Dora. You can do only your part, not his. I thought you were well suited to each other; you complemented him. But that was during a sort of interlude. Perhaps to him it could not fit into the rest of his existence. The summer may have its own meaning."

"Or maybe he found another woman down in Venezuela. Maybe there's a whole string of them, past and present, from Wyoming to South America—the route of the broken hearts. At least, he didn't *betray* me, since we were, after all, only friends, and he promised nothing; only my own hopes have done that."

"However that may be, please don't dwell on it. Knowing Wes was an episode, a sketch, not your life."

"But what *is* my life?" she said, pleadingly, almost in tears.

I couldn't answer. About two years later, Dora met and married a widower, C.J. Garrick. I know now that it was not a happy union for her. The man she'd really wanted was somewhere out in an oil field, or flying to a new job in one direction or another, or maybe fishing again on the Rio Grande, where the sunlight would bounce off the water and bronze everything and dazzle anyone who walked along the riverbank and set fires in hearts that flamed and glowed as if forever, as if such a moment would not pass.

ICONS

"GOOD LORD, THAT'S EDWIN Abends coming in here! I hope to heaven he doesn't see us!" I spoke in a low voice but not without a tone of panic. Quickly I turned on my bar stool, though not before noticing that Abends seemed to be accompanied by a strange, rather dramatic-looking woman, noticeably European in dress and demeanor. Trying to keep my head down and make myself unnoticed, I gestured to the bartender and ordered another glass of Chardonnay.

I was seated with my colleague Elinor Perrin and her husband, Roger, at the bar of the Restaurant Métropolitain in Paris, on the quais. It has a lovely view of the Seine, but that evening the rain was falling hard, blurring the windows and transforming trees and façades into an Impressionist painting. After stops in Austria and Germany, I'd gone to Paris to do some research. Elinor and Roger were already there—he was attending a meeting on international law—and we arranged for a number of outings together. We did not, however, expect to have to deal with an unpleasant colleague from the past; for Americans, part of the charm of European cities is the anonymity of their crowds and the distancing they afford from one's routine and the actors in it. And here, suddenly, was someone with whom an encounter would be very unwelcome.

Elinor and Roger, like me, had turned their backs to the door and remained as quiet and unobtrusive as possible. Elinor merely gave me a nudge as Edwin and the woman, shaking their umbrellas, passed by the end of the bar. I cast a quick glance in their direction, then took another sip of my wine. A shiver of distaste at the thought of his presence offset somewhat the pleasurable feeling of the liquid flowing into me. The whole period of our acquaintance with Edwin, with its multiple vexations, rushed out from the corners of memory to which it had been consigned, and it was as if part of the past had suddenly come to life again.

The year I was thinking of, we had engaged a visiting scholar at the Orleanian Institute to give a two-semester sequence of courses. The museum offers two or three classes in art history every academic year, as one of its functions, along with research, preservation and enlargement of the collections, and organizing exhibits. The visiting lectureship was underwritten by an old and wealthy New Orleans family, the Moutons. It had donated to the museum its superb collection of icons and other art from Russia and elsewhere in Eastern Europe, and had endowed a one-year series of lectures as a way of attracting attention to the collection. The lectures were to be open to the public and were intended for general interest, but eligible students could obtain college credit through St. John's if certain conditions were met.

The scholar brought in to give this course of study, at a handsome salary, was the same Edwin Abends who now was taking a seat, with his companion, at a table around the other side of the bar, within clear view of us. He was in his mid-forties. His origins were Central European. If one wished to stretch a point, he could be called distinguished-looking: an Italian-cut suit, a small goatee, gold-rimmed glasses, and a glance that ranged between comprehensive and meddlesome. He commonly wore his suit jacket thrown over his shoulders, a habit favored chiefly by Continentals. Perhaps he thought of himself, the way Michel Foucault did, as a cultural icon—the image of European sophistication and superiority. But his thick waist and spatula fingers detracted from the impression of supple *bonhomie* suggested by his other features.

Whether he truly cared for art as a dimension of human life I don't know; I tended to believe, ultimately, that for him it was mostly a passport, his knowledge of Eastern European styles serving to impress people at cocktail parties and conferences and to get jobs. He favored "theory," then coming to the forefront of art history studies, and he constantly cited Foucault, Tzvetan Todorov, the Marxist Raymond Williams, and other cultural critics who want to take the art away from the artist and even the patron. He had been trained in Germany, and, except for the fact that his command of spoken English was poor and he didn't try much to improve it, his credentials were excellent, almost too good; I suspect that before he came to us, somebody elsewhere had wanted to get rid of him. It was never clear, however—since he deliberately created fog around facts—whether he was on leave from another institution, between jobs, or just plain jobless. He had occupied a post in Boston at one time, it seemed. Reginald Mullins, the director who hired him at the Institute, assured us that we were fortunate to have him and that his immigration status was regular. We knew nothing about his personal life: employment laws forbid delving into such, and it wouldn't be pertinent anyway, if he carried out his tasks properly.

He turned out, unfortunately, to be a very troublesome, unreliable colleague. Among other things, he was a hypochondriac, inclined to miss classes, and something of a drunk: it was known that he'd walked into an oak tree one evening when he was going home from a bar near his rented place on Magazine Street. I don't think that accident was due to his alleged foot problems and so-called trick knee, which, he claimed, prevented him on occasion from walking, even standing. I was persuaded that those infirmities, as well as the sporadic gastric dysfunctions of which he complained, were mostly imaginary; the real disorder was in his personality. A terrible snob, he did not hide his scorn for his students and constantly intimated that his great talents were being prostituted in the circumscribed art world of New Orleans.

He was also a first-class skirt-chaser. I recalled the day I'd come upon him in the office where Sharon, secretary to Mullins, presides. She is an attractive dark-haired woman with a great deal of style, and Edwin had taken a fancy to her, as she explained to me with some embarrassment. She wanted nothing to do with him and tried to keep her distance, treating him coolly. That day he must have had a couple of noontime drinks at one of the bars within a short distance of the museum; for what I saw upon entering was Edwin pursuing Sharon around her vast mahogany desk. Attempting to grab her jacket, of a beautiful plum-colored linen, he moved quickly—the trick knee notwithstanding—but she was more nimble still. "Don't touch me, Edwin!" she shouted. "I've warned you ..."

"Oh, Sharon, yust a little kiss ..." he answered, still circling the desk and lunging at her, though losing ground.

I stepped between them and pulled his sleeve. "Edwin, for heaven's sake, stop it. What on earth do you think you're doing—in the office, of all places? Leave Sharon alone."

Though clearly somewhat intoxicated—his breath smelled of liquor and his eyes were unusually bright—he did yield to my gesture, and began to look somewhat disconcerted.

"Oh, Harriet, I didn't mean any harm, really, I just ..."

Sharon spoke up then, very sternly, as to an extremely naughty child. "You heard what Harry said, Edwin. What a spectacle you've made of yourself—you're disgusting. For the last time, I'm telling you, *no*—no dates, no kissing! Now, go back to your own office and try to sober up, or else go home; you can't be good for much work this afternoon."

"Sharon," I said when he'd left, "his behavior really is blatant sexual harassment; it's obnoxious. You could file a complaint against him."

"Oh, I know, Harry, but I don't want to go through that. He's not a real threat to me—he doesn't decide my salary or what I am supposed to do. He's harmless, after all—just a nuisance. You know I can outrun him. And he'll be gone after this year. Think of what the Mouton family would say if any word of scandal about him leaked out. I don't even want to tell Reginald, who would be outraged—you know how proper he always is—but would not wish to do anything about it because that would create complications."

"Well, let me know if he gives you any more trouble, or tell Elinor or *someone*. We could warn him and threaten to tell Reginald. He might take that threat seriously."

After that episode, Edwin seemed to lose interest in Sharon. As a replacement, he chose a young woman named Elizabeth Quigley, a museum intern who was also an auditor in his class. Like Sharon, she had dark hair and good coloring—his type, I guess—and often wore dark greens, blues, and reds that set her off to advantage. For a while I didn't know about his courtship (if it can be called that)—art, not gossip, is my line of work—but it finally became clear even to me that he was pursuing her. Although it's unprofessional, even unethical for an instructor to become involved with one of his students, in this case she was just sitting in on the course, so their relationship was not really that of professor to pupil. Still, she was an intern, in a subordinate, thus vulnerable position. Elinor and I talked it over with our friend Greg d'Hannis but did not interfere, since it was not a clear-cut case. None of us knew Elizabeth well enough to warn her.

One day Elinor caught me in the hall and said, "I've been talking to Elizabeth. Did you know that she's married—well, officially so, but separated, or so she says? Her husband is some sort of instructor at UNO. And she admits that she has been going out with Edwin Abends."

Just then Edwin and Elizabeth came by, stopping briefly at the water fountain. They'd been to the museum café take-out counter, for Elizabeth was carrying a plastic food carton with our logo. He had only a yoghurt—suitable for soothing his dyspepsia, or as a way of calling attention to himself as a sober eater. He was holding her by the arm, in the European fashion. I saw them stop at the office where she was working; he kissed her briefly before they parted.

"I see what you mean!" I told Elinor when they had disappeared. "No, I knew nothing about her private life; I scarcely know the girl, since she's not assigned to any of my projects. She must be about half his age, or maybe a little more. Maybe she's attracted by his maturity—you know, experience, solidity, authority."

"Well, Sharon must be grateful that he's chosen someone else to pursue, especially since the pursuit seems to be successful."

"Yes, you're right," I answered. "But, with respect to Elizabeth ... well, it's complicated, isn't it? Even if she's separated, it might be preferable for her not to get involved with someone else—from the legal point of view as well as the personal."

During the following weeks, Edwin and Elizabeth were seen together frequently, although there were rumors also of his being extremely cozy in his office with certain female students from St. John's. That was something for the dean to handle; perhaps Edwin received a warning. Greg, for whom Elizabeth was doing some work, reported to us that he'd come upon the two of them one Saturday morning at the copy machine. There was no one else in the office complex. They were, he said, *very* intimately connected to each other, limbs all intertwined as in some erotic painting.

"Did they see you?" I asked.

"Oh, yes, I nearly walked right into them, having no idea anyone was there."

"Why don't they just do that at home? Well, maybe not at *Elizabeth's* place—who knows whether her husband is still around, or might come in—but at Edwin's."

"Well, that's what I told them, more or less—just suggested that the office, even on a Saturday, was not the place for intimacy and that, if Mullins were to defy the odds and pop in on a weekend, he would be scandalized. I don't know what he'd do to Edwin, but Elizabeth could lose her position without further ado."

They had no more passionate trysts at the office, as far as we knew. But a few weeks later, there was an incident. I had been working late, when most of the offices were closed, though the museum galleries were still open for visitors, since it was a Thursday. Walking down the hall, right by the drinking fountain where Elinor and I had seen them, I heard great sobs coming from one of the workrooms. At that moment, Edwin burst out of a door, shouted something back inside, shut it with a bang, and ran off. In seconds, Elizabeth herself was at the door, looking out and watching him round the corner to the main foyer and exit. She looked utterly distraught, her eyes terrified, her face blotchy. For a few moments, she didn't notice me, but finally glanced where I was standing. I remembered what had happened with Sharon, though the copy-machine incident suggested that this time the object of his pursuit would have yielded without demurring. Still, I was concerned.

"Did he do or say something in there, Elizabeth ...?" I began, not knowing quite how to finish with this young woman with whom I was not well acquainted and who was much my junior. "Has he acted improperly ... or hurt your feelings?"

She managed to get out a few words. "Oh no, Dr. D'Aquin. It's just that ..." Sobs took over again and she couldn't continue.

It occurred to me that she might be at fault for this scene as much as he—for I had no way of knowing what her demands might be. Sentimental blackmail, or some other kind, can't be ruled out. I waited a moment; I simply didn't know her well enough to do anything else.

"I ... We ... Edwin had told me he would marry me, but now, he ...."

"But, Elizabeth, I understand that you're already married."

"Yes, but separated ... and getting a divorce, that is."

"That sometimes takes a long while."

"That's the problem—too long. He says he has to find someone to marry right away so that he can stay in the States—get his green card, that is. His visa has expired and the immigration people are after him."

Way to go, Reginald, I thought to myself. Mullins was perhaps in good faith in believing that Edwin had a green card already, but at best he had not checked properly with the Immigration and Naturalization Service. Edwin had doubtless given him assurances and maybe even fabricated evidence.

"When is he going to do this? Does he risk being deported before his course ends?"

"I don't know," she answered through her tears. "All he said is that he's found a widow—some volunteer here at the museum—who is willing to marry him now."

I couldn't ask her if Mullins had been apprized of Edwin's precarious legal situation; she was, after all, only an intern, and for her it was wounded feelings that counted, not the implications of his immigrant status. I tried to calm her by saying a few commonplaces and just standing at her door. She finally gathered her things from the room and left. I hoped that she had friends to whom she could turn that evening.

Mullins is going to hear from me if he hasn't already heard it from others, I reflected. But surely, the INS officers would have gotten in touch with him as Edwin's employer.

In fact, I didn't have to take up the matter with him. The next morning, at a meeting of the curatorial staff, Mullins himself raised it, saying that he had been informed by the INS, which had apparently traced Abends to New Orleans and the Institute, that Edwin's immigration status was irregular. He, Mullins, was going to plead Edwin's case and ask for an extension for the expired visa, on behalf of the museum, the students from St. John's, and the public, so that the course would not be interrupted.

"It appears to me," said Greg, "that this man deceived you deliberately."

"Yes," I added, "he surely knew when the visa was to expire; and even if he applied for an extension meanwhile, he never informed you about it, did he?"

"He ... he told me that his visa would be extended automatically with the assurance of this position at the museum; I wrote him a letter to give to the INS, stating that he had the job and what the salary was. That was back last June."

"He stretched the truth, to put it politely," said Elinor. Or perhaps he *thought* ..."

Greg is both fair and kind, but he doesn't suffer departures from what he believes to be the truth. "No, he didn't. He's not a *naïf*. The INS doesn't make such pacts without further documentation. He knew he was in hot water and tried to hide it."

"Perhaps I should add something here, Reginald," I said. "It is my understanding" (and here I looked pointedly at Greg and Elinor to indicate that I'd tell them more later) "that Edwin plans to marry a widow he's met here; that would change his status and there would be no further difficulty, I should think—that is, if he can get it done while the matter's pending, before he's deported. Doesn't his case have to be considered by an administrative court?"

We could say little further on the matter except by way of encouraging Mullins to arrange things somehow so that Edwin could finish his course. About him I cared not a whit, but the students needed to be taken care of and it would be difficult to find a replacement lecturer.

All these scenes came back to me there in the Métropolitain in Paris. I remembered how, in fact, Edwin had remained long enough to finish the course of lectures. Through the last weeks, Mullins would say nothing other than to confirm that the case was indeed in administrative court, then to reassure us later that everything was going to turn out all right. Edwin was very cool to me, refusing to speak; after all, I had witnessed both his pursuit of Sharon and the unpleasant episode with Elizabeth. No one ever saw the widow he was supposed to marry, or heard anything more about it. Nor did I see him with Elizabeth again, and she said nothing more to any of us concerning him. Anyhow, she left the same summer, having completed her internship.

After his last lecture, Edwin simply disappeared. When Sharon attempted to telephone him concerning practical end-of-term matters, she discovered that his telephone had been cut off and he'd moved out. He did not give final examinations, contrary to the policy at St. John's, and he left on the desk, unmarked, the dozen or so term papers turned in by those taking the course for credit. But at least there *were* papers; two members of the curatorial staff read them and assigned grades. (His last salary check had just been deposited; Mullins had not been wary enough to withhold it until all work had been completed.) Edwin took with him valuable books from the Institute library, including some donated by the Mouton family, and two small icons.

Seeing Edwin in Paris was not, after all, a great surprise; he had come from Europe originally, and he might be expected to return there, quite likely to Paris, the magnet of expatriates. But earlier he had given the impression of wishing to remain in the United States; wasn't that the whole idea of breaking up with Elizabeth and marrying the widow? I was, moreover, puzzled by the appearance of the woman who now seemed to be his companion. She wore a hat, and her well-cut, very European-looking navy-blue suit was enhanced by a scarf arranged in a Parisian knot. She didn't look at all, in short, like a New Orleans woman.

Elinor, Roger, and I finally consulted with each other, in low tones, and decided that we needed to get a table and order our meal. We could have gone elsewhere, were it not for the fact that a colleague of Roger's was to join us there after a commission meeting ended. We summoned the bartender, paid the bill, and asked him to have the headwaiter show us to a table away from the section where Edwin and his companion were seated.

Unfortunately, as we were getting settled, I glanced up and saw Edwin look our way. He rose from his table, put his napkin down, then approached us. Arrogance still radiated from him. "Vell, vell, Harriet D'Aquin! And Elinor, and Roger! What a surprise to meet you in Paris!"

It was an absurd remark; he knew perfectly well that my field is French art, and anyhow it should surprise no one that cultured Americans would travel there.

"Yes, Edwin, I'm here to do some research; and Roger is attending a law meeting."

"And how are things at the Institute?" He made a gesture of rubbing his hands together.

At that moment his companion, who had risen likewise, approached. She was distinctly older than he—old enough to be a likely widow, certainly—but I *still* didn't believe it was his New Orleans bride.

"Oh, let me present to you Frau Schieffenbach, from Leipzig; Isolde, these are some of my former... colleagues, from the Orleanian Institute ... Dr. D'Aquin and Mr. and Mrs...." He broke off; he might have forgotten Elinor's last name.

"How do you do?" Frau Schieffenbach said in a formal tone, extending her hand first to Elinor, then me, finally Roger. Her accent was heavy, though one could see she was well-bred. She had very noticeable jewelry—heavy gold earrings and choker and two large rings.

"And are *you* here to do research—perhaps for a new book you're writing?" I inquired of Edwin. It was a challenge, but, after all, he'd asked for it; he could have left us alone, as we'd ignored him.

"Oh, no, Frau Schieffenbach and I have just come to enjoy the cultural resources our Gallic neighbors have amassed." The words had a veneer of sarcasm, revealing the Germans' old, grudging envy of French cultural superiority. "You know that I have returned to Germany."

"No, Edwin, we didn't," said Elinor.

"I thought you were desperate to stay in the United States," I added. "Remember all the problems you caused Mullins with your expired visa?" Out of courtesy to the woman, I said nothing about his dropping Elizabeth on the pretext of needing to marry immediately.

"Oh, that would have been foolish. I left for Europe as soon as my course at the ... *Institute* was finished." He emphasized oddly the word *Institute*, as though to empty it of its value by suggesting its pretentiousness. "After all, the real center of art historical studies is here, not in America."

"That may well be," replied Elinor, "in your field. Still..."

"Still," I interrupted, "you were the cause of considerable worry; Mullins had to call the INS, and write letters, and ..."

"He ... *overreacted*, I think you say."

All this time Edwin and Frau Schieffenbach had remained standing. Good manners would have dictated that we ask them to sit a moment. But, remembering his conduct with Sharon and Elizabeth, the papers that our staff had been obliged to grade for him, and the purloined objects, I rejected the dictates of courtesy, hoping to get rid of him faster.

"And where are you working now?" Roger asked.

"Yes, Edwin, please give me your address; I should like to send you an offprint." I hoped by this request to find out exactly what he was doing.

"I have many offers, many offers. I shall be in Berlin next year, Berlin." Nothing more specific was said.

"And how are your ... health problems these days?" I thought to inquire. "I see that you are enjoying a good French dinner." Whether he caught the implication I don't know.

"Ja, my knee, it is bothering me still ... Isn't that so, Isolde?" he finished in a sly way. "We must go back to our table now."

"Goodbye, then, Edwin. So good to have made your acquaintance, Frau Schieffenbach."

He limped off in a Byronic manner, though I hadn't noticed any lameness as he approached us. Roger rolled his eyes; Elinor sighed. Happily, the waiter, who had doubtless been lurking at the side, came to take our order.

"We didn't think to say anything about the library books and those two icons," said Elinor suddenly, as we were studying the menu.

"I imagine they're gone forever," Roger replied. "Perhaps sold to a bookseller along the Seine or a dealer in the Beaux-Arts district, or on

Frau Schieffenbach's shelves, where he can consult them if he needs to—if he ever gets a post and does any serious research."

Later, we saw Edwin—the new Tristan, perhaps—and his Isolde leave the restaurant, greeting us once more with a sort of bow. It was a relief to see them go; we felt freer during the rest of the meal. Finally, the encounter left us with a feeling of satisfaction, the sort one gets when the last scene of a drama, even a rather tawdry one, is over. We had been able to take his measure once again, and he was found wanting. It was clear that, having lied to numerous parties and prolonged the controversy over the visa until he got his last check, he had then run off. He'd landed on his feet, certainly—that kind always does. Maybe he was even being supported by the art-loving Frau Schieffenbach, whom he may have considered his personal *objet d'art*; but there was no evidence that he'd gotten any position at all, still less a prestigious one.

Perhaps the best part of the whole affair was the fact that, not too long after we all returned to New Orleans, I ran into Elizabeth and discovered that, if there had been heartbreak, at least it had mended. I was on Magazine Street, near the Beaucoup Books shop, when I happened to look across the street and saw her. "Hello, Elizabeth," I called.

She crossed as soon as there was a break in the traffic. "Oh, Dr. D'Aquin, how nice to see you!"

"How are you? It's been a while since we've seen each other—four years, I guess."

"Oh, fine," she replied. "Did you know that my husband and I went back together, a while after I stopped working at the Institute? We don't even live here anymore; we're here just to visit his parents. He got a good position at UIC in Chicago, and I'm going to finish my postgraduate studies there."

"Congratulations! I hope that you will like living there—winters and all."

"You know, I'd like to apologize to you, for that scene ... you remember."

"Of course; but you don't need to make excuses. The fellow was a cad. I'm just sorry that ... you got involved with him and he misled you. You got off lightly, you know; he might have strung you along even more." And I explained how we'd run into him in Paris and what we had learned.

"That's not surprising. And as for me ... well, I'm the wiser for it, certainly."

To accompany that good news there was another development: Sharon, a year or so later, married a man she'd met at Trinity Church. I'm sure she never gave Edwin a thought. As for the widow, so-called, either she existed or she didn't. He may have invented her to deceive Mullins and the INS a while more and get rid of Elizabeth, if he was tired of her. If there really was such a woman, I hoped fervently that, after Edwin's precipitous departure from New Orleans, she realized what a fool she'd been to fall for him. Quite likely she would find, or had already found, a more reliable man. Perhaps, among the crowds that come into the museum on good viewing days—the sort of gray, sluggish, vacuous day that brings out the unoccupied, or a lethargic Saturday when one *simply* must get out and do something worthwhile—she will stop in, anonymous, look at the exhibits, stop especially in front of the Mouton collection, and think to herself, "These icons are wonderful— but good riddance to the expert!"

Chiaroscuro

"PLEASE, I WANT SO much to have lessons—and I cannot afford to take a college course. And I'm not interested in *commercial* art." The voice on the telephone was clearly not that of a high school student; I couldn't know the woman's age for certain, but perhaps forty or so. She spoke with a definite Spanish accent, though her English was completely understandable. I didn't wish to insult her by suggesting she was no longer young, but I wanted her to understand that I did not normally take pupils in middle age. At the same time, it was essential also that I avoid giving the impression that she would be disfavored because of her accent, that is, because she was a Mexican-American.

"You are not a high school student, are you? Generally, as my advertisement suggested, I accept pupils in high school who want to study art but can't get any art courses in school—or else only very inadequate ones. I am myself not much older than they; I'm working on a doctorate in art history." In fact, I was twenty-five.

"I understood that from your ad. But I wish you would consider taking me. Your price is ... so reasonable, and, as I said, in my position I can't manage a college course, not the fees and probably not the time. It might not be quite right for me anyway. I'm not advanced, but I ... have acquired *some* skills." The woman, who told me her name was Elena Hernández, sounded utterly sincere. The argument about the college fees was plausible, and her manner was persuasive. I agreed to meet with her in my studio the following Saturday afternoon, on the understanding that I would postpone any decision about accepting her until that interview was finished.

That summer I had returned to El Paso to spend three months, taking time off from my studies at New York University. When I first went away to study, I came home every summer, and it was then I had conceived the idea of offering to take private pupils youngsters to whom I could teach some techniques and whose talent and interests I could help develop. Even in a mid-sized city there are many children born with talent; in El Paso, where so much of the population is of Mexican descent, you could find hundreds with a wonderful inborn aesthetic sense, but it often was undernourished, like their bodies too, sometimes. The city, like other border towns, was poor, and the level of education low; the schools needed to concentrate on basic English, history, math, science, and written Spanish, and could not afford, either financially or otherwise, to have art programs of quality.

So, in the late spring each year, I put an ad in the El Paso *Times*, and when I returned in June I would go through the responses and choose the most serious and ablest students, after interviewing them informally and seeing their work. The lessons went on throughout the summer, once a week. Some pupils came back summer after summer. I charged about what an ordinary piano or singing teacher might ask, and even families in modest circumstances could sometimes afford that. After a few years, I started spending most of the summer in New York and thus gave up teaching, but this time I had come home again. My mother had not been well and would be hospitalized for a while; I wanted to be near her and help my father at home. It seemed reasonable to take pupils again, and, now that I had spent a few years at NYU and was going to Paris in the autumn to study at the Ecole des Beaux-Arts, I should be more mature and better prepared than before, through my developing acquaintance with art history and my own range of technique and understanding of how techniques serve style. Still, I wasn't sure that I should try to handle a middle-aged pupil, a woman maybe fifteen or twenty years older than I, who could not be expected to have the energy of an adolescent, nor the artistic malleability.

Years before, when it had become clear that my passion for painting would not go away, my parents had built for me a small studio on the north side of their house, a Mexican-style structure of ochre stucco, designed around a central patio. One could gain access to the studio from the entranceway and patio, without going through the living quarters. With its privacy, which adolescents cherish, its large windows and skylight, letting in the superb West Texas light, pristine and dry, and some of my art books—though most were in New York—along with the wide selection of supplies that I kept for students—paints, chalk, inks, pastels, paper and canvas, easels—it had served well as a teaching studio.

Elena came promptly, at three. I think of her from the beginning as "Elena," since she wanted me to call her that, but at first I tried addressing her by her last name.

"Come in, Mrs. Hernández. Or would you like to be addressed as 'Señora'?"

"Oh, please, call me Elena. Not that I mind Señora; I was born in Mexico" (she pronounced it *Méjico*). "How awkward that English doesn't have such a word by which you can address someone whom you don't know well! But you are going to be my teacher—at least I hope so; you'd better call me by my first name and treat me like the pupil I am. I want to be your *apprentice*." She gave a little laugh, which struck me by its modesty and sweetness. "And I shall call you ... Señorita? Señorita Harriet, perhaps?"

"Oh, no, call me Harry; everyone does—all my friends and family, I mean." (Did I have an intimation then that we would become friends?) "Won't you sit down—that armchair, or here at the drawing board? I want to see some of your work."

Elena took a seat on a stool near the board. She had the expressive features one sees on many women of Spanish descent. Her hair was black, thick, and straight; contrasting with its darkness, her eyes shone in a light hazel, and her skin was a beautiful pale olive. She wore no wedding ring. She cast a quick glance around my studio, and examined, discreetly, paintings that were hung or standing against the wall—mine, though she could not have been sure. She then opened her portfolio. I had told her she must bring samples: whether she was satisfied with them or not—and she professed not to be happy with them in the least—she was to show me what she had *tried*.

"Here, I've brought, as you said, some sketches—recent sketches. And I have older work too, including these wood-block prints, made years ago, and ... a new canvas." She sorted rapidly through the sketches and prints and put a few in front of me, on the drawing board. I saw immediately that they suggested unusual command of her art. Without making any comment, I leafed through them briefly. Then, from a case she carried, she pulled a canvas in a tube, unrolled it, and handed it to me. It was stunning. One could see that Mexico had not been far from her thoughts, although the scene was more oneiric than representational. Strong and muted colors setting each other off, bold lines, large, generous forms, and good meridional light: they made a spectacular landscape of the mind. While I did not wish to pre-judge either her range of skills or her limitations on the basis of this quick glance at her work, since she was convinced she needed direction, I could scarcely conceal my admiration; it would not have been fair to hide it.

"That is a splendid painting! You must realize that it is not amateurish in the least. Are you sure that you need lessons from me— or from anyone? Tell me why you are here; tell me about yourself."

What she said that afternoon was, not surprisingly, only a small part of what I learned subsequently. Even later, she was loath to reveal herself completely, giving of herself, through conversation and art, only what she chose to give, and in her own way. As our Mexican-style house allowed only its exterior, partly windowless, to be visible to the public, protecting a private interior patio, with its garden and open doors and windows, a human being may wish to practice exterior reserve, letting only a few into the garden, the *huerta*, which is also the heart. How can one not respect that? In her case, the reserve, which was genuine, not a pose, served perhaps to set off the candor, even the passion of her painting, all the more powerful because it had to overcome personal restraint.

That day she did tell me some things, however. "As I said, I am from Mexico, originally; I was born in Cuidad Chihuahua. I attended school there, a convent school, since my family was a respectable one, not rich but... how do you say it? *genteel*. Going to the university would have been out of the question; my father would not have allowed it. But I learned to ride at a *hacienda* belonging to friends of ours, and I had piano lessons and French lessons from a French woman who'd gotten stranded there (we also had French in school). So my experience was not so limited as you might think for a well-bred Catholic girl. What I became most interested in, though, was drawing. There was no art teacher suitable for me, my parents thought; I taught myself, rather, drawing at the window of my room, in the patio, on the hacienda."

"Was there no art course in the school?"

"No. That sounds strange, with the love of Mexicans for *las bellas artes*; but art, for the nuns, was rather like theater, I think—something that respectable people didn't practice. Remember, too—you must know this if you've studied art history—that Mexican art in our century has been very socially advanced, very ... revolutionary; if the nuns knew anything about it, they must have thought it would be poison for us."

"Yes, I understand—Rivera, Orozco, Siqueiros. So you had no instruction?"

"Not really. An aunt of mine, who had traveled to Europe, owned some art books—with paintings from the Prado, the Louvre, the Uffizi Gallery—and she followed my interest, sharing her appreciation, pointing out things that she had learned about composition—I don't know how. She encouraged me to try painting in oils. My parents did not object, as long as I did it simply as a pastime. That is how I began."

Elena paused. "Perhaps there is not really much more to say about ... my original interest. It has never left me, even through ... difficulty." She paused again.

"You do not need to tell me much more. I should like simply to know how you view your work and its development—what skills you think you have acquired, what you have tried to do, perhaps failed, what you want to accomplish—and also, how you did these." I gestured again to the sheaf of sketches, fanned out on the drawing board, and to the canvas, which I still held on my knees. "If I can do anything for you—and that is by no means certain, since you are far more advanced than any pupil I've ever taken before, and you appear to have an excellent command of your technique—then I need to understand how you see your own strengths and weaknesses, and what you wish to be able to achieve. I do not have great experience, you realize; *you* have more than I. And this will be only for three months, as the newspaper ad said; I leave for Paris in September. But it is true that I have studied art formally for years, and perhaps my skills in some media might be useful to you."

"I am certain of it. But you want to know how I did these ... I must explain, I think. After I left Chihuahua, I did not paint or draw for years. All I did, at most, was to think about it, and to look—not at painting, very much, for it wasn't possible, but at things—everything, all sorts of things, trying to see them as I would if there had been a chance to draw or paint them."

"Perhaps you looked inside, too."

"I did, I did; that was the only means I had of ... feeling and looking *freely*. The Iron Curtain isn't the only way to stifle free expression, you know. I should explain—I hope you will understand, though you are young: I married an American man, an Anglo, someone my family did not approve of. (My name is really Holland; but socially I have started calling myself Hernández again.) I met him at the house of friends; he represented his company down in Chihuahua. He brought me to Texas—not so far in miles but such a different world, inhabited by Anglos, businessmen, Protestants ..."

At the time, I had little understanding of what *looking freely*, or *not freely*, might mean. I had seen misery in love, with my roommate, an actress in New York, but I had not glimpsed the sort of censorship that Elena must have meant. Looking back, I am grateful to the gods for keeping from me, as a girl, that knowledge—while I understand, of course, that such innocence could not last forever.

"Of course," she continued, "I got used to some of those changes. I like El Paso, and I have the advantage of being a U.S. citizen. But in many ways I was ... *alienated* is the word, I believe—from the art that I had just started learning to master a bit, I think, and also from my culture and my family; my parents disowned me for marrying without their consent, with only my aunt continuing to write to me, to care."

"Tell me again when you did the work you have shown me just now." I did not want her to dwell further on unpleasant memories. Clearly, she had married for worse, not better.

"The sketches and oil are from the last year or so. My oldest child has left home. He gave me a lot of trouble, like his father. The two younger ones are in high school. I work full-time, of course, to support the three of us, and I am trying to put aside money for a down-payment on a little house. Once I ... had taken myself back, I bought materials and started drawing and painting again, even though there's not much free time. These samples—really, I cannot be satisfied with them. But at least they are... *authentic*—totally different from what I did as a girl. I must have been painting them in my mind, even through my unhappiness, for twenty years."

"That is why they have depth. What do you want to achieve this summer with me—assuming, and it is a big assumption, that I can really help you? You have to take me on faith; you know less of me than I know of you, now."

"But I've seen some of your work here, already—that is, if all this is yours." (She gestured; I nodded.) "And ... I like you. What I'd like to do is more of these imaginary landscape paintings, like the canvas I brought. It is a reflection, of course, of the real Chihuahuan desert, but it is my own desert also, my own dream."

"You have enough skill already to express how you see that world. You draw it from your imagination. At best, I could be your critic."

"That is what I want, a critic! I am not experienced enough to be my own critic. Also, I want to do some still lifes—and you have many here, I see. That pear on a linen napkin, for instance—wonderful!"

"Oh yes, these are mine. The still life is one of my preferred genres. Perhaps I can really assist you a little; but you must understand, as I said before, that I'm used to working with adolescents, with raw, tender, untried talent, sometimes a lot, sometimes not very much. They have no experience; they haven't much technique; you have both. Still, if you still wish to study with me, I shall do my best with you."

Her earnestness, along with her achievements, had convinced me. In fact, what she needed most was companionship in art: encouragement, subtle guidance, another set of eyes. Art mediates the world to us; but between art and the artist there must likewise be *others*, and that is the role of the viewer, the critic, the collector who hangs someone's painting at home.

Elena was one of a half-dozen pupils I had that summer, and of course was by far the best. Every Saturday afternoon—the most suitable time for her, when her children were both working at summer jobs— she brought a portfolio of work, not extensive, but always thought-out, whether a finished drawing or a sketch. I encouraged her with her still lifes and showed her plates by the masters of the genre. I was at work on some myself, with characteristic objects of my surroundings—chile peppers, pottery, a serape-like tablecloth, a vase with a few branches of desert willow that I had cut from the tree in the patio; and we ended up by critiquing each other's work.

I also urged her to paint outdoors. The house she rented near Ysleta had, she told me, a cramped garden, without much of a view; but, when I suggested that she do the house itself, with its vines and desert trees, she brought back a pleasing canvas, its greens, pinks, and yellows making me think of Bonnard. On a few occasions she visited friends on the New Mexico border and did some landscapes where her personal vision and the desert scenery before her transformed each other in a way that heightened each. She excelled with foliage.

Whether they were broad, full, and bursting with a dark, chlorophyllic green, suggesting a rain forest in the mind, or small, pointed, blue-gray and dusty, like sage, close to the heart, her leaves were always extraordinary, both robust and sensitive.

The summer passed rapidly, for me at least; visiting my mother in the hospital, then assisting her at home, helping my father, seeing my pupils, trying to advance my own work, and thinking about Paris filled the time. From New York, I had arranged for El Ocotillo Gallery, owned by Vivian and Paul Connell, to represent me in El Paso, and I spent some time choosing the paintings and hanging them. Elena told me repeatedly how much her lessons meant to her. She had discipline by herself; but perhaps being disciplined by, or being a disciple of, someone else strengthened her resolution, and it also helped her socially: it gave her a new and very legitimate type of self-importance and self-confidence with others, and she related to me how she had explained to her children that she had *her* "homework," just as they had theirs. She *thought* her work was developing well, both in technique and understanding; and, in all activities of the mind and hands, there is a point, not easily reached, at which to believe so is to make it so.

In early September she came for the last time, bringing me her final portfolio, including things I hadn't seen at all, on which she had labored secretly for weeks. I persuaded her to visit Vivian Connell, to whom I'd spoken already and who would like her work, I believed, so that they could discuss the possibility of showing some in the gallery. Elena made me promise that, if circumstances were ever to bring me back to El Paso for a lengthy stay, I would make time to take her as a pupil again.

In fact, that happened, two years later. I was about to finish my degree at NYU but left to spend a month in Texas, where my mother, again, was very ill. Picking up with Elena seemed like a matter of course. From what she said, I first thought that her life was going well. The younger boy, still at home, had finished high school and was to start at the university, where he had a small scholarship; the girl seemed steady and serious in her high school studies. Elena's job was stable, and she had pursued her painting and drawing and had developed her acquaintance with major European artists by using the library. A large portfolio that she brought contained a selection of her recent work.

"This is very impressive, Elena, in some ways. I like that landscape! And those garden scenes are very well composed; the color is just right also."

"Thank you. I have worked in that garden almost every weekend—painting, I mean. I haven't yet been able to afford to move."

I leafed through some more samples. "You seem, however, to be holding back. It's not a question of having reached a plateau—that happens to all artists, from time to time. And it's certainly not one of those 'blocks' you hear about. It's something else; I'm not sure what, and I do not know that I can do anything for you."

"Well, at the least you can say what you just said. Maybe you can keep me going, or push me ahead. You can share with me what you did during your year in Paris, and critique my work the way your teachers did yours. Maybe you can give me ... darkness, as well as light."

"Darkness?" I did not know quite what she meant. We were surrounded, literally, by the brilliant, searching light of a late May afternoon, pouring in from the skylight; maybe, although high summer was not yet upon us, the light was almost too keen. Perhaps that was it. I reflected how deep and tranquilizing darkness is when it falls in the high desert, with its clear air, strangely softened textures, crisp but shadowy outlines of hills, and stars as if in blessing. Full understanding of the other is not always essential for communication, in any case; much mediation—like prayer, I suppose—takes place unknown to the subjects, or at least operates in the sort of *chiaroscuro* that she was then evoking.

"Think," she said, "of the paintings of Rembrandt, El Greco, Le Nain, La Tour, Zurbarán: shadows are essential. Perhaps I have not been unhappy enough in these last years. Is that possible?"

I concluded then that during the previous two or three years I must have discovered *something* about human experience, though nothing like what I would learn in the following twenty. Her statement was profoundly disturbing, precisely to the degree that I too had discovered the potency of unhappiness.

"Whether it is so only you can judge," I answered. I thought of Van Gogh and others on whom I had been writing. "Disorder seems essential, sometimes—the Dionysian impulse—and restlessness of the soul may be a powerful impulse to expression. Yet it cannot be too great without paralyzing the desire and the ability to create something: art requires the availability of the mind. To identify and live within one's personal balance of disorder and order, and to keep distress and dissatisfaction at a distance, or, since they are inevitable, to know how to tame them and transform them into creative energy—that is the artist's challenge."

Whether the sessions Elena and I had together during that month were of any value to her I do not know. Although she pressed me to accept payment, I could not charge her: the tutor-pupil relationship had evolved into friendship on an almost equal footing, and I certainly couldn't pretend to do much for her in a few hours.

In the following years, when I was an assistant curator at the museum in Florida, I returned home frequently, but for brief visits only. Elena sent me a few short letters, and I would reply and telephone her when I was in El Paso, but did not see her often, being occupied with family matters and then family sorrows. The year I was home for my mother's funeral, I tried to call her a few days after the ceremony; I was surprised to discover that the phone number was no longer in service. I didn't want to attempt to reach her children; perhaps they didn't even live there anyway. When I stopped by El Ocotillo Gallery to deliver some paintings, there were several of hers for sale. I inquired about her from Vivian Connell.

"Oh, she's in Mexico now."

"Mexico?"

"Yes, didn't you know? I'm surprised that she didn't write to you about it; she told me some months ago. She married a man from Mexico and now has gone to live with him in Durango. It seemed to be rather sudden. As you see, we still represent her; these are some of the paintings that she finished before leaving. Two others have been sold. But she has sent us nothing new."

"But I am astonished! Maybe not at her marrying again—but at not letting me know. You have her address, don't you? I should like to write to her; at least I can offer congratulations on these latest pictures, and on selling two."

Her silence seemed strange. Or was it that the difference in our ages, which at first was not important, since my youth was offset by my training, finally had become significant? Friendships change, and often die without drama. She had a past already when I knew her, her children were now all grown, she had married again and launched a new life across the border; and she certainly didn't need me as a teacher any more. In the note I sent her, I did not know quite what to say, but mentioned how much I liked her paintings at the gallery, and then added best wishes to her and her husband.

For years, there was no reply. Vivian did not get news from her and received no additional canvases to show. Then finally, one Christmas— by then I had moved to New Orleans—a letter from Elena reached me at the museum, forwarded from my old gallery in Florida. "Unhappiness," she wrote, "makes correspondence difficult—as it does painting. I did not make the same mistake again; I made a different one. Please forgive me for not answering your note of congratulations on my work displayed at El Ocotillo and for not writing to you otherwise. Things cannot be as they were. It would be too difficult for me to change and start anew again. I cannot even find a way to draw from my life here some deeper sort of art." She sent good wishes for the coming year and for my work.

I thought of how the high desert and the Sierra Madre, as well as Durango itself and the surrounding villages, would have appealed in the past to her painter's eye and hand—churches, squares, markets, flowering trees, the clear light and vast Mexican skies of Madonna blue; but somewhere in that brilliant sunshine, or in the obscure recesses where men and women, living side by side, hate each other—or down in her own heart—she had found the darkness she had spoken of—the deep shadows that can either set off the glow of a single lamp or devour it.

FAMILY VALUES

WHETHER OTHERS HAD NOTICED that Ted wasn't looking well, I'm not sure. It didn't strike me until the evening of a large reception at the museum, to which he had accompanied me. Ted and I were simply friends, good friends. He and Jack, my husband, had known each other since childhood, and after Jack's death, Ted, who had long been divorced, had been attentive to me, inviting me occasionally to lunch or dinner, sharing with me his even temperament and understanding mind, being available at the margin of my life for moments when I needed someone. He and Jack were so much alike—not through temper but from five decades or so of common experience, which make people resemble each other the way all portraits from the same historical period do—that his presence gave me a familiar, reassured feeling. And he liked painting.

The reception was another of those affairs that mark the cultural life of any city: invitations go out, but to accept one must pay, and those who pay the most get their names printed on a program or in a bulletin and are the object of attention from other patrons, the board, the staff, and the director. Those who pay less get at least to look at the others and say they have attended. Philanthropic, one might say, or philaesthetic; but essentially, it is a way to circulate socially and thus retain, possibly advance, one's social standing. On this occasion we were launching a new campaign for capital improvements, which had already gotten a good start with the anonymous gift of $250,000. (Of course we on the staff knew who the donor was and knew that at end of the campaign her name would be revealed, noisily, along with the announcement of a final, matching amount.) But since you have to have something new to show off at such a moment, the launching was arranged to coincide with the opening of an exhibit featuring paintings from our collections as well as from private ones, and calculated to attract local interest and even to flatter some potential donors: "Family Values: Portraits of Louisiana Families from Three Centuries."

157

My attitude toward such a public event was ambivalent. As a staff member, I had to endorse it officially, and my interest in the exhibit was genuine. I had lent for it oil portraits of members of Jack's family by the Woodward brothers and other New Orleans painters. Moreover, I truly care about art, which I view as a superior, even transcendent aspect of life—being both experience and reflection of experience, reproduction and refashioning, and, ultimately, creation. And of course I wish to see good museums prosper, whatever their administrative failings. Where else, after all, can one see so much of the past, and who else pays the salaries of art historians?—except universities, and they're even worse. Still, I do not enjoy the enforced proximity to donors, in a setting where money, jewels, dress, and other bragging rights count for more, really, than the ostensible purpose of the gathering. My silent reflections on how certain angels got the fortunes with which to support culture and on what they *really* think during rare moments of cerebration did not make me mellow.

That was one of the reasons that I appreciated Ted's presence. Very successful himself in business, he could enjoy the exhibit and at the same time move comfortably among the crowd, without the unflattering reflections to which I was given, speaking easily to people he knew, putting to use his indulgent wit, and thus sharing with me—without purposing it especially—his sense of belonging.

It wasn't even I who first remarked that, despite his cordiality and easy socializing—at that moment, he was in a crowd of handsomely dressed people on the other side of the hall—he didn't look well. Elinor, who had met him on numerous occasions, was standing with me at the buffet, getting a plateful of hors-d'oeuvres. As we moved aside and exchanged a few observations, she added, "Is Ted overworked? He looks worn."

"Oh, he's had those deep lines in his forehead—as long as I've known him, that is."

"It's not just that; his whole face looks drawn, and there's an expression of fatigue even in his eyes."

"Perhaps you're right; I hadn't thought about it."

The topic was dropped for a few minutes. Looking for Ted, I found him at the bar. Strange how another's words are necessary sometimes for us to take off blinders. Armed with Elinor's observation, I saw a different man from the one who had picked me up not much more than an hour before, the lines in his face deeper, the complexion and eyes grayish. Some while later, as little groups eddied around in the general flow, I again found myself with Elinor and took her aside.

"You're right," I whispered; "Ted doesn't look good. I don't know why it didn't strike me before."

"Actually, it's worse than I thought. By chance, I noticed his feet. His ankles and insteps are horribly swollen; his feet hardly fit into his shoes. That's not a good sign."

"Of course not. Thanks for telling me. Not that it's any of my business, really; after all, we're just friends. But I'm concerned nonetheless."

"Surely he must realize himself that something is amiss—diabetes, perhaps, or gout, or cirrhosis?" Elinor added.

"Yes, it could be any of those, I imagine—or something else. I wonder if his son knows. He lives in Lafayette; I don't know how frequently they see each other."

Does one always choose the same friends and the same failings? I reflected how, despite their different personalities and concerns, Ted and Jack had in common not only nearly a lifetime of schooling, socializing, and business interests together in the same city but also a liking for drink, dating back to prep school days and never corrected. Alcohol had been both friend and enemy to Jack, seeing him through what he wouldn't have been able to manage otherwise, I suppose, but exacting a high price. I wondered whether Ted, more successful and serene—despite (or possibly because of) a dissolved marriage—

nevertheless had purchased some of that success in the same manner and was now paying with disease.

It was not many weeks afterwards—weeks during which Ted and I spoke by telephone once or twice but didn't see each other—that he asked me to lunch on the following Saturday. "We won't be lunching alone," he added; "I want you to meet someone."

"Of course; that will be lovely," I answered, while wondering who the person might be. An out-of-town friend, who, he thought, might be a romantic partner for me? But I wasn't interested in romance; he knew that. Perhaps a prosperous, even wealthy acquaintance who might wish to buy one of my paintings? That would be welcome. Or a potential museum donor who would be more likely to respond favorably to me than to the blandishments of professional fund-raisers?

"Good. Meet us at Commander's Palace at noon, all right?"

I walked over to the restaurant, just five blocks away from my place, and timed my arrival exactly. Ted was already there, however, waiting in the entranceway. "Hi, Harry, good to see you. Let me introduce you to" (and he turned aside slightly to a well-dressed woman standing a bit behind him) "someone you should know: Aileen Cooke. Aileen, this is an old friend, Harriet D'Aquin."

Aileen Cooke appeared to be about thirty. Well made-up, her blond hair carefully coiffed, and dressed in a navy-blue suit, with heavy gold earrings, a Hermès scarf at her throat, and an alligator-hide Kelly handbag (they had just come back into fashion), she made a handsome picture. We exchanged brief salutations ("Call me Harry, please," I was able to say), then allowed the *maître d'hôtel* to show us to a table. Though Ted was smiling broadly and spoke in a spirited manner, as we sat down I could not refrain from casting a critical glance at his face, where fatigue and tension offset his expression of happiness. I could not see his feet.

"What would you like to drink, Harry?" Ted inquired as the waiter stood by the table, expectantly.

"A Bloody Mary would do nicely," I answered.

He transmitted the order, though the waiter was already writing it down. "And for us, mimosas, please—or would you prefer a champagne cocktail, Aileen?"

"No, our usual mimosas will be fine, thanks."

Usual mimosas, I wondered? But to voice the reflection would have been inappropriate, especially at the beginning of our acquaintance. Someone needed nevertheless to launch the conversation while we waited for the drinks. Of course the first move could have been hers, or Ted's, but each declined the role—for reasons of drama, I now think. Deprived by the fact that her accent gave her away as fourteenth-ward uptown New Orleans, the *crème de la crème*, I could not ask, plausibly, where she was from and thus needed a different opening. Eschewing the repertory of chestnuts, such as "And how do you know Ted?" or "Are you enjoying this splendid autumn weather?" I took a gastronomical tack, knowing that cuisine is always an acceptable topic here. "Commander's is still one of my favorite places; its turtle soup is the best in New Orleans, don't you agree?" The trouble with such an opening is that it doesn't necessarily take you far.

"Oh, certainly," answered Aileen. Not much.

But Ted let the remark lead him. "We've been here a number of times together already, haven't we, Aileen?"

The cocktails arrived at that moment, along with hot garlic croutons. "A toast," proposed Ted. He lifted his glass slightly. "To Harry, a good friend, and to the memory of Jack, my oldest friend." He touched his glass delicately to ours, then raised it to his lips.

"Thank you, Ted," I answered; "thanks in particular for mentioning Jack."

We all took sips, sampled the croutons, and studied the menus, which a waiter had handed around discreetly. There followed more gastronomical talk, as one would expect, then ordering. I still didn't know much about Aileen, but Ted's remark about frequenting Commander's with her was suggestive.

Ted presently changed the topic to the museum. "Harry is curator of French art at the Orleanian Institute; I told you that, didn't I, Aileen?"

"Yes, you did." She turned to me. "Ted has said many favorable things about your achievements there—shows and collection-building."

I dreaded what might follow—meaningless compliments, inane, saccharine remarks on how wonderful it must be to work with art all day, reminiscences of visiting the Louvre or "when I studied at the Sorbonne"—the sort of empty phrases I get so often. But Aileen was much too smooth for such, remaining satisfied instead with that simple acknowledgment. Nor did either one of them raise the subject of my painting—so she wasn't a collector, I gathered. As we finished our drinks and croutons, then started on the main course, we talked of miscellaneous things—preservation and restoration in the city, which seemed to interest her, the new symphony conductor, the seven-month summer that had finally ended. Travel formed another knot of the conversation; I gathered that she liked to go to the Caribbean. Whether by chance or otherwise, I did not learn much about her particular circumstances or her family—just that she had gone to the Academy of the Sacred Heart, then St. Mary's Dominican, and that at one time her family had owned a plantation upriver. She herself seemed to exercise no profession. The food was delicious, as always, and although we did not trade samples—that is only for close friends—after the plates had been cleared we reverted to the topic of gastronomy, commenting on the pecan trout and red snapper in sauce.

After dessert, coffee was proposed, and, along with it, Ted suggested a brandy. Well, since it was Saturday and I didn't expect to get anything done, why not? When the snifters arrived, Ted proposed another toast. "This time, Aileen, it's to us. Harry, the reason I've invited you is to share our news: Aileen and I are to be married."

Many events are attended by both expectation and implausibility. I couldn't say that the announcement astonished me; their remarks and a certain *je ne sais quoi* in their expressions and gestures had suggested close acquaintance, and the bond between them did not appear to be professional. Yet his marrying again, and marrying her, struck me as incongruous. Ted was almost twice Aileen's age; he had remained divorced for twenty years or more; he was, perhaps, ill. There was no leisure to reflect at length on these discrepancies; I had to answer somehow.

"Well, this is news, certainly! And very good news." (White lies are indispensable in social intercourse. For all I knew, maybe it really *was* good news.) "Best wishes to you both!" And I touched my brandy glass against theirs.

At Commander's one may linger at the table. We sipped our brandy as the afternoon grew fuller and talked about their plans, which were to hold the ceremony in two months or so and go to New York for their honeymoon, in order to enjoy the opera and theatre. I assured them that I should be happy to hear later about what they'd seen and heard, and wished them a very fine stay. It seemed opportune then to excuse myself. As I picked up my jacket and bade them both goodbye, Ted rose. I could see then, in the quickest of glances, that his ankles and feet were still swollen, as Elinor had described them to me.

Walking home, I pondered the ways of Eros—if it was indeed Eros, not Thanatos, at work here. Ted was surely feeling his age. The need for youth and beauty, to reinforce or replace one's own, is all the more powerful as one feels deprived of them—until, in old age or decay, there is finally no more energy for feeling desire, and even the imagination of youth is gone. To have beauty at hand, own it, take it into your bed, seems rejuvenation; but it is Thanatos who helps fill the older man's veins with desire, as an oblique homage to the power of death. As for Aileen, did she love Ted—for his experience, success, distinguished good looks? Or was the inspiration that of Midas? Wearing a Hermès scarf doesn't preclude being a golddigger; in fact, in certain cases, there is a correlation, especially if one comes from a genteel family whose fortunes were founded on cotton or sugarcane plantations instead of gas and oil, and if the new-mode sugardaddy is no longer young—even, possibly, ready to cash in his chips.

The relationship between Ted and me thenceforth was changed; I would not have expected otherwise. In fact, I did not see him again for several weeks, and then only briefly, by chance, on Royal Street. Any opportunity that might have arisen for me to inquire discreetly into his health—assuming I could have brought myself to ask a direct question—was now gone. Two or three acquaintances—mostly old friends of Jack's—whom I ran into mentioned him, but there was no one with whom I could raise the subject of his condition. About three months after the lunch at Commander's, an engraved card came announcing the wedding, some weeks before, in the chapel of the Sacred Heart, of Aileen Leblanc Cooke and Theodore W. H. Livaudais. The address on the envelope was that of Ted's house on Henry Clay.

Eventually, one would suppose, Ted and Aileen—whatever her motivation in marrying—would have invited me to some function at their home, either a cocktail party, dinner, or small private lunch. But fate did not allow them much time to get accustomed to having guests—time required especially, perhaps, before she would consent to entertain a woman friend of her husband's. In the winter, not many months after their wedding, I learned that Ted was in Touro Infirmary in very bad condition. Aileen didn't telephone me; it was another friend who called. I told Elinor what I'd found out.

"Not surprising, is it?" she replied. "I'm sorry to hear it, though."

"Jack, if he were alive, would be there to visit him tomorrow, and the next day and the next. I think I should go, don't you? But it's a little awkward; though Ted invited me, as a courtesy, to meet Aileen before their wedding, neither one has called me since."

We were walking through the main foyer of the museum, past the posters advertising the next big exhibit, which I'd organized—"The Art of the Still Life." "You're right; it's awkward," Elinor replied. "But, after all, you knew him very well; and no one else can act in Jack's stead. Why don't you consider going anyhow?"

Her advice, as usual, was apt. I decided to telephone Aileen to inquire whether Ted could have visitors; perhaps she would tell me more about his illness. At first I was only surprised when someone I took to be a housekeeper informed me that Mrs. Livaudais was out of town. It was a strange moment, I thought, to be absent, with her husband seriously ill in Touro. Of course there can be more than one emergency at a time—perhaps a brother or sister in need elsewhere? No date was given for her return. Knowing that, I simply called the hospital, and, upon being informed that Ted could receive visitors for very short periods, I decided to walk over the following day after returning from the museum, even though I felt somewhat reluctant to visit another woman's husband in her absence.

He appeared pleased to see me; but it was obvious that his capacity for enjoyment, and for showing it, had diminished greatly. No wonder: he looked awful, his face drawn, his voice diminished, his hands suddenly old-looking, both wrinkled and spotted (maybe they'd been that way before, but I hadn't noticed) and at the same time swollen at the wrists. As best I could, I chatted with him, enquired about the hospital routine and his therapy, without knowing exactly what was wrong with him—if anyone did—and wished him rapid progress in regaining his health. "Come back soon, Harry," he said as I left.

The next day I reported the visit to Elinor. "He did not mention Aileen; how could I? You don't suppose she's left him already! Not that it's my business. But he and Jack knew each other for more than fifty years ..."

In fact, I returned to Touro once the next week and twice the following, finding Ted in no better condition, and learning nothing further. Though more information might have been useful, I did not dare call the house; if Aileen was there, it would be awkward to speak with her, since I'd already visited him on my own, and if she wasn't, it would strike me as worse. As it turned out, whatever I might have found out about his disease—ultimately acknowledged as cirrhosis of the liver—such knowledge wouldn't have helped me get through the next visits, because there weren't any. The last time I tried to see him, late one Wednesday afternoon, I was informed by a nurse at the desk on his floor that he couldn't receive visitors. I first supposed it was because of the hour; but a young assistant let out the information that he'd been taken to the intensive care ward.

A rush of memories, sickening and yet emboldening, came over me from Jack's illness, his long, agonizing, and futile treatment, and his death. I had scarcely left his side—and Ted had been the most faithful of friends. I wasn't going to drop this. "And Mrs. Livaudais ... is she here? Perhaps, if she's in a waiting room, I could speak with her—I'm a friend." (Of whom, I didn't say.)

The same young woman, really only a girl and probably inadequately trained, answered before the nurse could silence her. "Oh no, she hasn't been here at all; he keeps calling for her."

Ted died a few days later. The obituary appeared promptly in the *Times-Picayune*, giving the cause of death, listing the survivors, and announcing the funeral service, to be held at Holy Name Church, his family parish for generations. Aileen managed to show up for the occasion. She looked stunning. It may have been the same navy-blue suit, but the scarf was different. Ted's son, called Ted, Jr., and his daughter-in-law and grandchildren were there from Lafayette—it was obviously they, seated across the aisle from her—along with what I took to be cousins, business associates, and scores of friends. Whether others were present from her family, I can't say; those might have been friends seated in her pew. Nor could I guess what Ted Jr. might know, or suspect, of her conduct during his father's illness. Lafayette is nearly three hours away by car, and he had his own business and family to tend to; still, it was likely that he had become aware, at some point, of her very noticeable absence from Ted's bedside at Touro.

I followed the funeral party to the cemeteries at the end of Canal Street. Since in New Orleans you can't bury corpses underground (they would ooze up), there was no final casting of dirt upon a grave—dust unto dust or, here, mud to mud. The old above-ground family tombs being just about full, with no room for building more, Ted was buried in an "oven"—a drawer—of Love Eternal Mausoleum, cold and sterile-looking even on the warmest of days—and that day was wintry. A small number of mourners assembled for the final rites and dismissal under the main arch, where two immense stone angels, of dubious taste, appeared to guard the gates to Paradise. Aileen was again there, of course, along with the son and his family. Her demeanor was unobjectionable, although I was persuaded that no real regret underlay it. The others stood slightly apart from her—just enough so that one could interpret it as respect for her bereavement. At the end of the service, I spoke to Ted's son for a few minutes—he knew who I was, of course—and then turned to the widow, who was speaking with a younger woman.

"I am very sorry about your husband's illness and death," I began, extending my hand. "He was such a good friend to Jack and me. It seems like the end of …" She started to interrupt me, I think, but the son suddenly turned toward her. "You know that's Harriet D'Aquin—the widow of Jack, Dad's best friend." His tone was sharp, and it seemed to me as if the words *best friend* had been emphasized strangely.

"Yes," she said, "I do remember, Ted—you don't need to tell me." There was nothing more; she turned back and resumed speaking with the other woman.

What can be added? In small groups or singly, we walked back to our cars, parked on Canal Street. Some of those present would probably head toward the river and stop at Michael's Mid-City Grill or Mendina's for an early drink at the bar, followed by a poor-boy or spaghetti; others would return home, like most of those who'd been at Holy Name, talk to their children or spouse, and fix themselves a good stiff whiskey around 5:30. I couldn't blame anyone for seeking cheer and company, but I was glad to be alone. What Aileen would do I didn't quite know, but it was easy to imagine that she would soon be out of town again, flying off perhaps to the Caribbean or San Francisco or Paris, tasting the blue of freedom and the gold of a widow's usufruct.

Above the cemeteries, the skies were lumpy and gray, their clouds misshapen, ragged, as if in mocking imitation of the ancient stone monuments below, pocked and crumbling, where restless souls agonize, bereft of bodies long decayed. A few breaks in the cumulus merely showed more cloud beyond, the way the lacy designs of spires and turrets on some of the tombs let in nothing but a cold, macabre light. Jack, too, was in one of those enclosures, space having been made for one last body in the D'Aquin vault. No matter how full, however, its essence was emptiness, not plenitude. All my art, too, seemed vacuous, powerless, emptied of beauty and, even more, of love. If *art* could not endure the slow, undermining sabotage of time, what about the petty calculations of selfishness and greed? I got into the car and joined a line of traffic headed toward the river, wondering when Aileen would awaken to find dust on her tongue—the remnants of desire, like the dust of old pressed flowers that fall to bits under one's fingers, or crumbled statuary around a grave.

THE CHARM OF LOVE

IN NEW ORLEANS— "The City That Care Forgot"—or anywhere else, really, if one knows how to look and listen, the ordinary and the odd are often mixed together in such a way that the results are both expected and startling. Don't exceptions prove the rule? Any event— Carnival ball, parade, art opening, stroll in the French Quarter, concert, opera, school fair, dinner at a fine restaurant, even a church coffee— may provide the setting for *commedia dell'arte* scenes and moments so revealing of human truths even as they surprise us that they seem scripted by puppeteers. Sometimes the odd elements reach the extreme. And what begins as farce can end as melodrama.

Bastille Day is marked in South Louisiana on the days preceding July 14th and the date itself. The festivities are not without irony. What exactly is celebrated? The Acadian population of Lafayette, where French-language masses are offered, dates from the 1750s and has more to resent from the British in Canada than from the French monarchy. The earliest predecessor of St. Louis Cathedral on Jackson Square was founded with New Orleans in 1718. That the revolutionaries of 1789 had in their hearts and their platform a deep loathing of the Church and the will and power to destroy it, wreaking havoc, murdering nuns and priests, banning the sacraments, confiscating or setting fire to church properties, seems forgotten. At these masses the *tricolore* is everywhere, and the good pastor carries on as if the banners in the church still bore the gold *fleur de lis* on a white ground, while secular songs are sung, notably "La Marseillaise." Club parties and private *fêtes* abound, some in fine houses to which the 1789 rebels would gladly have set the torch. Does that make the celebrations phony? Certainly not—though falsehood and error are often hard to untangle. Moreover, human nature easily accommodates knots of contradictions, and much history consists in forgetting.

One July, I attended the French mass at the cathedral, accompanied by Robert Hughes, a former Orleanian Institute junior staffer and a good friend, who, after earning his doctorate in eighteenth-century French painting, got a position at another museum. Neither one of us is RC, and Robert is thoroughly Voltairean, but we were pleased to hear the hymns, homily, and readings in French. After the service, as we joined others trailing along the aisles, someone came up to speak with him and then was introduced to me. Franklin Lacour, called Frank, was a friend from school years, I learned. We three chatted briefly, Frank turned to go, and then Robert and I made our way out, retrieved his car, and left to attend a small reception at a house on Henry Clay.

Four days later, I was in the crowd milling around the street, alleyway, and back garden at the Alliance Française, on the uptown edge of the Lower Garden District. I had walked the four blocks from my condo; Robert, who had decided to come and be my escort, was parking as I arrived. Because I am responsible for the Orleanian French collections, for me the event was a command performance. Other staff members were there and former interns; Laura and Charles Trevelyan greeted me in the alleyway where the ticket table was set up. When I reached the garden, I spied Sylvia Croft and her sister Roz, on Adirondack chairs (much too large for Sylvia's small, misshapen body, but low, at least). Sylvia looked far better than on the day when she'd tried to throw herself from Hugh Legendre's balcony. A musical duo—man and wife, maybe—were playing Cajun music. Following a short pseudo-folkloric performance by four women, a few couples danced, even though the grass and gravel were uneven. The scene made me think of Renoir's "Le Bal du Moulin de la Galette." *Bleu, blanc, rouge* were everywhere. The steamy heat notwithstanding, men in jackets, including Robert, and women attired stylishly mingled with those casually dressed. Some guests wore French sailor shirts and berets, or bouffant skirts supposed to recall the gowns of Marie Antoinette (before she was shrouded). Roz was elegant in a form-fitting white dress with a tricolor sash. I sported a red top with a blue-and-white neckerchief.

By chance I noticed Frank Lacour in a small crowd near the tent set up for the band. He was looking intently at the players. He turned and started to move toward us, just as a woman, with hair the color of rose gold and a good figure, coming from the bar, approached Robert and me, to stand on a bit of lawn beside us. She was perhaps thirty years of age. I reflected later that she had very good genes. She wore an attractive dress in medium blue, with a string of large red-and-white beads. Frank must have caught sight of her, for suddenly, as though pursued, he broke into a run and came up to her, eagerly. "Oh, hello; I've been looking for you."

Desperate men, with little to lose, take desperate measures. The phrase was not strange to us; but she was surprised. Was it just a ploy? Oh, no. "I'm Franklin Lacour; I'm a lawyer. Please call me Frank." Somewhat startled, she seemed about to reply ("You must take me for someone else") when he burst out even more abruptly, "Are you married? If not, will you marry me?"

A Bastille Day party is not part of pre-Lenten Saturnalia, where fools rule. But we took the question as a joke. Robert responded with a loud laugh, heard (I could see) by a couple to our left. I smiled and offered a compliment. "What a witty self-introduction, Frank!"

The target of his wit, though perhaps slightly taken aback, added her agreement: "Oh, yes, thank you for thinking of me!"

"No, I mean it! You are beautiful, the image of my dream as a wife. I mean it! On Sunday, after the Bastille Day mass, I saw you briefly, dressed in blue , as you were leaving the cathedral; but you were too far ahead, and I lost you. Here I see you again—lightning strikes twice! Will you marry me? I see you're alone; you're not married already, are you?" (The *coup de foudre*, I reflected. It was doubtless the same dress—her French outfit.) So he was, in fact, searching for someone to wed and had conceived the proposal on the spot. Goodness, how improbable! I was as if hypnotized.

The woman's expression changed visibly; her face showed how she was grasping for words. "Well, no ... I mean I'm not married. But

I don't even know you! And I won't marry you!" She gasped. "What do you mean, coming up to me like this?" "Marry you!" she added. "We've not been properly introduced!"

Frank's courtroom experience in confronting an unexpected statement from the opposing side or a judge's admonition at the bench would have allowed him to respond, doubtless. But Robert intervened, his tact and social training, like that for a law court, coming to the fore automatically. As if he were under oath, he assured the woman that the man was really Frank Lacour, really a lawyer, and known to him, though he himself was an art curator. He introduced himself.

"Well, I don't know you either, Mr. Hughes!" But an afterthought burst from her lips: "Oh, maybe I do. Are you connected to the family that owns the Hughes Building, in the CBD?"

"Yes. Since our father died, we have all been the owners, though my brother Ed is the chief officer and manager."

"Ah, yes. Someone in the office where I work knows your family, on Palmer. And I'm Miranda." (No surname.)

Somehow, this exchange had defused her hostility and brought the confrontation back into the bounds of the normal. Socially reassured on one count, visibly less unsettled, the woman nevertheless returned suddenly to the proposal of marriage, which, having fallen in our midst like a live grenade, remained on the ground, sputtering. "Still ... Mr. Lacour, if that's who you are, what business of yours can my matrimonial condition be?" She lapsed into French (which, we learned, she knew well, having a French mother). "*Je n'épouse pas le premier venu.*" She then turned to me, showing continued irritation but a bit of embarrassment too. "And you?"

"My name is Harriet D'Aquin; people call me Harry. I'm with the Orleanian Institute and something of a Francophile. Oh, and Robert is a former colleague of mine. —Excuse me please; I'd like to go speak to friends who have just arrived." And I crossed the grass to greet Elinor and Roger. Extricated thus from the knot of people speaking, it seemed, at cross-purposes, I made my way toward my good friends. Robert joined us soon, leaving Frank and Miranda to themselves. When he had a chance, he remarked to me, "How odd!" nodding toward the twosome. Later, we could hear them speaking French. Not only did Frank have French lineage; he had, we learned, studied the language seriously.

Subsequently I saw them pull chairs together. Frank turned to go for fresh drinks; Miranda seated herself to wait for him. He was attractive, generally, though his complexion was slightly marred, and he had a pleasant smile. Was she entranced by his eagerness, his astounding proposal? Did his general good appearance or the word *lawyer* have special appeal? Was she among those women who respond to a man's unusual need, an unconventional or even crippling feature—a slight stutter, a Byronic limp? Either a rare daring or a flaw could be an aphrodisiac.

Robert and I circulated for a while more, listened to the band, which I applauded vigorously, and prepared to leave. I thanked the servers and said my goodbyes, then, on the sidewalk, thanked Robert also and turned toward home.

In time, it became clear that he and I were like witnesses to a traffic accident or a criminal act in a store or on the street: despite ourselves, we would become involved in Frank and Miranda's story by the simple fact that we were there and *had seen*. Robert did not know much about Frank's present circumstances; they'd simply been at school together at Country Day and had spoken again at a few games and reunions. Frank, he learned, was not associated with a major firm such as Phelps Dunbar; he had a practice of his own. His brother managed the jewelry store that their father had owned on Magazine Street. But Frank was not obscure; his name was listed on the membership rolls of the Alliance Française and the Orleanian as well as Country Day alumni. Robert had a vague notion that he had been married before—having shown up with a wife at some school event; but the memory was not entirely trustworthy.

It was not long afterward that Frank telephoned to invite Robert and me to lunch with him and Miranda on a Sunday. He mentioned the café at the Institute, but, pointing out its modesty, I suggested meeting elsewhere. He decided on an Uptown place, Au Bon Goût, with its fine menu and *terrasse climatisée*. At the table that day, he was ebullient. We learned that his ancestors were Bretons, from le Morbihan. His parents, doubly patriotic, had named him Franklin in honor of the great Benjamin, who had arrived at Saint-Goustan in 1776 to represent the Thirteen Colonies at the French court. Miranda seemed a bit timid in our presence but not unfriendly. Her roots were, it appeared, in Greenville, in the Mississippi Delta; her accent fit well into our Creole-inflected speech. Beyond revealing that she had gone to Newcomb and worked for a New Orleans company with which her family seemed to have some connection, she revealed little about herself. I did not pry. Such reserve may or may not cover a sensitive soul. She responded very warmly to Frank, however. They made allusions to what they had done together already and would do. He inquired of Robert and me about our work at our respective museums, and asked about our families (yes, I had a daughter, married in New York, and Robert spoke of his two nephews).

Knowing that Frank was already familiar with the Orleanian, but not sure of Miranda's acquaintance with it, I suggested that they stop by sometime, together; if they phoned beforehand, I would show them workrooms where we carry out restoration of materials and prepare exhibits. Thus in time I had a chance to watch them together and observe what seemed to be their growing romantic relationship. Robert and I had decided that I might invite them to a cocktail buffet in my condo, with a few additional guests, including Roger, Elinor, and Greg—good judges of character, all, albeit not perfect. The couple seemed pleased, and it was arranged. The little party in my place went well; my colleagues were charmed by the pair and by their romantic story, which Frank could not keep from recounting. I still did not know, however, the impetus for his inspired choice of Miranda; even less clear was her initial willingness to sit with him instead of walking away. To this day I do not understand her well. Maybe the common interest in things French, a taste for Cajun music, or some deep, imperceptible need had created the first bonds.

Sometime in the following weeks, an acquaintance, another Country Day alumnus, happened to mention Frank to Robert over coffee in the Marigny. Funny: until July Robert hadn't thought of Frank for a long while, hadn't run into him; yet here his old schoolmate was again drawn to his attention. Having heard about the engagement, the acquaintance mentioned it and inquired whether Robert knew the background story. The story was easy to summarize. Frank had indeed been married once. Hoping to have children, he was shocked, and dismayed, when he found contraceptive products in his new wife's dresser. Not giving in to fury, however, he simply removed and destroyed them. Of course, she discovered what he had done. The upshot was an annulment. How much time had passed since then wasn't clear. Having been badly burned by that fire once, for years he may have been reluctant to launch out again. Finally, he must have whipped up his determination to remarry and have children; it was clear enough now. Attraction, love, desire or sheer lust: whatever name it bears, whatever its form and appearance, the need to create the next generation is strong, like that of primitive man, determined to mate, heedless of difficulties, or a stag going after a doe.

But time had passed; Robert was no longer among the young contenders. Courtship, a skill, like another, is enhanced by self-confidence; fortune favors the bold, and lack of assurance can be fatal. In order to take the step at all, perhaps, he had to throw himself at a woman. A timid man, once launched into boldness, cannot pull back. He wouldn't have reflected that his desperation would probably keep women away. They often sense, under the respectable, even attractive exterior of a man some weakness, something that says "Loser." Maybe he had tried the tactic previously, without success; but one win would be enough. Or had he been especially inspired that evening by a sixth sense telling him that she too was vulnerable?

Lightning-like love affairs are supposed to end in marriage. The wedding took place in early October, in St. Mary's Church. Thus Miranda did, in fact, marry *le premier venu*—at least the first who came along at the Bastille Day party.

The wedding party included a maternal uncle of Miranda's from Greenville, who gave her away, a young cousin of hers, then in New Orleans, who was her maid of honor, and Frank's brother, the best man. Frank wanted to have Robert at the altar also, a second best man, so to speak, as if Robert had been responsible for Miranda's appearing at the magic moment. Frank's sister-in-law was there also, of course, among a sizeable crowd of neighbors and friends. In homage to the happy day of their meeting, the groom wore a navy-blue suit, white shirt, and blue tie, with a red *pochette* in his jacket pocket. Miranda was in white, with a bouquet of red roses and blue irises. I could see their faces as they stood opposite each other during the opening part of the ceremony. He was radiant, offering smiles on all sides. When the officiant, in his remarks, spoke of the happy home the two would make for themselves and the children they would have, if it pleased God, Frank beamed even more and lifted his face to heaven. Miranda showed little emotion, remaining demure, though not with downcast eyes. At the reception, she showed off her engagement ring—a large diamond solitaire—and her diamond wedding band.

Three months or so passed before we were invited to their home, a shotgun house with a side addition, which Frank had occupied by himself, on Soniat Street. They received us in the combined living-dining room at the front. The affair was simple—a cold buffet—but with champagne. We were the only guests; Frank's brother and sister-in-law had been invited but could not come. No matter, it turned out; they already knew what the little affair was to announce: Miranda was pregnant, and with twins. Two heartbeats! Frank was ecstatic. Miranda evinced considerable pride. Robert seconded me in showering the couple with congratulations and good wishes. The expected birth date was given as late August. Frank urged her to show us her new dinner ring, a lovely design with rubies, fashioned for her, he said, in gratitude for the happy expectation.

Later they showed us the house and the room, in the side addition, that was to be the nursery, not yet prepared; it was to be painted a soft yellow and have sheer curtains. They'd get twin bassinets. I made a mental note to look for baby gifts in yellow. They had chosen names, they said, for either a boy-girl combination or two of one sex (it was too soon to know); but they did not reveal the names. They planned to engage a part-time nurse and housekeeper; Miranda would work only part-time. Whether anyone from her family in Greenville would come at the time of the birth was unclear; her cousin was no longer in New Orleans.

We stepped out through the kitchen, passed their bedroom, and then were taken into another side room, a den, where tall bookcases in polished wood, with heavy glass, displayed Frank's impressive collection of old books, among which, he pointed out, were valuable early Louisiana imprints as well as French classics in nineteenth-century red-leather bindings. We glimpsed the back yard and a little garden, then, with many thanks, made our way out.

Oh, the turns of Fortune's wheel! I'd been at the Bastille Day party when an unknown woman came to stand beside Robert and me; Frank saw her, ran over, and drew her into an amazing conversation, to which we were witnesses. Some while later, chance would lead to my being the auditor to whom the principal character in a classical stage tragedy recounts the subsequent terrible events. Like Eliot's "attendant lords," Robert and I were thrust into the drama again by virtue of being the personae present at the first scene.

On a Saturday morning, I was in my condo, redding up things, doing laundry, thinking of very little. The phone rang; it was Frank, or so he said. Yet the voice was distorted—that of another. "Harry, may I drive over to talk to you? I must! I can't stay here!" Of course. A little more straightening of a desk, a quick wipe of the table, and the place was acceptable. Not that he would have cared. I told the doorman to send him up. In just a few minutes there was a sharp ring at the door. The man I let in was a man transformed. He took a few steps and collapsed onto the little sofa. "Harry, she's gone! She's gone." His voice cracked, and a great strangled sob came. It took him a while to get out the words; he remained somewhat incoherent and repeated himself. But of course the heart of the matter became clear. Why had he come to me first (as I learned)—rather than going to his brother, another friend, or Robert, whom he'd known, if casually, from school years? Maybe even in his frenzy and desperation, maybe even because of them, he could not face his brother or anyone else in the family—could not admit what had happened. And women are the sympathizers, who recognize need and reach out. "Oh, why did she leave? We did not quarrel; I was good to her, or at least I tried to be. She could see that! How could she go off, with our twins inside her? I cannot believe it. It is lunacy." I thought of King Lear on the heath: "Is there any cause in nature that makes these hard hearts?"

He paused briefly, then started again. "She's taken her car and her jewelry; there isn't any left in her dresser drawer. Her closet is half empty!" I wondered whether she'd packed things in her car trunk days before—items he wouldn't normally miss.

"But when did she leave—and how?"

"She must have driven off in the night—last night. She was in bed when I went to sleep. I can't understand why I didn't hear her!"

He recounted how he had awakened, gotten up, but, not finding her in the bathroom or kitchen, looked elsewhere, ending up by searching the entire house frantically. Looking outside, he had seen that her car, normally parked at night in the side drive, was gone. He noticed that the bookcases, locked but with their keys in the old-fashioned locks, had been left open; one shelf had been partly emptied. None of the silverware Frank had inherited from his parents appeared to be missing; but he and Miranda had received numerous pieces in their pattern, and he discovered right away—his suspicions devouring him—that she'd removed what she must have considered her half. Her laptop was no longer on the desk. What cash she might have had he could not know; but of course she owned credit cards (one in her own name, one on his account, he specified) and a checkbook for her Maxi Savings Account, which was like cash. They seemed to be gone, along with various other things that struck him by their absence.

Thoughts of the law swirled around my head but were probably very far from Frank's mind. He knew Louisiana property codes, of course, and laws concerning kidnapping. Secreting away children, including one's own child from the other parent, is aggravated kidnapping. But the question at the core of the abortion controversy struck me in this new context. Is a foetus a child, that is, a person? In Louisiana, it is, basically, but perhaps not in all respects. He veered onto the question of where she was—Greenville, probably. Did she have an accomplice? Another man, perhaps? "Greenville is not far, really, but it takes some hours to get there ... Oh, God." And, suddenly, a new concern,: "What about prenatal care, her examinations, then the birth itself?"

In the face of such misery, kind words, gestures showing understanding, are just sandbags or worse—old quilts and other trash—piled to stop a torrent. I responded as sympathetically as possible, with the usual worn expressions. It occurred to me to ask what must be true: "But you haven't called your brother? You must tell him."

"No, not now! I could not endure it." He would stall for time. Pride, perhaps, reinforced the thought in the back of his mind, unacknowledged as yet: Miranda would surely come back! She would return by herself, as she had taken herself away, or be returned by fate—and the nightmarish event would be interred, eradicated, before it must be known to others.

"Wouldn't you like to go consult with Robert? He is your friend; he cares about you. And he's discrete."

"No, no. Oh, maybe yes. I could drive to the Marigny if he's at home. Or he could come here. Would that be all right? I know I'm imposing awfully on you ... But, yes. Please telephone him. You'll do better than I."

So Robert came to join us, to talk with the suffering man, reason with him, assist him with useful remarks. How would one trace Miranda, for instance? Except for the valuable books she'd taken—to sell, or just to spite him?—she had removed mostly what was hers, or a fair portion of the community property. She hadn't committed yet any fraud. Do highway patrolmen look out for wives who have left home? Probably not.

Our thoughts, speculations, bits of information embedded in ignorance, ranged through the present, past, and future. Frank had not yet gone through all the papers in her desk; he was far too frenzied for that. Knowing that the poor man needed to *do* something, we persuaded him to return home to start searching for clues in letters and bills. Robert would follow him in his own car to see that he got in and was as settled as possible. He could not stay long, however. Full of pity for Frank, I nonetheless thought I could not keep him company the rest of the day. He would not go out, we could be confident; like criminals, those who are in misery return to the scene of events. In the house that Miranda had abandoned, the evening would be nightmarish and the night nearly sleepless.

On Sunday morning, Robert, after phoning, drove to Frank's again, to be a sounding board and offer any help he could. Around 11, they called to ask me to join them and pitch in; they suggested that a woman would have a keener sense of what might be concealed and where. (Maybe so, maybe so.) We decided to look more carefully through Miranda's dresser and the pigeon holes of her desk. We rummaged also in kitchen drawers, where she might have dropped reminders or addresses and phone numbers. We found no personal letters at all; I supposed that she used the telephone and emails to exchange news with her family in Greenville. A few credit card bills, in no order, and statements from her Maxi account looked promising but yielded little.

Frank looked for physicians' statements also, the sort that list services rendered, fees, and insurance payments. The medical insurance plan for his law firm was through Touro Infirmary, with which Miranda's gynecologist was associated; he kept expecting to run across statements and print-outs with the Touro letterhead. Nothing. She could have taken the medical reports, of course, to show another doctor, somewhere. Given what he knew presently to be her deceitfulness, he did not rule out anything far-fetched. Did she know, for instance, some handsome doctor elsewhere who would take care of her?

Once, that afternoon, the telephone rang, echoing loudly, it seemed to me, within the emptiness she had created. Frank hurried for it. "Oh, maybe it's Miranda." But it was a wrong number. Returning, he said, "I hoped ... Oh, I am deluded."

Then, slowly but brutally, a terrible thought came into his consciousness: that the pregnancy was a sham, a horrible fraud. Thus, she likewise was a sort of fake. With a groan, almost of self-loathing, he looked at me, looked at Robert, and pronounced what he saw as the awful truth. "Oh, it cannot be! No, dear God! She concocted it all! She's a phony and the babies were too!"

It was another horrible moment for him, morally marooned, his world turned against itself. His thoughts churned over until, poor masochist, he came up with an even worse hypothesis. What if the pregnancy were real but Miranda had left him to seek an abortion in a state allowing the procedure at any time? She'd need to go north for that. He groaned again as he let his thoughts out. "Oh, what if she's gone to have an abortion? Oh, Jesus, oh, dear God! No! May it not be. Please make it that it not be!" Then he added, "The Touro statements from her doctor's visits and the first ultrasound test would provide her with the required documents."

I didn't want to believe it of Miranda; she didn't seem to me the sort to carry out such a deed. After all, she attended church voluntarily. But did I know her, really? Since this hypothesis was worse than any other, I tried to tamp it down. "Oh, from what I've read, even girls of fourteen or so, who've had no doctors' visits, can get admitted in a 'women's health center' where no questions are asked, no records requested. So she wouldn't have needed those statements, would she? Their absence doesn't prove much."

"Maybe she's killed the babies and herself!" he countered.

No, not her way, I reflected. Though she was foolish as well as unkind to have undertaken such a charade as hers, she was cool. In his despair, Frank would be a more likely candidate for suicide. "But look," I countered, "she's taken valuable things with her; she planned her disappearance well. She just ... Oh, I don't know!"

Robert and I each left at twilight, after we'd succeeded in making Frank drink a glass of wine and eat a small plate of cold food. We begged him to try to rest, sleeping on the sofa if need be, to avoid the bed they had shared. What else could we do? Frank had said he would call Touro the next day; hadn't Miranda said her doctor's name, Diaz, perhaps? Yes, yes, of course.

As we dreaded, he reported in the morning that the keepers of the main Touro records would let out no information; when he said his name, though, a clerk, probably only half-trained, in the offices of Diaz and partners let out that they had no record on her. This response did not, of course, keep Frank from creating various scenarios, going over the past, supposing at once the worst and the best, even the most implausible of each.

What a schemer Miranda was, from the outset, I supposed, though maybe she had just found marriage unpleasant and had devised a way to leave, with a few extras. Robert and I commiserated with Frank as well as we could. What additional sympathy he got we could not know. We hoped he was acquainted with a good counselor on the staff of St. Mary's or another church. What a shabby and disheartening story. Why hadn't Miranda left earlier, without the bother of the sham pregnancy? The ruby ring, perhaps, promised as a gift at the right time. Or was it a sort of mania?

Though she had apparently engineered her own disappearance, Frank filed a missing-person report with the police as though foul play might be suspected. After all, a woman can be abducted *with* her car. He phoned people in Greenville whose names he remembered, starting with the cousin; no one cooperated with him, either denying all acquaintance with Miranda or, like her uncle, refusing to answer questions. He could have driven there himself; but some good instinct, that of self-protection, perhaps, warned him not to do so. An agent hired to trace her movements did turn up evidence of her presence in Mississippi, but at first he was unable to determine much else. For practical purposes, she had fled, but of her own volition, and she had broken no law, except for prima facie theft of a spouse's property, a theft Frank had not reported.

In any case, she changed her mind about keeping the books; before long he received a shipment through FedEx, insured but with only a commercial P.O. box as the return address. Eventually, he was obliged, of course, to tell his brother and sister-in-law and others in the family as well as associates in his office who would be involved in filing legal papers; but otherwise he shared his changed circumstances and his sufferings with few, I think.

Ultimately, agents found Miranda, whom he sued successfully for divorce on grounds of desertion. She did not attempt to recover her portion of the common income during the short marriage. Good riddance, I could not help but reflect. I thought of Sylvia Croft. She, at least, escaped what would have been a miserable union with that cad from Crowley, who was after her money. The consequences for her of such a marriage would have been dreadful; she was spared. Even saved, though, she remained heartbroken.

Frank had been devoted to Miranda; that was over, with only the memory remaining. Robert and I paid him a visit after the turmoil of the divorce had ended; he spoke of her wistfully. "When I first glimpsed her, leaving the cathedral, in her blue dress, with her beautiful hair, I loved her—I wanted to love her." We recalled the Bastille Day party, the lightning effect a second time. "Oh, the charm of love!" he added. "The charm! But she killed it; it's gone!" He had also loved in utero two infants, who turned out to be fake. His hope for children was given form in her announcement of pregnancy and developed as mental pictures of their future. The yellow room! But, simulacra, those infants could not be buried; they could not be mourned. Yet, even as fantasies, they continued to occupy his mind, he said. Mental stillbirths, that's what they were. How could he begin again a second time? Was his soul so resolute, so loving, that he could try?

ALONG THE DANUBE

THE PLANE BANKED, dropped, and straightened, approaching the runway. I hoped to glimpse the Danube, but it was not visible from my porthole. I would see it shortly at close hand, however; although Karl, my host for this visit, kept an office and apartment near the Ringstraße in Vienna, he had invited me to stay first at his principal residence forty or so miles upstream, in the Wachau Valley, and the drive there would take us along the banks of the river. I would see it even better from the windows and terrace of his house, almost at the water's edge.

Karl is both an old and a new friend. I knew him rather casually in New York many years ago, when I was studying art there and he had a Fulbright exchange scholarship to take a master's degree in architecture. A mutual acquaintance introduced us, and we had a few outings together—dates, you could call them, I suppose, according to the usual definition, but not signifying much to me. He is some years older than I, and at twenty that makes a difference; moreover, he was a sophisticated European, or so he appeared to me, whereas I was still a somewhat diffident girl from El Paso, bent on a career in art but scarcely worldly, as he was. Living in mid-century Austria would mark any man; although at the time he did not speak of them, surely he had witnessed and experienced things known to me only very generally, from written accounts. The friendship was not pursued after he returned to Vienna; only passion—if anything—could have overcome the obstacle of such a distance.

Again through friends, we met briefly more than three decades later. Learning that I was planning a European journey not long after this reunion, he invited me to visit him in Austria, explaining that he had retired from the full-time exercise of his profession, while still doing consulting work all over the world, and thus could arrange to be free to act as host and guide. He had been married for many years, he said, but was now divorced, and his sons were both grown. I had been in Franz-Joseph's great imperial city once before, but a return visit was certainly warranted; and I had never seen the Wachau. Besides, it was a pleasure to become reacquainted with Karl, in a mode appropriate to our situation; we could speak as old friends, yet also exchange new selves, as experienced practitioners of our respective arts, comfortable at once with the similarities we discovered shortly and with the differences bred not only by our respective experiences, gender, and nationality but by time itself. I understood that this was no attempt at seduction. *En tout bien, tout honneur.*

As the plane landed, paused, then slowly taxied, it was clear that it would arrive early. That is sometimes awkward. After the brief immigration and customs procedures, I was out in the arrival hall some minutes before the time Karl could have expected me. I put down my suitcase and briefcase and looked around for him in the considerable crush; no Karl, it appeared. Like a mechanical mannequin, I slowly turned, surveying the crowd. Quite some time passed; I began to wonder whether he'd come but missed me, or there had been a contretemps of some sort. Should I telephone? But chances were slim of reaching him at either of his two addresses; he must be en route. Furthermore, I had no Austrian coins; and, often frustrated by public telephones in America and France, where at least I know the language well and the system, more or less, how could I have dealt with a Viennese pay phone? Anyhow, it was better to remain in one spot. So I just stood, waiting. Wavelets of people, occasionally a large breaker, washed around me. Suddenly, there he was, well toward the right, straining to see over and through the crush. He must have just arrived. Whereas I was wearing denims and a casual jacket—it has been years since I dressed otherwise to take a plane—he had on a tie, a white shirt, and a jacket of a traditional Austrian cut.

"Karl!" But he could not hear. I picked up my luggage and, like an icebreaker on the Arctic Circle, made my way toward him. "Karl! Here I am."

He turned. "Harriet! *Gott sei dank!* I was worried when I didn't find you. I'm late; apologies. When I saw from the board that the plane had landed a while ago, I feared you were wandering around looking for me—or perhaps hadn't come."

"In fact, you are not really late; the plane was quite early."

Karl gave me a warm hug of welcome, took my suitcase in hand, and led me through the crowd, outside, and into the parking lot. "Are you tired?" What a question. Of course one is always tired after a transatlantic flight; yet, if one travels by choice, and has beauty and pleasures to look forward to, it is an energizing experience.

"Not really—not too much so. It is wonderful to be here. You look well, Karl."

"Thank you. I *am* well, though too busy for someone who has retired. Come, here is my car; let me just get these things in the boot and I'll open your door."

Within a few minutes we were heading into the city, where he needed to stop by his flat before driving me to his country house. Once in the center of Vienna, close to the Ring Road, he parked in a taxi zone and ran up the stairs to his apartment, leaving me for a moment on the sidewalk, where I took a few steps and breathed the fresh, invigorating air, some thirty degrees cooler that what I had left in New Orleans—air that helped offset the fatigue of sitting up sleepless during the short night. We then headed away from the Ring, crossed both branches of the Danube, and took the expressway upriver. I admired the splendid deciduous trees, whose grayish-green leaves showed lovely silvered undersides, and their conifer companions—long-needle pines and immense firs, so dark they appeared almost black.

Karl's country house is slightly upriver and across from Krems, a town that recently celebrated its 900th anniversary. It also has a splendid view of the medieval ruins of Dürnstein, high above the site of one of Napoleon's battles as well as an eighteenth-century chateau, now turned into a hotel and restaurant, where we dined one evening. To become better acquainted again with Karl during the next three days meant getting to know his area—his house, which he designed himself in a traditional Austrian style and which he showed me with pride, the Danube and its bridges, the town of Krems, with its marvelous Piaristenkirche and its ancient, winding streets, and other villages up and down both sides of the river, each with a splendid baroque church. A strong, visceral bond seemed to exist between the man and his surroundings. Perhaps that is truly the soul of architecture. One day he took me to the nearby monastery of Gottweig, high above the river, and the even more imposing *Stift* of Melk, an immense gilded structure, whose main chapel could almost blind the viewer by its dazzling gold. On another excursion, we drove by fine hillside vineyards and visited the new wine museum in Krems, toured Stein, its neighbor, and Spitz, had lunch on the terrace of the Hotel Rose above the river, and chatted with Karl's friends encountered here and there.

On the third evening, at the cocktail hour, we were seated on his deck, with the garden behind us, shrubs and trees dropping off sharply below to the road and the river bank, barges and a tourist boat passing by, and great green slopes rising on the other side. The baroque church of Stein, directly across, was illuminated by long sunset rays. It was time for trying to express more thoughtfully than before my appreciation of Karl's beautiful region.

"What a fine house you have built here, Karl, in the place that you chose. With your eye for design, your interest in the past, and your deep Catholic faith, you seem to have strong affinities with your environs. I am so pleased to discover the Wachau, thanks to you."

"It is lovely to have a guest who appreciates it."

"This valley is not only beautiful, but dramatic, with the ancient, powerful river and its companion hills, the contrasts of forest and sky, and the great arches, naves, and towers of the churches. I discern, though, something tragic, too—like a late Mozart symphony, or, even more, a motif from Tchaikowsky's pathos-laden work. You are very far east here."

"Yes, Harriet, you are right—both in seeing the beauty and drama of the Wachau Valley and in sensing disturbing memories."

After a moment, I continued. "The battle of Dürnstein in 1808, for instance—commemorated in that monument you pointed out to me. Think of the Austrians, French, and Russians who died there, many of them conscripts or raw recruits! I like the intense, dynamic paintings of the Empire by Géricault, Gros, and Horace Vernet; but I cannot accept the destruction and distress that Napoleon brought to Europe, with his megalomania and overreaching ambitions. Art cannot vindicate such history."

"I quite agree. Sometimes the valley appears too peaceful to me, a disturbing disguise of its past. But here, Harriet, let me top up your glass" (Karl's English is marked by Briticisms). He poured from a bottle of a local wine, a variety that we had sampled earlier at the museum.

"Besides," I added, "think of how many invaders came along this route long before Napoleon. One is not always fortunate to live in a fertile valley along a major waterway; others come by and want to seize the place for themselves." "I paused for a moment, thinking of much more recent history. The Pangermanism of the Third Reich was not in itself irrational, but in the hands of a great madman it became destructive on an apocalyptic scale. "Didn't you see some of that yourself, Karl, after the Anschluß? Of course, I think of the Second War and its immense destruction chiefly in broad, general terms—those of historians. Or else in those of art history—its consequences on individual artists, those who were not themselves destroyed in the cataclysm."

"Quite naturally," he agreed. "At this remove, I sometimes think as you do. Often, though, the war remains a concrete experience to me. You know my older brother was captured and put in a prison camp; I suppose he was lucky, for he was fed regularly. We had less and less to eat ... At the war's end, we went for several days without any food whatsoever, not even runt potatoes from someone's back garden."

"What a terrible, bloody century we live in. But look at its achievements! There is not an epoch in human history where great achievements in the arts and sciences have not been paralleled by violence, aggression, upheaval. Look at Renaissance Italy, Elizabethan England ... or, farther back, the Assyrians, the Egyptians. Art seems to thrive in such turmoil, perhaps to require it. It thrives, too, in the turmoil of the individual soul."

"Too much so," Karl replied. (Only later in the visit could I understand what he had in mind.) "Even architecture, the most functional of the arts."

"Does that make all art tragic? Or should human existence be looked upon as a soil whose purpose is to produce culture, at whatever price?" I thought of Nietzsche's ideas on tragedy and the necessary sacrifice of the masses so that superior specimens might flourish; I thought also of his insanity ... "Inevitably, the name of Nietzsche arises in this connection."

Karl thought a moment, then remarked, "You know that I am an industrial and urban designer—the lowest variety of architect, some would say. I cannot be on Nietzsche's side. Collectivities are my concern, although I recognize that they are, and can be, composed only of individuals, who must remain their measure. Somewhere this side of Hitler's oppressive state architecture, intended to support his ideology, and even Franz-Joseph's imperial Vienna, there must be art for and with the masses, neither abusive nor repressive."

"The chapel and the rest of Melk, if I may say so, seem a virtuoso achievement, too grandiose, designed less for piety than for an artist's ego. Where is the thought of God and others in that gilded splendor? Please forgive me; my tastes run to Romanesque and early Gothic."

"Of course."

Karl paused and refilled his glass. I watched a multi-deck cruise ship move slowly upstream, white and seemingly as smooth as a swan. Perhaps it was time for a change of topic.

"What a large vessel, Karl."

"It's Ukrainian. Just think how things have changed since the fall of the Soviet Union. That ship descends the Volga, goes through the Black Sea, and cruises up the Danube, with hundreds of tourists. Look, you can see some on the upper deck, drinks in hand. Dinner will be served soon, I suppose. And, speaking of dinner, let's go down to the restaurant of my friend Raimund Thierry. He is from a French family who settled here generations ago. You will like his place."

Indeed I did. Located on the river road, not far, it was a charming, rustic establishment, featuring basic Austrian cuisine and some French dishes. We chatted with Raimund and his wife (my spoken German is not fluent, but at least I can handle the subject of food), ordered, and took our time over beet broth, a cold cheese and meat plate, a dessert, and another local wine.

Back at Karl's, we again went out to the terrace; it was damp and cool, and I went to get a sweater to put on under my jacket. The golden walls and towers of the church in Stein, now brightly lit by spotlights, stood out against the sky; farther along, the Dürnstein church, half-blue, half-ochre, was illuminated dramatically from below. Karl was pensive, but finally spoke. *In vino veritas.* "You know, Harriet—I'm sure you will understand—it is not just the drama of history I see, or imagine, here. There is my own, also. This house was built for my wife and children as much as for me. The boys have grown and left to start their own careers; that is to be expected. But I could not have expected Helga to leave me. We had been married for twenty-eight years. One man's disappointment is nothing, I know, against the river's flow, the turning of the seasons, the waves of invaders over millennia, the death of all. But the individual response is everything; it is the way that man knows the river, the seasons, the world; history would not be, without the individual intelligence to apprehend it. I have been very unhappy since she left, and the divorce has not freed me, merely made my misery official."

No one can live through a few decades without understanding unhappiness. The causes vary, as would the solutions, if there were any; but the core experience is much the same, and the body's ways of feeling it basic and few. Now that he had let it speak for him, I could see, on Karl's fine, responsive face, with its lines of thoughtfulness and its distinguished shock of white hair, genuine pain, not merely that of vanity wounded.

"And is she happy, in her new state?" Despite the wording, the question was concerned less with her than with him; he might take comfort, upon reflection, in having afforded the one he loved most a new contentment, even at his own expense.

"I do not believe so, though of course I cannot be sure. She seems brittle and driven, under a surface of gaiety. My information is fragmentary, gleaned from our sons, who are, understandably, protective of her, and from friends who run into her sometimes in Vienna. I should explain that she was an actress when we met and married. Strange, that I should fall in love with someone from the theatre, whose life was so uncertain and whose art so subjective. For her, everything is performance, directed toward an audience—theatre-goers, preferably, or friends, or me … But the ultimate audience is herself—for which, however, she needs others, to reflect it. She does not mind the ephemeral; in fact, that is her element. She is too dependent on others for her identity to have a stable self. My work *must* be stable. Her temperament is very much unlike mine."

He was silent for a moment, before resuming his musings aloud. "She continued acting for several years after our wedding. Then, when the boys were young, she dramatized her role as mother. She was both emotional and permissive. At first, the children were an attentive, devoted audience; ultimately, they became impatient with her demands. After they were grown and we two were alone, she had almost no outlet for her performances; she felt stifled, and we had … difficulties. Still, I loved her—perhaps even more, or more urgently. Maybe even my own work, scientifically grounded though it is, fed on our conflicts; I don't know. The sense of distance between two people can be discouraging—but maddeningly exciting, also. Are we not drawn to what differs from us, wanting to seduce and conquer it?"

Thecontradictionsoftheirrelationship,withitsdeeptemperamental differences and misunderstandings, yet attraction, were nothing new, really. Beyond the appearances, however, lay mystery, which I could not pretend to penetrate. No one can understand anyone else's marriage from the outside, and few understand their own.

"Of course. Love has always fed on difference. Still, you have not said whether she loved you in return, whatever that might mean from her point of view."

"I cannot say. She was jealous, certainly—of my friends, my projects, of women in our social circles. Does that imply love? Or did she simply enjoy the drama of jealousy? My pride wanted to believe that she still adored me ... obviously, a foolish masculine idea. The evidence went more and more against it, but I hoped at least, in my most sober and rational moments, that the tension between us, wearisome to me, would satisfy her. Instead, she decided to return to the stage—acting again, this time older roles, and also getting involved in production. She is very talented."

Karl's refined courtesy toward me and toward the world, as I saw it, did not disguise—indeed underlined—the fact that he had been bred in another time; he seemed put off, still, by the emancipation that her decision indicated.

"Karl, I am a woman too, one who chose a profession early and has exercised it all her adult life, enjoying the identity and the autonomy it affords, even under difficult circumstances. Helga and I must not be many years apart in age; I can easily imagine how, with her children grown and you well established in your career, she would want to return to what she had done earlier—developing her talents, which you say yourself are considerable, beginning again, as it were. We live for many decades, now."

"But I did not oppose her resuming her career. Perhaps ... perhaps I was not sufficiently enthusiastic. Doubtless I did not *reflect* her well enough. She spent all her time in the flat in Vienna, coming here at first only for holidays. That was not hard to accept; our life was already divided between two residences. Meanwhile, I was away a great deal—out of the country, I mean, working on contract for various governments in Asia and Africa. That should have given her a sense of freedom; perhaps, though, she felt abandoned. Finally, she asked for a divorce. I was generous to her, but she also has money of her own, so she can afford a very stylish bohemian life. I have wondered, of course, whether she found someone else, less rationalistic, less ... bourgeois than I" (he pointed to his necktie, with a wry expression) "—maybe an actor or producer, or more than one. But she has not remarried; I would know that. To her, fantasy is preferable to reality."

"Excuse me, Karl, for saying this. But remember, you said yourself that architecture is for others, and so is drama. In fact, we all need fantasy. The theatre has good credentials, starting with the Greek tragedians; it can be at the core of a culture, the nexus of what *is* and what we dream of, whether grotesque and fearful, or fine and beautiful. To say that the art justifies the artist—as perhaps we should do in Helga's case, although I know it is very difficult for you, who have been hurt—does not mean one subscribes to Nietzsche's view, or to the most extreme version of art for art's sake, as the Symbolists claimed to practice it. In fact, it is a question of human happiness."

"That is so."

"You understand, don't you, that I am lecturing myself also. Who among us will not accept *others'* sacrifice? Giving up our *own* projects, our *own* art in the realization that they must not be based on exploitation of others, since the aim of art should ultimately be moral—that is entirely different."

He nodded.

We were still on the terrace, which had been designed to resemble the deck of a ship; nautical flags fluttered in the night wind, and lights on the river and the opposite bank twinkled as if in reply to some signals we might have made, navigating in the darkness along the currents of thought. A telephone rang in the study behind me; Karl rose to answer it. I could hear his voice through the half-open window, but couldn't make out the German words.

When he returned after a few moments, he did not speak immediately. I got up to lean over the railing and gaze more closely at the water, swirling and dark with its swift motions.

"Strange," he said, finally. "That was Helga herself. It is the first time in many weeks that she has rung me up."

I waited for him to continue, but he seemed to need a prompt. "How curious that she called as we were speaking of her."

"Isn't it? And of course that added to my ... confusion, I guess you would say, or awkwardness. I was startled to hear her voice; I'm not sure now quite what I said, or, rather, how I said it."

"Do you ... I mean, if you wish to go call her back, please do so; don't let my presence interfere." That is a senseless thing to say; being present is never the same as being absent. It was, nevertheless, the best I could do to invite him to conclude our evening, whether he wanted in fact to call her back or simply wished to be alone. I could retire to my room upstairs and read, or, if I wished, stare out at the blackened river and the deep pits of stars.

"No, no. That would displease her greatly anyway; she wishes to—how do you say it?—call the shots."

We nevertheless moved toward tying up for the night, straightening chairs, gathering glasses and plates left from the cocktail hour, and carrying them through the French doors, which Karl locked. I said something about wishing to retire—an extra hour of rest is welcome even days after a transatlantic flight.

"Good night then, Harriet."

After a day or so more in the Wachau Valley, touring other towns, churches, and nearby vineyards and forests, or just reading, conversing, or listening to music—surely to be expected in Austria—we returned to

Vienna. Karl was to leave shortly for an organized architectural tour of Russia, and I had a train ticket for Munich, then Paris. We would spend the last three nights at his Vienna apartment; in the daytime he would make final preparations for his journey, and I would do some sightseeing alone, on foot or by tram or subway.

Not long after we reached his place and he showed me to my room, the telephone rang in his small office. He emerged shortly to tell me that the tour would depart the following day—two days earlier than planned. "It is a bore, really; I hate to abandon a guest like this. But it cannot be helped; everything is arranged and paid for, and my protests against the change of date had no effect. But of course you may stay here just as we planned; the flat is yours."

"Thank you so much, Karl. And do not worry about leaving me; I understand entirely. I will be fine. I'll walk around, go to the museums, and try to get a ticket to the opera one evening. Just give me the keys before you leave and show me how to lock up and do anything else that's necessary. I'll get a taxi to the train station on Friday."

As we were talking, the phone rang again. The office door was open, and I could hear most of Karl's end of the conversation, begun in a normal tone but soon louder. It did not take long to conclude that Helga was on the line. I realized that she had discovered he was entertaining a woman. When she had called him at Krems, it was apparently without knowing I was there; but someone had alerted her in the meanwhile. "Nein, nein," he almost shouted, "eine Freundin, nur eine Freundin; eine amerikanische Frau, die ich vor dreißig Jahren in den Vereinigten Staaten kennengelernt habe." After he reiterated that I was just a friend, that he'd known me in America thirty years before, I could hear him explaining that I was an art historian, interested in Austrian art—true enough, if not quite the whole story. He continued to protest, while she, obviously, continued to accuse him—irrationally, of course, since they were divorced and it was she who had walked out—but nonetheless violently. She clearly knew how to play with him when she wished, holding onto his emotions by the very act of making accusations: she was not an actress for nothing.

There was a short pause, and then I heard him explain that she could *not* come by later in the week to do or get something (it was unclear what) because he would be away. She must have made some threat, or at least intimated that I too would surely be gone. "Nein, sie wird noch zwei Tage hier bleiben." Upon her hearing that I'd stay another two days, further explosions ensued; she seemed unwilling to let go. At last he came back to the salon, where I had sat down.

He did not try to disguise matters. "Pardon all this, please, Harriet. It is dreadful; it is embarrassing for you, I know, and for me, both humiliating and enraging. *That* is the woman I loved, and whom, if truth be told, I should like to win again. I confess I have tried, attempting to be delicate. What a fool I am."

"Did you ever read Balzac's *La Peau de chagrin*? The shagreen, or piece of leather, has magical power to grant wishes, but shrinks each time, shortening thereby the owner's life. Art may be parasitic, as we suggested when we spoke on your deck, feeding on passions and violence, drawing its power from misery of one sort or another, contending against, even draining away morality; but life itself is parasitic too, and our desires, which are like lamps casting light ahead of us, can destroy us if they are fulfilled. Forgive me for saying that if she came back you would be miserable—more than you believe you are now."

"Oh, you are right, you are entirely right. As it is, I feel old. I cannot afford any more ... pain. You are a good friend, Harriet, to suffer this embarrassment with me and let me see things through your eyes—the eyes of common sense."

We spoke no more about Helga, but instead left by tram for the Ringstraße. I visited the Karlskirche and some other monuments while Karl tended to pressing business. That evening we ate at a pseudo-American place near the Schwarzbergstraße, which had on the menu club sandwiches, hamburgers, and something purporting to be chili. Maybe he looked upon the place as relief from the atmosphere of a city now made oppressive by the thought of Helga.

Later that evening, as he was packing, he interrupted his preparations and returned to the salon, where I had turned on a television news program. "Harriet, I shall have to leave early in the morning. No need for you to get up. You will not even hear me go." He gave me the keys and explained a practical thing or so. "Ignore the telephone when it rings—unless you are expecting a call yourself."

"No one will call me in Vienna; I've left no forwarding address and phone number except for my hotel in Paris."

"Good. Now, let me tell you goodbye. Thank you for coming; please come again."

"I am the one who should thank you. The visit has been lovely; you have done a great deal to make Austria memorable for me. Won't you please fly down to New Orleans the next time you are in America?"

"You know that I shall try—although New York, where I usually land, is still not close to you."

"No matter; try to arrange it anyway. Goodnight, Karl, goodbye, and *gute Reise*."

As planned, the next morning he was gone by the time I woke up. He had left everything I needed—breakfast and lunch things, a city map, extra coins, notes on where to catch the trams and find the museums and opera house. After getting my ticket for the next night's performance of *Der Rosenkavalier*, I wandered the streets, stopped at the Central Café, visited St. Stephen's again despite the impediments posed by tourists, beggars, and sidewalk performers, and looked in the shops, admiring the handsome shoes and their handsome prices; the next day, I would stroll through the Volksgarten and do a museum or so. At evening I would have drinks somewhere, then could find easily the same American-style restaurant—appealing, I'll admit, after some heavy Austrian meals. But first I went back to Karl's flat to rest and change; the Viennese eat dinner late anyhow.

While I was there, the telephone rang, and then rang again, persistently. It could be anyone—a colleague, a client, one of his sons, whom he hadn't informed of his premature departure, even Helga, though Karl had said he would be gone. If it was she, she must be trying to speak to me—to find out what I was like, if not to accuse or at least intimidate me. The caller eventually hung up. I was not without misgivings; hysteria is capable of anything. She might call back, perhaps in the middle of the night, and let the telephone ring until I answered, to get some quiet. She would have the advantage—I could hardly defend myself in German.

I dressed and went out, first to a café, then the American restaurant. Returning from dinner, I took the tram, which stopped a few feet from Karl's building. Upstairs, I fumbled a bit with the keys and locks. As I managed to get the door open, I caught a glimpse of a figure inside the apartment, coming along the hallway from the office—Helga, obviously. My heart pounded brutally against my chest, and, as I remember it, I jumped, making an indeterminate sound—a mixture of surprise, fright, indignation. What seemed logical in a way, almost inevitable, fulfilling dramatic expectations—the scene between wife (or ex-wife) and "other woman" (which she erroneously took me to be)—was nevertheless startling. The apartment was strange to me, but at least I had expected no human presence; it had not occurred to me that she might come during the evening, though it wasn't surprising that she had kept a set of keys. Immediately I began speaking in English, not bothering to reflect that she might not understand me. "Good heavens, who are you? (though I knew)—"and what on earth are you doing here? You have frightened the wits out of me!" There was a table by the entry. Not bothering to lock the door from the inside, I threw down the keys and my briefcase. "I am Karl's guest. How dare you come thus and ... and ambush me like this?"

How well she could follow my words I cannot say; the drift must have been clear enough, for I was truly upset. My immediate thought was to wish I had gone to Munich that very morning; perhaps, foregoing my opera plans for the next evening, I could leave right away, on a night train. But as I was wishing this she was already haranguing me, in German, of course; for the moment, I was caught. She told me she was Helga, Karl's wife (maybe she said "ex-wife"); that she knew he had left for Russia and that I was... something, perhaps "dishonorable" (*unehrlich*), and other things I could not follow. I was still standing at the front table, my hand on my briefcase. My knees seemed to be giving way beneath me; but I did not make a move toward the salon—would I want to sit down and discuss things with this deranged woman? As she spoke, I just stared at her. The wine from the evening did not give me courage, exactly, but gradually, as the shock lessened a bit, I felt something like indifference, together with increasing indignation. I also became aware, finally, of her striking appearance—a truly beautiful woman, with a haughty air, almost young-looking despite having grown sons, well-dressed if somewhat too dramatically, with black and red predominating, contrasting with obviously-bleached hair.

At some point, I interrupted her. "I know who you are," I replied in German, "I know all that. I know also that I am Karl's guest, that you and he are no longer married, and that he is free to do as he wishes." My grammar was doubtless not perfect, but the meaning was clear enough. Abruptly I switched to English. "You are talented, he says so himself; you are obviously beautiful; you are theatrical. For God's sake take your acting back to the theatre and leave me alone. Get out of here!" I reached for the doorknob, turned it, and opened the door wide. "Raus! Raus! Leave!"

She cast a strange glance at me; her face was a mask, as of wax. Then, abruptly, the mask melted; what had been smooth and severe decomposed into a mass of trembling flesh, white as tapioca, around two frightened eyes. She uttered a kind of shriek, put her hands to her face (only then did I note she was wearing gloves), and began sobbing.

It all may have been more or less performance; I don't know. What she saw as the uses of art and its relationship to life, and even whether she distinguished between art and life: that was unclear. Karl and I had spoken about the relationship between the two, their osmosis, their tensions; but I doubt that she could have added any rational reflections to our discussion. I ended up showing her out to the landing, walking down the steps with her, more or less leading her into the street, and helping her get into a taxi, providentially free in front of the building. She was incoherent, but I supposed she could give the driver her address. I managed to make it up the stairs again, my knees trembling more than before, my stomach feeling knotted. It would take me at least an hour to get rid of that feeling—as if *I* were the one at fault. Inside the apartment, I closed and locked the door and shoved the table against it; she could have pushed it aside, but seeing it there made me feel better. I did not really expect her to return; the play was over, or at least that scene.

The following day, I went, as planned, to the garden and a museum, visited the Piaristenkirche, and saw *Der Rosenkavalier* in the evening. The phone rang once or twice while I was in the apartment, but not lengthily, and Helga did not come back. On Friday morning I left, suitcase and briefcase in hand, to take the train for Munich, then Paris in a few days. Along the Danube and through the Tyrol, I would see charming country houses, imposing churches, and beautiful and serene landscapes. Inevitably, I would reflect on what was hidden behind them, wondering what passions and griefs and deaths had fed their beauty and tranquility. On Karl's desk I left a note of thanks, merely adding that the opera had been splendid. About Helga, I did not say a word.

A Little Nightcap

THE PINES AND OAKS CANOPIED the grounds, and the soft, moist air of a Florida twilight in spring lingered on our skin. Helium balloons and ribbons in bright colors had been attached to the fences, and on the lawns and lampposts Japanese lanterns glowed with pastel lights. Hibiscus bushes blossomed in reds and yellows, and the white tablecloths were dressed with bouquets of iris, lilies, and other flowers. The sight reminded me of Sargent's "Carnation, Lily, Lily, Rose" in the Tate Gallery; some of the women's dresses, light and filmy, even had ruffles, reminiscent of the gowns of a hundred years before. My own was made of chiffon, in an abstract print, mauve and sea green.

The painterly quality of the spectacle was appropriate, since the event was the opening of a visiting show at the Gulf Coast Museum, south of Tampa, where I was an assistant curator before moving to New Orleans. It was I who, at the Orleanian Institute, had organized this touring exhibit of mid-twentieth-century French painting, with works from our own holdings and many from galleries and private collections in France, New York, and elsewhere. After its initial showing in New Orleans, it was to move to four other locations, including the Gulf Coast Museum, and since I had worked there and still had connections, I had been invited to set it up and, of course, be there for the gala black-tie *vernissage*, which was a small triumph for me, marking my return with a major exhibit I had assembled.

The museum doors were open, but the party had been set up outside. In the crowd gathered around the bars and buffet, I recognized very few people, for some of the staff I had known had left, and, in my former position as assistant, I did not have much to do with donors and other supporters. I didn't know the new director at all. Still, there was the small cluster of friends who had worked with me to arrange the show there. We moved on the grass in small circles, like ice skaters, smiling, shaking hands, returning to the bar to get more ice in our drinks or fresh napkins to replace those turned soggy from the condensation in the moist, sensual air. Having been told that I had done the show and catalogue, several people whom I didn't recognize came to speak to me. My greetings were mostly casual: "Oh, hello, nice to see you again; thanks for coming to the opening" or "I hope you will enjoy the exhibit." A few people had actually been inside already and made appreciative comments.

Among those standing near one of the bars was Mavis Watson. She had joined the curatorial staff of the museum about the same time I had. I had been warned by my friend Louise Garfield that she was still around, though, given her shortcomings, how she kept her position was a mystery. The museum had major holdings in Baroque art, which was supposedly her field; but when I was there her work had not been equal to the collection it was supposed to publicize, and Louise had told me that recently she had done almost nothing. Her weaknesses were both intellectual and personal: lack of true understanding of what she should be doing, lack of commitment, and—the worst—a bad case of lunacy, combining paranoia with what I took to be schizophrenia. We had often said that there were many inmates in the state asylum fitter than she to work in the outer world. Yet I never believed that she was *entirely* without responsibility for her actions; you could sometimes see her mind clicking, sorting through lemons and apples and oranges like a slot machine and trying to arrange them to her advantage. With me, she had been saccharine-sweet on some occasions, aloof or downright nasty on others; you never knew.

"Well," I said *sotto voce* to Louise and another acquaintance standing near, "there's Mavis; I need to go talk to her, but shall be circumspect. Better to get this over with; I'll come find you later."

So I moved over to the bar, got a half-refill, and popped a small sandwich into my mouth, chewing and swallowing it hastily. Then I turned to Mavis, standing alone. She had an absent-minded, distant look. We had been colleagues; I had to say something. "Mavis, how are you?"

"Well, Harriet, fancy having you back!" (She had known, of course—unless she had paid no attention—that I'd be there for the opening of the show.) Throwing back her head a bit, she gave a little laugh. Her voice was high, nasal, artificial. Her dishwater-blond hair was done, as before, in a bun, but at least she had put on makeup and for once looked less like an old maid and a bit younger than her thirty-five years or so. Thin lips, the bun, the tweed suits she often wore, and a rather otherworldly air she put on had contributed to my image of her as the type of the Presbyterian preacher's wife; but that evening, in a blue gown, with jewelry and lipstick in a camellia-pink shade, she did have some femininity about her. I wasn't sure quite how to answer her sweet-and-sour greeting.

"And it's very nice to be here and to see everyone again. The grounds look lovely for this event. Are you enjoying it?"

"Yes, as much as I enjoy any of these events. You know my private life is what really interests me. My life, you know, is very intense. *Some* people even think that I have affairs."

That was just like Mavis—to dramatize herself, speak needlessly of personal matters, without any lead-in, and call attention to what should have embarrassed her. Her sense of reality was clearly inadequate; she had no understanding of how this sounded to others. In the matter of her private life, she was telling the truth all right, and not merely in the way in which most of us could say, at any time, that our personal concerns were paramount. And, regarding the purported affairs, she understated the matter: when I was at the museum, it was common knowledge that she pursued men, almost always younger, and had liaisons, often torrid but not lasting. She was known for frequenting the Cuban-American community of Tampa, and not its higher layers. I'm not sure how she met these men—probably in bars. Why she chose Cubans wasn't clear to anyone; she was certainly not of Cuban extraction herself, nor did she even speak much Spanish.

Perhaps what attracted her was what she saw as their insecurity. Ybor City, the Cuban section of Tampa, is old and well established, but, since the Castro regime established itself, there have been influxes of newcomers, many of them of the lower classes and ill-educated; and some of them were, in a word, easy prey for a professional woman who might offer them, they supposed, various advantages. She couldn't have much self-confidence, surely, if she needed to look for men in social circles so different from her own. I'd seen her myself, once, eating at the Columbia restaurant with a dark-skinned man, distinctly her junior, who looked uncomfortable in a jacket and tie. Some years before, I recalled, she had gone after a football player at the university at Gainesville, one who certainly was no star and wasn't a good student either, and thus didn't appear to have much of a future; only the intervention of the coach had made her desist.

With Mavis, one often felt that conversation was not quite real—something more like a tentative draft of a script, or a rehearsal where one actor was missing. It was difficult to answer her; but I had to say something. "Of course," I replied breezily, "our personal lives engage us the most; isn't that true for us all? Still, this profession we exercise is one of the most interesting, isn't it? We work with things that, for us, have meaning. And because of that, our professional and personal lives are close—unlike those of, say, an assembly-line worker. How fortunate we are. That doesn't mean, I'll concede, that all these receptions and other events are scintillating!"

"As a matter of fact," she added in a rather distracted way, "I am looking for ... someone. *So* good to see you, Harry." She pursed her lips a bit as she spoke; then she turned away and walked off under some trees. Not a word about the exhibit. That was all right; I didn't wait on praise from her.

Twilight was turning into early darkness; the Japanese lanterns looked brighter. Waiters turned on low lights along the walkways and lit hurricane lamps on the larger tables. Among the small swirls of bodies, a few more people spoke to me, and then I went to find Louise and my other friends. They were near the entranceway. As we stood chatting, I noticed a young black man, wearing a suit, coming from the parking lot. He seemed a bit uncertain. There were other people there of black or Hispanic descent, of course, but mostly couples. Louise, happening to turn then, saw him.

"Goodness, that's Mavis's latest."

"What do you mean?" I hadn't quite heard.

"That's the man Mavis has been seen with recently. In fact, it's been going on for a while, and it's quite dramatic—more so than usual."

Robert somebody—I hadn't caught the name, but a new colleague of Louise to whom I'd been rapidly introduced earlier—had come up next to us, with his wife. "You're right!" He explained, in low tones, that the news was all over the museum. "The fellow tried to break off with her—probably a little frightened of her, or realizing that such an arrangement could do little for him, ultimately, and was making him look like a fool at home or with his friends; but she wouldn't agree."

"How could she prevent it? I mean, if he wanted to break off ..."

"We don't know. She must have something on him. All of this we have had to put together, from bits and pieces—what little we've seen, things she has mentioned, usually in that enigmatic way of hers, and what others have said; there's someone on the staff who apparently knows his family. So, after we hadn't seen them together for a while, he's started showing up again—I mean, in public with her."

The man had left the walkway by then and was crossing the lawn toward the bar. Of course he knew no one but Mavis. I had never thought of her as a sex siren, but perhaps she had magnetism I hadn't been able to identify, to which men responded strongly; maybe they wanted to see her take off that tweed suit uniform. I reflected, too, how the strong animal urge of men to mate—something entirely natural to them, inherited from the survival behavior of ancestors eons ago—often makes them vulnerable to predatory or simply silly women, whose superficial appeal draws them into a net of social, sentimental, or financial difficulties from which extrication is nearly impossible, or who end up by making them look like fools. They too are creatures of biology, and one has to feel for them.

"This would be comic," said Louise, "if it weren't basically unfortunate; she takes advantage of these fellows, and then usually drops them. She'll get tired of him after a while, probably, and then end the affair. It's really a type of exploitation. Meanwhile, she hasn't been easy to live with."

In a moment or so we saw the two of them, in the light cast by some Japanese lanterns among the pines. They were walking slowing toward us, heading for the building, probably. They were holding hands, though the man looked ill at ease. Heaven only knew what absurdities Mavis might tell him about the paintings, or any of us. Her expression was odd, suggesting some mania or possession by a force she didn't understand. As they passed by, Robert, his wife, and Louise all said some undistinguished words of greeting to Mavis, and I smiled again. Robert put her on the spot. "Going in to show your guest the exhibit, Mavis?"

"No, we are going in for a little *nightcap.*" The word, as she spoke it, sounded as if it were in quotation marks. What on earth did she mean? Drinks weren't being served inside; the only bars were outdoors. The man wasn't even carrying a glass; I guess she hadn't gotten a drink for him.

"Louise," I asked after they passed us, "do you think she has a bottle of brandy or something like that in her office? What could she mean, otherwise, since the bars are out here?"

"I can't imagine. Maybe she does have a bottle, something better than what's out here, though usually she acts as if the rest of us are alcoholics when we have a cocktail or so. You know how erratic and strange she is. Her office must have lots of surprises in it—one part utilitarian, with books and papers, one part sybaritic—she's gotten a new chaise longue and a small Oriental carpet. Remember, Harry, you used to call it the *capharnaüm.*"

We continued talking and circulating a bit, picking up hors-d'oeuvres and sandwiches from trays, getting some more ice, shaking a few hands and smiling generally. I made a point of standing for several minutes near the director, Arnold Porchon, so that, if there were any important patrons whom he wanted to flatter by introducing them to a visiting curator from New Orleans, he could do so. I wondered whether Louise, who had invited me to stay with her and thus spared the museum the expense of a hotel room, might wish to make her final rounds and leave. As I approached the circle where she stood, there was a noise from the building behind me—the sound of an engine backfiring or something exploding. It was immediately followed by another. It took me several seconds to realize that those must be gunshots.

"Louise! Did you hear that?" (Of course everyone did, even those so engrossed in their own talk that no other human speech could have reached their ears.)

"That's gunfire!" exclaimed Robert.

Movements, cries, shouts, jostling animated the crowd in an instant. Some men ran along the walkway, up the steps, and through the entrance. Guards from the regular museum staff who had been at the door, plus some policemen who had been hired, since the crowds were large and the entire museum was open, had already darted inside. I supposed—since *some* supposition had to be made—that there had been a robbery attempt, perhaps of one of the paintings in the visiting exhibit, for which I was responsible.

"Good heavens! If anything happens to one of the paintings lent for the exhibit it will be a disaster! Think of the repercussions for your museum, for mine, for me... Most of those canvases are on loan to us from Europe or New York. Everything's entirely insured, as you know. Still, those works are, strictly speaking, priceless."

Louise followed my thoughts, a bit melodramatic but not implausible. "A robbery, maybe. I suppose some thief thought that a party, when people were milling about everywhere, would be the ideal time for an attempt. Even if he's caught—maybe the policemen or guards have him right now—well, the canvas could be cut out, or torn, or even have a bullet in it."

It was true that certain paintings on loan were small, and there was no alarm system or other technical security, just that of guards, so that a robbery attempt did not seem fantastic, especially given the publicity this opening reception had gotten and the number of misfits and street criminals in every populous area, especially a port. I put down my drink on a nearby campaign table and started walking toward the steps of the building, but I didn't intend to enter until things got cleared up: no point in getting in the way if security personnel were trying to get someone under control. From the building came tremendous noises of banging. Some guests were hurrying to the parking lot and getting in their cars; others milled about nervously, the way cattle must be before a stampede, all twitching and making noises. There was more coming and going on the museum steps. Leaving his wife with Louise and me, Robert started walking toward the entrance.

Suddenly we saw guards and policemen silhouetted against the light from the open foyer of the building, yelling to each other and motioning to the small crowd gathered at the door to get back. It still wasn't clear at all what was going on. Robert moved up a few steps, trying to get a better look and catch their words. Porchon, meanwhile, who must have been standing at the far side of the lawn, hurried past us as fast as his little porcine legs would allow (I reflected how well his name fit him), calling out, "Here I am!" as though they had been asking for him. Waddling in his tight tuxedo, he got his hams up the steps. Robert came down after a moment and reported to us that he had heard a guard say, "They've called an ambulance. And someone is trying now to find a couple of blankets, or at least a raincoat ...," and then Porchon disappeared inside.

I don't know how many minutes passed before an ambulance appeared in the circular drive to our left, where a *porte cochère* gave access to a wing. There was more commotion on that side as the paramedics got out, but we could still hear shouting from the main foyer. Since no more shots had been fired, I decided that, on the grounds that I was the curator of the exhibit, I could try to inquire about the incident. Louise, Robert, and his wife all followed me up the steps. As we got to the landing at the top, in front of the open doors, we saw a most extraordinary sight: Mavis's paramour pushed by the paramedics on a guerney through the lobby toward the *porte cochère*, and Mavis herself pulled along, unwillingly, by three policemen, with museum guards right behind. She still had on the high heels she had worn for the party and was attempting to dig them into the floor as she was being dragged. But instead of a dress, she was clad in an oversized man's mackintosh.

We heard more shouting from the officers: "Get her into the squad car!" "Come along or we will charge you also with resisting arrest!" "Out of the way—get everyone out of the way!"

From Mavis herself came volleys of words, in her high, whining voice. "Let me go! *He* did it! He's the one you should arrest!"

I supposed that one of them had tried to vandalize a painting; odd for an art historian, but with Mavis anything was possible. Still, that wouldn't explain the body and stretcher, unless the guards had fired... I couldn't intervene at the moment, but as soon as the group was past me and down the steps I spoke to a guard who remained. "Has there been some sort of attack on paintings in the exhibit? I am the curator for this touring show, in charge of everything, most of it on loan from France and New York."

"No," he explained, "nothing has happened to the art work. It's just this woman." He gestured to Mavis, now being escorted against her will to a police car in the parking lot.

Robert asked the guard, "What happened—what did she do? We saw the man carried out on the stretcher." And he added briefly that he also was on the museum staff.

"Oh yes, I recognize you, Mr. Lejeune. She attacked that man in her office—I mean, shot him with a shotgun—through the neck and shoulder."

"Good God!" two or three of us said at once. Robert added, "He isn't dead, is he?

"No, just wounded and bleeding badly. I can't say how serious it might be. You know who she is, don't you? That woman in office 120—I can't remember her name."

"Mavis Watson," Louise said.

"Yes, that's the one. She shot him. The door was locked; we had to break the frame around the bolt to get in. He was lying on a sort of couch she's got in there. She must have whipped out that shotgun and fired before he could do anything. Oh, I should add that apparently he was holding a glass, and dropped it. There was a bottle of whiskey on the desk. When we broke in, she was standing in the corner, crying ... Mr. Lejeune, and you, ladies" (he looked at me, then at Louise), "I'm sorry to say this, it's shameful for the museum, but she was standing there in her underwear."

"But did he try to attack her?" I asked. "You know... Maybe she shot him in self-defense."

"Well, of course the police will have to determine that, or the courts. But I can tell you now that her dress and some other things were folded neatly on the desk, with some jewelry lying on top. He certainly hadn't ripped off her clothes. And from what I could see she didn't look injured—I mean, she hadn't been cut or bruised. He didn't have any weapon—there's nothing in the office but the shotgun—which she's not supposed to have, as you know: firearms are strictly forbidden on museum property except for the security staff. Now they've sealed the room, of course."

It was too extraordinary: even when someone is unstable, we are always astonished, almost incredulous, when some gesture or words that we long sensed aborning and dreaded finally come out. It was difficult to take it all in. But I thanked the guard for informing us, and we started down the steps, as the ambulance drove away with the siren screaming. It was clear that the party had come to an end: what would otherwise have been a tapering off, as glasses were emptied and the waiters stopped refilling trays, had been terminated abruptly and dramatically. Louise and I had planned simply to return home after the reception was over, but as we walked with Robert and his wife to our cars they invited us to follow them and go to their house for coffee—"or something stronger, if you think you need it, as you well may." At least I didn't need to say goodbye to the director, who was still inside.

We spent a couple of hours drinking coffee and brandy and going over the evening's events, trying to piece them together, exclaiming about Mavis's extraordinary behavior. The trouble is, we were rational people, attempting to make sense of irrationality; it didn't work well. The next morning, at Louise's house, I saw that the newspaper didn't mention the event; fortunately, it had occurred too late, after the paper had been put to bed. Louise, like the rest of the staff, had to go to her office. Since I had one free day before returning to New Orleans, I had planned to drive in a rented car down to Sarasota and St. Armand's Key, but I postponed starting out until she telephoned me with more news.

Of course, as Louise later told me, there was talk of nothing else at the museum. By late morning, she called with a report. The man Mavis had attacked was in stable condition at a hospital and expected to recover completely: neither the neck nor shoulder wound was deep. No charges had been filed against him. The preliminary investigation had revealed no signs of struggle, no injuries at all to her such as strangulation marks, lesions, bruises, cuts. Nothing that could have served as a weapon for him, not even a bookend, seemed to have been touched. Mavis was in police custody, charged with multiple offenses: attempted murder, assault with a deadly weapon, inflicting grievous bodily harm, and illegal possession of a firearm.

"What about this business of her being undressed? Was she trying to seduce him?"

"Apparently. Remember that I told you he had tried, unsuccessfully, to break off their relationship. Why he came back last night—and to this public event!—isn't known, but he may have chosen this moment to tell her again that he wouldn't go on with it. She tried ... changing his mind, and when that didn't work, she shot him. A different explanation is that, fearing she was losing him, she had plotted all along to kill him then—for that's what the police are persuaded she tried to do. She probably thought he would bleed to death from that neck wound. She got undressed to make it look as if he tried to rape her. No one knows how long she'd had that shotgun in her office. The preliminary police report, which Arnold has gotten wind of somehow, with his connections, concludes that she took off her own clothes—before she fired the shotgun, or maybe afterwards, since a few minutes passed before the police broke down the door. They'll do tests on the dress to see what it shows."

"Do you recall that strange comment she made as they were going inside—something about a nightcap?"

"Yes, I do. Furthermore, she repeated it to the police, it seems—saying that is what they were doing when he, supposedly, jumped her. 'I just wanted a nightcap,' or some such phrase. Perhaps it was a code word for—well, either for making love, or for what she planned to do. She is *so crazy*; she has always thought people were plotting against her, and here she cooks up this plot against that man, whom she may have tricked into coming. For all I know, she'd be capable of offering him money. The police didn't want to disturb her folded dress and half-slip; that's why they wrapped her in a man's raincoat, which a guard found in the main office."

"Has Porchon tried to get in touch with the newspaper and television stations—to hush it up or at least make it seem less ... degrading? A scandal such as this is not good for a museum. Just think of what the 'angels' are going to say—whether they were there or not. And it's bad publicity with the general public, which already thinks of the art world as ... you know, strange. They won't distinguish between Mavis and the rest of you, and the argument that she's plain crazy won't help."

"Well, I imagine that Arnold has called the editor and news directors, though what will come of his efforts I don't know; the newspaper here pulls its punches with the university and the museum, but I don't have confidence in the television stations."

"Well, whoever she gets as a lawyer is in for it. Trying to defend a *rational* person who's charged with a felony—I mean, one who is more or less sane from day to day, even if he lost control at some moment or just *wished* to commit a crime—that's one thing. With Mavis, how could one establish a defense? She cannot cooperate with anyone, including her own lawyer, probably, and she's had delusions as long as we've known her. Insanity will be the defense, I suppose—and it wouldn't be inaccurate. I'll have to come back for the trial, if you'll invite me!"

I said that in jest, but in fact, I did return—though not as a witness, for there were many others who had seen and talked to Mavis that evening and knew her habits and could quote her. I just used the trial as an excuse to myself, having been pleased to renew contact with Louise, who again invited me to stay with her, and telling myself that a few days on the West Coast of Florida in the autumn could be very pleasant. During the trial, at which Louise, Robert Lejeune, Arnold Porchon, and numerous others testified for the state, the prosecution argued, very convincingly, we thought, that Mavis had lured the man, who was a gardener and whose name turned out to be Orlando García, into the office with the express intent of killing him, and had set up the whole scene to make it appear an act of self-defense. (*Orlando*! Maybe because the name made her think of *Orlando Furioso* and thus of the Italian Renaissance and Baroque.) The state's attorney was able to cite numerous facts to support the charge of attempted murder, among them, the angle and distance at which the bullets had entered his body, which indicated that she had not shot him while he was attacking her physically. García family members were especially useful in the box, and García himself, entirely recovered, testified against her.

All the evidence was in favor of conviction on all counts. The only possibility her lawyer would have had for arguing that the shooting was an act of self-defense—that García was blackmailing Mavis, using threats rather than physical force against her—was apparently deemed weak, in light of the absence of any evidence, and in any case, blackmail doesn't justify assault. Having very little on which to build a case, the attorney persuaded her to change her plea to guilty by reason of insanity. The way she had chosen a public place and a public occasion for liquidating her lover, and her obvious naïveté about how the crime would appear to investigating authorities, made that plea entirely plausible; the only surprising thing is that the lawyer got her to agree. Perhaps, as I had thought, she really could make distinctions when they were in her immediate interest as she saw it; he'd persuaded her that she'd be convicted, and the state hospital sounded better to her than prison.

The museum would have to hire a new Baroque Painting specialist. "Perhaps it will be someone competent this time," Louise observed to me, "without a shotgun. For all we know, she might have shot one of us sometime!"

"I wonder," I mused, "whether the doctors can do anything for her; she always seemed like a hopeless case. But who knows? Meanwhile, she may end up giving lectures to her fellow inmates; you'll open the paper one day and see a headline such as: 'Criminally Insane Women Benefit from Courses in Baroque Painting.' Well, if she does something for them it will be more than she ever did here! They might even get college credit that they can apply to a degree if they ever get out! Therapy and credit too!"

Dora's Dying

THE FRANKLIN MOUNTAINS were as dry and brown as usual when I flew into El Paso; with rare exceptions, when there has been unusual rainfall and the desert has taken on green, they are the same throughout the year. I noticed yellow leaves on the maples and other imported trees planted along the road leading from the airport. I had picked up my rented car and was driving toward the Airport Holiday Inn, a convenient place to stay on this visit, since it was not far from the hospital where Dora was confined. I would need the car not only to go there, but to visit an old friend of my mother's, still alive, and my one remaining friend from high school days, who lived in Las Cruces. I would also go by the cemetery where my parents were buried.

Aunt Dora—really Dorothy Kathleen—was not my blood aunt; she was the widow of my mother's brother Joe. She had come to the Southwest from Ireland by way of Canada, and had married Joe, though she was ten or so years younger than he. But by the time I am speaking of she was the only family I had left, outside of my McDonald cousins in Colorado and my daughter; what was more important, *I* was the only one *she* had left. Joe had died many years before; they had never had children. Later, she had remarried, and that husband, C.J., also was deceased. She had continued working at the bank where she and Joe had met. Her one stepson lived in Washington State. As for her own family back in Ireland, I think there was no one but a brother. So, in practice, I was the closest thing she had to a relative anywhere near home. When I was a child, she was good and generous to me, and she had followed with interest my career as a painter and art historian. She always referred to me "my niece," and the affection was, I'm sure, genuine.

In earlier years she had written regularly to me, but that had ended, since arthritis in her hand and wrist made writing difficult.

217

Then I started telephoning her frequently so I could find out how she was. At age eighty, she had cleared out her house and moved into an assisted-living place. She had been told that there were incipient heart problems, and often she complained of having little strength. In the previous weeks, her voice on the telephone had been feeble. "Aunt Dora, how are you?" I would inquire.

A sort of timid squeak was all I could hear; sometimes I imagined she was saying "All right."

If it was the right time of day, I would ask, "Have you had your lunch? Did you have a good meal today?"

The answer, again, was feeble, but she never said that the meal had been good. Sometimes I asked whether she had any appetite, whether her arthritis was bothering her, or whether she had watched a baseball game on television. Uncle Joe had followed the sport and she had often watched games with him; a Cubs' game on the cable from WGN might entertain her.

Two weeks before, when I dialed her number, I got a nurse, who told me that Dora was not doing well. She was going into the adjacent hospital that very afternoon, for tests.

I could not suppress a remark: "Well, I hope the tests won't kill her. She's not strong, you know."

"These tests are necessary," the nurse answered, in a rather snappish manner.

"I know, I know," I said. I wasn't convinced that doctors might not subject her to Nazi-like torture just to get more data for their articles, but didn't want to vex the nurse, who might be in a position to help or hinder Dora. I asked a few practical questions and hung up, resolved to go spend a week or so with her. That could be arranged, since at the museum I usually have accumulated vacation time. A later call confirmed that she had undergone certain procedures, that more were coming up, and that there was no prospect of her going back to her apartment soon. So, having arranged to be away ten days, there I was on a Sunday afternoon in El Paso, checking into the Holiday Inn, then studying my old map to be sure I could find the hospital. It had been so many years since I had lived there as a girl that the city was barely recognizable. Still, the Franklin Mountains and the river were where they were supposed to be, along with Fort Bliss, the Sun Bowl, and Cuidad Juárez; I would find my way around.

It was already 4:00 by then. I called the hospital and asked to speak to Dora—who had been informed of my coming visit—and was told she was unavailable, whatever that might mean in those circumstances. It would be better, the speaker said, for me to go see her the next morning, since dinner was to be served shortly (I doubted she would eat much) and then the place would close up for the night. Meanwhile, I could take a swim, get a drink, and have dinner.

The next morning, I drove over about 9:00, thinking that breakfast and consultations would be over. Dora had a double room; though the beds were separated by sheet curtains, they were open. Dora was by the window, fortunately; I passed by the other bed without looking at its occupant.

"Aunt Dora!" I said, cheerfully, as I entered the room.

"Oh Harriet, my dear, thank you so much for coming. You have made my day." (The expression, now so famous, was droll in her mouth.)

"How are you? Are they treating you right here?"

"Well, as you see, I'm not very well, or I wouldn't be here!" She gave a little laugh; her sense of humor was always keen. "I am so weak; in the last few weeks, I could barely walk. I thought it was arthritis, but the doctors think it's something else, since they keep poking my insides." (Later, I realized that she too suspected something grave but had hidden it.)

"Have you eaten anything here?" She was always small, with a bird-like appetite; now she seemed like a child, whom one must try to feed.

"Not much, dearie. The food on the tray usually looks awful—some unrecognizable main course with an awful gravy poured over it."

"In college we called that 'mystery meat.'"

She chuckled again. "And the vegetables have no color or taste. There's not much fresh fruit. The nurse brings me orange juice in the morning, even though I've told them I'm allergic to it! I usually eat the Jello, a little bouillon in the afternoon, sometimes a little piece of cake. That is, when they'll let me eat at all. Sometimes I'm fasting before a test, or sick after one."

"What sort of things are they doing to you? What are they looking for?"

"I have no idea, dearie. You know, the patient is always the last to know."

"I shall try to find out for you. Are you strong enough for me to stay here a while today?"

"Oh yes; I feel better just having you here."

"Do you have to have any more procedures now?"

"Not today, at least. Yesterday they put me to the wheel."

So I spent the morning there; I straightened her things a bit for her and gave the nurse a lecture concerning the orange juice. When lunchtime came, around 11:00, I sat with Dora and encouraged her to take a few bites; then I went down to the coffee shop on the ground floor to get a sandwich for myself.

When I returned, Dora's roommate was talking to her. Dora had not been able to confide to me what she thought of her; but I had caught some coolness in her attitude toward the woman, who was big, with coarse features and an outsized stomach, which created an obscene bump under the sheet. She had a large mole near her mouth. I crossed the room to Dora's side and sat, listening to the woman's babble, directed toward us. The drift wasn't clear at first—something about neighbors—but after a while she moved to the topic of religion, making some reference to her preacher at the Temple of the Pillar of Fire. She carried on for a while in a fundamentalist vein. "God heals," I heard then. Very well, doubtless; but He seems to call on therapeutics and pharmacopoeia as intermediaries. Meanwhile, she and Dora and all the others there had diseases or dysfunctions. "I have faith. Do you have faith? Have you been *washed*?"

In that setting, the word was so comical that I wanted to laugh, or make a crack about the nurse's having come by with a wet cloth, at least. But this was Dora's scene, not mine; I was at the periphery and should remain there.

Dora waited a moment, then replied: "I may very well be dying—I think I am. But even dying, I do not answer personal questions from someone I barely know."

A silence followed; then the woman reached up to the sheet curtain, grabbed it at the edge, and jerked it around the ceiling track, closing off her bed from our view.

Later that afternoon, a clergyman came in, wearing a clerical collar. He was rotund in a middle-aged way, sandy-haired, somewhat ruddy in complexion, and had sky-blue eyes. He came over to Dora's bedside and announced that he was Father Flaherty, from St. Patrick's Church. He was Irish, all right; his name was matched by his accent, stronger than Dora's, which had been eroded by years in the Southwest.

I supposed he'd gotten the wrong room, but he continued, "You are Dorothy Kathleen Garrick, aren't you?"

Dora answered, with a disarming directness, "Yes. But I'm not RC."

"I know that, but I've come anyway." It turned out that she had written "Church of Ireland" in the "religion" blank on the admissions card. She had done it, I supposed, because it was, strictly speaking, the truth, but also because it would keep ministers of God from coming round; she was so independent in thought and manner that she and organized religion were a poor fit. It occurred to me that she might be especially impatient with any visitor of the cloth after she had been obliged to endure the roommate's babble about faith. But that turned out not to be so.

The priest continued. "I know you're Protestant—Church of Ireland. But I thought that you might let me pay a call anyway; at least I'm *from* Ireland."

"So I hear. I should thank you, and I do. I'm usually called Dora, by the way. And this is my niece, Harriet D'Aquin, from New Orleans."

The good man and I shook hands. "Call me Harry. I'm originally from West Texas; I grew up right here; I can even put on the accent." And I showed him.

I wondered what would happen next: would he attempt to proselytize Dora? dwell on her illness and demoralize her? speak condescendingly, as people do to children, the deaf, the aged, the crippled? (The nurse, for instance, had asked, like a bimbo waitress, "And how are *we* today?"—a question to which the only sensible answer is "I don't know about *you,* but I'm well"—or whatever applies.)

Oh, no. Instead, Dora and the Reverend Mr. Flaherty entered into a delightful exchange of pleasantries and reminiscences, centered on Connemara, County Clare, the river Shannon, and the Ring of Kerry. Soon they were telling Irish jokes; he even recited a limerick. Dora's spirits, which were already better when I was in the room than on the telephone, seemed to rise even more.

Finally she said, "Now, don't tell me any more jokes. I've laughed so hard my sides hurt."

So we talked about Dora's marriages, and life in West Texas, and how a Flaherty from Ireland had gotten there and how he could stand living without mist, rain, and green fields. "Ah, the Lord's work, the Lord's ways!" he exclaimed. "You know, Saint Patrick lived in Ireland, but Our Savior didn't; He was over there in the desert, almost like ours here, where the soil is recalcitrant, the sun burns, and a river is a miracle."

"How familiar some of those Biblical things seem to me," said Dora. "The milk was probably goats' milk, which many of the Mexicans still have around here, and the honey—perhaps it was like our cat's-claw honey, the most fragrant I know, from wild bees. As for balms and perfumes—you know, the ointment Mary poured on Christ's feet— some of them may have been made from sage and desert flowers."

"When I think of Christ preaching by the wayside," I mused aloud, "I imagine Him in a grove, but not composed of the giant oaks of Louisiana, or huge, pagan pines, but instead smaller, thoughtful trees, both delicate and tough, with deep roots—mesquite or huisache."

Dora added, "Yes, and He walked in sand. What a pleasure the oases must have been, with their underground streams or wells. You know, with cactuses, a few small trees, ornamental rocks, and a well and sprinkler, I learned finally to create my own oasis here. That is how I conceive of redemption—water welling up, refreshing earth, creating life anew, everywhere."

It was striking how Dora's image echoed the roommate's peremptory question about being washed. There are only few truths, I suppose; the style in which they are expressed is everything.

Dora reflected a moment, then asked, "But how did Saint Patrick and Saint Columba get their converts in Ireland and Scotland to picture the wilderness of Palestine? How could *they* imagine it?"

"They gestured to the moors and the peat bogs," the priest suggested.

It was a lovely image—the ex-slave and the prince of the O'Donnells, missionaries to the Gaels, preaching the gospel to the heathen, beside the heath, using their humble experiences to help them imagine new ones. Father Flaherty's manner was somewhat similar: to find the paths that were already there, and walk down them with someone, disclosing new ways of seeing.

A nurse came in; it was time for Dora's late afternoon medication. Father Flaherty bade Dora goodbye, and I followed, promising to return the next morning—earlier, so that when the doctors came I could be there to try to interpret their delphic pronouncements and press for more precise information.

It was a good thing I was around on Tuesday morning when one of the team came by. (Later I asked Dora whether he was her chief physician. "Oh, I don't know," she answered. "You can't tell who is in charge. The doctors come and go, all looking and talking alike, with no explanation about why they've come instead of someone else.") The fellow, dressed in a white lab coat, of course, with a stethoscope and some other gadgets poking out of his pocket, spoke in a brusque manner. He inquired who I was.

Dora answered, "My niece."

"Your blood niece? It says on this sheet that you have no blood relatives in the United States."

"That is true, but she's my niece anyway; I've always considered her so."

"Well," he said, turning to me, "you'll have to leave; I need to talk to this lady alone."

I do hate it when people use the word *lady* that way; what's wrong with *woman*? Of course Dora *was* a lady, in the true sense, but I doubt that he was refined enough to recognize it, and anyway it's not his place to judge.

I thought of protesting about having to leave—not on my account but for Dora, who would certainly wish to have me there; but instead I stepped outside, then decided to go downstairs and get coffee in a carry-out cup. When I returned, the fellow had gone. I sat beside Dora and put my cup on her table. She looked at me, rather strangely, it seemed, and said, "Harriet, bad news. I've got cancer, all through my middle; it's eating me up from the inside."

"Oh, Aunt Dora, dear Aunt Dora! Oh, that's terrible. Tht's what the doctor told you? How do they know?"

"Well, all these tests—tests where they dye my blood or fill my bowels with chemicals and put me in a machine to be x-rayed, tests on blood samples, probes put into me, biopsies, and who knows what else."

"I'm so sorry! That's awful." I put my hand on her arm, thin as a small girl's, and rubbed it, back and forth, as though that gesture could impart through her skin a bit of my own vitality. "What ... can be done? You couldn't stand surgery; it would kill you faster than the cancer."

"But that's what this doctor says they'll do—cut me open, take out my intestines, part of my stomach ..."

Her stomach was already barely working. What part they left would shrivel up. A radical removal of the intestines would be worse. The cancer was probably lurking elsewhere, anyway, and that would mean radiation and chemotherapy, which can scarcely be endured by even a strong person. Besides, she probably wouldn't be able to bear the surgery; just the anesthesia might kill her. You don't have to be trained in medicine to see when a body can be broken like a bundle of dry sticks.

"Aunt Dora, do you want the doctors to operate?"

"No, I don't want it. I said so. I don't even have time for anger and revolt. I've seen your uncle Joe die, and C.J., and my own father before I left Ireland; one recognizes when the end is coming. But the doctor says the operation is *needed*. In truth, I don't have many more needs—maybe what I really need is death."

"You sounded better yesterday, though, when you were talking with Father Flaherty and laughing at his jokes."

"Yes, but I knew something serious was wrong; I've felt it for a while—a bit, I guess, like a dog that knows he's dying."

Dora reported a few details of her cancer and the proposed operation and therapy. She hadn't been told much, really. I persuaded her to give some reflection to the surgery and to consider accepting it, despite everything. Meanwhile, I resolved to seek out the sawbones in his lair and get more information, especially his prognostic for recovery. Finding him was difficult; getting information was impossible. He was less amenable even than when he'd been in Dora's room. He kept taking refuge in the pretext that I was not of blood kinship to Dora.

"But since she has no one else?"

"That makes no difference. You have no right to her medical information and you cannot advise her."

"Well, about the information you may be right, at least until she names me her agent; but I *can* and *shall* advise her."

It occurred to me that he might accuse me, then or later, of practicing medicine without a license, because I spoke of *advice*; but, though cocky, he cared about his time and was not going to run after that hare.

It was not too late to return to the hospital room. Dora and I talked the matter over. Just to understand, she resolved to insist on getting a fuller account of her disease and share it with me; yet she also said that she was loath to undergo hours of surgery, no matter what she was told. "It is my life; I should decide. Let no one speak of murder. This is not a matter of abortion or euthanasia; it's a question of dying, in the natural course of things, and *how* I want to die."

On Wednesday she showed further resolve about the surgery. Not sleeping well anyway, she had reflected on it again during the night. She would not give permission, she said, for any radical measures.

"I still have my wits about me! An operation will not save me now, Harriet; or, if it does, it will save me simply for further treatment—days of drugs, and radiation, and misery. My body is not up to it. Operating on someone in her mid-eighties, with a weak heart, devoured by cancer... what good will that do?"

"I wish that were not so. But I understand ..."

"My life seems now to have acquired its shape, including its end, from the young woman that I was until now. Strange that I should see it that way, complete; for often it has appeared to me as a failed design, with its possibilities only half-fulfilled—my coming here; my marriage to Joe; the vagueness of our middle years; two husbands' deaths; aging and disappointment—not just that we had no children, Joe and I, but also, with C. J. ...he was very mean-spirited, tyrannical, miserly of words and gestures and soul, because *his* life had not been very well fulfilled either."

"Old men are so often that way. The dreams they dreamt as boys and young men become hollow; those around them must pay."

"But it makes little difference now. Adding days and weeks will not change anything. What do you think, dearie?"

"I think that you are right to see your life whole, and close it as best you can. *You* must find its meaning. Think of all the paintings that I live among at the museum. The colors, lines, and textures are givens; but the eye is the essential thing. If the Neo-Platonists were right in saying that the eyes are the windows of the soul, don't truths pass in the other direction also, the sense of the world moving inward through images, which we make ours? But *we* do the interpretation."

Dora sighed, less at my philosophy, I think, than at her own reflections and resolution, which had taken courage and had fatigued her. You could see, though, that she had been a reader. "I'll be back tomorrow," I assured her; "don't let them cut on you meanwhile. Just take your medicine, try to be comfortable, and eat something; ask for a second Jello if you can stand it."

That evening, I went to see my mother's old friend, and called my chum in Las Cruces to arrange something for the weekend, when she and her husband would be free. The following day—it was Thursday by then—I returned to the hospital in the early morning. A gaggle of doctors were gathered at Dora's bedside, along with someone who, I learned later, was the "hospital counselor." One of the former, solemn, was lecturing her; the others, standing like supporting troops at a distance of two or three feet, reinforced his views. "Absolutely necessary ... No reason why you can't make a full recovery ... . We can't let you decide against it ... ." and other bromides. The solemn man added, "We cannot be responsible for you otherwise; you would have to leave our care and this hospital."

One of these omniscients was the doctor to whom I had spoken two days before. Noticing me, he interrupted the platitudinous peroration of his colleague. "I'm Dr. Neal. We spoke earlier. You are not a blood relative, you said; you do not belong at this consultation."

Dora had not even seen me come in; the curtain, which had remained partially drawn ever since she had refused to talk religion with the roommate, blocked her view. She looked around at me now. "Harriet, dearie! Oh, I'm glad you're here. Please tell all these gentlemen that my mind is made up; they should leave me alone, for they are wasting their time. Do tell them."

But telling them anything proved difficult. Neal came over, took my arm, and began showing me out.

"Wait," exclaimed Dora; "I want her to stay."

There was some consultation among the doctors, in low tones. Then the chief member of the team, or so I supposed, announced,

"That is all right; we are leaving anyway. Mrs. Garrick, we will set up surgery for Monday. The nurses will get you ready."

They trooped out, leaving behind the "counselor," a husky woman with a stern expression and voice. "Now Dora, I'm here to make you understand." She didn't even have the courtesy to address the patient, much older than she, as "Mrs. Garrick."

The doctors I could do nothing about; but with her, I thought I could prevail. "She is to be called Mrs. Garrick. And I believe she does not wish to understand—at least not from you. Is that right?"

"Yes, dearie." She turned her head on the pillow. "Please ... go away."

The woman protested some more, peevishly, but finally left. I wanted to talk to Dora about the practical ways of avoiding the surgery and yet providing for her care—having the insurance company arrange for her transfer to another hospital and other doctors, or to a hospice, or for home care. But she was exhausted.

"You must rest, Aunt Dora. I'll leave you now, go out and do some shopping, then come back later this afternoon—but before your dinner."

Seeing her will count for so little was wearing down what little resistance she had left. I hoped she would sleep much of the day, then be able to talk later. I knew who her insurer was, and decided to return to the hotel to call the 800-number. All the information I got was general—other hospitals that were associated with the network, other doctors; no one would discuss her case with me specifically because I was not a blood relative and did not have her proxy. After calling and getting lunch, I still had some time. I shopped at a Mexican-imports market, looking at wood carvings, silver, and glassware, always good for Christmas presents; then I drove to a nearby mall where there was a large Western outfitter store, in order to look for a new hat. There were some lovely models on display, but the one I liked most was too large. The master hatter there said that he could create a custom-made one that very day. He did it beautifully, and I wear the hat with great pleasure; but it took an hour or so. By the time I got back to the hospital, it was nearly four. I wanted to show off the new hat, knowing that Dora, who had such a sense of style when she was younger, would admire it. But when I reached her room, and saw her plugged up to two or three tubes and a machine, I realized that she wasn't in any condition to do so.

"What has happened?" I asked the nurse.

It was a good thing that she didn't challenge me on the blood-relative issue. "She had an attack a while ago. Fortunately, I was just coming in to check on her. We have her rigged up now to the heart monitor and are giving her an IV. She hasn't responded well, though; the vital signs are very low."

"Aunt Dora, can you hear me?" Hearing, I knew, was the last sense to go.

"You really shouldn't try to speak with her now," said the nurse.

"I don't know why not. When *will* I speak to her, if not now—it may be the end, and you know I am the only one here with her. All her friends are gone or are in the old folks' home." (Dora and I never called it "the golden age center" or any such euphemism.) "Anyway, if she's conscious, she won't mind hearing my voice. If she's not, what difference does it make?"

There seemed to be no objection to my staying; Dr. Neal was not around, luckily. I sat with her throughout the rest of the afternoon and evening, leaving only to get a Coke and a sandwich in one of those triangular plastic boxes. Dora did not show any signs of consciousness, as far as I could tell. Two different nurses came in to check on her and read the monitor. I have no technical knowledge of pain, or the body's failures and the means for combating them. She seemed calm, at least. When did I notice that there was a slight change in her breathing, her presence? It happened so subtly that I could not be sure. Some minutes passed. A nurse popped in then; it was she who told me that Dora was dead.

The funeral was arranged for Monday; the doctors would have to find someone else to operate on. She would be buried in the same cemetery as my parents. Out of courtesy, I informed her stepson, whose name and town I knew, in Washington State, but of course he merely sent regrets and a wreath. She hadn't told me whether her brother was still alive in Ireland, but I persuaded the staff at her residence to let me consult her address book, found a telephone number, and called him, as well as some names I recognized as those of former neighbors of hers. A few of them came to the service, and some of her new associates at the residence, whom she had not found her type but who were good people, at least.

I had telephoned Father Flaherty at St. Patrick's; he agreed to read the graveside service, a basic rite, which, in the modern English version, was not too different from what she would have had in the Church of Ireland. He read from Isaiah, chapter 35: "The desert shall rejoice, and blossom as the rose. It shall blossom abundantly ... Then the eyes of the blind shall be opened, and the ears of the deaf shall be unstopped. Then shall the lame man leap as an hart, and the tongue of the dumb sing: for in the wilderness shall waters break out ..." The tears spilled over my eyelashes and made rivulets down my cheeks as I heard in my mind Handel's exquisite recitative on the passage and thought of Dora's feeble, destroyed body, and how she had loved the desert and now was returning to its dust.

On the weekend, I would go, as planned, to visit my friend in Las Cruces. I spent all Friday in Dora's apartment, making arrangements for her few things to be disposed of, and taking care of some immediate business, as she had asked; the rest, I could do by telephone from home. She had wanted me to have anything of hers left that I wished as a keepsake or for practical use, but all I took was a silver bowl, engraved with her name and Joe's, for an anniversary, some perfume that she'd never opened, and her diamond-and-ruby ring. After the funeral on Monday, I visited my parents' graves. On Tuesday, I flew back to New Orleans. From the porthole of the plane one could see the narrow strip of cultivated fields and groves in the river valley, and, around them, the harsh, lonely landscape of the Chihuahua Desert. It seemed to me that I would not return for a long time.

Cubist Angles

FOR TEN DAYS OR SO there had been Carnival parades along St. Charles Avenue almost every weekday evening and on Saturday and Sunday afternoons, and we were still in the pre-Mardi Gras weekend, to be followed by Lundi Gras, with its two elaborate parades, and then Carnival Day itself, given over entirely to revelry, from the marching clubs waking us up at dawn, through Zulu, Rex, the truck parades, and, at twilight, something called the Krewe of America—made up of Bostonians, we were told. Sounds of the street activity, both organized and spontaneous, had risen to my condo windows again and again. Some of the principal parades had jazz bands on floats, playing traditional but amplified tunes such as "Mardi Gras Mambo," and there were always school marching bands, which stepped to the beat of bass and snare drums and occasional notes of brass, usually the same few musical measures repeated over and over—a fact suggesting that the young musicians were thought to be incapable of learning an entire Sousa march, for instance.

Surrounding like murmuring water the music and beat and the hum produced by the tractors pulling the behemoth floats, from which krewe members tossed out trinkets, was the noise of the crowd, competing with the blaring bands, rising and falling in rapid tidal movements according to the ebb and flow of the spectacle. Shouts and howls punctuated the *basso continuo* of the human swell. Sounds rose from the side streets, as parade-goers walked to the avenue, then back, or simply camped out for a few hours near the intersection, and there were parties at houses on or near the parade route, with barbecue pits set up in the front gardens and their own amplified music competing with the parade sounds. Well into the night after the organized activity had passed by, I still heard voices, some joyous, others angry, from the street or the neutral ground between the lanes of St. Charles. The sounds floated in my consciousness, sometimes in my sleep, the way bits of blue and red float on a canvas by Miró or Chagall.

Indeed, the whole spectacle of the days leading up to Mardi Gras and then the great celebration itself could have been seen as a materialization of modern painting. It was not just that the clowns, harlequins, and jugglers seemed to step out of Cézanne, Picasso, and Rouault, or that other scenes appeared to have been anticipated by Ensor and Dufy; in an eclectic mélange of forms and colors and late winter light in New Orleans, one could experience in three dimensions the visions of the Impressionists and Post-Impressionists, the Pointillists, Fauves, Futurists, and above all the Cubists, whose overlays, collages, distortions, and bent planes were suggested by the strange perspectives from my balcony and the juxtaposition of disparate visual elements half-glimpsed through the budding trees and the crowds.

On Sunday before Lundi Gras, after an early supper, I went down to the avenue well before the Bacchus parade—the evening extravaganza. In a plastic cup tossed by some krewe the previous year, I carried my dinner wine, which I hadn't finished. Work had become impossible; my ability to block out the sounds and the images they evoked had been strained in the previous days and finally exhausted by the Iris and Thoth parades earlier Sunday. In the interval between those parades and Bacchus, there had been a continuous milling around, producing swirls not unlike those visual mixtures made by the slow stirring of paint. The crowds either hadn't gone home or had gathered again, bringing back their ice chests and lawn chairs and stepladders, to which were attached seats for children or baskets for collecting trinkets or both. For some while, the lanes of St. Charles heading downtown had been closed to all but mounted patrolmen and a few police cars and sheriff's vehicles, moving slowly, so I wandered up and down and loitered in the intersection, listening to the random activity and watching twilight start to seep fog-like through the heavy canopy of live oaks. A blimp bearing the logo of a sportswear manufacturer was still visible in the pale sky over the river, and helicopters buzzed above like hornets.

Here and there appeared faces familiar to me, including those of a few neighbors from my condo building, but I saw no one with whom I wished to converse particularly until Laura and Charles Trevelyan appeared in the crowd. Years before, Laura had been an intern at the museum, where she was assigned chiefly to me. She and I had worked closely together and she'd become a good friend. After her marriage, she ceased full-time museum work; she now does mostly free-lance writing in art history and also teaches an occasional course. Charles takes her to France frequently so that she can keep up with the latest on the art scene there. They live farther uptown but like to come to my neighborhood for the parades. Charles, who manages his properties, is witty and personable. So I went over where they were leaning on the iron fence that surrounds the condo garden.

"Harriet, how good to see you!" Charles exclaimed, bending down from his considerable height to kiss me on the cheek, just as Laura, wrapping her arm around my shoulder, said, "Harry! How are you?"

'Oh, very well, thanks. It's good to see you also. Happy Carnival!"

"And to you too," she answered. "Harry, we've got a guest with us whom I want you to meet; in fact, we came here in hopes of running into you so that you two could get acquainted." Turning to her left, she gestured toward a figure I could barely glimpse. Then I moved, the figure moved, and I saw that it was a child—no, an adult, a cripple, with the upper body of a man, normal in shape and size, and broad-shouldered, but with twisted and abnormally short legs. Laura turned back to me. "Harry, Jacques Lemarignac, un ami parisien. Jacques, je vous présente mon amie Harriet D'Aquin."

I put out my hand. "Enchantée de faire votre connaissance."

The grip of this Frenchman was solid—the kind I like—and bespoke, I thought, sincerity and strong character. His face was handsome—square-jawed and masculine. We said a few more words in French; then he added, "But we'd better speak English because of Charles, shouldn't we? Anyhow, I need the practice." And he smiled in a winsome manner.

Jacques Lemarignac, it turned out, was a painter whom Laura and Charles had met in Paris some years before at a show of his own work; later, at the home of mutual friends, they had encountered each other again. I remembered having heard of him from Laura and reading about his work in art magazines. The acquaintance had developed enough in the course of several visits to Paris, Laura explained, for them to invite him to New Orleans; they had lured him with reports of gastronomical and visual delights, especially the spectacle of Carnival. That year, finally, he was able to accept the invitation. He had brought slides of his canvases and hoped to find a gallery to represent him. But that would be later: he had just arrived, and Bacchus was his first parade.

It seemed strangely appropriate that he should turn up for Mardi Gras—the pre-Lenten season being a time for Saturnalia, the extraordinary and exorbitant, whether in behavior or physique. Jacques's deformed body was itself somehow carnivalesque—the sort of figure Brueghel might have put into one of his kermess canvases, or Rouault might have added to a tragic clown's face. Jacques struck me as being even somewhat Cubist, his legs bent at odd angles. As I stole glances at him, I thought also of Toulouse-Lautrec; I could almost imagine Jacques wearing a vast, sloping Lautrecian beret. (I trusted that my face did not betray my thoughts, as the painter's silhouette superimposed itself on Jacques's image in my mind; he must have been too aware of the obvious resemblance to wish to see it mirrored in another's glance.)

"Look, wouldn't you three like drinks? I've got lots of wine and plastic cups and can just pop upstairs and get you something before the parade arrives."

"Oh, thanks, but we've got our cooler, right here." Laura gestured to an ice chest they had placed at the foot of the nearest oak tree. As if that were the signal to serve, Charles went over and pulled out a magnum of wine from the cooler, filled three cups, and then offered me some. The four of us exchanged bits and pieces of talk—whether Jacques was a born Parisian (no, he was originally from the Gers), how long he was staying, what medium he was currently using, what my special interests in painting and art history were, and so on. Laura praised his style for its strength and originality and assured me of his high standing in Paris. I liked his manner—youthful for a man well into middle age, enthusiastic, almost passionate when he spoke of others' painting, but modest about his own. I told him about the Orleanian Institute, invited him to visit our collections, and assured him that I could arrange to show him our library and workrooms as well as some holdings that would interest him especially but were not then on public display. His eyes were bright with sympathetic understanding and interest, and I found his smile—soft and generous in his rugged face—utterly delightful.

At that moment a squad car passed in the street, followed by the cherry picker from the electric company, a sign that the first floats were not far up the avenue, and we could hear the beat of the first band. Voices started to swell in anticipation; it was time to get our places for watching. The crowd was already surging in waves. I picked a level spot by a signpost, right at the curb, with Laura, Charles, and Jacques to my right by the nearest oak. It would be a long evening, with thirty floats and who knew how many bands, military units, flambeaux bearers, dancing girls, baton twirlers, and second liners—and thus I was happy to have some firm ground, my own island in the crush of bodies. Jacques would need it also; the spectators, particularly children, could get rowdy and I supposed that his balance was not excellent.

The Krewe of Bacchus puts on an impressive show each year, with oversized floats that just barely clear the oak branches above them and carry dozens of riders. Thousands of colored lights blinking through the trees and growing brighter in the deepening dusk give a cinematographic impression, and the bands are sometimes professionals. Without ties to old New Orleans money and traditions, the organization does not eschew the garish, nor the common; on this occasion, a Belushi brother was king. Shortly, the royal float arrived, followed by others, all spectacular, and by bands thumping out what they thought of as music. As each float approached, voices around us roared in excitement; once, when floats were stopped right in front of us and couldn't proceed, the bellowing did not diminish for ten minutes or so.

Like nearly all other newcomers to Carnival, Jacques was almost silent for some minutes, just watching, wondering at the insanity, I suppose; he held back, making no attempt to catch some of the doubloons, beads, and plastic cups being tossed out abundantly and fought over by seasoned parade-goers. Finally, though, he overcame his reserve and started yelling and waving with the rest of us, being careful, however, not to leave his place by the oak tree, which afforded some protection. He smiled at me several times and exclaimed, "Magnifique! Magnifique! Ah, Madame D'Aquin, *Arrhee*, si je peux me permettre … Ah, c'est splendide." (He had heard Charles and Laura call me "Harry.") Like those of a child, his expressive features revealed his delight at the spectacle, almost his passion, and I recalled how, at first, I had believed he *was* a child.

During a long pause between floats and bands, Charles refilled our drinks and passed around some cheese tidbits on a paper plate. Jacques was beside himself with enthusiasm. "Que c'est beau! Toutes ces lumières... toutes ces couleurs." He saw the spectacle, as I tried to do, in painterly more than social terms, but his gaze was fresher than mine and he was not disturbed by the sort of reflections I could not help making on how Hollywood was taking over Carnival. "How *dynamique*," he observed to Charles, as a mounted sheriff's posse approached, the men and women, in Western dress, sitting high and proudly on their horses. For a moment, the whole parade was held up again, and the posse stood at arm's length from us. "Quels beaux chevaux," observed Jacques; "j'adore les bêtes—chiens, chats, oiseaux, et surtout les chevaux." I knew then that, like me, he liked horses for themselves and for their beauty.

Then the procession resumed and new floats arrived in a seemingly endless flow. Suddenly, above the general yelling and calling, there was a scream, close by, followed by eddies of movement. It was impossible to tell what had happened. Perhaps a child had been kicked by a horse—though I had seen no one running through the posse—or had gotten too close to a tractor or float and fallen under the wheels; or someone had been stabbed—once in a long while there is an incident of that sort along a parade route. A second scream and a sort of groan struck out at the night. All at once there was a thud, nearly beside me, and I found myself looking down at a condo neighbor, Régine Dupuy, a spinster of some years whom I barely knew. She was lying supine, her hair disheveled and eyes glazed, among the tree roots and several pairs of feet, including mine. The ensuing confusion was considerable, with gestures and shouts and orders coming from all directions; but I could distinguish nonetheless her startling words: "I hear them, I hear them, the voices, they are coming, they are in me ..."

She was obviously deranged or having hallucinations. She wasn't of the generation that indulged in LSD or Ecstasy, but she could have taken a prescription medication that had misfired, or taken too much of it; or perhaps she'd been hit on the head or had some sort of seizure. Charles, followed by Laura and then Jacques, had come up at my right, and I could feel Charles elbowing a few onlookers out of the way. Because he's tall and very strong and also has an air of authority, he's the sort who steps in when an incident takes place and sees what needs to be done. Soon he had opened a little space for himself and was bending over the woman. Jacques stood then right beside me, about a foot shorter than I, his face below my shoulder. In the light of some float or another that was passing—we had ceased paying attention to what its theme might be—I saw his face transformed, showing no longer his delight at the parade but instead a concern, a sympathy that were overpowering.

"Jacques!" I said, "what is the matter? You don't know that woman, do you? You can't possibly know her."

"Non, non, bien sûr que non, mais ..."

In fact, he was simply moved by the incident—the woman's cry, her sudden fall and apparent inability to rise, her hallucinations. Such a reaction on a stranger's part could have struck me as foolish; instead, it touched me, revealing still another angle of his character and leading me to wonder whether it was his own physical vulnerability that made him so easily affected by another's. He stood by watching as Charles, seeing that Régine did not appear to be injured, got her to sit up and lean against a tree trunk, while paramedics were summoned and I explained to him who she was.

Meanwhile the floats and bands continued to file by. After an ambulance pulled up at the intersection via the side street and Régine was carried off to Touro Infirmary, we turned again to the parade and started catching worthless trinkets, but we could not recapture our mood: the drama of Régine's collapse had broken the spectacular illusion and dampened the spirit of participation. Finally, I said, "Wouldn't you like to come upstairs and let me prepare you real drinks in glasses?"

"That's a good idea," Laura said, "if Jacques won't mind missing the rest of this show tonight."

So we spent the rest of the evening in my place on the seventh floor, conversing, admiring the city panorama, and catching phrases of the sporadic parade music, somewhat muted by the height. More, doubtless, than Charles and Laura had anticipated—for they had not thought of being matchmakers in the circumstances—Jacques and I found ourselves enjoying each other's company: two artists, one slightly older than the other (but what difference did that make?), having made painting our lives, reacting to sights and sounds in the same ways, the one with a deformed body, the other with—well, something like internal mutilations …

At the end of the evening, it was agreed that I would look for them all in the street around twilight time the following day, Lundi Gras, before the Orpheus parade, which would reach my neighborhood about 8 or later. But I didn't see them—perhaps they'd not been able to get through the traffic. On Shrove Tuesday, I knew, they were all to be at a party on Napoleon Avenue, given by some acquaintance of Charles. So we had no more Carnival celebrations together. But, as planned, Laura drove Jacques to the museum on Thursday and left him in my care. I showed him our offices, library, and workrooms, gave him a few numbers of the *Bulletin*, introduced him to my closest colleagues, and persuaded him to show them the slides he'd brought at my urging. Then I took him through some of the exhibit areas, leaving him alone to wander through others by himself. After lunch in the café, we went into the storage areas so that he could study several portfolios of French drawings not usually out for view and some huge canvases for which there simply isn't room on the display walls. As at the parade, he evinced great appreciation for what he saw: my work (a few samples on my office walls), our holdings and public exhibits, and the arrangements for research. He made incisive and keen observations on the paintings and drawings, and again I felt that his comments were sincere, not perfunctory.

Rather than let him call Laura, or walk several blocks and then take the streetcar, I offered to leave early and drive him back to Laura and Charles's house; I'd worked late so many days in January that the museum owed me a lot of time. I put down the convertible top—it was a splendid day of bright blue sky and tender leaves—and chose a long and circuitous route, through the far end of the French Quarter, then along Esplanade Avenue, where Degas had lived, Bayou St. John, and parts of Mid-City. He was full of admiration. "Oh, *Arrhee*, comme tout cela me plaît—la ville, le bayou, les avenues, le beau temps ..." He said he would like to come back to New Orleans to paint—not like Degas, who had feared the bright sun and stayed indoors, but in the streets and along the bayou. "Et peindre surtout le Carnaval ..." The prospect of his rendering Mardi Gras in paint was appealing; having seen his slides, I could imagine the colors, the shimmering quality he would succeed in putting on canvas. Again, I reflected how well his whole person seemed to fit the celebration of life and disorder and desire that precedes Lent.

He turned to me then. "Et vous, vous êtes adorable, adorable ..." That's a Frenchman for you: not many days into an acquaintance, he is already telling a woman he barely knows that she's adorable. In this case, moreover, it was a man who, you'd think, might have reason to be sensitive about women and keep them at arm's length, in the knowledge that his deformity made rejection likely. Perhaps the words were just offhand, a Gallic conditioned reflex; but I didn't think so. "Voulez-vous bien dîner avec moi ce soir?" And he explained that, Charles and Laura having some real estate banquet they had to attend, he was to be left on his own for the evening, and had supposed he would fix himself a sandwich from cold cuts in their refrigerator, but now had a vision of our dining out somewhere, maybe at a "grand restaurant" that I would choose.

Proust says, I remember, that when a man shows desire for a woman who has no interest in him, it usually puts her off or even offends her; but sometimes the effect is the opposite—a sort of contagion that alerts her to her appeal and, through it, to his. Maybe she must feel a latent attraction already in order for his desire to operate and her interest to crystallize. Sensed obscurely, that may be what leads the man initially to venture glances, compliments, invitations. I had already enjoyed Jacques's company and seen the quality of his tastes and his mind; I suppose I was vaguely drawn to him, without quite being aware of it, and his charm may have magnetized me more than I realized. Desire is all around us and is often diffuse, I think—and not just sexual desire. But usually we don't act on brief flickers of attraction and little tropistic movements toward objects. The beauty of an emerald ring or a bracelet that I vaguely covet in Adler's windows, for instance, or a handsome man, just glimpsed—I'm drawn to them, like most other women; but for all sorts of practical reasons one usually lets these wisps of attraction just blow away. A word, a glance, a gesture may capture them.

Anyhow, I said yes. We dined at Arnaud's in the Quarter, still reliable and easier to get into than Gallatoire's and Commander's. It was a lovely evening, with undercurrents of flirtation in our conversation, the selection of wines and the toasts ("A mon retour à la Nouvelle-Orléans ... à nous deux," Jacques finally said), and the long, leisurely meal. He did not feel ill at ease, I'm sure; nor did I—why should I? Anyhow, I never feel compromised. An appealing, boyish kind of self-confidence beamed from him—that of his achievement as an artist, that (perhaps) of a man who is dining with a woman whom he finds attractive and whose choice by him is ratified by other men's glances. So much the worse for them if a few diners made reflections on his "handicap" or supposed it was pity that had brought me there. Whatever it was, it wasn't pity, surely. They would not have seen how all the strength that would have been distributed *evenly* in the body of a whole man was condensed in him—his searching eyes, his masculine chin, his large, sensitive hands.

Amitié amoureuse—that's what Stendhal called the sort of "affair" that we were, possibly, embarked on—"love-friendship," maybe "erotic friendship." Even now I don't know how well or how long such relationships can work, or whether they inevitably turn into something else. An ocean between the partners wouldn't be of much help, one would think, if it were to be *amour*. I could not forget that Jacques was to return to Paris in two weeks or so, and that my visits there, even if yearly, or his to New Orleans (he did shortly sign a contract with a gallery on Magazine Street) were not enough to nourish a love affair. The love part was, I reflected as we drove back to Charles and Laura's house, a bit of a nuisance, anyhow, if not simply a fantasy of mine, a delusion that sprang from having been single too long. Perhaps he was merely being polite. On that score, at least, Jacques soon set me right. "*Arrhee*," he said, as we reached the house, "voulez-vous sortir avec moi encore une fois—tous les soirs même tant que je serai là?" Go out every evening! An invitation of that sort could not be entirely casual.

"Volontiers, Jacques," I answered, but then corrected myself to explain that I wasn't free for two or three of those evenings, though he might like to accompany me to one engagement—a reception on Saturday at a rival museum. Scruples made me add, in English for some reason, "But you are not being fair to yourself—you will surely want to go out more with Charles and Laura, meet other friends of theirs, especially people who might like to acquire some of your work; or maybe you want to travel over to Lafayette to visit the Cajun country ... And you said you needed to work on your English."

"No, no," he answered, tit for tat, as if to show that he could really handle the language. "I mean, I certainly enjoy their company, and am so grateful to them for inviting me here—especially since I met you" (and his hand brushed my arm, briefly); "but—well, maybe except when you are otherwise occupied anyway, I should like so much to ... to spend the evenings with you—if you will drive me around, that is, suggest bars, restaurants, spots where we could listen to good jazz, if you would like, or go to a play, a concert ..."

How might one paint a love affair, I wonder. It would be harder still to depict a non-love affair, an unrealized possibility. We had almost a dozen outings together, dining, I remember, at Café Degas, Mr. B's, and Bayona's (I managed to get a reservation, mentioning the museum and identifying Jacques as a visiting artist), hearing the symphony play on Thursday, driving to the lakeshore, attending that reception I'd mentioned and afterwards going to the Bombay Club to hear live jazz. On Sunday, I took him to lunch in Ascension Parish and we drove back by way of Madewood and Oak Alley plantations, which he admired from the exterior but declined to visit, all those stairs being a bit of a bother for him. He seemed to enjoy every minute, listening attentively to the orchestra, taking time over the menu in the restaurants and proclaiming his delight at New Orleans gastronomy, exclaiming with glee when we roared along the road with the convertible top down, marveling how the ocean-going ships on the Mississippi as we saw them from the Sunshine Bridge looked like toys. What good times we had, what good conversations. I felt a bit like a girl again, as if the spirit of that child I'd taken him for were infectious.

Yet, between the *amitié* part of the pair I'd identified and the *amour* part—right at the space that joins, yet separates them—there was, I discovered, a gap that I could not quite abolish; my feelings were, I suppose, more on the friendship side. Was I wrong to venture as far as I had? To mislead others, or oneself, is never fitting. But without the current of romance, the very tasteful flirtation Jacques had initiated and I had allowed to develop, no pairing at all would have come into being for us; there would have been just a superficial professional acquaintance, friendly enough and conceivably useful to one or the other in the future but otherwise insignificant and unmemorable. As it was ... well, did I know how it was, know at all?

As the date approached for Jacques to leave, it occurred to me that at the end of our time together he might say nothing at all beyond expressing his thanks, with an urbane touch of realism: the interlude in our lives would be over, like Carnival. Or, if he were more serious, he might only throw me a look that would invite me to divine more, so that any further gesture would be up to me. French though he was, emboldened culturally, he was a cripple ... For him to say nothing would be more discreet, and easier for me to handle, than saying—just what, I wasn't sure. But do women really like discretion and reserve? Do they not prefer declarations, which are undeniable homages? In any event, Jacques did not leave things unsaid. Since, very tactfully, Charles and Laura had held their official farewell dinner for him, inviting me also, of course, two days before his departure, he was able take me to dinner the last night. He had asked my advice on restaurants; I had managed to get us an early table at Commander's Palace. Beforehand, we had cocktails in my apartment, then walked over (he wanted to go on foot). On the way we passed by Lafayette Cemetery, and went in, on an impulse—his impulse. Twilight was about to settle, but the gates were, unaccountably, still open, and we took a few moments to walk among the raised monuments, some as large as gardener's huts, with their stone angels and saints, their little iron-work fences, and their inscriptions for all eternity. I told him that Régine, whose collapse and hallucinations had been caused, it turned out, by interactions of four or five drugs, had died that very day.

Death—that is, the thought of death—is an aphrodisiac; the tombs doubtless put Jacques in mind of time's passage, of the needs of the heart and the body, while it is here. With his departure merely hours away, if he was to speak he had to speak soon. He waited until we had ordered and the server had brought a bottle of champagne, opened it with a flourish, filled our *flûtes*, then retreated to the opposite wall. There was a discreet clinking of glass, with Jacques's eyes, dark and searching, finding and holding my own. Then he took my hand in his.

"*Arrhee*, n'y a-t-il personne dans votre vie?"

No, there was no one in my life—in the romantic sense of that phrase, at least.

"Alors, pourriez-vous un jour m'aimer?"

To be asked whether one could love someone someday is to be asked whether one loves at the moment. Although I did not have the delusion of being unique for him—there are thousands of women in Paris who can talk about art—it seemed to me that a great deal was riding on the question—not the outcome of a vulgar attempt at seduction, certainly, but rather a man's sense of himself, as man, not artist. I thought of Schubert and other gifted, passionate creators, geniuses at the palette or piano keyboard but miserable in life, who would have given all their art in exchange for the wholehearted and lasting surrender of a woman they loved.

My immediate reply was cowardly. "Jacques... Ce n'est pas le moment..."

But he retorted that then was the moment if ever; wasn't he about to leave to return to Paris, perhaps never to see me again, or instead, conceivably, to see me often, to be closer to me in the future, to ...

Just then the waiter acted on the compulsion to come refill my champagne glass, from which I had taken another sip or so, nervously, as Jacques was speaking. The interruption was gauche but briefly useful; we both paused for a minute. Jacques resumed, though, more intensely than before, as if the pause and the passing minutes had added to his desperation.

"Pourriez-vous m'aimer comme je suis, même ... infirme comme je le suis, estropié ..." And he glanced down at his body and his twisted legs, hidden by the tablecloth but always present to him, doubtless, as he knew others registered them always. For the first time a touch of sardonic bitterness played on his lips. "Parce que je sais, voyez-vous ... je sais que je ne suis pas joli à voir."

"Oh, Jacques!" And I could scarcely get the words out fast enough to tell him that he was, on the contrary, handsome, "très beau, Jacques, très beau, vous devez le savoir, tout de même," and I ventured to tease him on a light tone, asking whether many women hadn't told him so.

"*Arrhee*, soyez sérieuse, je vous prie." He asked again whether I could love him, a cripple.

"Il ne s'agit pas de ça," I replied—a way of saying, "Don't put the question in those terms."

"Pourquoi non? Il s'agit de moi, comme je suis, comme vous me voyez ...il s'agit de moi et de vous."

A question of him as he was, of us ... There was no mystery, but I did not know what to answer. Silent, I took a sip of champagne, then nibbled like a rabbit at a piece of garlic toast in a basket.

"Bien. Je vais poser la question d'une façon différente." And he proceeded, indeed, to frame his question differently, asking, since I hadn't said yes to loving him someday, whether I could love him— could have loved him—if he weren't crippled.

Again there was an interruption, the waiter appearing with our starters, shrimp rémoulade.

Suddenly I recalled that the philosopher Pascal had inquired how ancient history would have been changed had Cleopatra's nose been longer, or shorter. We weren't dealing with world events, Jacques and I, but the "What if...?" question still receded into infinity.

All this time Jacques had held my hand in his, pressing it once or twice, although I was almost unaware of it. I suddenly put my other hand over both of ours, as if in acknowledgment, but perhaps judgment also, of their joining.

"C'est une question insensée," I ventured. Certainly it was nonsensical, with no possibility of answer or meaning: I could not love a hypothesis. Since I had retreated from his earlier questions, it appeared also that, when confronted with the need to decide, I could not, or did not, love Jacques as he was, with everything that implied. Yet I wasn't sure I could not imagine it ... So many angles—so many ways of seeing and being oneself ...

I had to continue. "Mais, finalement, *non*, Jacques, puisque vous me le demandez de cette façon. Finalement, que vous soyez infirme ou non n'a rien à voir avec la chose. Je ne peux, je pense, aimer personne." Wasn't that the most tactful way of saying no—to tell him that I really could love no one? I hadn't known it myself, but supposed, as I said it, that there must be some truth in the statement for it to have come out. It was as if, pressed by a friend, I had drawn myself, and some feature, some inner shadow I had not suspected had appeared in the likeness.

All this discussion had not been much of an appetizer. I had removed my hands, both of them. I thought again of the cemetery and the nothingness that filled the tombs. Something of a sense of failure and futility hung over the table for a few minutes, while we ate our shrimp in silence. But we were both too resourceful to let the evening end quite that way, and soon we were talking again, sipping champagne, chatting about painting, commenting on the main dishes when they arrived. Jacques's sensitivity to others, evidenced so clearly at the Bacchus parade, was again displayed as he asked more about my future painting projects, the way a very close friend might inquire, a mentor, an angel ...

We walked back to my building and got into the car, for me to drive him to Laura and Charles's. Laura would take him to the airport the next day. From the back seat I got a little gift I'd chosen for him—a book on New Orleans architecture. He unwrapped it silently. "Oh, *Arrhee...* Merci" was all he said. At Laura's, I stepped out of the car, walked around to the passenger side, and met him as he was climbing out. "Au revoir, cher Jacques, au revoir." He held me briefly in an embrace of disequilibrium, then turned and limped to the steps, his twisted legs made even more angular and grotesque in shadows around the veranda. At the door, he turned and gave a brief wave. My heart felt as shattered as his body, contorted with emotion, all angles and broken planes, beating violently, and as if the blood were gushing out.

I got back in the car and started the engine. Tears had already overflowed my eyelids and were turning cold on my face, chilled by the evening air. "I suppose that I do love you a little bit anyhow," I murmured to myself as I looked in the rearview mirror, then pulled away.

A Day with Cyprien

CYPRIEN HAS BEEN ON my mind since last week, when I put on again the blue Daum earrings that I brought back from Paris a few years ago. I hesitate to wear them when I am going out, although they don't seem loose and the hooks are not flimsy. What makes me nervous is just the thought of having more than $100 worth of an artisan's work in glass dangling from my ear lobes, as I walk on the sidewalk or get onto the streetcar. Nevertheless, I put them on for a wedding last week in the French Quarter, since they are such a perfect match for the blue garden-party dress I had chosen, and since the wedding was that of John Howard, a former intern of mine who truly is steeped in French art.

I bought the earrings because of Cyprien, but not *for* him, as a coquettish woman might buy something to please a man. That summer, I was in France for a few weeks. He had come up from Bordeaux, where he is a museum curator, to Paris, just for a day, especially to meet me. It was the first time I had seen him since the 1960s—thirty years or so. You could call it a reunion, but perhaps it was more a coda to the music of the past, the old phrases replayed briefly, in a different key. Not that the past had been dramatic; we had been friends, with just a bit of romance thrown in, of the passing sort that flavors a friendship between a man and a woman without changing it into something harder to manage. I suppose, had things been different, that it could have been transformed into love. The instruments for our sentimental coda were ourselves, considerably aged; as the date of our meeting approached, I did not know whether the effect of time should be counted as mellowing or destructive, or perhaps some of both ...

His full name is Jean-Luc-André-Cyprien Cazenave. Born on St. Cyprien's Day, he received that name along with those of his father and a grandfather, and it was that one which stuck. His father's family was from Bayonne, where he was born; his mother was a Spanish

251

immigrant who ended up working as a chambermaid in resort hotels in Biarritz and later in Bordeaux. She was probably a very intelligent woman, though her schooling had not advanced far; Cyprien was, I thought, brilliant as well as a very good painter. Social mobility was so limited in Europe, for so long, that circumstances weighed heavily on an individual's chances. His mother was, after all, a foreigner, a sort of *Gastarbeiter*, from a relatively poor and politically retrogressive country; France had looked good to her, but, without family connections or any higher education, she could not hope to go far. She was very pious, in the typically Spanish way. Cyprien's father, a teacher, was the opposite, a freethinker and left-winger—a communist, I had suspected, though Cyprien had never admitted it to me, fearing, I suppose, an American's knee-jerk negative reaction to the very word. Having a free-thinking father and a devout mother is so common in France that it scarcely needs comment; in many communities, few men go to mass. But theirs appeared to be an extreme case. At any rate, Cyprien's father died, in circumstances unclear to me, toward the end of the German Occupation; quite how, I'm not sure, but I know now that he was involved with a communist Resistance network. As a boy, Cyprien received help for his schooling from his father's family, and thus was able to finish the lycée and go to Paris to study at the Ecole des Beaux-Arts; he also had some help from an association of former members of the Resistance.

We had first got acquainted, long ago, at a café right near the Ecole, and learned that we would be students there together. I remember that I was seated by myself, with a coffee cup long emptied. From his table he had examined me, looking doubtless like the foreigner I was, but obviously an artist, since I had a large portfolio with me. He had nodded slightly, then said, using the all-purpose student greeting, "Salut." After a pause, he added: "Would you like to come join us?" He gestured to his friends: Christine, André, Claire, Philippe, Marie-Hélène, and so on. We shook hands all around. That was my introduction to the little band of fellow students who remained the center of my social life throughout my year's study in Paris. Thinking about it after three decades, and walking along the Boulevard Saint-

Germain and the rue de Seine to the art quarter to meet Cyprien again, brought back details as though I had returned to the stage set of my past.

We had decided to meet again in the same neighborhood, but we would do things more elegantly this time: we would have lunch in the dining room of L'Hôtel—that is its full name—where Colette had lived and Oscar Wilde had died, in the rue des Beaux-Arts. Then we would go to the Musée Nissim de Camondo, which I had never visited, on the Right Bank near the Parc Monceau—a collection of eighteenth-century furniture, *objets d'art*, and paintings in a handsome townhouse that a rich collector gave to the nation as a memorial to his son, killed in the Great War. Cyprien's curatorial responsibilities in Bordeaux cover a vast area, but his scholarly speciality is eighteenth-century art— porcelain, *faïence*, furniture, bibelots, paintings. That was how I had discovered him again, after years when we had lost track of each other and neither had any idea what the other was doing: in an art history magazine, I had come across an article signed Cyprien Cazenave concerning some of the everyday objects in Chardin's still lifes, and had written to him at his museum address in Bordeaux. Subsequently, I had informed him about my forthcoming stay in Paris and we had decided to meet.

Having a few extra minutes, I walked rather slowly—on the very narrow sidewalks of those old streets near the Seine, crowded at midday, you can't make fast progress anyhow, especially near the open market stalls—and I cast a leisurely glance or so at the windows of the antique shops and art dealers. I was looking at some engravings of ships when I sensed someone at my elbow. "Pardon," a voice said, "might you be Harriet D'Aquin—I mean my friend Harry?"—the name pronounced *Arrhee*, of course, as a Frenchman would say it; we had always used French together, his English being halting. "It's really you?"

I turned quickly. "Yes, Cyprien, it's I." We shook hands, in the French manner. "I was going to wait for you in the lobby of L'Hôtel, where you would have guessed that I was the gray-haired woman in the green jacket. How did you recognize me here on the street, after all these years?"

"Ah, *Arrhee,* I couldn't have missed you. How many women in the rue de Seine have your style—your very *American* French style? You are as charming as ever—the same tilt to the chin, the same eyes. Those eyes! How good it is to see you!" (He used *vous,* of course, as I had in writing to him—the familiar *tu* of distant student days replaced by suitably professional address.)

"Oh, Cyprien, it is grand to see you too. Such a long time it's been since we were students here! And you are still the dear flatterer. Come, let's go have a drink and lunch." And off we went, turning into the rue des Beaux-Arts, finding the right number, and making our way to the rear of the dining room, where a table was set up for us near the fountain. He ordered a *kir royal* for each of us—"You would enjoy that, wouldn't you?" Signaling clearly to the *maître d'hôtel* that this would be a leisurely meal, we laid aside for a while the menus that had been thrust into our hands. Time to talk, it was; we would oblige time to give us back a bit of what it had taken. And what it had taken was, I acknowledged, all too obvious. Cyprien could not have missed noticing the changes in me; and, despite the cordial greeting, the display of Gallic charm, what I saw was an ascetic-looking man of "a certain age," as the French say, *bel homme* but a bit stooped in the shoulders and thin-chested, with a thatch of white hair and thick lenses, his forehead deeply lined, his skin stretched taut over prominent cheekbones.

Where does one begin, at a retrospective? He inquired about my life and my work, of course, following up on the bare sketch I had given in my letter, so I filled it in briefly: my return to New York after Beaux-Arts, getting my degree, my struggle to paint and get my works shown, my first curatorial positions, then my settling in New Orleans and marriage to Jack. He told me more about his position in Bordeaux, where he had ended up, some years after finishing not only Beaux-Arts but also the prestigious Ecole du Louvre.

"And your painting? You still paint, surely; you were one of the most gifted, Cyprien, much more than I." Looking at his stretched, yet lined face, I thought of the masks that some great painters acquired over their features—the masks of their true selves, exteriorized and molded to their face by an intense identification with their art.

"*Arrhee*, I must tell you the truth: I have not painted for many years. My painting is still ... latent, as it were. Only recently I have thought that I might ..." The words trailed off.

His admission fell like a stone onto the table. We had finished our kirs by then. The waiter, sensing a pause, came over to enquire about another *apéritif.*

"No, thank you," Cyprien replied, "but please bring the wine list, and now we will look at the menu and order." He changed his glasses, putting on a pair of small reading spectacles.

We chose according to taste, and according to our ideas of what such a luncheon should be: I had snails provençal, followed by a Basque paella in honor of Cyprien's home region, while he ordered prosciutto with melon—it looks so lovely on the plate, like a small Chardin painting—and Dover sole, the latter perhaps an oblique homage to Wilde. He selected a dry white Bordeaux to accompany the meal. As we ate and drank, we wove a conversation composed of bits of information on ourselves mixed with comments on the food and wine, reiterated exclamations on the time that had passed, and some news, which he shared with me, of our fellow students, now scattered around Europe.

"Cyprien," I ventured shortly before the plates were cleared away and the desert menu was announced, "please tell me why you gave up painting—you must tell me what happened." There are dozens of questions that, out of politeness, I would refrain from asking, but to remain silent on what he had cared about so deeply, at one time, would have betrayed old friendship and commitment to what we had been. Anyhow, artists can be like that—mercilessly probing a wound or a rip in the vision, reaching for the hidden springs of creativity or the source of paralysis, in themselves and others. I knew why *I* had left the brushes alone for quite a few years; but then, I am a woman. I now imagined the worst—some critic's column having devastated him so that his creativity was paralyzed, perhaps a vow he had made to the Virgin (I remembered his mother's piety) in exchange for the cure of a sick child, or an obscure mental or physical disease that gnawed him from the inside and took away the inner vision.

"You remember Corinne Lapeyre." Indeed I did. She was from Bayonne, and went to the university in Bordeaux while Cyprien was in Paris at Beaux-Arts. After I had known him for some months, she came to visit for a few days; I understood that their relationship was not the same as ours. He told me then that he would marry her when his studies were over—that he had loved her for years, and that was why he couldn't quite love me.

"Of course I remember Corinne. You did get married, didn't you?"

No, they had not. He paused, then began to explain what had happened. She came from a conservative upper-bourgeois family, very right-wing, which all along had viewed the youthful romance with disfavor, in light of Cyprien's origins—his mother an immigrant of the working class, his father an intellectual, a radical, perhaps worse. Her parents objected also, he told me, to the fact that he was an artist: among proper families, the old stigma against pursuing literature, the stage, music, or art as anything but a pastime had not disappeared. It is true that in the 1960s even conservative French parents did not often presume to forbid outright such a marriage, and they had to acknowledge, he added, that, by going to the Ecole du Louvre, Cyprien was preparing himself, officially, for a career in the national museum system, thus a stable and respectable position.

"But they made inquiries."

"What sort of inquiries do you mean? Into your finances? Your exam results? Your circle of friends?" I could not imagine what he meant—his own finances amounted to nothing then, and they knew it, and French examination results are public. Did they think he was a fraud, claiming to be a student, living instead a life of dissipation in Paris on who knows what unsavory means?

"They ... *Arrhee*, they ... inquired into my father's activities during the war. You know, I never told you; all that was too close to me then, too fragile—since my memory of him was all I had and I didn't want to touch it—and you might not have understood how it was possible for someone ..." He paused, then resumed. "Anyway, my father was a communist, in the *maquis* in the Southwest. After the landings in 1944, as the liberation troops moved closer to Bordeaux, he and other *maquisards* began their program of clearing out the worst of the collaborators in the Gironde—factory owners who had profited obscenely from furnishing goods to the Germans, and actively collaborationist mayors and other officials. Those were terrorist operations. For years I had known he had done things of that sort—my mother told me. But I didn't know exactly what actions he took part in. M. and Mme Lapeyre, at any rate, had ways of finding things out, and learned that my father had been in one of those Resistance cells that didn't wait for official justice."

"But, Cyprien ..." My impulse was to say that by the mid-1960s that was water under the bridge; but of course it was not true, and still isn't true for those whose families were closely involved in what, toward the end of the Occupation, had turned into a civil war.

"That's not the worst of it, anyhow. They found out—or at least claimed so to Corinne—that my father was one of those who assassinated the mayor of Castelfort. He was Corinne's uncle."

His voice had fallen, and he looked down, as though dismayed all over again. By then, we had ordered sorbets of black currant and lemon, and as he spoke I had taken small spoonfuls of mine, letting the cold sweetness dissolve in my mouth. "My poor Cyprien," I murmured.

He went on to explain that M. and Mme Lapeyre had then forbidden absolutely that he and Corinne see each other. Corinne herself had written to break the engagement. "It is better this way," she had added.

He was, he said, devastated. Paris, Beaux-Arts, and the Ecole du Louvre had been for him not only a threshold to a career, but also a way of earning Corinne. Nevertheless, he took his competitive examinations, one after the other, and got a position as a curator in a very small provincial museum, before he moved to Bordeaux, where he was happy to remain. She married someone "from her world," as he put it. He had never married (and I reflected how that helped explain the long, severe, almost ascetic face, which had not smiled over a child nor been rejuvenated by seeing itself renewed in a grown son). He had not stopped painting immediately; rather, for a while, he had thrown himself into his studio work, seeking release or oblivion. "But unhappiness did not help me to paint; I don't know how to make art out of anger and pain—not from that kind of raw hurt, anyway. It paralyzed me."

Luncheon was over, and the sorbet dishes had been cleared away. We drank our coffee without dallying too much. Two hours or so had passed; we needed to get on to the museum. It was sunny and almost hot in the streets; Cyprien put on his dark glasses. We walked to the *métro*. To get to the Monceau neighborhood, it would have been possible to choose an itinerary allowing us to change trains only once; but Cyprien—whether because he was upset from having told the Corinne story, or because he had really lost the art of being a Parisian—consulting one of those booklets that show the subway lines, with maps of every neighborhood, decided on another route, with two changes. I could have advised him but didn't wish to. After waiting on three different platforms, we finally emerged at Villiers and started along the rue Monceau toward the museum. Suddenly, he stopped me, saying, "Let me look at the map again." He fumbled in his pockets, got out the *métro* booklet, then reached in his shirt pocket for his reading glasses. They weren't there. "I must have put them in my jacket pocket." He fumbled again and pulled out a pair—but they were obviously not the right ones, for they had oversized tortoise-shell frames.

"Cyprien, how many pairs of glasses do you have with you?"

"Five," he admitted, "counting these sunglasses." He continued searching in his pockets—jacket, shirt, even trousers pockets; finally, he had to acknowledge that the reading glasses were missing, though the slim leather case was in a coat pocket. He looked panic-stricken.

"You must have left them in the restaurant."

We found a street telephone back at the Villiers intersection and he called. I could half-hear the answer through the receiver: "No, Monsieur, no one found any eyeglasses on the table when you left. But we shall look again."

Cyprien whispered to me, "He's sending a waiter back to look." But no glasses could be discovered anywhere.

"Do you suppose you dropped them in the *métro*? Did you take them out to look at the map on the platform or in the train?"

He could not remember, but it was plausible. So we went down the steps to the ticket booth. Villiers is a large station and it was quite crowded; he had to wait in line to report the loss. He said afterwards that it had been necessary to list the three different lines we had taken to get to Villiers and the station where we had begun the trip, as well as describe the glasses and give the name of his Paris hotel and his Bordeaux address. He had been told to call the Lost and Found later in the afternoon.

He fretted as we turned up the stairs to the intersection and once again started for the museum. "They were a new prescription, you know. And I cannot read without them." Nevertheless, he seemed determined to act as a good guide and attempted to be cheerful. We got our tickets at the museum and walked around the spacious rooms, which displayed paintings by Hubert Robert and Guardi and the very finest eighteenth-century furniture and art objects. His knowledge was detailed and dazzling. "That piece of *marqueterie* is from the 1750s," he would say; or "That cabinet was made by Riesener, that splendid example of *orfèvrerie* by Roettiers." He was especially good with porcelain and *faïence*, identifying pieces by their region and workshop simply by a glance (he was wearing by this time yet another pair of spectacles—designed especially, I supposed, for viewing art displays). Our visit was thorough; it's the sort of museum you do in a couple of hours, and few other visitors were there to interfere with our movement and examination of the collections. But I could see how preoccupied he was still.

When we left, the afternoon was drawing on. We had already planned to have an *apéritif* somewhere before we said goodbye at the end of the day. I was obliged, unfortunately, to attend a semi-official banquet at 8. I was staying that summer on the Right Bank near the Louvre; it was decided that we would go back and stop at a café in that neighborhood. We walked toward the Villiers *métro,* talking about the collections. Though I had been looking at Cyprien, I happened to turn and cast a glance toward the street. Prominently propped on the hood of a car was a pair of eyeglasses, of the reading sort. "Cyprien! Look! Might those be your glasses? There, on the car!"

He turned quickly and, after the moment required for him to grasp what I meant, ran toward the car. There they were, not crushed, not bent, waiting for their owner. Earlier, he must have gotten them out absent-mindedly, then dropped them, at the very moment he stopped to look at the map; then a stranger, considerate but probably in haste, had seen them and propped them on the car hood. Cyprien almost wept with relief. "Oh, *Arrhee*! It's wonderful." Feverishly, he put them in the empty case. I embraced him—the sort of thing I don't do much with anyone, and particularly not on a Paris street. "You know," he said, almost embarrassed, "I said a little prayer to St. Anthony." I thought of his Spanish mother; whatever other views Cyprien might have on the world, including, possibly, his father's radicalism and surely his own aesthetic vision, which constituted, perhaps, the most important lens of all, those views had not overcome entirely a faith he must have learned from her.

We continued walking down to the intersection; Cyprien was beaming. In the *métro* station, he went to make another report, saying that the lost glasses had been found. I don't know whether he told the clerk he'd picked them up on the street; if so, she probably didn't believe him, concluding that they'd been in his pocket all along. We rode to the Palais-Royal station, near my hotel. In the huge square and the rue de Rivoli, the stores were still open. "Let's go look a minute in the shops over there," Cyprien suggested, his high spirits showing in his step and voice and easing a bit the lines of his face. We passed by the Daum shop windows and, drawn by the pure colors and graceful designs, went in. He looked at the glass birds and vases; I was drawn to the earrings. In the euphoria of the found eyeglasses, I felt the strong need to make a gesture—a sort of offering in acknowledgment of the way Fate, or Providence, had taken care of Cyprien this time, and so often takes care of us all. To acquire something beautiful by which to remember the day and the friendship it celebrated seemed fitting; I chose eardrops of a frosted blue.

With my purchase in hand, in a white box, tied with ribbon, we went over to the place André Malraux and sat down at the Royal. Cyprien had not bought anything chez Daum, but he too felt the need to mark the end of our day as extraordinary. He ordered champagne, and, in the long, almost motionless cocktail hour—not twilight, since night would not fall for a good three hours or more—we sat, as intoxicated with pleasure as by the wine, studying obliquely the nuances of pale and darker blue in the sky, watching the passers-by, with the fountain and leafy chestnut trees and theater in the corner of our eye, and the time we had spent together already slipping into the past, in a mellow way. It was drawing on toward 8; soon I would have to say goodbye, run back to the hotel, and then leave for the banquet. I hoped that Corinne had vanished from Cyprien's thoughts, to which my questions had summoned her, and that perhaps, when he returned to Bordeaux, he would find it easier to take up again the painting that had helped make us friends. I could imagine him in his studio, getting out his brushes and a clean canvas, telling himself that it was time to start afresh, under the good geniuses of friendship, beauty, and the reconciliation that comes with time—and watched over by some angel with great wings, who would see the masses of blue and green taking shape on the easel and think, "Yes, those are the skies and trees of a Paris afternoon, when you were happy again."

TWO GRAY HILLS

WHERE HAD WE SEEN that old Navajo before? Although on the surface there was nothing extraordinary about him—like innumerable other Southwestern men of his age, he was lean, slightly stooped, with reddish-brown skin and a face as deeply lined as weathered ponderosa logs, and he was wearing jeans, a plaid shirt, and a battered Western hat—I was confident that we'd run into him earlier on our journey. Now, he was standing outside of my tent, saying nothing, just staring. I'd heard the pick-up, with its shaky muffler, come along the road and stop right near us, and had crawled out by my tent, where I'd been putting some things in order, to see who had pulled up so close to our campground site at Canyon de Chelly. He had parked the old vehicle, a dusty and dented Ford with faded sage-green paint, right alongside my Jeep. It didn't make sense: our site was obviously occupied, with two tents erected and things spread out on the wooden table, whereas there were some empty sites on both sides—and anyhow, he looked like a local, not someone needing to camp; and any driver with a Louisiana license plate would scarcely have been the right person to answer questions about roads or other practical matters.

It suddenly occurred to me where and when I'd seen him: the previous day, at a combination gas station-motel-beer outlet-general store at the crossing of the San Juan River called Mexican Hat, in Utah, not far from the Arizona line. The territory on one side of the river is part of the Navajo Reservation; on the other side, it's Utah state land, and although there are rather strict liquor laws, beer and wine can be sold. Nigel, Anne, and I had stopped to buy a map, a six-pack of what Nigel, as a joke, called "barley water" while we were on Indian territory, and two bottles of wine, or "grape juice," red and white; I now recalled that the old man had been in the store, getting beer. Presumably he was going to smuggle it back onto the reservation, where all alcohol is strictly forbidden, and drink it under the cover of night. That was risky, but less so, I supposed, than drinking it by the river's edge and then driving back intoxicated. We had similarly brought in contraband, cooling our bottles surreptitiously in the ice chest, opening them inside the tent toward sundown, and pouring the contents into opaque plastic mugs brought for the purpose. Every evening, as the long twilight took on plenitude and the mesa colors of orange, violet, and red spread through the sky, we had sipped the cool, ebullient drinks under the cottonwoods and willows.

Seeing the old fellow standing before me, mute, in the powerful afternoon sun, which the trees barely filtered, I wondered whether he was still, or again, somewhat under the influence of his beer and had become disoriented, or—a more disquieting thought—had suddenly taken offense, as a Navajo, at the presence of Anglos on his tribal homeland and wished to challenge us. Nigel and Anne weren't with me at the moment; they'd gone up to the park office a half-mile or so away. Could he have seen them leave and decided to approach me because I was alone? Well, the only thing to do was greet him, since he didn't seem ready to speak himself.

"Good afternoon. What can I do for you?"

He remained silent, his countenance immobile, his expression impossible to interpret—indicating perhaps suspicion and hostility, or humility and reserve. It occurred to me then that perhaps he didn't speak English. Without any knowledge of Navajo, I could try Spanish, at least.

"Buenos días, señor. ¿Qué desea Ud.?"

That time, it worked; he must have attended a Spanish-language school for a few years. "Sí, señora, gracias, muchas gracias." He abruptly removed his hat and held it against his chest, but still hesitated a moment before continuing. Through a somewhat halting exposition, he led me to understand that he had noticed my Jeep, with its Louisiana plate, at the Mexican Hat store, then had seen us drive away in the direction of Bluff and turn toward Mexican Water and Round Rock. He had followed us for a while, lost us (it wasn't clear why) and had returned home, but had driven that morning to

Chinle and the Canyon de Chelly campground and looked for us. "Sabía que yo los encontraría a Uds.," he said, explaining that he'd heard us pronounce the name Chinle and supposed we wanted to visit the canyon; he added that he knew the territory well because he lived on the reservation, just over the line into New Mexico.

The story was strange; why should an unknown man, a Navajo, want to speak to us? He didn't seem intoxicated, after all; either the beer had been drunk up without ill effect or he'd hidden it for another day. I remained somewhat apprehensive, while reflecting that, if he meant to insult or threaten us as invaders, he surely wouldn't go through such a narrative. The most plausible explanation was that, like scores of his tribal brothers and sisters, he wanted to sell us something—jewelry, sand-paintings, hand-woven or Mexican machine-made blankets, pottery, even rocks, the resort of the least resourceful. Perhaps he'd decided that we looked prosperous or vulnerable. But so far he had said nothing about any goods he had for sale; and why drive all that distance just to catch up with three tourists, when he could have waited for others along the roadside?

Gesturing to the picnic table a few feet away, I invited him to sit down. "Siéntese Ud., señor. And tell me, why did you want to find us?"

"Porque pienso que mi hija ... mi hija Consuelo, vive cerca de Uds., en Luisiana, en la Nueva-Orleans." He gave a heavy sigh, almost a groan. His words struck me as being buoys, cast out into the unknown in the hope of rescuing something.

Explaining that only I was from New Orleans, my companions being *ingleses*, I then asked him more about this daughter, Consuelo, who, he thought, lived there. He explained that, as a girl, she had left the reservation to go to the Indian school in Santa Fé. The family expected her to return home after she graduated, but instead, she remained in town to work, then suddenly left. A friend from the school told him later that Consuelo had gone to New Orleans with a man she'd met. Since then, he'd had almost no news; more than ten years had passed. Once someone had telephoned for him to the information service there; no one by her name was listed. It had nearly broken his heart, he added. To go off into a different state, in a different culture ... maybe he could have understood, yes, he could have understood and accepted that. But to cut him off, send no word ... That was too much.

"So you do not know whether she is still there, after all this time?"

"No, señora, no sé. Quisiera saber si ... si ella vive todavía, donde está, si ... si es feliz, si es casada, si tiene niños quizás ..." They were the wishes anyone would express about a son or daughter who was long disappeared—the desire to know where and how the child was, whether there were grandchildren ... "Me gustaría saber también como ... como imaginar la Nueva-Orleans, si es muy grande, bonita, si hay árboles ..."

It had become clear what he wished of me—first, simply the contact with anyone whose life had some association with the young woman's, however remote it might be, and who could, at least, speak of where she lived; then, more practically, assistance in tracing her. In a moment, he said as much, adding that his love for her was stronger than ever. He then paused and took out a large pocket bandanna with which he wiped his forehead. After the ordeal of explaining himself and asking for help, he looked drained. I invited him to put on his hat again: "El sol es muy fuerte, y hace mucho calor."

Tracing missing people is the work of agencies, I reflected; but almost surely he couldn't afford the cost, and anyhow, where would someone whose life and whose neighbors' lives were circumscribed by the reservation and a few nearby towns be able to get in touch with one? Clearly, I had to agree to look her up once I returned home. He had the barest information: her surname, of course, her age—over thirty by that time—and the name of the fellow with whom she'd gone off. He showed me a worn photograph, taken during her last year at the Indian school. I tried to explain to him that this was not much, that I had no particular skill in such matters and that New Orleans was a very large place, much larger than Chinle, or Shiprock, or even Santa Fé. Moreover—and this was delicate—it was necessary to remind him of what he already knew: that *she* was the one who had not come home, who had disappeared ... Some people didn't want to be found, I pointed out. Nonetheless I took down his name and his post office box number in Shiprock. I wondered whether he would be able to read Spanish well, but didn't dare ask.

In his proud, restrained Navajo way, he was nearly overcome with gratitude. "Gracias, señora, gracias. Ud. es muy buena. Me gustaría darle algo a Ud...." And he rose, before I could stop him, and went to the pickup, from which he brought over a box, a piece of pottery, well protected in plastic bubble wrap, and a Two Gray Hills blanket, small but very fine and valuable, the sort you display on a wall. He thrust them into my hands. The box, which he opened for me, contained a large and handsome turquoise, polished but unset.

"No, I cannot accept these gifts," I tried to explain. "You are very kind, very gracious, but I simply cannot take such lovely things—after all, what I am doing is very little, and I do not know at all whether I shall be successful."

Just then Nigel and Anne came around a clump of cottonwoods on the other side of the road. Anne told me later that she supposed, upon seeing me at the table with the Navajo things, that the old man was trying to sell them to me. The two of them came up to the table, ready to help shoo him off. I hastened to explain what we were talking about. The old fellow pressed the gifts on me again. "La calidad es muy buena," he insisted, fearing perhaps that I believed them to be cheap. He explained further. "The rug comes from Crown Point. No two rugs sold down there are alike, and each bears the signature—in symbols—of its maker. See the patterns ... black for the basalt rock of our land, white for the sands, dark broken lines for the hills and the far horizon ..."

"I know," I assured him, "the rug is very beautiful, the stone is exquisite, and doubtless the pottery also. You are very kind. But no ..."

Finally it was decided that I would accept the turquoise ("I have many others," he assured me) and that, should I locate his daughter, he would have the rug shipped to me; he would not agree to anything less. I described New Orleans to him a bit. "Yes, there are many trees, huge trees with branches extending over the streets, and beautiful old houses painted in many colors with lush gardens; and it rains a great deal"—all of which seemed marvelous to him.

Even assuming that she still lives there, how does one find someone without a telephone listing in a city and suburbs with a population of well over a million? That evening, Nigel, Anne, and I talked of little else as we sat with our illegal cups of wine and watched our steaks grill over the fire, while the western sky flamed with gold and crimson. I had asked the old man what Consuelo had studied, in particular, and what sort of jobs she had held in Santa Fé. As one might have expected, he knew little, or perhaps there was little to know, but he emphasized that she had learned both English and Spanish, although the family spoke Navajo at home, and that she had a great deal of artistic talent, which had been developed at the New Mexico Indian School. "She paints and does pottery," he had specified, "like her grandmother, who made this pot"—which again, he had pressed upon me, unsuccessfully. I had encouraged him by telling him that I too was a painter, with many contacts in the art community in New Orleans. Around the table, with our wine cups refilled and the steaks on their platters, Anne, Nigel, and I agreed nevertheless that the outlook wasn't good; even if she could be located, would she agree to write or telephone her father, or let me send photographs? Yet, looking west where the broken skyline, resembling the pattern in the Two Gray Hills rug, turned ashen as the last blood-red light paled and then collapsed into itself, I had a presentiment that perhaps, after all, she and I might be drawn together.

Months later, it was, appropriately, the rug that did it. As I wrote to Anne, I had first spent many hours in futile searches of the ordinary kind. After looking in vain in the telephone book, just in case, for Consuelo's name and that of her erstwhile lover, probably long gone, I had phoned a Hispanic club and a number of churches with large Spanish-language congregations; I even inquired for her in a few bars on Magazine Street that cater to Spanish-speaking clientele. I also tried telephone listings for the rest of the state, the Mississippi Gulf Coast, and both San Antonio and Houston, whose large Hispanic population might have attracted her. Of course she was really Navajo, and perhaps had broken her ties with the Spanish culture that had surrounded her in New Mexico. Each time there was a major crafts show—for Spring Fiesta, Jazz Fest, and other events—I took time to visit its booths, on the outside chance that she would be there, displaying her work. In New York, my daughter searched for both names in the phone books of every borough. All that was fruitless. It was like looking for the dead, trying across distances and darkness to call up an image and a voice out of nothingness. Maybe, truly, she was dead. At Christmastime I sent the old man a greeting card with a picture of the oak trees on St. Charles Avenue to wish him Feliz Navidad and assure him that, though I'd not found Consuelo after searches in telephone books and other efforts, I hadn't abandoned the quest.

One might have foreseen it: though I had not a scrap of new information for him, and thus contrary to our agreement, he had the Two Gray Hills rug sent to me anyway. A card inside the package, written in English by a post office worker, explained that my letter had been read to him and said that he wanted me to have the rug, in thanks for my willingness and friendship. So much for so little, I thought. Still, knowing that someone hundreds of miles away was thinking of his daughter, as he thought of her, was perhaps to him worth more than a rug, no matter how fine. We made an axis of hope, he and I, wishing together for something, and trying to believe that wishing could make it be.

Perhaps it can, sometimes, through intensity of thought and other powers of the mind. Love can cross great distances, and art, which bridges the real and the ideal, can act as a magnet not only for the eye but for something deeper in us, drawing us together. The following spring, Ángela Martínez, a new acquaintance of mine who has a gallery of Southwestern art and jewelry in the French Quarter, happened to mention that she was putting together a large show of Hopi, Zuni, Navajo, and Pueblo Indian work. The previous autumn, she had been out to the Rio Grande pueblos in New Mexico and the Hubbell Trading Post and had bought fine weavings, Gorman prints, pots by followers of María Martínez, and many other pieces, some very valuable, others of modest price. She wanted to attract buyers' and art lovers' interest by displaying additional objects, not for sale, from collectors—more as an education for her clientele than anything else. She did not know at the time about my Two Gray Hills rug.

When I told her about it—keeping quiet about how it came to be in my hands—she was delighted. "Won't you please let me display it, at least for the opening of the show?"

"Of course; I'll be happy to lend it, although the wall in my study will look bare for a while! It was a gift," I added without further explanation. With my permission, she used its design in the advertising posters and fliers, which were sent out to the usual gallery and art-loving crowd. I made just one stipulation: that, in addition to my being listed as lender, the piece be identified as having come from Crown Point.

The *vernissage* was a small event, compared to a museum opening, but still, a lot of visitors walked in and out during the course of the evening. My colleagues from the curatorial staff dropped by, of course, and several other friends, and Ángela saw to it that we were well provided with wine, finger-sandwiches, and other tidbits. Though Consuelo had been on my mind, earlier, at the moment I was no longer thinking about the futile search for her and the affinities between her and what was on display. People came in, stared for a bit, got drinks, looked around some more, and went back into Chartres Street; a few stopped at the desk and arranged with Ángela to purchase something. I stayed most of the evening, taking special interest in the whole show and pleasure in overhearing compliments on my rug and others.

At one moment, through the monotonous chatter and occasional high-pitched exclamations, I became aware that someone was commenting in an unusually knowledgeable way on several displays— pottery, jewelry, painted *santos,* and tinware. It was less a single remark than their number and consistent perspicacity that finally got my attention. The speaker, I observed, was a woman, who appeared thirty-five or more, with straight hair, black and shiny as coal, wide cheekbones, and the brown skin of the Four Corners area. She was handsome, but not fresh like a young woman. She was dressed in a black velveteen ensemble that set off a massive turquoise squash-blossom necklace and heavy silver earrings. Can I say that I knew then it was Consuelo? That would be presumptuous; at first, I simply recognized the type of the Navajo woman. She had been examining some Ácoma Pueblo pottery; she turned then toward the wall where rugs and other weavings were displayed. Only when I heard her comment on my rug did a sense come to me that *of course* it was Consuelo. I could imagine her as an older version of the girl pictured in the old man's photo. I could have been wrong, with a hundred different wrong women; instead, I was right. I went over and stood by her.

"Pardon me," I said as soon as there was a pause, "I am Harriet D'Aquin, from the Orleanian Institute. I heard you speaking a moment ago about the Ácoma pottery, and just now about these rugs. This one" (and I pointed) "is on loan from my collection."

Her dark eyes shone in admiration, and, in an accent that barely suggested English was not her native language, she spoke with confidence. "I saw it pictured on the gallery ads; that's why I came tonight, really—I wanted to meet the owner. It is a very beautiful example of work by Two Gray Hills. I congratulate you on your taste."

The belief that I was indeed talking to Consuelo was nearly overpowering. But to ask her identity directly, without preparation, would be a tactical mistake. I didn't know even what to say next. She helped me out herself.

"The most extraordinary thing is that I'm convinced I've seen that rug before. I thought I recognized the design in the flier, and now it strikes me even more. It is puzzling ... I should explain that ... originally I'm from New Mexico—rather, from the Navajo Reservation, although I went to school in Santa Fé. Oh, pardon me, I should introduce myself also." She drew from her purse a business card. "I'm Consuelo García; I teach art at the University of New Orleans."

Despite the different surname, that was enough confirmation for me. How pleased the old man would be by her success, if he had not been so hurt by her silence. But it was still hardly possible for me to speak of him and his search and all it implied, including her indifference, if not callousness, even betrayal. And I could not explain how I'd gotten the rug without mentioning him. I had the presence of mind to ask her whether she had been at UNO for several years.

"No," she answered, "this is my first year in the department. I lived in New Orleans a few years ago, but left to take my doctorate at Texas and returned just this fall." Either that fact or her changed name could explain why she hadn't been found earlier in the telephone book.

"Please, take my card also," I said, handing her one. "Have you met Ángela Martínez, the gallery owner?" Shepherding her over toward the desk, I left her with Ángela and determined to arrange some sort of meeting at which, after preparing myself, I could tell her what I knew. But she would find it odd if I invited her home. Before she slipped away, I caught her arm and asked her if I might show her around the museum sometime—"including new acquisitions and certain works not currently on display that you might like to see." It was bait; I hoped she was curious enough—about the rug, about me—to take it.

A week or so later I telephoned her office and left a message. When she called me back, I invited her to come to the museum on a Friday for a tour and then lunch in the café. Waiting for her, I was as nervous as a high school boy before a date, reflecting on how much happiness might hang on my diplomacy. She may have thought at the time that my behavior was strange, although my interest in art of all sorts helped to cover me as we chatted. At the Orleanian Institute we have very little Southwestern art, and perhaps she knew that; it turned out, fortunately, that she'd done her doctorate on Spanish painting of the seventeenth century, though at UNO she taught survey courses. I remember that she stopped for some moments in front of our Degas canvases—two race track scenes, the usual dancers and scenes at the barre, and one painting done in New Orleans—and talked perspicaciously about their movement and tones. She admitted that she was very fond of horses. I showed her some new holdings and took her through part of the warehouse where we were collecting and setting up things for a large exhibit.

Lunch didn't amount to much; I had little appetite and she ordered only a tuna salad. Over coffee, I finally had to raise the subject that had been in my mind ever since the opening at Ángela's gallery. "You say you grew up on the Navajo reservation and went to school in Santa Fé, and your name is Consuelo. I believe I know who you are"—and I gave her father's name. It was risky; if I was right, she might simply have risen from the table and walked out, though at least that would be evidence of her identity and I could report to him what I'd learned. Or there might have been an outburst. Instead, she put down very carefully the spoon with which she had been stirring her coffee and looked at me deeply, even suspiciously, yet with a certain frankness in her eyes. "Yes. So I was right to recognize that rug you own; for I remember now that my father bought it at Crown Point, just before my last year in Santa Fé, having some money then, and wanting to invest it in the only sort of riches that, to him, have significance. How did you get it—and why are you interested in me anyway?"

I was about to answer, when she burst out, as an afterthought, "Did he have to sell it? Oh, God!"

"No, Consuelo, he did not; he *gave* it to me. But he has suffered more than if he *had* sold it." And then I was obliged to relate everything— how he had seen the Jeep in Mexican Hat, traced us to Canyon de Chelly, begged me to look for her in New Orleans, then sent the rug after Christmas, and, what she knew already, the good fortune of our encounter at the gallery. But I had to say also what was obvious—that her father was old and unhappy, living so much in the thought of her that he had followed a car with a Louisiana tag. "He wants to know everything—where you are, and who you are, I suppose, and why you do not communicate with him ..."

She had the sort of proud self-knowledge that I like, even as she dredged up the failures of love. "Imagine," she said, "what it was like to go to school away from the reservation, even if it *was* to an Indian school, and to see Santa Fé, and the modern Hispanic culture, and even more the Anglo culture, with its success, its wealth, its denial of the old. Imagine being eighteen there, having a bit of education, living with friends in an apartment instead of a hogan, earning money—right after graduation I got a job at the museum in the Governor's Palace— and then imagine my father and mother's appeals (she was alive still then) to return to the ranch and the traditional society they knew. My father was obstinate, not understanding that, if appeals didn't work, threats wouldn't either. We quarreled; he said ... harsh words. You know how traditional fathers are—if you displease them, they predict the worst, almost as if they were hoping for it."

She explained then that his forebodings had been realized, at first; as he knew, she'd gone off with Glenn, a truck driver she'd met, falling for his broad shoulders, handsome features, and deep brown eyes, even though sense told her that to do so was to cheapen herself. "He brought me to New Orleans—he worked for a trucking line based in Texas but had always wanted to live here, and could work out of here just as well. I was young, you must understand. Ours was a slick-paper life for a while, since he made good money. Of course he wasn't interested in art and didn't understand either what had made me, among the Navajos and in Santa Fé, or what I wanted to become."

"Did you not write to your father, or telephone?"

"Once, after Glenn and I started having serious difficulties, the sort you can guess, I did call. It was a moment of weakness; I thought briefly that I wanted to go back home. My parents had no phone, but I called some neighbors outside of Shiprock, who said they would convey the message. But, when I telephoned again, I was told that my father had refused to listen to any news from me. My mother had died, and he held me responsible for it—for not being there, for letting her die without knowing where I was. Now, I realize how wounded he was; I am older. But *I* was wounded also. That's the trouble—I'm his daughter, just as proud, just as stubborn. How could I be otherwise?"

God, the power of words to hurt, to destroy, to create chasms over which no ropes can be thrown. Actions can sometimes be undone, or at least forgiven, but words, brilliant as jewels but often venomous as serpents, remain in the heart.

Our coffee was lukewarm at best, by this time; she had not taken a sip since she'd put down the spoon. "Tell me what happened then, as I drink this coffee; fortunately I don't mind it tepid."

She stirred hers again, out of nervousness, doubtless, and took a few sips. "I left Glenn, not before we had terrible fights. I hadn't married him, thank heaven. Living in sin was one of the things I did right, though my mother would not have approved. And we didn't have any children. I already had a job, just a cashier's job, but then I learned some computer skills and got a better position. I went to UNO part-time, then full-time, got my B.A., then went to Austin to get my doctorate."

"But ... your name, García—are you married now, or... did you change it?"

She'd married, she said, an anthropologist she'd met at Texas, of Mexican-American extraction, who, like her, had found a position at UNO. "It is a new life, for both of us. We even have a little boy."

What remained to be done was persuading her to get in touch with her father. "He wants to hear from you—letters, photos, any news at all. Most of all, he would like to see you and your child. Imagine, a grandson he doesn't even know about! Whatever happened, however bitter it was, he loves you still—he said, *even more*—and needs you now. He is too proud to acknowledge his role in your estrangement, I suppose, but no matter: old as he is, he drove over a couple hundred miles to speak with me because I'm from New Orleans."

It was only because the soil of her heart, long parched, was already prepared for reconciliation that my words, like steady rain, made a difference. Sitting that evening in my study, near the Two Gray Hills rug, now returned to the wall above the piano, I composed a carefully-worded letter to the old man, as Consuelo had agreed I should, telling him about meeting her in an art gallery thanks to that very weaving, and then about our lunch. All her current circumstances were set out; I did not mention the long-gone truck driver or the quarrels and resentments of the past. Whether he would know what a doctorate was I doubted, but studies in Texas he would understand, and teaching, marriage, and especially the little boy. I assured him that, as she had promised me, she also would write to him, in a few days, and send photographs. "Quisiera decirle a Ud.," I assured him, "que su hija es una mujer muy bella, muy elegante, muy trabajadora."

She kept her word, I found out, and did more: in the summer, after more letters and telephone calls arranged through the neighbors, she and her family traveled out to New Mexico to spend some time with the old man. Before they left, I invited them to my place to see the turquoise he had given me and look at the rug again, so she could tell him how I'd displayed it. "You must express to him my thanks once more. And please give him my best wishes for health."

"But *he* will want to thank *you*. And I do too."

It could have been expected: when they returned in August, they brought me not only snapshots of the four of them together, but a pot—the very one, I supposed, that he had offered me, and another Two Gray Hills rug, of a different but compatible design, which Consuelo herself had purchased for me. It hangs in my study next to the other one, its stylized black shapes suggesting the monumental basalt rock formations of the Four Corners, where I can imagine the crimson sun glowing at sunset, coloring the sky, like the thick blood of love.

ABOUT THE AUTHOR

CATHARINE SAVAGE BROSMAN is Professor Emerita of French at Tulane University and Honorary Research Professor at the University of Sheffield. She spent her girlhood in Colorado, where she was born, and in Texas. She took her B.A. (Phi Beta Kappa) and M.A. at Rice University, studied for a year in France as a Fulbright scholar, and then returned to Rice for her Ph.D. Her teaching career took her to schools in Virginia and Florida, then, in 1968, to Tulane, where she was named Andrew Mellon Professor in the Humanities (1990) and held the Gore Chair in French. Her years in New Orleans (just short of forty) allowed her to develop the close acquaintance with the city that is visible in these stories.

Dr. Brosman has published widely in the fields of late nineteenth- and twentieth-century literary history and criticism, with books on such authors as André Gide, Roger Martin du Gard, Jean-Paul Sartre, and Albert Camus. Among her other volumes are *Jules Roy: Art as Testimony* (1989); *French Culture, 1900-1975* (ed.) (1995); *Images of War in France: Fiction, Art, Ideology* (1999); *Existential Fiction* (2000); and five edited volumes in the *Dictionary of Literary Biography* series. In addition, she is the author of four studies in American literature, dealing with Louisiana Creole literature, poets of Louisiana and Mississippi, and women writers of the Southwest. Her scholarly interests include painting and its connections with literature, explored in book chapters, reviews, and papers.

She is the author of four chapbooks and fourteen collections of poems, issued by the University of Georgia Press, LSU Press, Mercer University Press, Green Altar Books, an imprint of Shotwell Publishing, and others. Her latest is *Arm in Arm* (2022). In 2023, Green Altar Books will publish *Aerosols and Other Poems*. Her poetry has been anthologized frequently and featured on the radio and literary sites such as Poetry Daily and American Life in Poetry.

Her collections of non-fiction prose are *The Shimmering Maya and Other Essays* (1994); *Finding Higher Ground: A Life of Travels* (2003); and *Music from the Lake* (2017).

Catharine was active in the South-Central Modern Language Association, of which she was president, and the American Association of Teachers of French, which she served as assistant editor and Managing Editor of *The French Review*. She has given talks and read from her verse in many American cities and abroad. Since 2007 she has been poetry editor of *Chronicles: A Magazine of American Culture*. She was in New Orleans when Katrina hit the city. For unassociated reasons, she moved to Houston in December 2007. She has a daughter, Katherine Brosman Deimling, who lives with her husband and children in Brooklyn. In fall 2021 Catharine acquired as a second residence a small pied-à-terre in New Orleans.

Additional information on the author can be found on Wikipedia. org, in both the English-language and French versions.

GREEN ALTAR BOOKS
SHOTWELL PUBLISHING

www.ingramcontent.com/pod-product-compliance
Lightning Source LLC
Chambersburg PA
CBHW050125030726
47505CB00007B/2038